Praise for *Second Chance*

PENGUIN CANADA

SECOND CHANCE

JANE GREEN is the author of nine bestselling novels, including *Swapping Lives*, *The Other Woman*, *To Have and to Hold*, and *Jemima J*. She lives in Connecticut with her family.

ALSO BY JANE GREEN

Second Chance

JANE GREEN

PENGUIN
CANADA

PENGUIN CANADA

Published by the Penguin Group

Penguin Group (Canada), 90 Eglinton Avenue East, Suite 700, Toronto, Ontario,
Canada M4P 2Y3 (a division of Pearson Canada Inc.)

Penguin Group (USA) Inc., 375 Hudson Street, New York, New York 10014, U.S.A.
Penguin Books Ltd, 80 Strand, London WC2R 0RL, England
Penguin Ireland, 25 St Stephen's Green, Dublin 2, Ireland (a division of Penguin
Books Ltd)
Penguin Group (Australia), 250 Camberwell Road, Camberwell, Victoria 3124,
Australia (a division of Pearson Australia Group Pty Ltd)
Penguin Books India Pvt Ltd, 11 Community Centre, Panchsheel Park,
New Delhi – 110 017, India
Penguin Group (NZ), 67 Apollo Drive, Rosedale, North Shore 0632, New Zealand
(a division of Pearson New Zealand Ltd)
Penguin Books (South Africa) (Pty) Ltd, 24 Sturdee Avenue, Rosebank,
Johannesburg 2196, South Africa

Penguin Books Ltd, Registered Offices: 80 Strand, London WC2R 0RL, England

First published in a Viking Canada hardcover by Penguin Group (Canada),
a division of Pearson Canada Inc., 2007. Simultaneously published in the U.S.A.
by Viking Penguin, a member of Penguin Group (USA) Inc.
Published in Penguin Canada paperback by Penguin Group (Canada), a division of
Pearson Canada Inc., 2008. Simultaneously published by Plume, a member of Penguin
Group (USA) Inc.

1 2 3 4 5 6 7 8 9 10 (OPM)

Copyright © Jane Green, 2007
Excerpt from *The Beach House* copyright © Jane Green, 2008

Excerpts from "Goodbye My Friend," words and music by Karla Bonoff, Copyright
1998 Seagrape Music. Used by permission. All rights reserved.

Manufactured in the U.S.A.

Library and Archives Canada Cataloguing in Publication
data available upon request to the publisher.

ISBN 978-0-14-305196-1

American Library of Congress Cataloging in Publication data available

Visit the Penguin Group (Canada) website at **www.penguin.ca**

Special and corporate bulk purchase rates available; please see **www.penguin.ca/**
corporatesales or call 1-800-810-3104, ext. 477 or 474

*This book is dedicated to the memory of Piers Simon,
who will always be missed*

ACKNOWLEDGMENTS

I am often dubious about extended acknowledgments, but there have been so many angels in my life this past year who have guided me through with their love and support, and to whom I remain eternally grateful. My gratitude and unending thanks go to the following . . .

Deborah Valentin and Dani Shapiro, for their extraordinary wisdom, advice, and love.

Roe Chlala, Jody Eisemann, Brian Russell, Kathy Steffens, Nicole Straight, and all the many friends who showed me, with grace and humility, that there is another way.

Joan Burgess, Fiona Garland and Andy Bentley, Anthony Goff, Kim and Niv Harizman, Bob and Jane Jacobs, Steve March and Rob Rizzo, Lisa Miller, Louise Moore, Deborah Schneider, Gail Sperry, Jonathan Tropper, Susan Warburg, David and Natalia Warburg.

And finally to Ian Warburg. For bringing me back to myself. And for everything else besides. I love you.

Second Chance

PROLOGUE

The wine has been drunk, the pasta demolished, three-quarters of the tiramisu polished off. Were you to peer through the window you might think you were looking at a group of old friends laughing, catching up, having a wonderful time, never seeing the gossamer-thin threads of grief that are woven between them, that have brought them together again after all this time.

Look a little more closely and you'll see the way the brunette—Holly—has a tendency to drift off into space. How she'll gaze into her wineglass, lost in a memory, a tear welling up in the corner of one eye; how the blonde—Saffron—will lean over and ask gently if she's okay, lay a hand softly on her arm with a squeeze; how Holly will nod her head with a smile as she blinks the tear away and gets up to clear a dish that doesn't yet need clearing, wash a bowl that doesn't yet need washing.

Observe how the thin girl with the short, mousy bob watches them both with concern, her eyes softening as she sees how Saffron is able to comfort, how after all this time apart Saffron doesn't feel the slightest bit awkward about reaching out and making Holly feel better. There is a part of Olivia that wants to be able to do this too, but she has spent years trying to find comfort in her skin, in who she is, in being someone who has not followed the paths expected of her, not being a lawyer, or a doctor, or a super-successful, high-flying businesswoman, and, while she thought she was happy, finding herself surrounded by her school friends has brought back those insecure feelings of old: not being good enough. Clever enough. Ambitious enough.

His name is not mentioned for a while, they are too busy focusing on catching up. They go around the table, haltingly at first, as they fill one another in on who they are now, where their lives have taken them.

"Short summaries, please," Paul requests with a grin. "No more than two sentences to start off with, I think."

"Christ." Saffron looks at him in amazement. "Over twenty years since we left school and you haven't changed a bit. Still trying to be the boss."

"Fine, I'll start," he says. "Freelance journalist for various newspapers and a few men's magazines. Quite successful, quite enjoy it. Evenings and some mornings spent writing, as I said, the great British novel. Small house in Crouch End but fast car to make up for . . ."

". . . small penis?" Olivia remarks.

"Not small, average, I think, but no complaints from Anna."

"Tell us all about Anna." Saffron raises an eyebrow.

"Swedish, thirty-nine, gorgeous. Also highly tolerant, given she puts up with me. As you know, founder of Fashionista.uk.net. As a result, she is frighteningly trendy, which is stunning given she's married to me. Desperate for children, have been trying for two years, and currently undergoing yet another bloody round of IVF after which I think we may have to resign ourselves to having cats. Anna is the best thing that has ever happened to me, but starting another cycle with this awful Synarel nasal spray that turns Anna into the hormonal horror from hell, so not particularly looking forward to it.

"Hopefully," he looks around the room and attempts a smile, "this time will be the last time, hopefully this will be successful. Keep everything crossed for us . . . Saffron? Your turn."

"That was more than two sentences." Saffron says softly. "But I will keep everything crossed for you. So . . . me. Actress, a bit of theater, hopefully big role coming in major film with Leonardo DiCaprio. Split time mostly between LA and New York. Am very happy with someone, but complicated so can't talk about it. No children, animals, or other dependents, but good circle of friends, although have to say, nothing like being with people you've known almost your entire life." She looks at each person sitting around the table and smiles. "Having a shared history is something you just can't create with the new ones. No matter how much you like them, it just isn't the same."

"And . . . time's up," says Paul, looking at his watch.

"My turn?" Olivia sighs. Here it is. "Um. God. Where do I start?"

"At the beginning?" Paul offers helpfully.

"Okay. Did drama at university, which was ridiculous really as nowhere near confident enough to be an actress." She looks nervously at Saffron, who gives her an encouraging smile. "Played around for a few years doing various jobs—worked at health food store, ran bookshop for a while, then asked to volunteer at animal sanctuary. Seven years later, run the place and love it. Gorgeous flat in Kensal Rise, and . . . " she takes a deep breath, wondering why on earth this should be so hard given that it has been six months since George left. ". . . and still single. Was in relationship with George for seven years, but he upped and left and is about to marry ghastly American girl called Cindy, and now I am planning on turning into the crazy old woman with a million cats and dogs."

"No one else on the horizon?" Paul is surprised.

"Well . . . oddly enough Tom put me in touch with someone from his American office. We've been e-mailing for a few weeks, and he's coming over here soon, but what was fun and sweet seems just awful now, since . . . everything. I feel really weird about even meeting him."

"Bollocks," Saffron says. "You have to meet him, especially if Tom set it up."

"You're probably right. I just feel completely unready for a relationship," Olivia confesses.

"Darling," Saffron shrugs dramatically, "who's talking relationship? I bet you haven't been laid for six months."

Olivia blushes and looks over to Holly for help.

"Okay," Holly laughs as she interjects. "My turn. That fine arts degree wasn't a complete waste of time as

I've managed to make a somewhat decent living over the years. I'm an illustrator for a card company, although my dream is to work on children's books. Met Marcus in Australia at twenty-five. He seemed, on paper, to be everything I was supposed to be looking for in a husband, now rather think no one should get married before the age of thirty." Olivia raises an eyebrow and Saffron's eyes widen slightly. "Whoops," Holly said, knowing that she had drunk too much. "Did I say that out loud? Oh well. Two gorgeous children, Oliver and Daisy, and truthfully Marcus is a pillar of strength. Really. So strong. He could move mountains. Harbor secret fantasies of running away with kids but know that's just typical of an old married woman thinking the grass is always greener. Have to say, in all, life's pretty good."

Holly pauses. "And to finish, I sent Tom an e-mail because I hadn't spoken to him in ages, and I never heard back. What about you lot? When did you last speak to him?" Holly looks up at each of them, and the tension, almost undetectable but nevertheless present all evening, now dissipates.

Finally it is safe to talk about Tom. They have spent the evening talking about themselves, reminiscing about school days, but none of them wanting to bring up Tom, none of them knowing the appropriate way to talk about him, knowing what to say. None of them ready to face the reason they are all sitting in this room. Friends reunited. After twenty long years.

CHAPTER ONE

Tom wakes up first. Lies in the blackness and sighs as he reaches over to turn off the alarm clock. Five-thirty. Blinking red, beeping madly, waiting for him to bang it off. He turns his head to see if Sarah has woken up, but no. She is still soundly asleep, rolled on her side, breathing heavily into her pillow.

He packed the night before, so accustomed now to these business trips, to getting up in the middle of the night, looking out of the window to check that the town car is waiting in the driveway, the driver killing time by reading the *New York Post*, a large cardboard cup of steaming coffee in hand.

The payoff, as he and Sarah both know, is that these business trips won't be forever. Soon his company, a large software company, will have finished buying the smaller start-ups and, as chief executive officer, he will be able to concentrate on growing what they already have. He's thirty-nine now, and in another three years or so, hopefully his annual bonuses will allow him to think about doing something else. Some money will have been put aside for the kids' college accounts, and he'll be able to retire, maybe buy his own business, do something that doesn't involve travel or a commute, time away from the family.

In the bathroom, he trips over Tickle Me Elmo and shakes his head in exasperation before smiling at the memory of Dustin, two years old, giggling uncontrollably alongside Elmo until his older sister, Violet, grabbed it away, leaving Dustin in floods of tears.

A hot shower, the last of the packing, and he's ready to go. Back into the bedroom to kiss Sarah on the cheek. "Love you, Bunks," he whispers, using their pet name for each other, a name they've been using for so long they don't even remember how it came to be.

Sarah stirs and opens her eyes. "Love you," she murmurs. "What time is it?"

"Just after six. The town car's here. Are you going to get up?"

"Yup. In a second. Have to get the kids ready for school."

"Promise me you'll take pictures of Dustin in the play, okay?"

"Okay, sweetie. Promise. Have a safe journey."

"I will. I'll call before I get on the train."

" 'kay," and Sarah smiles and sinks back into the pillows and falls fast asleep again before Tom has even made it to the front door.

Across the Atlantic Ocean, just as Tom's town car pulls out of the driveway, Holly Macintosh also wakes up: 11:00 A.M. Today she has taken the day off, exhausted from the past few sleepless nights when the routine is always the same: she stumbles through her bedroom, hits the light switch just outside the doorway of her tiny bathroom, and sinks her head in her hands as she sits on the loo. This has started happening every night. At more or less exactly the same time, Holly wakes up needing to pee, and by the time she climbs back into bed her mind is up and racing, and these last few nights she has still been awake when the sun comes up.

Last Sunday she had just managed to fall back into a deep sleep when Daisy came in, clad in mismatched socks, her brother's Spiderman pajamas, and Holly's favorite cashmere scarf wrapped around her neck. Daisy demanded Weetabix, and Holly stumbled out of bed shooting daggers at Marcus, who, she was convinced, was merely pretending to be fast asleep.

And last night she was up all night. She lay in bed, her eyes closed, trying to ignore the occasional snore or grunt from her husband, too deep in sleep to notice her. Usually when his snoring becomes too irritating to bear, even though she is wide awake and not even pretending to be attempting to get back to sleep, she will shove him over from his position lying on his back. "Snoring," she will hiss, suppressing the urge to push him hard enough to prod him right out of the bed.

Holly turned on the light last night, waiting as her husband stirred, then rolled over again, still sleeping. She gathers up a magazine from the pile on the floor next to her bed, resigning herself to yet another of those long, long nights, those nights that render her almost senseless in the mornings.

This morning, a zombie in oversized men's pajamas and moccasin slippers, Holly just about managed to get the children up and dressed. "Don't start," she said warningly to Oliver, who is never at his best in the mornings, and particularly not when his four-year-old sister has discovered exactly which of his buttons to push to start the tears falling, and with huge enjoyment has incorporated it into her daily morning routine.

The au pair stumbled down at the end of breakfast, and Holly smiled gratefully as Frauke bent down to get the children buttoned up, slapping some ham and cheese on pumpernickel bread for herself and holding it in her teeth as she took Daisy and Oliver by the hand.

"I'm not working today," Holly said. "But I'm exhausted. Another bad night. Would you mind organizing a playdate or something this afternoon? I'm just desperate to sleep. Is that okay?"

"Yes," Frauke nodded, with her stern morning face—the result of having gone out last night with six other au pairs, and staying up until much too late drinking Starbucks. "I will phone Luciana, although the last time I tried to see her she was thirty-six minutes late, which was not good. But I will try again. Don't worry, Holly. I will keep the children out of the house today. Perhaps a museum."

Holly sighed with satisfaction. She finds herself describing Frauke to friends as "my grown-up daughter from my first marriage." Her other friends complain about their au pairs, but Holly feels constantly and consistently thankful that Frauke has come into her life. She is organized, strict, loving, and happy. When Marcus goes to work and it is just Holly and Frauke alone with the kids, the house always feels lighter, happier, the energy changing entirely.

So now, awake again at 11 A.M., Holly gets up and makes herself a cup of tea, loving how quiet the house is in the middle of the day. This is the house she and Marcus lived in together well before the children were born. It is the house she bought expecting to fill it with children and animals, neighbors and friends popping in at all hours of the day and night. A house we can grow into, she thought. A house that will truly be a home.

Holly's mother was an interior decorator, and every house Holly had lived in as a child had been a project. As soon as the project was finished, the Macintosh family was on the move again. Holly had had bedrooms in every color of the rainbow. She had had blue fairies, yellow Laura Ashley, hot fuchsia, and gold leaf. She had attempted to stop attaching herself to these houses, but couldn't help the secret hope with every new move that perhaps this house would be the one her mother would fall in love with, perhaps this time she would finally have a home.

When she and Marcus found this house in Brondesbury, Holly knew that she would never leave. Five bedrooms for all the children she was convinced they would have, a large garden for barbecues and swing sets, a huge, dilapidated kitchen that Holly started mentally reorganizing as soon as they first saw it.

There is no doubt at all that it is home. Holly bought

every piece of furniture herself, trawled through dusty, fusty antique shops, spent months going to car-boot sales looking for that one special find, even buying several pieces on eBay, and getting burned only twice. (One time it was a sofa that was supposed to be in great condition, but it turned out that the picture on eBay was of a different sofa, and the other was an antique cherry sideboard that turned out to be riddled with woodworm.)

In so many ways, Holly has exactly the life she has always wanted. She still gets pleasure every time she comes home, and still, at least four times a week, she finds herself wandering around her house, leaning in doorways and looking at rooms, smiling at the home she has created.

She has her gorgeous, adorable children, Daisy, who is like a mini-me of Holly, and Oliver, who is more serious, pensive, more like her husband.

She has a career she loves—she is a freelance illustrator—and a husband who would appear to be the perfect husband. He is successful—a lawyer in one of the top family law firms, he has become the divorce lawyer of choice for several celebrities of late. He is tall and distinguished looking in his bespoke suits and natty silk ties, the salt and pepper of his hair giving him a gravitas he only aspired to when he and Holly met. He has changed enormously, but Holly tries not to think about it, or at least tries not to dwell upon it. His old friends have even tried to gently rib him about changing his name from Mark to Marcus, but it has gone down like a lead balloon, and the few friends remaining have learned not to tease Marcus about his past.

Did he have humor? Holly supposes so. She remembers a time when he used to make her laugh, when they used to go out with friends and she would wipe the tears of laughter away from her cheeks. She doesn't seem to have laughed with him for a long time, Marcus working longer and longer hours as his career has continued to shoot upward.

They haven't seen friends either, for that matter, not for a while. Holly, who loves cooking, would regularly host dinner parties in the old days. She didn't actually want to have dinner parties, would have preferred casual kitchen suppers, friends standing around the island with giant glasses of wine as she threw together a salad, but Marcus insisted on doing things properly.

Marcus insisted on the best crystal being out, the silver cutlery. He insisted on eating in the dining room at the mahogany pedestal table with the Chippendale chairs, but they had been a gift from a great-aunt of Holly's whom she had always hated. They are beautiful, naturally, but they seem so formal, so out of place with the life she had envisioned for herself.

One night they had gone to the neighbors for dinner, and the dining room was a light, bright room, French doors leading onto a terrace, every wall a floor-to-ceiling bookshelf lined with books, the wooden floors painted a white gloss, an old round table with retro Formica chairs. It was hip and warm and fun, and Holly had loved it.

"Wouldn't our dining room be wonderful like that?" she had said to Marcus as they climbed into the car at nine o'clock. (Holly had wanted to stay later, had been dying to stay later, having not had that much fun in ages, but Marcus had insisted on leaving because he was in the middle of a big case and still had work to do when he got home.)

Marcus had shuddered. "I thought it was ghastly," he said. "Dining rooms are for dining in, not for reading in."

Oh fuck off, Holly had thought, rolling her eyes as she turned her head and looked out of the window. Since when was he the expert on dining rooms?

Marcus has an awful lot of theories, particularly about what is *right* and what is *wrong;* how one is supposed to act; how children are supposed to behave; what is *common* and what is not.

Most people are fooled by Marcus, believe he is as he appears, but there are many who are not. Holly, though, does not realize this. Not yet. Holly thinks that people take Marcus at face value. She thinks that he has perfected his image as someone who comes from a good family, from old money, from aristocratic intelligentsia, and has managed to pull it off. Why he would want to do this in the first place is something Holly does not even try to understand.

Some of the time Marcus does pull this act off. Admittedly, the few remaining friends from university who remember his parents, his childhood home, know that it is all an act, but they are still in his life because they have learned the art of discretion.

So he has acquired manners and tact and graciousness and charm from Holly, but because he is mimicking her, mimicking those around him whom he is trying so hard to emulate, and because none of it comes naturally to him, the charm has a habit of falling off, the manners have a tendency to disappear, particularly when Marcus is feeling superior.

He tries desperately to keep his mother in Bristol, terrified that she will give his past away; and poor Joanie, who longs to spend time with her grandchildren but doesn't know how to be around a son she no longer recognizes; Joanie who sits on her own in her little house, surrounded by photographs, utterly bewildered.

Bewildered at how she produced a son like this, a son who she has come to realize is more than a little embarrassed by her. A son who keeps buying her Hermès scarves and Burberry raincoats, not because she needs them or because she asks for them but because, she well knows, he is trying to turn her into something she is not.

Her plastic rain scarf is fine, thank you very much, and her mac bought from M&S all those years ago still does a great job. When the gifts arrive, she bundles them up and takes them down to Oxfam unless, of course, she's having a bridge night beforehand, when her friends get to choose.

She doesn't know what to make of this son who speaks with more marbles in his mouth than the queen. She's extremely proud of what he's achieved—she is the only mother in the town with a son who's a lawyer and working his way toward becoming a partner. A partner! Who would have thought! But on a personal level, she has to admit she doesn't like him very much.

She feels awful saying that about her son. How could she possibly feel that about her own flesh and blood? But Joanie Carter is nothing if not matter-of-fact, and while he will always be her son and she will always love him, she is quite clear that she doesn't like him.

Who does he think he is? she finds herself thinking when another scarf arrives. But she already knows the answer. *He's Marcus Carter. And he thinks he's better than all of us.*

She thinks Holly is wonderful because she is so down to earth. Joanie can see Marcus growing more and more self-important, more and more puffed up with pride, and she hopes, has always hoped, Holly will knock it out of him. She doesn't know how Holly puts up with her son, and is so pleased that Holly acts normally and doesn't obey Marcus when he's not around, which seems to be most of the time these days. But she can't help but wonder what they're doing together, can't help but think that this may be the most peculiar match she's ever seen.

She thought it was an odd pairing from the beginning although she was delighted. Marcus took her and Holly out to tea at the Ritz, and Holly was so effervescent Joanie was worried she might just fizz up through the ceiling. Thank God, she thought with relief. Maybe my son has a chance after all. Maybe this lovely, real girl will knock the stuffing, the stuffiness, out of him.

And then the engagement and a diamond ring that was bigger than anything Joanie had ever seen, and plans that took on a speed and energy of their own. Holly had phoned and said it would be small, maybe in a little hotel or a service in their local church and a lunch for their friends.

It had ended up being at the Savoy. Two hundred people. Holly glorious in her Jenny Packham sheath dress, but strangely subdued, Joanie had thought— serene and stunning, but there was a hint of sadness that she pushed to the very back of her mind, refusing to acknowledge what it might mean.

Even Holly refused to acknowledge what it might mean. Marcus had proposed, exactly as she had known he would, on bended knee next to the river Thames beside the Southbank Centre. He had the ring, exactly as she had known he would, and she couldn't think of a reason to say no.

After all, he was everything she thought she ought to have been looking for, and soon she was swept up in the momentum of planning the wedding—so very much more lavish than she had wanted, but this was Marcus's day too—and she didn't stop to question her doubts, didn't stop to allow them space to breathe and grow.

Looking back, an observer might say that Holly seemed heavy on her wedding day. Not heavy in weight—Holly was positively tiny on the day itself, the stress of keeping Marcus happy already having taken its toll—but there was a weight on her shoulders, a flatness of spirit, a heavy energy.

She kissed Marcus, she danced, she greeted her guests and lit up when talking to people she loved, but it wasn't perhaps what you would expect from the bride on a day that is supposed to be the happiest day of her life.

Joanie had not been able to put her finger on it, but if you asked her, if you gave her the words, she would nod in wonder for that is exactly what she felt. And all these years on, she worries that Holly isn't happy. Worries that, despite outward appearances and despite the children, Marcus has become too difficult, too imperious for Holly to stay.

Holly could judge Marcus, could find the faults his mother finds unbearable but, on the whole, she doesn't. She knows that there is a different Marcus, wouldn't be with him still, surely, if there wasn't a different Marcus hiding behind the pomposity and grandness.

Holly knows that deep down there is a frightened little boy who doesn't feel good enough; and in order to try to feel good enough he has to surround himself with people he deems worthy; fraternizing with anyone less than himself would diminish him in other people's eyes, so he doesn't bother with anyone he regards as inferior.

It was one of the reasons he fell in love with Holly. She came from the background he wished he had, was the ultimate trophy wife. Except once he had her, he had to subtly put her down, make sure she never thought she was better than he was, make sure that he was still able to feel superior.

Despite all this, Marcus has good points. Of course he does; why else would Holly have married him? For starters, he loves her, or at least Holly believes he loves her. He performs random acts of kindness, thoughtfulness. When he passes the newsagent on the way home from work and sees the latest *Hello!* or *heat,* he will always pick it up for her. He frequently sends her beautiful flowers, and occasionally comes home with a Crunchie or a Kit-Kat, Holly's favorite forbidden indulgence.

He is, when home, great with the children. Not for very long, and only when the children are behaving as he thinks appropriate, i.e., no screaming, whining, crying or hitting—all the behaviors, incidentally, that Holly has to put up with all the time—however, the children are too terrified to behave in ways anything other than exemplary, and on those occasions Holly's friends will watch him approvingly and murmur what a wonderful father he is.

And he is a wonderful husband too, Holly tells herself during those moments in the middle of the night when she wakes up gripped by panic, panic that her marriage won't be forever, that she has never been more lonely than she is now, that she never sees him, that she has nothing in common with him, that they are growing further and further apart.

Marcus wouldn't see this. Why would he, when Holly, like most women, is a consummate chameleon? During the day, when Marcus isn't around, she can be herself, can have girlfriends and their children round for lunch, throwing together salad, pita bread and dips to eat around the kitchen counter as the kids make a mess of fish fingers and ketchup around the kitchen table.

She can break open bottles of wine and put Shakira on the stereo, she and Frauke shaking their hips while Daisy, attempting to imitate them, shocks Holly at how a four-year-old can appear to be so mature, so womanly, so—good Lord, she can't believe she thinks this—sexy. But she can have fun, can throw on ratty old cargos and trainers, hoodies and no makeup, and not worry about impressing anyone.

And when Marcus comes home, she can slip into what he likes. If they're staying in, she'll swiftly change into crisp, dark jeans and a cashmere sweater, small diamond studs in her ears, or, if going out to supper, smart woolen trousers, high-heeled boots, a velvet jacket.

The music goes off, the cushions are plumped to perfection. Holly finds herself running through the house every night before Marcus comes home, checking that all is exactly the way he likes it. The children are not allowed to build forts out of the sofa cushions in the living room, and Frauke is in charge of making sure Marcus doesn't know that almost every afternoon every cushion in the house is piled up in the center of the room.

The children are also not allowed to run "naked like savages" through the garden, and, on the rare summer afternoons when Marcus announces he's coming home early, she and Frauke beg, cajole, and plead with the kids to put their swimsuits back on before Daddy comes home.

Her own father had stopped showing interest in Holly soon after the divorce. She remembers very clearly being fourteen years old, her father taking her to the soda fountain at Fortnum & Mason for tea and, over a huge chocolate sundae, telling her that he loved her, would always be there for her, and that no matter what happened he was going to see her every week and every other weekend.

He didn't say that the reason for the divorce was his persistent infidelity. Holly only found that out later.

For a while, he kept his word about seeing Holly. For six months. And then he met Celia Benson, and suddenly he was jetting off to Paris, or Florence, or St. Tropez with Celia, and soon he had a new family, and Holly was largely ignored.

Her father, she realized as an adult, was weak. Celia Benson didn't want the child from his first marriage around, and he acquiesced, allowed himself to give her up. To this day Holly blames Celia.

Is Holly happy? Happiness is not something Holly thinks about very often. She certainly has everything a woman could want in order to be happy, so how could she be anything but? The fact that they sleep in a king-sized bed, both on the far edges, a huge expanse of space in the middle, Holly furious if a leg or an arm should wander over to her side doesn't mean she's unhappy, surely? The fact that they rarely have sex anymore, and when they do it's perfunctory, doesn't mean she's unhappy, surely? The fact that Holly finds herself withdrawing more and more from life, having already given up several friends Marcus deemed "unsuitable," doesn't mean she's unhappy.

Surely?

Distractions do a wonderful job of keeping her mind off the fact that her life is not quite what she expected it to be. There are her children, for starters. Her house. And, of course, work. A freelance illustrator for a greeting card company, Holly can lock herself away in her studio at the top of the house and lose herself for hours in a delicate watercolor of a little girl and a puppy, only coming out of her reverie when she hears Frauke and the kids returning from the park. A couple of days a week she goes to the studio at the company, but mostly to keep her hand in and to remove herself from the isolation of working alone at home, to feel part of the company.

She hasn't been in that much recently, not least because of her exhaustion. Sleep is becoming a growing problem, and Holly's defenses are nowhere in sight when she wakes up in the middle of the night, her heart pounding with fears she refuses to acknowledge. She is finding herself sleeping more and more in the middle of the day, yet however much sleep she gets, she never feels truly energized.

Now, sitting at the kitchen counter after another daytime nap, Holly finds herself thinking about when she had last been truly happy. School? Well, no. She hadn't been happy there, but outside school, when she, Olivia, Saffron, Paul, and Tom had been together, then she'd been happy.

And at university. She and Tom, best friends, in love with one another since the day they met at fifteen, but somehow never managing to make it happen . . . Those had been happy times.

Holly smiles as she remembers those days. She hasn't spoken to Tom for weeks. They kept in touch for ages with phone calls, then dwindling e-mails; but once Tom had met Sarah while she was working in his London office, then moved to her hometown in America to marry her, their friendship never seemed quite the same, although Holly always thought it was just a phase.

Olivia, she has discovered, works for an animal charity. Every now and then Holly will spend an afternoon Googling friends from a previous life, hence her discovery of a picture of a smiling Olivia holding a kitten at a benefit to raise money for her charity. She had looked the same, other than that her beautiful, waist-length hair was now in a short bob. Holly had sent her an e-mail, years ago, to which Olivia had responded warmly, but somehow they had never managed to follow through.

Saffron, as befits someone named Saffron, is now a semi- famous actress trying to become a movie star in Los Angeles. She has been in several low-budget British films, has had tiny parts in major films, and is often recognized in the streets. She is regularly profiled in British magazines and newspapers as the next big thing; however, at thirty-nine—even though Saffron would never admit it—Holly knows that Saffron is unlikely to be the next big *anything* in Hollywood movies.

Holly hasn't seen Paul for years. He and Tom have

kept in touch. Tom, in fact, seemed to keep in touch with everyone, albeit sporadically, but now and then he'd send Holly an e-mail, making her laugh with stories of what Paul, the eternal womanizer, was up to.

Tom would say, once he married Sarah, that he was able to live his life vicariously through Paul, but Holly remembers that Paul got married a couple of years ago, to a beautiful girl, someone successful, if Holly remembers correctly, and Paul had sworn to Tom that she had changed him completely.

Holly remembers sitting at the hairdresser's, flicking through *Vogue*, and stopping short when she turned the page and suddenly came across Paul, lounging across an oatmeal-colored Eames sofa, dressed head to toe in Prada, looking suspiciously like a male model, with a gorgeous blonde draped between his legs, a Chloe dress on her spectacular figure, her head thrown back, hair like a silken wave over his arm.

Her mouth had dropped open as she started reading about the marriage of this new power couple: Paul Eddison, journalist and man-about-town, and Anna Johanssen, founder and CEO of Fashionista.uk.net.

Of course Tom had told her that Paul was getting married, but she had no idea it was such a big deal. She had pored over the pictures, stunned at how trendy Paul had become, but when she'd phoned Tom to squeal about it, Tom had just laughed.

"It's not what he looks like," Tom had said.

"But I saw it with my own eyes," Holly had insisted. "He looks like a bleeding model. What happened to the permanent stubble because he couldn't be bothered to shave? Paul's hair was always a complete mess, and frankly the Paul I used to know wouldn't have known Prada from a pencil."

"Trust me," Tom had cracked up, "Paul's still exactly the same. I was his best man, and I had to stand over him with the razor and supply the hair gel to make him look half decent. He's still happiest in his scruffy old jeans and T-shirts with holes in them."

"I don't know," Holly had said dubiously. "It sure as hell looks as if he's changed. What's she like, anyway? She looks terrifying."

Tom had sighed in sorrow. "Don't be so bloody jealous, Holly. She's lovely. You think she must be a bitch because she's beautiful but she's not. She's incredibly sweet, and she adores him."

"You're right, you're right. I was making assumptions because she is completely stunning. Lucky Paul. Lucky couple." She'd sighed. "Looks like they have a completely glamorous, perfect life."

"Not so much," Tom had said, serious now. "*Vogue* made it look like that, but trust me, their life isn't nearly as glamorous as it looks, and nobody's life is perfect."

"Mine is," Holly had said wryly, and Tom had snorted.

With these memories Holly gets up from the kitchen counter and switches on her computer. Why not e-mail Tom now? It's been, what, seven months? Eight months? Ages, anyway, since their last contact, and she misses him. He and Marcus had never seemed to gel, and Sarah wasn't exactly Holly's cup of tea, hence their drifting apart.

Not that Sarah wasn't nice, she had always been perfectly pleasant when they'd attempted to get together on the rare occasions Tom had brought Sarah back to England to see his family, but Holly had found her cold, unyielding. Polite without giving any more than she had to.

Holly first met Sarah after she got back from Australia, the trip on which she met Marcus, marrying him a year later.

She hadn't spoken to Tom the entire six months she'd been away, but soon after getting back she got in touch again. It was long before Tom started talking about this cute American girl who was working in his London office.

"How's the Yank?" Holly would tease, secure once again in their friendship now she had Marcus, unable to believe that she had ever had feelings for Tom, ever thought of him as anything other than her best friend, even after that night . . .

"She's pretty amazing actually," Tom would say hesitantly, going on to tell Holly how much she would love this Sarah, how he couldn't wait for them to meet, that they should all get together as a foursome.

And so they did. The four of them going to a pizza place in Notting Hill one night, Holly excited about meeting this girl that Tom had been talking about for so long, who had now become his girlfriend, who he was talking about moving in with him.

Holly wanted to love her. Was convinced she would love her, but she approached Sarah with a warm smile and an open heart and found Sarah to be prim, proper, and cold.

"God, she's awful," she hissed to Marcus when they were safely in their car on the way home. "What does he see in her?"

"She's quite sexy in a standoffish kind of way," Marcus said, instantly regretting it as he watched Holly's eyes narrow.

"Sexy? What's sexy about her? What? Because she's clearly addicted to the gym? Is that why she's sexy? She's had a complete sense-of-humor bypass as far as I'm concerned, plus she's intense beyond anything I've ever known. Christ, do you think she'd even crack a smile? Gender politics all evening. Please. Does this woman even know the meaning of the word *relax*?"

"You liked her, then?" Marcus had said with raised eyebrow and a grin.

"Did you like her?" Tom phoned first thing from the office.

"I thought she was great," Holly lied smoothly.

"Isn't she? I knew you'd think so."

"She's quite serious, though," Holly ventured.

"Is she? I think it's probably because she doesn't know you that well, but you'll get to know her much better now she's moving in."

"What about us?" Holly's curiosity got the better of her. "Did she like us?"

"Oh yes," Tom lied smoothly. "Very much. She thought you were both great."

And that was the thin end of the wedge that lodged itself into the heart of Tom and Holly's relationship. At first it was just a splinter, but the more the four of them endured one another, attempting to find a way of turning Holly and Tom's friendship into an equal friendship among the four of them, the larger the splinter grew until Holly and Tom were forced to sneak in the odd lunch or phone calls from work. It was a friendship that suffered from lack of contact but became more precious precisely because of it.

Years ago, Holly would call Tom in Massachussetts, praying that Sarah wouldn't answer the phone, praying that she wouldn't be forced to go through the obligatory small talk. Eventually she had stopped phoning.

Holly always thinks of Sarah as Scary Sarah. It had slipped out once, by accident, when she and Tom were having lunch, and Tom had almost spat out his drink, he was laughing so hard. It is still a shared private joke between them, something that indicates the intimacy they had before.

"Hey, stranger!" Holly taps into the computer, her need to get in touch with Tom suddenly all-consuming.

Have been wondering where/how you are, my friend. Not sleeping well at the moment and finding myself thinking about my past and realize it's been AGES since we spoke. How are you? How's Sarah? And those little munchkins? My own munchkins are as delicious as ever. Have you been in touch with anyone? Read something about Saffron the other day—she's got a small part in some new film with Jim Carrey—whaddya think?—could this be the big time we've all been waiting for? (Unbloodylikely, I'd say. Ouch!) How's Paul? Any little ones yet? Would love to hear from you. Actually, would love to see you— can't you do a business trip over here? Just think, we could have long liquid lunches like in the old days. Anyway, thinking of you and sending you much love. Send my love to Scary Sarah. Big kiss, Holly xxxxx

Much later, Holly will find out where Sarah is at the precise moment she hits the send button on her computer.

Sarah was, at that moment, shouting up the stairs to Violet to hurry up or they will be late for school. Violet is four, in her last year of preschool before starting kindergarten, and as slow as molasses, particularly when her mother is in a hurry.

"Come on, honey!" Sarah shouts. "It's your field trip today. You can't be late. Oh Violet!" she says, as Violet appears in the doorway of her bedroom, naked, clutching her threadbare pet elephant. "I asked you to get dressed!" Sarah snaps as Violet starts to cry.

"Oh God," Sarah mutters. "Please give me patience this morning." Last year she complained to Tom that it was like this every day, always running late, having climbed out of bed too late and spending too long over breakfast, forgetting to get the kids' clothes ready the night before, not able to find the car keys.

Every day last year she woke up and vowed that today

would be different, today she would be fun, nice, loving mommy; and by the time they all piled into the SUV in the driveway, she was back to being stressed, shouting mommy, hating herself for doing it, but somehow being unable to stop.

Sarah takes a deep breath. *I will not shout at the kids this morning,* she tells herself. *So what if we're a bit late? It's only preschool, for God's sake. It doesn't matter.* Feeling calmer, she grabs her camera from the dresser in the bedroom and takes the kids down to the car.

An hour later—so many mothers to catch up with in the car park—Sarah is about to get in the car when Judy, another mother, races up, her face stricken.

"Have you heard?" she says, her eyes wide with excitement and horror.

"What, what?" The mothers clamor around her, some turning as cell phones started to ring simultaneously.

"Another terrorist attack! Right here! They bombed the Acela!"

Sarah's focus shifts as everything becomes fuzzy. The Acela Express. The high-speed Amtrak train that covers the Northeast. That can't be right. Tom is on the Acela.

"No! What happened? Is it bad?" comes the babble of voices, and then groans of, "Oh God, not again."

"I don't know," Judy said as one of the other mothers shouted over. "Bodies everywhere. Happened just outside New York. Oh God, we're bound to know someone." And all eyes suddenly turn to Sarah, who finds herself sitting on the ground of the car park, her legs having given way.

"Sarah?" A voice, gentle, on level with her ear. "Sarah, are you okay?"

But Sarah can't speak. These things are not supposed to happen to people like her and Tom, but now it seems they have.

CHAPTER TWO

Holly Macintosh wakes up, as she has woken up every morning since she heard the news, and feels the weight of grief settle upon her chest.

It is all she can do these days to get out of bed, to go to the kitchen and pour herself a coffee with a shaking hand, to sit at the kitchen table lost in a cloud of memories, of things unsaid, of might-have-beens and of missing Tom—the Tom she grew up with and the Tom she will never see again—so very, very much.

She shakes it by breakfast, has to for the sake of the children. Marcus has been wonderful. The night she found out she collapsed in tears and Marcus wrapped his arms around her, the children looking on from the kitchen table, fear etched in their little eyes.

"Why is Mummy crying?" Oliver asked.

"Mummy's sad because she's lost one of her friends," Marcus said softly over the top of Holly's head.

"Shall I help you find her?" Daisy said after a pause, and Holly was able to smile through her tears, which only started a fresh round of sobbing.

Just three days earlier, Holly had watched the footage on the news with Marcus. One hundred and forty-seven people dead. She had shaken her head with her friends and said how unbelievable it was, how they lived in a different world; they wondered whether it could ever end.

And then one morning on the Internet, she'd found a list of names on the BBC News Web site. *I wonder if I know anyone,* came the thought. She'd known it was unlikely, and odd, given that tragedies had come and gone throughout her childhood—various IRA bombings, none of them far from where she lived—and never had it occurred to her that someone she knew might be involved, but this time she'd clicked on the article and started to read.

Names. Brief biographies. A banker from Islington, in New York for a business trip; a mother and daughter from Derbyshire, there on a brief holiday; Tom Fitzgerald, a software genius . . .

Holly had kept reading, then her eyes went back to his name, and she reread it a few times. Tom Fitzgerald. A software genius. Tom Fitzgerald. *Tom.*

Tom.

But it couldn't be. How could it be? This happened outside New York. Tom is in Boston. Tom has to be fine.

Confusion had swept over her as she picked up the phone to call Tom at work, but it would be nighttime there, and she dialed the home number.

"Hi, this is Tom, Sarah, Violet, and Dustin," Sarah's voice had sung down the phone, lending this phone call a normality that had made Holly think perhaps she was imagining all this; she must, surely, be imagining all this because how could the answerphone indeed be so normal, how could the message still be the same if something terrible had happened to Tom?

And she'd looked back at his name, jumping out at her from the computer screen.

Tom Fitzgerald.

"Oh, hi. Sarah, Tom, it's Holly." She'd spoken haltingly, unsure, Googling Tom's name as she spoke, looking for more information. "Um, I just . . . I was reading . . . God. Sorry. But can you call me? Please? I . . ." There'd been nothing else to say. Another article had appeared. *Tom Fitzgerald, chief executive officer for Synopac, was on the doomed Acela Express on his way to a business meeting . . .*

The phone had been placed back in the receiver in slow motion.

"Holly?" Frauke had come into the room, had observed Holly's trembling back. "Is everything okay?"

And Holly had turned to her, stricken. Her face had filled with grief and shock, and when she had tried to speak, nothing had come out in the way it was supposed to.

"It's Tom," she had managed to whisper eventually. "He's my oldest friend. On the train . . ." and she had stopped speaking as the sobs took over, collapsing in Frauke's arms when Frauke had rushed over to comfort her.

At thirty-nine years old, perhaps it is not surprising that Holly has not fully known grief. She has a passing acquaintance—various elderly relatives have died over the years—and Holly was naturally upset at the time, but there was a sense that this was all in the natural order of things. People you loved got old, sometimes they got ill and occasionally this was earlier than it was supposed to happen, and eventually they died.

You could accept that this was their time or, if not their time, they had at least managed to live a full and fulfilling life. They had done what they were supposed to have done while on this earth; and they left those who loved them with happy memories albeit some wishes that there had been less left unsaid.

But this? This is something entirely different. This is a deep, searing, tearing, raw grief. This isn't just emotional. This is physical. This unexpected grief is with Holly all the time. It wakes her up in the morning by settling itself on her chest, sinks down on the floor with her as she collapses in sobs next to her desk, works with its friend gravity to pull her eyes and mouth down in an expression of such deep sadness that strangers come up to her in the street and in shops and ask her if she is all right, then have to hover awkwardly as Holly nods, tears streaming down her cheeks.

She took a week off working altogether, after going back into the studio at Jubilations feeling numb, but thinking she would be able to cope, thinking that she would be better off being surrounded by people, having to make conversation, having to act as if everything in life was normal.

Sitting in a meeting with the marketing department,

someone had asked Holly an opinion, someone who worked in a different building and had heard that Holly had lost a person she knew, but didn't understand how it could be different to losing, say, a grandparent.

"I heard you knew someone who died on the train," the man had said nonchalantly. "Awful thing, wasn't it?" He'd shaken his head, preparing to move on to the business at hand—Holly presenting her drawings of elephants for their new line of belated birthday cards. "Such a shame. I just can't believe what's happening in the world today."

And Holly had immediately replayed in her head the tape of the train blowing up in flames (a tourist had captured the precise moment on film: grainy, blurred, the train way off in the distance, but the only film that existed) and watched the moment of Tom's death as she'd seen it on television, trying to imagine whether he knew, whether it was quick, whether he had burned to death or had been blown apart by the bomb.

Holly had looked up at the man, and then the tears had started falling again.

"I'm sorry," she said, "I just don't understand. I don't understand how this could happen to Tom. This just doesn't make sense to me. . . ." And her shoulders had started heaving, her body wracked with sobs as her colleagues had looked at one another nervously, none of them knowing quite what to say with this oh-so-public display of grief, none of them knowing how to fix it, but all of them wanting to climb back into their comfort zone, to have the old Holly back.

"I'll take her out," Simone mouthed, leading Holly out through the door and into the small kitchenette, gathering her in her arms and letting Holly sob.

"You need to take a break," Simone had said when Holly had finished. "Grief is a process and one you have to work through, and you certainly shouldn't be in here. You've worked incredibly hard on the elephant campaign and we're not in a hurry. Take some time. It can wait a month, at least." Holly had nodded mutely and looked down at her hands, unable to meet Simone's eyes.

Things like this aren't supposed to happen to people like me and Tom, she'd thought, as she gathered her things and allowed herself to be put in a radiocab to go home. *This is not what my life is supposed to be.*

This was not supposed to happen.

But she can't sit at home doing nothing, replaying in her head all the memories, all the horror stories of how Tom might have died, how it must have felt. Did he know, was it quick?

Do the others know? Their gang from school, people she hasn't spoken to for years, but who suddenly seem as close as the day they finished their A-levels, old friends she now feels compelled to see.

She phones Paul first. Given his high-profile wife, he is easy to track down. A phone call to Anna Johanssen at Fashionista, an urgent message left with the assistant for Paul to call, and he rings later that afternoon.

"Holly Mac!" he says when he phones. "How lovely to hear from you, what a tremendous surprise!"

"Well, actually—" Holly pauses. She hasn't worked out what she is going to say, the right words to use. A couple of phrases had come into her head but they sounded so clichéd, so completely out of a film that she knew the best thing to do would be to just phone and hopefully the right words would come.

But of course there are no right words to say that someone you both love has died. Holly has cried more tears these last few days than she thought possible. Her head feels woolen, she is exhausted with the constant thump of a headache from too much crying. And now, now that she has Paul on the phone, Paul with whom she knows Tom is still in touch, Paul who has remained friends with Tom, Holly cannot believe that she is the one who has to give Paul the news.

She half hoped Paul would know. Paul does not know; she must now be the one to tell him.

"It's not good news, I'm afraid," Holly says, her voice dropping. "It's Tom." She waits to hear whether Paul might know.

"Tom?"

"Yes. You know he and Sarah live in Boston. He was on a business trip to New York, and he was on the train that was bombed. . . ." Her voice is remarkably calm. She was expecting to burst into tears again, but if grief is indeed a process, then perhaps this is the first part of the process, that you are able to be the bearer of the worst news you have ever had to give anyone in your life, and you are able to give it with pathos and sadness and without breaking down in floods of tears.

There is a gasp and a long silence.

"You mean he's dead?" Paul's shock comes down the phone in waves.

"Yes. Tom's dead."

Another long silence. Then a whisper. "I don't believe it." There are a few muffled moments as Paul turns away from the phone. When he comes back, his voice is already starting to break.

"I'll have to call you back," he says, and puts down the phone.

An hour later he calls back.

"I don't know when the funeral is," Holly says.

"It's family only," Paul tells her. "Saffron spoke to Tom's dad. He said they knew how many people wanted to come, so they decided to do two memorial services. There's one in America, I think, and then the one here at the family church that's open to everyone, because they're keeping the funeral private. So the service is on the thirtieth. I thought maybe we could all go together. I've spoken to Olivia and Saffron's flying over. I know this is crazy, that none of us have seen each other in years, but I just want us all to be together again. I thought maybe we could all have dinner the night before . . ."

"Yes," Holly says quietly. "That's a wonderful idea. I'd love you to come here."

"Then we will," Paul says. "October the twenty-ninth?"

"October the twenty-ninth," Holly repeats. "I'll see you then."

Paul puts the phone down in the cradle, not noticing how much it is clattering, how his hand is shaking uncontrollably.

He makes his way from the desk to the sofa, numb, not aware that the kettle is still whistling on the stove, that he hasn't saved the piece he was working on when he took a break to call Holly, that it is quite possible, given how his computer has been playing up recently, he will lose the damned thing, but he doesn't do anything other than sit on the sofa and stare into space.

His thoughts are a jumble. The phone rings and he can't move, can't pick it up. It was all he could do to call the others, but he had to, had to do something before he could call Holly back. But he hears Anna's voice on the phone as she starts to leave a message, and he rushes over, the safety and familiarity of hearing the woman he loves bringing him back just for a moment.

"Hey!" Anna says as he picks up. "Where were you? I thought you were going to be stuck to your desk for the whole afternoon. I got your message. Is everything okay?"

"I . . ." He doesn't know how to say it, how to fit his mouth around the words.

There is a silence and Anna takes a sharp intake of breath, knowing suddenly that there is something terribly wrong.

"What is it, Paul? What is the matter? What has happened?"

"It's Tom," he says, his voice flatter and darker than Anna has ever heard it. "He was on that train in America. He's dead."

Another sharp intake from Anna, and then her business side takes over. "Stay where you are," she commands. "I am coming home now."

Anna walks in to find Paul exactly where he was after they spoke on the phone. He is sitting on the sofa, still in his boxers and the T-shirt he slept in last night, a shower now the last thing on his mind, and he is staring at the wall.

He looks up slowly as Anna rushes over, and she is speechless at the shock and pain in his eyes. They look at each other as Anna sinks down next to him and puts her arms around him, and for a while he just leans his head on her shoulder as she strokes his back, too raw to cry, too raw to do anything other than stay right here where it is safe and warm and good.

The girls' school where Holly, Saffron, and Olivia met sits high up on a hill in one of London's leafier suburbs.

ST. CATHERINE'S PRIVATE SCHOOL FOR GIRLS reads the sign outside. Although if you drive past at 3:20 P.M. on a weekday, you won't see the sign for the swarms of girls, large and small, identically dressed in burgundy pleated skirts and white shirts, the little ones bundled up in hats and scarves, the older, cooler ones, thinking they can't be seen, sprawling on the bench under the gazebo around the corner, cigarettes in hand as they give disapproving mothers the evil eye, resplendent in their teenage truculence.

Nestled in the valley of the leafy suburbs, a few streets away, is St. Joseph's private school for boys, yang to St. Catherine's yin, home of St. Catherine's male counterparts, recipients of thousands of schoolgirl crushes over the years.

St. Catherine's girls and St. Joseph's boys were destined to be together. Some of the more rebellious girls got in with a crowd from Kingsgate, the comprehensive in Kilburn, but what was the point in traveling so far when all the choral societies, all the fairs, all the parties and social events occurred between St. Catherine's and St. Joseph's?

There was even a rumor that Mrs. Lederer, the steely eyed, firm-but-fair headmistress of St. Catherine's, had been having an affair for several years with Mr. Foster-Stevens, the steely eyed, firm-but-fair headmaster of St. Joseph's, but nobody had ever been able to prove it, although Adam Buckmaster in lower fifth swore blind he saw them snogging after the schools' joint performance of *The Importance of Being Earnest*.

Holly had been a late starter when it came to boys. The other girls in her class had seemed to discover them around twelve, but Holly, apart from a crush on Donny Osmond when she was a little girl, had not really understood what all the fuss was about. Olivia, her best friend since they had started senior school, was exactly the same; and both of them were slightly worried about Saffron, who had always been just like them but in the last six months had started going to Kensington market for black leather, impossibly pointed shoes, and had sewn her school skirt so tight it was less of a hobble skirt and more of a straitjacket.

Saffron, while still their best friend out of school, had started getting in with a crowd that already wore makeup, already had boyfriends, and met up after school every day with a gang from St. Joseph's, usually going to someone's house for games of spin the bottle or just to listen to LPs—Madness, Police, David Bowie—in someone's bedroom while a disinterested mother sat at the kitchen table with a cup of tea and a cigarette, chatting on the phone to a friend, unaware and probably not caring what a group of eight teenage boys and girls were doing behind a locked bedroom door.

And then came Saffron's birthday. Her fifteenth. Her parents had let her rent out a youth club, and she was determined to have the best party anyone had ever seen. Someone's older brother was doing the music, friends of said older brother were going to be bouncers because there had already been three parties that year at the youth club and teenagers from all over the area had come, whether invited or not, and a couple had gotten slightly out of control. (Nothing beat the story of Matt Elliott, who had a party while his parents were away, and gatecrashers burned down the staircase. Matt Elliott wouldn't be coming to Saffron's party—he'd been grounded for a year, and this was England, where they didn't even really know what grounded meant.)

Holly and Olivia were in almost matching outfits of gray rah-rah skirts, pink off-the-shoulder sweatshirts and striped leg warmers with—oh thank you, Mum! Thank you, thank you, thank you, Mum!—*jazz shoes*. Real, proper jazz shoes from Pineapple Dance Studios that everyone wanted but nobody had.

Holly went to Olivia's house, was staying the night, in fact, and they each curled the other's hair—not for the boys, you understand, but in a bid to look exactly like Jennifer Beals in *Flashdance*.

"You look fantastic," Olivia breathed to Holly after she'd finished singeing her hair with her mother's curling iron, not to mention burning her own hand three times as she attempted to curl Holly's hair without touching the bloody thing.

"So do you!" Holly had grinned, and they'd put on the soundtrack to the film and practiced their dance routine to Irene Cara's *Fame* in front of Olivia's mirrored bedroom wall.

The hall of the youth club was so dark it was almost impossible to see anything. As promised, Saffron had rigged up the disco ball, which spun slowly—small squares of light rotating around the room, illuminating the groups of people who had gathered in corners. In one were the bitchy girls. In another, the mixed group of boys and girls who met after school, each of them having a boyfriend/girlfriend, some of them already "getting off" with one another, not needing to wait for the slow songs. Duran Duran was quite romantic enough.

The bouncers turned out to be ineffective. It seemed the entire lower fifth year from St. Joseph's showed up, many without invitations. And got in. They stood at the side of the room, eyeing up the girls, putting on macho displays, a group of male peacocks strutting around showing their feathers as the girls giggled and played along.

"Do you want to dance?" Holly had been sitting with Olivia, and she looked up into sweet, eager brown eyes.

"Sure," Holly said awkwardly, turning to Olivia with a grin and a shrug as if to ask, *What could I say?* Self-consciously she followed the boy onto the dance floor, relieved the room was as dark as it was, knowing that every eye was upon them, that she would be the center of attention tomorrow, and finally having a slight understanding of what it is to be a girl, what it is to attract boys, and how addictive that feeling of power is.

"I'm Tom," he said, bopping in front of her.

"I'm Holly," she said, switching feet, hoping she looked cool.

"I know." He grinned. "I've seen you before."

"Oh. Okay." Pause for a few seconds. "Where?"

"Just around."

They danced to Adam Ant, Michael Jackson, and Human League. And then "Every Breath You Take" by Police came on. Tom raised an eyebrow and opened his arms, and Holly wrapped hers around him.

Together they stood, barely moving, rocking gently from side to side, and Holly had never felt so safe before, wrapped tightly in someone's arms, her head resting on someone else's shoulder.

Through Culture Club, then Lionel Richie, then Christopher Cross, Holly and Tom didn't move. Holly felt as if she had been waiting her whole life for this moment, and in a flash of light she knew what everyone was talking about. She understood about boys. She understood about love. And by the end of the night she knew that Tom Fitzgerald was her soul mate.

When Tom asked for her phone number, she thought she would burst with happiness. He phoned the next day, and they talked for an hour and a half. An hour and a half! She gleefully reported every sentence of their conversation to Olivia, who felt slightly left out and didn't quite understand what all the fuss was about. And so Holly turned to Saffron, and soon Holly and Saffron were sitting on the phone every night talking about either Tom or his best friend, Paul, whom Saffron conveniently fancied.

It didn't strike Holly as odd that Tom and she never kissed. She knew it was only a matter of time. What they did was talk. And laugh. They, and soon a large group of them, would go out every weekend. Saturday afternoons they would jump on a train and go out to the country. Someone's parent would drop them off at the theater. They'd meet up at the park and just sit on the swings for hours, a curious mix of adult and child, trying to act older than their years, yet still young enough to shriek with laughter as they squeezed down a slide designed for those far smaller and younger.

Soon, Holly's crush on Tom dissipated. Daniel joined the group—taller, louder, funnier than Tom—and within weeks Holly and Daniel were propped up against every available wall, snogging for hours. Holly, lying between Daniel's legs on a sofa at someone's party on a Saturday night, felt so grown up, so sophisticated.

Tom became her best friend. When Daniel dumped Holly for Lisa, one of the bitchier girls in her class, Tom was the one who comforted Holly, confessing that he had fancied Holly when they first met but that now he was glad they were just friends, especially since he'd recently started going out with Isabelle.

And of course Holly, who had gotten over Tom completely, found herself developing a major crush on him again. Except by the time he and Isabelle split up, she found herself going out with Dom Parks, and she and Tom drifted apart for a while—he and Dom Parks mixing in totally different crowds. The time Holly and Tom rediscovered their friendship, A-levels were looming and they both knew one another far too well for there to be anything between them other than friendship.

Olivia was a slow starter. She was more interested in animals than boys, but eventually, in the fifth term, as they were preparing for their O-levels, she developed a crush on her math tutor. Ben was a first-year student at UCL, only three years older than Olivia, but a math genius whose mother was a friend of Olivia's mother, hence the tutoring arrangement that Olivia was initially furious about.

Furious until Ben walked in. Quiet. Studious. Gentle. Olivia finally realized what everyone else had been talking about, and for the next two years she carried the weight of her crush in her heart, fantasizing about Ben turning to her over the calculator and admitting he'd fallen in love with her, dreaming of the day when Ben would see her as someone other than his little O-level math student.

The day finally came in the upper sixth. She had passed her math O-level with a B and had run out of excuses to see Ben. Her mother mentioned one day that she had to go over to see Ben's mother and that he was down from uni, and Olivia jumped in the car, desperate to show him how grown-up she was, how much she had changed, and how perfect she would be for him.

And he noticed. Noticed that this was a young woman standing awkwardly in the hallway of his house and not the child he had last seen two years previously. He noticed and he liked, and when they went into the den to chat about school and university, he was surprised at how easy she was to talk to, how sweet she seemed.

He took her to a movie that weekend and then out to the Queen's Arms for a drink a couple of nights later. Olivia invited him to a party that weekend, slightly apprehensive about Ben meeting her friends, worried he would find them too young, but after he told her how much he liked them, he kissed her, and Olivia floated up to her A-levels on a cloud of joy.

They all studied together for their A-levels. At the local library, Holly, Olivia, Saffron, Tom, Paul, and sometimes a couple of others, Ian or Pete, would grab a table upstairs, throw their books open and whisper to one another as they worked, all moving downstairs mid-morning, like a wave, to go to the local Italian coffee shop for cappuccinos and Silk Cut King Size.

Over twenty years ago and Holly remembers it as if it were yesterday. She remembers when they first met, when Holly loved Tom and knew that there would never be another Tom, how Tom and Paul had the same jacket in different colors. They had, in fact, bought them together one Sunday morning down at Camden Market, the five of them weaving their way through the crowds on Chalk Farm Road, cool, confident, indestructible.

Tom's jacket was navy. Paul's was green. Holly's heart used to lift when she saw Tom's jacket. Just a glimpse of navy in those early days would send her heart soaring, stick a smile on her face that seemed to last for weeks.

Holly remembers how Tom used to smile at her across the desk as they worked in the library. Sometimes she'd be buried in revision and she'd look up and catch Tom's eye and he'd grin; and even then, even when she was over her crush, knew that Tom probably wasn't the one for her, no longer spent nights crying in her bed as she listened over and over again to the soundtrack for *Endless Love*, even then she knew that whatever she and Tom had, it was special.

And thought that maybe, at some point in the future, they would find one another again.

Holly spreads the photos out on the floor and starts to move them around, sifting through for the photos from school, photos of Tom, needing to see him again, if only in a photograph.

She pulls one from the pile. It's Tom and some girl. Holly doesn't even remember who she was, only that she never liked the girl very much. Holly had been at Tom's flat when she had seen the photo; it was during one of her phases when she had been in love with Tom, but gently, one of the resigned phases when she didn't expect anything to happen, had been there so many times before only to have it pass. She had seen the photo and had demanded to have it because Tom looked so handsome, smiling next to the girl she hadn't liked. He looked almost model-like, and Holly had been so proud of knowing him.

Tom had cracked up laughing when Holly had said she was taking it. "I'm going to cut her out and stick me in instead," she had said with an evil glint, and Tom had shaken his head as if he didn't know what to do with Holly, which he didn't. She was, in turn, funny, delightful, warm, wise, insufferable, jealous, insecure, and impossible. He loved her but didn't know how he could live with her. He loved her but wasn't in love with her.

Not today, at least.

She just was.

Holly Mac.

A fact of his life.

Someone who would always be a part of him.

As he would always be a part of her.

Holly gathers all the photos of Tom and stares at them, one by one, thinking back, emerging from her reverie to answer a ringing phone.

"Hello?"

"Holly?" It's a familiar voice. A voice from a long time ago. It swims back through her consciousness, bringing the past back with it.

There's a pause as Holly nods, the voice trying to place itself, stopping her from speaking.

"It's Saffron."

"Oh Saff," Holly starts to cry. "Tom."

There are tears on the other end of the line. "I know," Saffron says, her voice uneven and small. "Tom."

CHAPTER THREE

Olivia steps through the door of her basement flat and flicks the light switch on as her three cats and two dogs come running to greet her excitedly. She bends down to cuddle them, folding her lips inward as the dogs lick her all over her face, then she walks through her flat turning on all the lights and all the table lamps until there is a warm glow throughout.

Grabbing the leads from the Shaker pegs by the front door, she clips them onto the dogs as they whirl around in joyous delight. She allows herself to be dragged up the front steps, turning once at the top to look back at her flat, which now looks warm and welcoming even from the busy street.

Olivia never used to keep all the lights on, but since she and George split up, coming home to a dark flat makes her feel far more alone than is altogether necessary, and her routine now involves whisking the dogs out for a walk and returning to a flat that could almost, *almost*, have a husband lying on the sofa reading the papers.

Except it doesn't. Not anymore.

Not that George was her husband, but since she was with him for seven years he might as well have been, and frankly she wouldn't have stayed with him all that time if she didn't think that at some point they would be walking down the aisle.

Olivia was thirty-two when she met George. Fantastically happy with her job as deputy director of the animal shelter, she was oblivious to the dating world unless one of her well-meaning friends set her up on a blind date—she had, much to her chagrin, unwittingly become something of an expert at these. Most of whom, Tom always said most of the dates would fall madly in love with her, but she was not particularly interested in any of them.

She had never wanted children—her babies were her animals, she said, and she was close to Ruby and Oscar, her niece and nephew, as close as she ever wanted to be—so didn't feel the pressing ticking of the biological clock that so many of her friends seemed to feel around the age of thirty, and was quite happy with everything in her life. Then George turned up one day to find a dog, and her life turned upside down.

It was his sweetness that did it for her. That, and the fact that he was as lovely with his three-year-old as he was with the animals. Not that she had given him any hint of a clue that she found him lovely—that would have been horribly unprofessional, but she leaned in the doorway and watched him play with one of her favorite dogs, Lady, a dog that had been in the shelter for months, that no one would adopt because she was eleven years old, not terribly pretty, and deeply terrified of people.

George had taken his daughter, Jessica, into the meet-and-greet room, and Olivia had brought Lady in, crouching down with her and soothing her as Lady looked frantically around for a corner in which to hide.

And George hadn't done what most people in this situation would do. He hadn't advanced on Lady, crooning in an attempt to make her feel comfortable, overwhelming and crowding her, he had just sat at the other end of the room, Jessica sitting next to him, and he had watched Lady as he talked to Olivia.

The usual questions. About Lady. About the shelter. How could she do it, didn't she want to take all the animals home? And then a little about her. How she started. Did she know she wanted to work with animals when she was a little girl?

"See?" He turned to Jessica. "You might grow up and work somewhere that helps to save animals when you're big." The little girl's round face lit up.

"We have an open house next Sunday," Olivia volunteered. "It's our big annual fund-raiser. We have stalls and games and pony rides. And the kids get to play with some of the animals."

"Oh we'd love that," George said. "Next weekend you're with Mummy, though, but I'm sure she'd let you come with me. Let's call her when we get home."

Ah, Olivia thought, her heart fluttering in a way she'd almost forgotten. *Divorced. But he can't be single, not this kind, lovely, gentle man. Surely he has a girlfriend, someone. And even if he were available, surely he wouldn't be interested in me. Not looking the way I look at work.*

Olivia spent far longer than usual preparing for the open house. Instead of scraping her hair back in a ponytail and wearing old jeans, a sweatshirt and wellies, she let her hair fall loosely on her shoulders and slicked on lipgloss and a touch of mascara. She wore cords and a shirt, and tiny silver earrings, and told herself that she was making this extra effort only because it was a special event, a fund-raiser, and as the deputy director of the rescue home she had to present a professional face.

Never mind that she had worn her old jeans and sweatshirt for the past four fund-raisers.

"Oooh," said one volunteer after another, after another, and another, when she walked in. "Don't you look *fancy!*"

"Off for a job interview?" They laughed.

And finally: "Why are you looking so *posh?*"

"Just ignore them," said Sophie, her able and lovely assistant. "You look gorgeous, Olivia. You ought to dress up more often."

"I'm hardly dressed up," said Olivia, who by now felt so self-conscious she may as well have been wearing a ball gown.

"But you look lovely nevertheless."

"Well, thank you." Olivia headed straight to the loo to check herself in the mirror, feeling overdone; but she wasn't, she realized—just more done than they had ever seen her.

George and Jessica came for the entire day. He bought twenty-four raffle tickets and won a course of pony rides for Jessica ("I think you may have to wait until she's a little older," Olivia said with a smile), a giant bag of dog food, and dinner for two at Chez Vincent on the high street.

"I hope that as the deputy director of the shelter," George said, having collected his prizes, "you'll be my guest at Chez Vincent."

"Oh . . . um . . ." Olivia flushed. "Well, yes. I'd love to."

"Good," the delight in his eyes was clear, "I'll phone you tomorrow and we'll organize it. And thank you for the most wonderful day. Jessie and I have loved every minute," and with that he leaned over and planted a soft kiss on her cheek.

She floated home.

One dinner became many, then became a relationship of weeks, which became months, then a year.

After a year Olivia's mother sat her down and asked whether George was planning on marrying her. Olivia's mother had divorced her father five years before, and Olivia was always surprised that, given this unexpected turn of events, her mother still seemed to think that marriage was the very pinnacle of achievement for a woman.

Olivia's mother continued to ask, on a regular basis, whether they were planning a wedding soon, inevitably sniffing and, on one occasion, stating, to end the conversation, "Of course he's never going to do it. Why buy the cow when you can get the milk for free."

"Mum!" Olivia reprimanded her sharply. She had heard enough, and Fern eventually backed off, but couldn't resist asking from time to time if Olivia thought it might be happening.

"I don't know when we're getting married," Olivia said. "Or even *if* we're getting married. I imagine we will at some point, but there's no hurry. Look at Goldie Hawn and Kurt Russell, they've never gotten married and their relationship seems great. We're quite happy as we are."

Which was true. Olivia had never thought she would need a ring on her finger to be utterly committed to someone, and there was no doubt in her mind that she and George were utterly committed to each other.

They had Jessie every other weekend, which was also easy for Olivia. Although Olivia had never been entirely comfortable with children other than family, Jessie loved animals, which always helped, so they bonded over the animals, and Olivia found a way of being Jessie's friend.

And Ruby and Oscar adored Jessie. Olivia's sister, Jen, would drop the kids at Olivia's almost every weekend they had Jessie, and when she and George went out with all of them, everyone would tell her what gorgeous children they had, and after a while she stopped explaining that none of them were, in fact, hers.

One year became two, then three, and after seven years Olivia knew that she was going to be spending the rest of her life with George, ring or no ring.

Until the night they went out for dinner and George announced that they were setting up an American branch of the advertising firm, and he was one of the people going out to New York to get it going.

"New York?" Olivia felt as if the air had been knocked out of her. New York. What could she possibly do in New York? What about the shelter? She couldn't leave now, not after she'd worked so hard to build it up, and where would they live? What about her friends? Her flat? But even as she thought that, she was thinking, New York! How exciting! How many people get the opportunity to even go to New York, much less live there!

"I'm going alone," George said gently, taking her hand across the table.

"What do you mean?" Olivia didn't understand. Still doesn't understand, for that matter. "What about Jessica?"

George sighed. "I know, this has been the hardest thing. I get her for the entire holidays, every school holiday, and I'm going to try to come back a couple of times a month, so hopefully it won't be so different. But when I say alone," he looked back up to meet her eyes, "I mean . . ." He sighed. "God, this is so hard. I'm not going with you, Olivia. I love you, I'll always love you, but I think this is a perfect opportunity for us to go our separate ways."

"What?" Olivia froze, feeling as if she were stuck in a bad dream. What had happened to her safe, predictable world? Why was it spinning out of control? "What are you talking about?" she managed. "Are you finishing with me?"

"That's not how I look at it," George said. "It's just that I don't see where this is going, it feels like we've been coasting, and I think this has happened for a reason, that it's time for us both to move on."

"But I don't want to move on," Olivia said, tears already welling in her eyes, hating herself for sounding like a five-year-old. "I want us to be together. I thought we were happy."

"We were," George said sadly. "But I'm not anymore."

Tom was the one who had sat on the phone that night as Olivia sobbed into the receiver.

"How could he do this to me?" she kept saying over and over again.

"I agree," Tom said from time to time. "Fucker. Do you want me to come over and break his legs?"

"I just want him back," Olivia sobbed, and this time Tom didn't say anything at all.

Six months on it was supposed to have become easier, but the truth was, it hadn't much. Tom checked in on her regularly, other friends dragged her out, and although she threw herself into her work, often the last one to leave the shelter, she still came home and lay on the sofa for hours, completely numb.

Bed offered no respite. She would wake up in the middle of the night and replay their relationship, wonder how it went wrong, think about the reasons why she wasn't good enough for him to stay.

"Oh Christ," Tom would say, his voice tinny on the line, as he sat at his desk at work in Boston. "It's not you, don't ever think it's you. He's obviously got some issues he needs to work out, but, Olivia, don't ever think it's because you weren't good enough for him."

She had even been on a couple of dates. Not willingly, it has to be said. She had hoped they would be a welcome distraction, but it was awful to have to be sitting across a table from a stranger, sharing your stories again, wondering how quickly you could possibly leave and crawl into bed. Olivia thought those days were over, thought she would never have to endure that particular hell again.

And then George phoned one night with some news. He sounded happy, as high as a kite, and Olivia expected waiting for those words she had been waiting for for months: *I've made a mistake. I miss you. I love you and I'm coming home.*

But instead George told her he was getting married. Oblivious to the pain that would cause, he went on to tell her that Cindy was someone Olivia would love, that he hoped Olivia would come to the wedding, and that he knew that Olivia would also find a love like this one.

"Cindy!" she had spat to Tom later that night on the phone. "How could he? How could he do this? And why is he getting married? Why didn't he want to marry *me*? What's wrong with me?"

Tom listened, and then, a couple of weeks later, phoned and said he thought the best thing for Olivia to do would be to have a fling, someone fun to take her mind off George, and he had just the person in mind.

"Oh God, Tom," she groaned. "Not you too."

"Look, I'm not trying to fix you up with the love of your life, but what harm could it do to go out and have some fun, at least recognize that George isn't the only man in the world, that there are plenty of great men out there who would be thrilled to be with someone like you. There's a guy in the office—Fred—who's really great, and he mentioned he's got a trip to London in the New Year, so I said I had a friend he should get together with who could show him around. He lives here, so I'm not thinking anything permanent, but you'd like him, and it could be a fun few days."

"Fred? Doesn't exactly conjure images of gorgeousness," Olivia said.

Tom snorted. "Yes, because George is such a sexy name."

"What about George Clooney?"

Tom sighed. "Okay, point taken. But you of all people know you can't judge a man by his cover. Or his name."

"So tell me about him," Olivia said reluctantly.

"He's thirty-three, single, freakishly fit—he does these Ironman competitions that are all the rage in our office and are completely mad and horribly addictive."

Olivia burst into laughter. "I suppose your idea of exercise is still ambling around a cricket field?"

"Yes, well. Quite. It was before I worked here. Have a look at his picture. It's on our Web site," and so Olivia looked while talking to Tom, and Fred was rather dishy, and even though she wasn't looking for anything at all, far too soon after George, maybe Tom was right, maybe a revenge fuck was just the thing she needed.

"Go on, then," Olivia said. "You can give him my e-mail address."

Fred e-mailed her the next day, and the two of them embarked on a fun, and rather more flirtatious than she had expected, e-mail exchange.

He sounded boyish and relaxed, and although she had always thought George was the perfect man for her, at forty-seven he was definitely set in his ways, and there was something about Fred's thirty-three years, his youth, that filled her with delicious anticipation.

"I wish I was coming over sooner," Fred wrote, "it seems so long to wait to meet you, until January. I was thinking maybe I could orchestrate a London meeting in November . . . what do you think?"

"I think that's a wonderful idea," Olivia wrote back. "I'd love to finally put a face to your name."

Olivia walks back into her flat, unclips the dogs, and feeds the animals before starting to think about feeding herself. She has become a creature of habit these last six months where food is concerned. When George was living here she would cook, would plan elaborate meals, or at least hit M&S food hall for something every night.

Now she can barely think about food. She keeps a stock of sliced turkey breast in the fridge, and usually eats it with half a bag of carrots and a couple of spoons of hummus.

When she remembers, she has Lean Cuisines on hand too. Not because she particularly likes them but because they are easy, because she presumes she is getting the nutrition she requires, and because she can throw them in the microwave and blast them without putting any thought or effort into it.

As a consequence, she has lost a stunning amount of weight. Not through choice, she is quick to tell everyone who asks her what miracle diet she has been on, but through stress and unhappiness. Her clothes are now hanging off her, and she knows she will have to buy new ones soon, but the thought of shopping for clothes has always filled her with horror.

Still. There are times when she feels like eating, and tonight is one of them. Sod's law, when she opens the fridge door, she is confronted with a nearly clear expanse of white: the wax rind of a slice of cheese that should have been thrown away when the cheese was finished, a clear plastic bag of greenish-black slime in the bottom drawer that she seems to remember may once have been mixed lettuce leaves, and half a pint of rancid milk.

The cupboard doesn't offer much more. A couple of Ritz crackers rattling around in the box, a full box of cornflakes, which doesn't hold much appeal without milk, and some tea bags.

There is only one thing to do on nights like this. She grabs her keys, heads out of the door, and drives up the road to Maida Vale. To her sister's house and, more specifically, her sister's fridge, which is always stuffed with delicious leftovers.

"Jen!" she calls out, throwing her coat on the chair in the hallway—something their mother has always hated, and something Olivia and Jen both started doing when they were about ten—except now that Jen is married and a mother herself, she hates it almost as much as their mother. "Jen?"

She knows she's home, her car is in the driveway, so Olivia heads through the hall to the kitchen, planning on rifling through the leftovers in the fridge while her sister makes her a cup of tea, able to do it now that both kids are fast asleep in bed.

As she opens the door of the kitchen, she sees Jen sitting at the kitchen table, and immediately she knows something is wrong. Her sister is just putting down the phone, and she is as white as a sheet.

"Jen?" Olivia feels fear grip her chest. "Jen? What is it? What's the matter? Is it Mum?" There is a touch of hysteria in her voice as it becomes louder.

"Oh Olivia," Jen says, her eyes filled with sadness. "That was Elizabeth Gregory, she's one of my friends from school. She knows . . . well, her husband knows your friend Tom. I don't know how to say this. I don't know how to tell you, but Tom was on that train."

"What train? What are you talking about?"

"He was on the Acela. In America. He didn't make it."

"What do you mean Tom was on the Acela? What are you talking about?" And then slowly it starts to dawn. "Tom? You mean *my* Tom? He's *dead*?" And without realizing it, Olivia sinks down to the floor, her body trembling like a leaf.

CHAPTER FOUR

"Thank you so much, darling." Holly reaches up to give Marcus a kiss on the cheek as he hustles Oliver and Daisy out through the door. "I can't tell you how much I appreciate this."

"You just remember this on the weekend when I want a lie-in," Marcus says. "Any message for your mum?"

"No, just tell her thank you and I'll call her tomorrow."

The kids are going to stay at Holly's mum's house for the night, and Marcus is going back to the office to work, leaving Holly to get dinner ready for the people she once felt she knew better than anyone else in the world, people she hasn't seen for years.

Twenty-one years, to be precise. And tonight this is not only their reunion, it is their private memorial service, their chance to support one another, to remember the Tom they all knew and loved. Continue to love.

Saffron has flown in from New York, where she was meeting with a film producer. She had been staying at the Soho Grand, had been right there when the train exploded. She, like many other New Yorkers who were instantly transported back to 9/11, had fled the city, thinking that this was just the first of a series of terrorist attacks. She had jumped in a friend's car heading out to their house in Bedford, crawling along the West Side Highway, shaking the entire journey, all of them stunned that New York was a target yet again.

Olivia had been at home, leafing through the *Guardian* as the dogs begged for food at her feet, not reading, mindlessly flicking pages as she tried to comprehend the tragedy, when Holly phoned her.

She had barely thought about Holly for years. She'd only spoken to her once since the summer after they all left school, when Olivia went off to Greece for a year and came back deciding to reinvent herself as a grown-up.

They had bumped into each other a year or so after university, and both of them had laughed at how different they were. Olivia's hair had been waist-length at the time, and Holly's curly mouse-brown locks had become a sweep of straightened gloss with mahogany lights.

Olivia would have stayed longer to chat, wanted, if not to become friends again, at least to find out more about Holly, but she had just started seeing Andrew, jealous, insecure Andrew, and he had hovered behind Olivia, nodding disdainfully at Holly when introduced, had created an atmosphere so tense that Olivia had allowed herself to be pulled away from Holly at the earliest opportunity.

And years later here was someone on the phone asking for Olivia, and how odd that the voice sounded just like Holly's.

"Holly?" Olivia finds herself saying, incredulously.

"It is you!" Holly says. "I wasn't sure."

"Oh Holly," Olivia said, as the tears started. "Isn't it just awful? Have you spoken to everyone? Have you been in touch with Saffron? And Paul?"

"I have," Holly said, finding her voice suddenly choking up. "I've spoken to everyone."

And speak to everyone she has.

All Holly wanted to do, leading up to the memorial service, was talk about Tom. All anyone talked about was this latest attack. She couldn't get away from it, and talking about Tom was a way for her to keep him alive. Even though strangers weren't interested in knowing anything other than here was someone who actually had a personal connection to the tragedy, Holly found herself talking and talking and talking.

Perhaps people were interested in the details, perhaps not. Nobody stopped her from talking, though; everyone wanted to share in Holly's personal tragedy, wanted to be able to go home and say they had met someone today who had lost someone in the Acela attack, as if they too were connected, had a different, deeper understanding of the pain and grief, the fallout from a tragedy such as this.

Marcus has been fantastic. Supportive when she needed it, giving her the space and time to cry when she needed that too. Since Tom's death, Marcus's behavior has reminded Holly of all that is good about him, and during those few moments when her grief subsides, she has been grateful for that. He was, she thought one day as she looked up at him, her pillar of strength, and immediately she knew that that was why she married him.

Everything about Marcus spells strength. From the set of his jaw to his quiet but firm insistence that his way is the right way. The first time Holly saw Marcus she'd known she had never met anyone like him before in her life.

And it helped that he was the diametric opposite of her father. She'd known he was loyal. She'd known he wasn't the sort of man who would have an affair, wasn't the sort of man who would leave his wife and daughter, to disappear into the ether leaving just a faint whiff of false promises. He wouldn't have an affair with one of her friends, as her last boyfriend, Russ, had ended up doing.

She had been at a friend's house in Sydney, having a cookout, when she met Marcus. Sitting on the grass in frayed denim shorts and a T-shirt, she was as brown as a berry from the traveling, the smattering of freckles across the bridge of her nose so plentiful, they almost created the tan themselves.

There had been tons of people there. Surfers mostly, and neighbors and friends, everyone arriving cheerfully bearing more food, more beer. Marcus had stood out, even then, with his odd formality. He'd looked like a stuffy English lawyer in his Ralph Lauren polo shirt, tucked into chino shorts belted with a plaited brown belt. Holly had watched him uncomfortably sipping his beer, not bothering to make small talk, and she had felt sorry for him. She had felt sorry for him as the only other English person there, as being a man who so clearly did not fit in.

"I'm Holly," she had said, clambering up and going over to him, extending a hand. "You must be Marcus," for she had heard one of the neighbors had a stuffy English lawyer staying with them, and he couldn't be anyone else.

His face had lit up. "You're English!" It had been a statement, not a question, and his gratitude at having been rescued had been sweet and endearing, and Holly had found she didn't mind spending the evening talking to him. And she hadn't minded when he phoned the next day to ask her for lunch, and she hadn't minded a couple of nights later when he kissed her as he was saying good-bye and dropping her off at her house.

He wasn't her normal type, but perhaps, she'd thought then, that wasn't such a bad thing. And where had her type got her, anyway? A series of destructive, disappointing relationships in which Holly had always seemed to be the one who got hurt. Maybe it was a good thing Marcus wasn't her type. And it wasn't as if he were awful. He certainly looked the part. He was tallish, not bad looking, clearly successful, and he seemed to adore her. Frankly it was bloody nice having a bit of adoration in her life.

I'll just enjoy it, Holly had thought to herself. *I know he's not the man of my dreams, but he's so different from everyone else I've been involved with, maybe this is better*

*for me, maybe this is what a real relationship looks like.
Maybe I was the one who was wrong, maybe I shouldn't
have looked for a soul mate, a perfect partner, maybe this
is what I am supposed to be looking for instead.*

Holly had been looking for safety. She had been looking for security at a time when she didn't feel secure.
Her heart had been broken one too many times, and
she didn't think she could do better, she didn't think
she deserved a happy ending. She told herself that
happy endings existed only in Hollywood films. That
friendship, security, and shared hopes and dreams were
far more sensible, far more likely to result in a long and
happy marriage.

She'd told herself that it was okay to settle. That she
could be a grown-up for once and make a grown-up
decision. That it would be enough.

But during her entire marriage, when Holly's thoughts
have turned to Tom, Tom has always been there as the
symbol of what might have been. He wasn't just the
one that got away, the road not taken, the love she
didn't choose.

Tom was the one Holly knows, deep down, she
should have been with. And so the loss is double. She is
grieving for her best friend, a man she loves, and she is
grieving for the life she was never able to have.

Tonight, at this preservice dinner, Holly is hoping for
something of a catharsis, is hoping that somehow they
will be able to share their grief, and move beyond it
onto a path of healing.

She is nervous about seeing the others. Is excited but apprehensive. Olivia had been bristly that one time she bumped into her at the cinema with an awful boyfriend who had seemed arrogant and rude.

"I can't believe I ran into Olivia and she was with this awful awful man," she said to Tom one night soon afterward, when they were sitting in a small Greek restaurant in Bayswater. "All these years of not seeing each other, and you'd think we'd have a fantastic reunion, but he basically dragged her away. You ought to say something to her about her taste in men."

Tom laughed. "It's none of my business, Holly. She likes him, isn't that all that matters?"

Holly sighed. "I suppose so, it's just that Olivia was always so sweet and so naïve around men and she doesn't seem to have changed. What's Saffron up to? Have you spoken to her recently?"

"You should ask her yourself. She'd love to hear from you."

"It's been too many years. I love hearing about her, but we've all drifted apart, and I doubt she'd want to hear from me anyway."

"I think she would," Tom said. "I'm sure she would. You all ask about everyone else but none of you will actually pick up the phone."

"It's because I honestly don't think any of us have anything in common anymore," Holly said. "Other than a shared history, and frankly how many times can you reminisce about slow dancing in church halls, wearing donkey jackets and monkey boots?"

"Oh God." Tom laughed. "I'd forgotten that. You looked terrible."

"Yes, well. You with your bad impression of Suggs weren't so hot either."

"Ah yes. I try to forget. But I do think you would have things in common with everyone, of course you would. There was a reason we were all friends."

"I don't know," Holly said doubtfully. "I think it was just being forced together for so long. You are funny, though," Holly said. "I can't believe that you're still in touch with everyone. How in the hell do you do it? I barely have time to answer the calls on my answerphone at night, let alone make time to phone a ton of people from my past. You're amazing, you know."

"I know. Isn't that why you love me?"

"Speaking of love . . ." Holly felt a familiar flutter. Here it was again. Like a constant merry-go-round, she was sitting across the table, aged twenty-five, looking at the face she knew better than any other in the world, her best friend's, and all she could think of was what it would feel like to kiss him. ". . . Are you . . . seeing anyone?" She fidgeted on her seat. Nervous.

"Why? Do you fancy me again?"

It had become a standing joke between them, this falling in and out of love with each other, but to Holly's embarrassment she found herself lost for words, a deep blush spreading across her face.

"Oh God." Tom was mortified. "I didn't mean that. Oh God, Holly. If you'd told me two months ago."

"Two months ago I was with Jake."

"I know." Tom smiled. "I was horribly jealous."

"Well, why didn't you say anything?"

"Because you were with Jake. What difference would it have made?"

"I might have dumped him for you."

"Holly, Holly, Holly." Tom put his head in his hands. "We're not destined to be together, you know that."

Holly's blush faded as quickly as it came. "I know." She sighed. "But what about if we're both still single at thirty? How about we make a pact that we get married if we're both still single at thirty?"

"Thirty?" Tom sounded slightly alarmed. "That's only five years away. Can we make it thirty-five?"

"Okay." Holly extended her hand across the table and Tom shook it firmly. "Thirty-five and we get married."

"Done."

"So go on," Holly said after a few minutes, mouth full of pita and tzatsiki. "Who is she, then?"

And on it went.

Holly has not had the heart to cook, but has made a salad, has picked up a gourmet pasta dish, a couple of baguettes, and a tiramisu from the Italian deli down the road. Several bottles of wine are chilling in the fridge.

Holly sets the table for four, everything taking five times as long as it usually does because she loses herself in a constant stream of memories about Tom.

She finishes getting the table ready, then goes to the bathroom to attempt to mask the pain her face has been carrying the last few weeks. Murine eyedrops to wash the redness from her eyes, tinted moisturizer to even out her skin, now blotchy from the streams of tears. Eye shadow to make her eyes bigger, blusher to bring color to her face, recently an unbecoming shade of gray.

Not gorgeous. Not now. But presentable. That's the best she can hope for. As the doorbell rings, Holly sighs and smooths her hair behind her ears, then she walks down the stairs.

She has often thought about a school reunion, but never thought it would be under circumstances such as these.

CHAPTER FIVE

Olivia is first. Standing awkwardly on the doorstep proffering a bottle of wine, Olivia is surprised at how naturally she and Holly fall into each other's arms, and when they pull apart, both wipe their eyes and smile, shaking their heads, too overcome with emotion to speak.

A Saab crawls slowly up the road, and they turn, Holly squinting at the car, a man and a woman peering out of the window. She waves furiously as they pull into a spot, and Paul and Saffron make their way up the path, all of them smiling sorrowfully at one another, before wrapping each other up, one by one, in huge tear-filled hugs, unable to believe they are together again after all these years, unable to believe what has brought them back together.

Holly is suddenly enormously relieved that the clattering group has made its way into her kitchen in her home. Olivia had suggested going out, didn't want Holly to go to the trouble of cooking, preparing a meal, but Holly had known she couldn't deal with this in a public space, needs intimate surroundings to talk about Tom, needs the warmth and comfort of a home.

"How are you?"

"You look fantastic!"

"Look at you!"

"Our friend the film star!"

"Oh my God! How long has it been?"

Their voices echo around the kitchen as they smile at one another, Olivia grinning at Saffron, Paul squeezing Holly's shoulders, Saffron feeling, for the first time in years, that she doesn't have to be Saffron Armitage, movie star, that she can finally be Saff. Just Saff.

"It's good to be here." Paul sinks into a kitchen chair, gulping from a glass of wine. "Horrible, awful circumstances but, Christ, it's good to see all of you."

"Forgive the movie cliché," says Saffron, emotion choking her voice, "but I feel like I've come home."

Olivia breaks the silence by prodding Paul. "You've obviously eaten well all these years," she says with a grin.

"Oh charming," Paul says. "I don't see you for, what? Twenty years? And the first thing to come out of your mouth is an insult. I see you haven't changed a bit."

Olivia puts her arm around Paul's shoulders and squeezes, leaning down to kiss him on the cheek. "You look great. I'm just teasing. Anyway, you should be happy I still feel so comfortable with you."

Saffron wanders into the living room looking at the photographs dotted around. She picks one up—Holly and Marcus grinning at the camera as they perch on a wooden gate in the country.

"Holly," Saffron calls, "is this your husband?" She holds up the photograph.

"Yup," Holly peers around the doorway, "and those are my kids over there."

"I can't believe it," Saffron shakes her head. "Holly Mac married. With children no less."

Holly comes back in from the kitchen with a smile. "Hey, Paul. Speaking of married, I saw some spread you did in *Vogue* when you got married. Mr. bloody Prada. I almost phoned you then just to laugh at you."

Paul dips his head sheepishly. "Ah yes. Did feel a bit of a poseur. Had the piss taken out of me for weeks, and only did it because Anna thought it would be great publicity."

"Was it?"

"Yup."

"God, I love Fashionista!" Holly says. "I used to spend a fortune with that other clothes Web site, but the service was crap. Everything always used to arrive about two weeks late because it was always out of stock, and they never apologized, which drove me bonkers. So now I only use Fashionista and it's amazing. Seriously, the packaging, the speed. Tell your wife I'm a huge fan and she's doing an incredible job."

"I don't suppose your wife would give us mates' rates?" Saffron attempts.

"Sure. You'd have to meet her first, and she'd have to like you, which is obviously a problem, but I'll work on it." Paul smiles.

"Why do you buy so much stuff from them?" Olivia asks.

Holly shrugs. "Two reasons. First, whoever is buying for the Web site has the most spectacular taste imaginable—"

Paul nods smugly. "That'd be the wife."

"—and," continues Holly, "it seems that one of my vices as I have grown older is compulsive shopping."

And so it goes on . . . As the evening wears on, inhibitions are loosened, and connections are being made again. Whatever it was that kept them from one another all these years has now disappeared without a trace.

Olivia, so nervous about seeing these people against whom she had always felt so inadequate, doesn't feel inadequate anymore, is surprised and moved to find that she no longer feels Saffron is prettier or that Holly is cleverer and, although it may still be true, it doesn't bother her now, doesn't provide a yardstick against which she constantly has to measure herself and find herself falling short.

Saffron is calmer, more measured somehow. The Saffron of old was a shrieker, but the Saffron sitting here today seems, even through her sadness, to be at peace. The drama queen of old has settled down, she is comfortable in her skin and far more beautiful today because of it.

Paul is the same. He hasn't changed at all, despite Holly dragging out the copy of *Vogue* (she'd gone out and bought it immediately). Tom was right, Holly thinks back with pain, remembering her conversation with Tom when she first saw Paul in *Vogue*. He is still a scruff, just one with the ability to scrub up incredibly well.

And Holly? Holly is the one you might perhaps worry about the most. She is the one who seems lost. Even here, among people who have known her longer than anyone else, although she appears comfortable, her feet tucked under her at one end of the long, squishy sofa, even here she looks lost.

"Tom was probably the most consistent thing in my life." Olivia reaches over to the coffee table and pours herself more wine as she sighs. "Whatever else was going on, whoever else might have left me, or however crappy my job might have been, Tom was always there. Not that I saw him that often, but he was so fiercely loyal in his friendships, he'd always be there for you. God, I tried to get rid of him in my twenties, but he just wouldn't bloody disappear . . ."

The others laugh.

"You know what I loved best about Tom? That he didn't change. That he was never impressed by people or things. He knew me for so long that he refused to be impressed by my acting or the films I was in. Used to piss me off enormously," Saffron admitted with a shrug. "After I was in that film with Dennis Quaid, I thought he'd finally treat me with a bit more respect, but he didn't give a damn. Actually, I think he even told me to get off my high horse once upon a time."

"Did you?" Paul looks at her with an amused grin.

"What do you think?" She raises an eyebrow as she turns her head slowly to look at him.

"Thought not."

"I know this sounds terrible," Holly says quietly, "but don't they always say you never appreciate what you have until it's gone? I spent years falling in and out of love with Tom, and then I met Marcus, and then obviously Tom and I were just friends, but I wish I'd spoken to him more, wish I'd shown him how much I loved him. I mean, how can you know something like this is going to happen?"

"Of course you can't," Saffron says, "and he would have known. He knew how much we all loved him. That's why he insisted on staying in all our lives."

"Let's toast," says Olivia. "To Tom . . ." she raises her eyes upward, ". . . . wherever you are."

"To Tom," they all echo. "We wish you were here."

"More coffee?" Holly sighs as she pulls her legs out from under her and hoists herself up from the sofa, knowing that there was a difference in her relationship with Tom but not wanting to share it with the others. Not yet.

"I think more wine," Paul says, as he drains the dregs of his fourth glass.

It was not long after the dinner in Bayswater. Before her trip to Australia where Marcus had swept Holly off her feet, before a time when she would look at Tom and see nothing more than a best friend.

Another dinner. This time in Holland Park. Not for any reason other than to catch up with each other. Holly had been to the huge Ghost warehouse sale that morning—had pushed her way through hundreds of desperate west London women to grab anything that looked vaguely her size, had thought nothing of stripping down to bra and knickers to try on her pickings in the middle of a room filled with clothes racks.

She had found a beautiful diaphanous lilac coat. Sheer, flowing, it wafted out behind her as she walked. It was tied around the neck with a delicate beaded string, and worn with sheer flared lilac pants and a camisole vest.

She looked beautiful that night. The afternoon had been a hot one. She'd met a group of girlfriends on Primrose Hill. One had brought an oversized blanket, another baguettes, another cheese. Holly had brought wine, and they'd all taken off their T-shirts, rolled up their peasant skirts as far as they dared, and basked in the sun as Frisbees and balls whizzed over their heads, dogs running up and trying to pinch some of their food.

Holly had the kind of skin that looked at the sun and bronzed. That night she tipped her head upside down and shook her hair out to achieve that slightly wild, sexy look, swept ultraglow on her cheeks, and popped silver hoops into her ears. She wasn't doing it for Tom but for herself, although she knew Tom would appreciate it.

He pulled up outside the flat at seven, beeped the horn, and Holly ran down the stairs and tumbled into his car.

"You look *gorgeous*!" he said in surprise as she leaned over and kissed him on the cheek.

"I know!" she said. "Ghost sale. Dirt cheap. Isn't it fantastic?"

"Yes, and how come you're so brown?"

"Mixture of Primrose Hill and makeup. You like?"

"You look the very picture of health. Come on. I've booked Julie's."

"Oh I say," Holly settled back in the car seat. "How romantic."

"I know. I was hoping I might get lucky."

Holly raised an eyebrow. "Play your cards right and you just never know."

They had a quiet, candlelit table in the corner of the room. For anyone other than Holly and Tom it would have been absurdly romantic, but instead of murmuring sweet nothings across the table, they chatted nineteen to the dozen and kept bursting into splutters of laughter over shared jokes.

They fought over the crème brûlée, clashing forks like swords as they each battled to get more, and when Tom pulled up outside Holly's flat, he did as he usually did, walking up the stairs with her for one last coffee.

It was a perfect evening. Neither one had fallen in love with the other, both of them just enjoying each other's company, no false expectations leading to disappointment.

Holly sank into the sofa next to Tom, and threw her legs over his.

"Careful," Tom said with a grin. "You wouldn't be leading me on, would you?"

"Not bloody likely," she said, sipping her coffee. "I've learned my lesson too many times before, thank you very much."

"I've often wondered . . ." Tom said, not looking at Holly but focusing on her lilac Ghost-clad legs instead, "what it would be like to kiss you."

"Oh stop it." Holly burst out laughing. "Don't tell me tonight you're actually going to make a pass at me?"

Tom shrugged and grinned. "I was thinking about it."

"Go on, then." She raised an eyebrow, knowing this wasn't going to happen—there was no sexual tension, no heat, no admissions of sexual attraction. "I dare you."

For a few seconds neither of them moved, Holly about to burst into laughter again with an *I knew you were just faking*, and then slowly Tom put down his coffee and turned back to face Holly, and all of a sudden she wasn't laughing anymore.

It was the slowest, most tentative, most thrilling kiss she had ever had. Even as his lips first met hers she didn't think it was happening, was still sitting there with a smile, not expecting Tom to really go through with it.

Soft, gentle, just the feeling of his lips on hers, and her smile disappeared. Then again, the kisses on her upper lip, her lower, until she dared lick his upper lip, ever so gently, and there they were. Kissing. Arms reaching up to stroke a face, trace a cheek, fingers running smoothly down the nape of a neck.

"Holly." A whispered sigh from Tom.

"Sssh." Holly dissolved into him, then pulled back to look at him. Tom. Her Tom. Gazing up at her through half-closed eyes glazed with lust. She didn't say anything, didn't want to spoil the moment, and leaned down again to kiss him more, quick clever fingers swiftly undoing the buttons on his shirt.

"Tom." A whispered sigh from Holly as she plants kisses on his chest, moved back up to reach his lips.

So familiar. So safe.

So this is what it's like.

Like coming home.

Tom left before morning. What felt so right and so natural under the cover of darkness started to feel increasingly unnatural as daylight approached.

Tom left Holly sleeping. He stood next to the bed and watched her as she slept, just before he crept out of the door, and he felt an enormous sadness. He never truly thought this would happen with Holly. He loved her more than he'd ever loved anyone and however attracted he was to her, you can't sleep with your best friend and then expect everything to be normal.

You can't sleep with your best friend and then start dating, going out for dinner, sharing your stories, seeing how it goes.

You can't sleep with your best friend and be anything other than an immediate "couple." There is no halfway measure. You sleep with your best friend and you have one of two consequences. Either way the friendship is over.

Tom loved Holly, but he didn't plan this, isn't ready for this. He was only twenty-five, not nearly ready to settle down with anyone. Not even Holly. He still had wild oats to sow. Jesus, he shook his head viciously. What on earth was he thinking? But Holly, so lovely in her lilac, so much lovelier later in bed, how could he not? How could any man resist?

And what was he to do now?

Holly called Tom the next afternoon. Got him on the phone whereupon they had an awkward, stilted conversation. The most awkward conversation Holly had ever had with anyone, but a conversation she was not unfamiliar with. These are the conversations you have with men who feel you are putting pressure on them, she realized. These are the conversations you have when you are about to be dumped, when you are clearly feeling so much more than they.

But how could this be? This wasn't just anyone. This was Tom. *Tom!*

They said good-bye and Tom put down the phone and sank his head in his hands. He hated this. The last person in the world he wanted to hurt was Holly, but what choice did he have? He knew he couldn't be her boyfriend, and how could they go back to being just friends after last night?

He'd take some space, he decided. Not phone her for a little while. Not abandon her, never abandon her, but they would both take a little space until they could pick up the friendship where they left off. Prior to last night, that is.

For several weeks Holly was devastated. She had had enough relationships over the years to know, with pain and shock, that Tom was no different from any of the others, that their years of friendship stood for nothing, and that things would never be the same between them.

Leafing through the back of *Time Out* one afternoon, she saw an ad for a three-month expedition in Australia. Life in England had never been bleaker, and the constant entreaties from friends to just get out and get on with life fell on deaf ears. She needed a change, needed to get away from the memories, needed to replace the videotape in her head with something other than that one night with Tom. That whispered "Holly" that she thought meant he loved her would never leave her.

Tom finally tried to get in touch when Holly was in Australia. He missed her. Had thought of many other things, but ultimately all roads led to Holly, all other girls were not what Holly was, and mostly he remembered the longing, the feeling of having come home.

"Tom? It's Holly!"

"Holly? Where are you? Where've you been? I've missed you, where the hell have you been?"

Holly laughed. "Australia. I was meant to go for three months but ended up staying for six. I've had the greatest time of my life, and I've met someone! Can you believe it? This is it, Tom, this is the man I'm going to marry. I can't wait for you to meet him."

Sweet Tom, Holly thought, having made a date for Tom to meet Marcus. How I've missed him, she thought. And she was too caught up in the rebound to hear Tom's confusion, to think that she might have broken Tom's heart in much the same way he had broken hers a few months earlier.

"I loved him," she wants to shout, to tell Paul and Olivia and Saffron, but she doesn't because she knows what they will say.

That they loved him too.

CHAPTER SIX

"Christ, there are a lot of people," Marcus mutters, turning the wheel hard as he circles the block for the third time.

"I imagine there's probably quite a contingent from America," Holly says, scouring the people walking up toward the church to try to find someone she knows. "Oh look!" she says. "There's Saffron. Saff! Saffron!" She sticks her head out of the window as Saffron turns and waves, hurrying gratefully over to the car.

"Oh thank God," she says breathily. "I didn't want to go in on my own."

"Can I get out and go with Saffron?" Holly turns to Marcus, only to see he is completely starstruck, and she suppresses a giggle. "You two haven't met, have you? Saffron, this is my husband, Marcus. Marcus, this is Saffron."

"How lovely to meet you." Saffron shines her most luminous smile on him, and Holly uses the opportunity to hop out of the car. "I'll see you in there," she says as Marcus regains his senses, thanks to a car behind them honking, and drives slowly down the road, leaving the two girls standing facing each other, laughing.

For Marcus can be charming. He can be quite the most charming man you could ever wish to meet. He is known on the court circuit as Jekyll and Hyde. One day he can be delightful and the next he will be so dismissive and curt that he will leave people standing still in shock, wracking their brains to think of what they might possibly have done.

And he is always charming when he is faced by someone he is seeking to impress.

"I thought your husband was supposed to be an arrogant wanker," Saffron says.

Holly should be upset, but she has long suspected that people secretly think this, and so it has ceased to bother her. "Most of the time he is, but, as you can see, he can also be devastatingly charming."

"Was it just me or was he a little starstruck?" Saffron giggles.

"Yes, well. It seems Marcus isn't quite so cool and collected when faced with genuine celebrity." Holly rolls her eyes as she links her arm through Saffron's. "Anyway, who told you he was an arrogant wanker?"

"Am I allowed to drop Tom in it at his own memorial service?"

"Figures." Holly snorts, and they join the hordes of people as they start walking up the driveway.

"So did Marcus see *Lady Chatterley*? He probably fancied me rotten when I played Lady Chatterley."

"I think everyone fancied you rotten when you played Lady Chatterley." Holly laughs. "Whoops, careful. Your head seems to be expanding."

"Oh God. Don't be silly. It wasn't me; they all fancied my character. First time I ever did full nudity and I'm still paying the price. I can't seem to meet a man these days without his tongue hanging out."

"Sounds good to me. Seriously, though, Saff. If you want Marcus you can have him."

"Thanks," Saff peals with laughter, "but my hands are perfectly full dealing with P."

"Is that what you call your luvver whom you refuse to talk about? P?"

"Easier than his full name, and no one would guess if they overheard anything. I . . . oh God. You can keep a secret can't you?"

"Of course."

"He's famous. Incredibly famous, so you have to swear not to tell anyone."

"Cross my heart and hope to die."

Saffron leans forward and whispers a name into Holly's ear.

"But . . . Isn't he married to . . . ?"

"Exactly. That's why it's so secret. Sssh," Saffron puts her finger to her lips as they approach the door, "I'll tell you more later."

They step into the cool lobby and follow the crowds into the church. Standing room only. The place is packed, several hundred people crowded in.

"Where are his mum and dad?" Holly whispers, looking toward the front.

"We'll find them later. I haven't seen them for years, have you?"

"No. I just keep thinking how awful for them to lose a son."

"What about his wife? Sarah, isn't it? Is she here with the kids?"

"She's got to be here. Excuse me. Excuse me. Sorry." They shuffle past huddles of people expressing the same shock and bewilderment until they can just get a glimpse of the pulpit.

"Let's stay here," Saff says. "At least I can breathe. Do you think your husband will be able to find us?"

"I hope not." Holly sighs, and Saffron frowns at her.

"Is everything okay with the two of you?"

Holly's laugh is hollow. "I'm just being silly," she says. "Ignore me."

"Holly Macintosh? Saffron? *Oh my God!*" Holly and Saffron find themselves looking up at a tear-streaked face, a huge dramatic black hat, a skin-tight fitted suit, and high heels with scarlet soles that immediately give the shoes away as Louboutin.

"I don't believe it!" the girl says, sweeping first Holly, then Saffron into a giant hug. "I haven't seen you since school, and isn't it so awful that this is the first time we see one another? Can you believe it? Poor Tom. And poor Sarah. I can't even think about the children, it's just too heartbreaking."

Holly sneaks a look at Saffron, a look that says, *Who the fuck is this?* But Saffron seems to know, or, at the very least, is doing a wonderful job of hiding that she doesn't. "I can't believe how wonderful you look," Saffron says. "You haven't changed at all."

"Now I *know* you're lying," the girl says, leaning forward slightly with a whisper. "My nose was about the size of this church at school. Thank God for plastic surgery and husbands willing to pay for it! Speaking of whom, this is my husband, Eric." A short, sweet-looking man steps forward and shakes hands with Holly and Saffron. "We were all at school together," she explains to Eric before looking back at Holly. "Didn't you and Robin go out for a little while?" Holly looks completely blank as Saffron lights up, realizing who this woman is, leaping in to save the day.

"Holly!" Saffron says. "You remember? You did! You went out with Robin Cartledge for ages. How funny that you should remember that, *Sally*." She shoots Holly a look.

Holly does a double take. This is Sally Cartledge? Sally Cartledge was the mousiest girl in the class, with a nose that earned her the nickname Concorde. She was one of the clever girls who never seemed to discover boys, who left school to go to Oxford and was never heard from again.

But how can this possibly be Sally Cartledge? This willowy, brunette beauty with immaculate makeup and legs that go on forever. Holly stands in shock and squints slightly at Sally, trying to see anything of the old Sally in her, but no. Nothing.

"We're going over there," Sally trills. "But so lovely to see you. Can we swap cards? I'd love to get together sometime."

As she and Eric walk off, Saffron breathes a sigh of

relief. "Jesus. Thank God she brought up Robin or I would have had no idea who she was."

"How is that Sally Cartledge? What has she done to herself? When did she become beautiful?"

"I'd say after she paid the plastic surgeon for the nose job, Restylane implants in the lips, Botox everywhere else, got her teeth fixed, and probably spent a few years doing something like the Zone."

"But *God*. I've never seen such a dramatic transformation. I wouldn't have had a clue it was her."

"Good, huh? I ought to have gotten her surgeon's name."

"Why? What would you have done?" Holly is horrified.

"Oh darling," Saffron laughs, "I've already had my boobs done twice, Botox is basically as essential as brushing your teeth, and I'd quite like to have my eyes done."

"What do you mean, have your eyes done? Have what done to them? They look fine."

"No. See these pouches?" Saffron points to the skin under her eyes. Holly leans forward but sees nothing.

"Nope."

"Get closer. See? This little bulge? It's fat that's dropped and I'm desperate to get it removed. The easiest operation in the whole world, and it should take years off me."

"Whatever happened to growing old gracefully?"

"Not in film these days, my darling. Now you have to use all the help you can get."

"I think you're bonkers. I can't see anything at all."

"Maybe not, but I can. All I see when I look in the mirror these days are pouches. Anyway, P said he'll pay for it."

"He will? Why?"

Saffron shrugs. "He paid for his wife's work, and he paid for my two boob jobs. At seventeen million a picture, I think it's just a drop in the ocean. Anyway, he enjoys it. Says he likes spoiling his little girl."

"Hmm. That sounds like a healthy relationship." Holly grins. "Oh shit. Marcus is over there. Quick. Duck." She grabs Saffron and scoots behind some other people.

"Yes," Saffron says with an ironic smile. "And you're clearly the expert on healthy relationships. Don't worry, you don't have to explain anything now, but there's definitely something up with you two. God, where *did* all these people come from?"

"Who knows? I mean, I know everybody loved Tom, but half these people don't look like they even *knew* him. Sssssh. They're starting."

Holly and Saffron stand quietly as a hush descends and music starts softly playing from the speakers, Linda Ronstadt's voice as clear as a bell as her voice reverberates around the church.

So good-bye my friend
I know I'll never see you again
But the love you gave me through all the years
Will take away these tears
I'm okay now
Good-bye my friend

And the grief that had been waiting at the door is welcomed in as, finally, people start to cry.

Tom's dad, Peter, is the first to speak. He walks up to the pulpit and clears his throat, and Holly's first thought is how very old he seems, standing up there. She remembers him as a big, imposing, hearty man. Not this little, lost, and, well . . . old man, fumbling for his reading glasses and shuffling his papers.

"On August the seventeenth, 1968, I was standing outside St. Mary's Hospital having a cigar in anticipation of the birth of my first child," he starts, his voice surprisingly strong and clear.

"In those days we weren't allowed to be present at the birth, or at least that's what I told my wife," a ripple of relieved laughter throughout the crowd, "and I wasn't supposed to be having the cigar, but it was burning a hole in my suit pocket and I couldn't wait.

"Well, it took the nurses half an hour to find me, but eventually they did, and they told me I had a beautiful bouncing son, Thomas Henry Fitzgerald. Good job I wasn't in the room because I had other plans for the name—Octavius Auberon was one of my choices . . ." more laughter, "but Maggie won and, more importantly, Thomas Henry completely won my heart.

"The name Thomas means dependable, and even as a little boy, Tom was always dependable. There are plenty of other words I could use to describe him, and those of you who accompanied him on his annual New Year's pub crawl could, I'm sure, certainly think of a few choice alternatives, but you could always rely on Tom, and he was the most loyal son, the most loyal friend any man could wish to have."

Laughter and tears. Pleasure and pain. The range of emotions throughout the service is so great that at times Holly thinks she can't stand it. She looks around and sees people looking blank, or whispering to one another, or laughing about something, and she can't understand how they can look so normal, how they can behave as if nothing is wrong, when she herself is struggling so hard to suppress sobs she can feel welling at the back of her throat, she thinks she is going to explode.

They are all so dignified, she thinks. His dad able to smile through his speech, his mum looking pale but strong beside him. Will, his brother, telling funny stories of things they got up to when young, ridiculous pranks they had played on each other, and how they were so close people would think they were twins ("Will being," he said, "the better looking, more charming, more successful one," which cracked up all of Will's friends who knew him to have a somewhat unreliable career).

One more friend, and then Sarah. Still and quiet, there is something mesmerizing about her lone American voice in this oh-so-British service. She talks about why she fell in love with Tom. About their children. About what a wonderful father he was. And as she is talking a little girl runs over and tugs on her sleeve.

"Mommy?" she says loudly. "Why are you talking

about Daddy? Can we see him now? Is this heaven?" And Sarah picks Violet up to comfort her as the church fills with tears yet again.

Sarah ends with a Christina Rossetti poem, her voice breaking halfway through "remember me when I am far away," and she struggles to finish, Chopin's Prelude No. 6 finally easing through the speakers, allowing people to hug one another and break down, file slowly outside, blinking in the glare of the sunlight as they fish crumpled tissues out of pockets and blow their noses, smiling sorrowfully at strangers.

Holly takes deep breaths to regain her composure, then turns to see Marcus joining them.

"Where were you?" he says sternly. "I was looking . . ." and he notices Holly's tear-stained crumpled face and stops, holding his arms out to hug her instead.

"Thank you," Holly says, disengaging herself after a few moments. "Wasn't it heartbreaking?"

"It was tough," Marcus agreed. "And I didn't even really know him. I thought Sarah was wonderful, though. So strong and stoic." *Ah yes,* thinks Holly. *How typical of Marcus to admire those qualities in a widow, or indeed in anyone.*

"I don't think it's necessary to go back to the house, though," Marcus says. "Far too many people, plus I've got to prepare for a court hearing tomorrow. We have to leave."

How very different we are, she thinks again; and then, as so often happens these days when she thinks about

Marcus, a word flits into her head, announces its presence, then disappears.

Arse.

She thinks but forces a smile. "I have to find his parents," she says. "And Paul and Olivia are here somewhere. And I think it's wrong not to go back to the house. Work can wait, surely. I mean, this is more important."

"More important than me preparing for a hearing?" Marcus says coldly. "I understand you're upset, Holly, but if you'd given me notice that this was going to be longer, I could have made different arrangements."

That's it, Holly thinks. *Make it all my fault as usual.*

"I'll bring her home," Saffron says brightly. "You go off and do your work, don't worry about Holly."

"Oh thank you, Saffron, that's incredibly gracious of you." Marcus smiles, giving Holly a perfunctory kiss, and then Saffron the standard double-cheek air kiss. They stand watching him stride off toward wherever his car is parked.

Arse.

Holly turns to Saffron. "Gawd. I'm surprised he didn't try to stick his tongue in your mouth." Holly rolls her eyes.

"Oh behave," Saffron says. "He'll get over it. Frankly it's bloody nice to be appreciated, though, particularly at a memorial service."

"Yes, nothing like a spot of inappropriate flirting at a memorial service," Holly says.

"Speaking of which, horribly and entirely inappropriate to even mention this, but did you see Will?"

"You mean, cute and cuddly little baby brother Willy, who we used to occasionally let in to watch us being horrible teenagers and play spin the bottle?"

"That'd be the one. But did you see him?"

"Big brown eyes, messy longish hair, gorgeous smile with dimples and an undoubted six-pack under the suit? That one?"

"That'd be the one."

"Nope." Holly shrugs. "Can't say I noticed him."

"Who would have thought he'd grow up to look like that!" Saffron says.

"Actually I think he looks just like Tom," Holly muses. "A messier, more laid-back, younger version of Tom. Imagine him with a short back and sides in a polo shirt and jeans, and he's basically Tom."

"Maybe, but I never fancied Tom and I do quite fancy Will."

"Saffron!" Holly glares at her. "That's sick. This is his brother's memorial service."

"I know, I know," she grumbles. "And I'm not actually interested, just observing, that's all. Oh come on, Miss Holier Than Thou, just because you're married doesn't mean you can't look. You're married, my darling. Not dead!"

"Well, ask me again when today is over. Right now I just want to find Tom's mum and dad."

Holly hovers a few feet away from where Maggie and Peter are greeting a line of people. Maggie looks up and catches her eye, turns back to the people who are giving her their condolences, and then she looks back at Holly.

"Holly?" she says, and Holly nods shyly, then Maggie opens her arms for her to go running up for a huge hug. "Oh Holly!" she says. "It's been too long. Years and years. Look at you, Holly! Peter! Look!" she calls over to her husband. "It's Holly Mac!"

After Holly's parents divorced when she was fourteen, her mother had moped for the year after the divorce, then had got out of bed, got a job in the trendiest interior-design shop, and suddenly turned into the mother from hell.

She started wearing tons of makeup, all the clothes that Holly and her friends wanted to wear but couldn't afford (although no one's mother was supposed to be wearing Vivienne Westwood, for heaven's sake), and going out clubbing every night, staying with a series of friends, each one seemingly younger and funkier than the last.

In short, she'd had enough of being a mother. Even though Holly, at fifteen, was more or less old enough to take care of herself, she didn't want to. Her friends adored coming over because, save for a Spanish au pair who didn't seem to want to have anything at all to do with Holly or her friends, there were no adults to tell them what to do.

At Holly's house, they didn't have to sneak cigarettes on balconies or stick their heads outside open windows in the middle of a freezing winter. Hell, at Holly's house, they could sit around the kitchen table and get high as kites or drunk as skunks, whatever the substance of choice happened to be that day. It was not dissimilar to life at Saffron's, except Saffron's parents were around. Liberal enough to let Saffron do whatever she wanted, at least they were there.

Everyone was jealous of Holly, and all Holly wanted was to be normal. She wanted boundaries. She wanted a mother who would tell her she couldn't wear makeup to school and a father who said she had to be in by eleven.

What she wanted was a family.

And what she got through her friendship with Tom was Tom's family. Their kitchen was filled with delicious smells from Maggie's cooking, the kettle seemed to have just boiled no matter when you walked in, and every cushion was plastered with hair from Boris the Labrador or one of the cats. It was messy, noisy, and fun. There was a constant stream of people dropping in and staying for meals, and Holly felt as much a part of the family as Tom and Will.

"I always wanted a daughter," Maggie would say, taking Holly with her as she ran up to the supermarket or taking Holly to M&S and treating her to a new jumper or a pair of shoes. "You're part of the family," she would say, and Holly knew she was.

They even gave her a bedroom. Actually it was the junk room, but they cleared some of the stuff off the bed so Holly always had a place to sleep, and Peter found an old turntable at a car-boot sale that he picked up for a fiver so Holly could listen to her beloved Police albums.

Holly and Tom would lie on the floor in his room (Tom had a much better turntable and stereo system, but that was okay, it was his house after all), and make compilation cassettes. Some were love songs, others dance songs, but they spent hours painstakingly recording their LPs and writing in all the songs on the tiny lines. "Tom, Will, Holly . . . supper!" would come up the stairs, and they would yell down, "in a minute," then Tom would complain and Holly would pretend to complain when, in fact, she was overjoyed to be treated as just one of the kids.

She stayed close to them until she got married. Even after marriage she saw them a bit, but then Tom moved to America, and, it was true, she hadn't seen them for years.

Peter's mouth falls open when he sees Holly. "My goodness, Holly Mac! You're all grown up," he says, and as he hugs her Holly feels herself well up.

"I'm so sorry," she says, looking from Maggie to Peter. "I wrote to you and I tried to call but I couldn't get through. I just wanted you to know how terribly sorry I am, how much I miss Tom."

"Thank you," Maggie says, squeezing her arm. "It's the most terrible thing that's ever happened to us, but you know he would have loved this service. He would have loved that Peter was still able to make people laugh, and weren't those stories of Will's funny? For as awful as this is he wouldn't have wanted everyone to stand around and be sad, he would have wanted to be remembered for all the good things."

"I know," Holly says, smiling; and then, out of nowhere, her face crumples and she starts to sob.

"Oh love," Maggie says, and putting her arms around Holly she finds that the stoicism she has faked so well for today, this day she has been dreading, disappears, and the pain of losing her son is so great she leans onto Holly and dissolves into tears.

They stand there for a long time, silently crying, and then they break away and wipe the tears.

"Oh Holly, I'm sorry," Maggie says. "I didn't mean to collapse on you like that."

"Maggie, it was me. I'm so sorry I had no right to cry on you after everything you've been through. I'm so embarrassed and I'm so sorry."

"Don't be embarrassed. Come back to the house and have a cup of tea. That should make us all feel better."

REMEMBER BY CHRISTINA GEORGINA ROSSETTI

Remember me when I am gone away,
Gone far away into the silent land;
When you can no more hold me by the hand,
Nor I half turn to go, yet turning stay.
Remember me when no more day by day
You tell me of our future that you planned:
Only remember me; you understand
It will be late to counsel then or pray.

Yet if you should forget me for a while
And afterwards remember, do not grieve:
For if the darkness and corruption leave
A vestige of the thoughts that I once had,
Better by far you should forget and smile
Than that you should remember and be sad.

CHAPTER SEVEN

It smells the same. Despite all the people crowding into the hallway, the living room, every available space, the first thing Holly notices as she walks through the door is that Maggie and Peter's house still smells the same.

Like home.

The same dhurrie rugs thrown haphazardly in the entrance hall, the same huge squishy sofa now covered with various throws under the giant mirror against the back wall.

Paintings Holly recognizes, new ones filling every square inch on the walls. Large oils in elaborate frames, Matisse lithographs, line drawings of interesting faces, landscapes, abstracts, all thrown together and all working perfectly.

And then, above a console table, a framed line drawing of the Fitzgerald family—Maggie and Peter grinning with their arms wrapped around each other, and Tom, Will, and Holly lying on their tummies in front. *Happy Anniversary 1984! Lots of Love, Holly* written at the bottom. Holly had copied a photograph with her Rotring pen, then had added herself as part of the family.

Maggie is, as always, in the kitchen. Unwrapping cakes and platters of sandwiches on the kitchen table as friends of hers bustle around refilling the kettle and making sure there are enough cups.

The kitchen table is still the same, the kitchen cupboards updated—no longer seventies pine and melamine counters, the cupboards are now a pretty antique white with thick butcher-block counters, but the dresser holding all the plates is still there, as is the old church pew serving as a bench on one side of the scrubbed refectory table.

"What do you think of the old place?" Maggie looks up and sees Holly. "Hasn't changed much, has it?"

Holly shakes her head with a smile. "Apart from the cupboards in here, it looks exactly the same. I keep expecting to see Boris leaping about the kitchen."

"Oh Boris." Maggie smiles. "What a good dog he was. A maniac, but a good one. Nowadays we have Pippa, who's a rescue dog, although quite pretty. We think she's spaniel crossed with retriever."

"Where is she?"

"She hates lots of people so we moved her bed up to our bedroom. Olivia has taken her out for a walk."

"Ah, of course. The animal lover."

"Thank goodness I was able to say we rescued Pippa—I think it immediately put us in her good books."

"As if you would ever be anywhere else." Holly laughs. "Do you need help?"

"No, love. I'm almost done. Anyway, keeping myself

busy seems to be the best thing for me at the moment. I love all these people coming over all the time. I just wish it wasn't under these circumstances." Maggie's eyes glaze over for a second, then she shakes her head to dislodge the thoughts and reaches behind her for some plates.

Holly leaves the kitchen and continues walking down memory lane, loving how so little has changed. She pushes her way between the people standing around with cups of tea in hand, sharing their stories of Tom, and she walks upstairs, knowing she has to see Tom's room.

Pushing the door open, she expects to see little changed. The rest of the house is exactly the same, why would this be any different? And of course in the movies, the bedroom is always just as it was. But bizarrely, this is the one room that is entirely different. The walls are a fresh yellow, framed prints of Babar and Le Petit Prince line the room, and there are pretty twin beds with teddy bears sitting atop the pillows.

Holly smiles. Of course. This is now Dustin and Violet's bedroom, where they stay when they come over here. She walks over to the window seat and sits down, leaning her head on the windowpane as she looks out on this familiar view, remembering when she and Tom would lean outside seeing who could blow better smoke rings.

The door creaks and Holly turns around with a start, immediately feeling guilty about being in Tom's bedroom, being somewhere she doesn't belong, although of course she does belong here.

If she belongs anywhere at all, if Holly has a home anywhere in the world, this is where it is.

"I thought I saw you at the service, and I had a feeling I might find you up here." Will stands in the doorway with a huge grin, then holds out his arms for Holly to run into.

"Oh Will," Holly says, leaning her head on his shoulder as she squeezes him tight. "Look how grown up you've become! I can't believe it! It's so good to see you, and you look just like Tom! Look at you—you're a long-haired version of Tom. Oh God, Will," she feels her eyes well up, "it's so awful. I'm so so sorry."

"I know," Will says, rubbing her back. "I still feel a bit numb, really, and it's so completely bizarre seeing all of Tom's old friends here, most of whom I haven't seen for years."

They disengage and both move toward the window seat, grinning at each other.

"You look great," Will says. "You've improved with age."

"Oh shut up," Holly says, blushing ever so slightly. "And I don't look great. Look at this gray hair and these lines." She raises her eyebrows to create a series of mounds on her forehead.

"Well, okay, you don't look so great when you do that, but, seriously, it's so good to see you. What happened to you? You got married, we all came to the wedding, had a couple of Christmas cards, and then you dropped off the face of the earth."

"I know. I can't believe I lost touch. I suppose life just got in the way. Husband, children, work."

"Ah yes. Those things that normal people do. I can't say I have much experience of them."

"No? Why? Are you still the reprobate son? Have you been trapped in time somewhere around 1989?" Holly laughs.

"According to my parents the answer would be yes." Will smirks. "I just don't think I'm the settling-down type."

"What? No devoted wife and six children then?"

"Hardly. I'm something of a serial monogamist. Thus far I've been accused, several times, of being a commit-aphobe, but I think I just haven't met anyone I've wanted to commit to."

"So how old are you now? Thirty-five?"

"Yup. Exactly."

Holly shrugs. "You have plenty of time. I got married in my twenties and frankly I think it was probably too young. Not that it was a mistake or anything, I'm incredibly happy . . ." She falters slightly, wondering why she is coming out with a lie such as this, and to Will of all people, but she feels safer in the lie. "I think it ought to be illegal to be married before thirty."

"Because?"

"Because you change so much in your thirties, how can you possibly predict whether you'll grow together or apart?"

"So," Will studies her face for a second, "have you and . . . is it Marcus?" Holly nods. "Have you grown together or apart?"

"Oh God, Will! Isn't this a bit heavy for Tom's

memorial service?" Holly won't answer the question. Can't answer the question. Doesn't want to even *think* about what the answer is going to be.

"Enough about me," she says instead. "What about work? Are you hugely successful at something? A millionaire with gorgeous models hanging off his arm?"

Will laughs. "Hardly. Well, I have had a few gorgeous models, and I'm relatively good at what I do when I do it."

"What is it?"

"I'm a carpenter, I suppose. Or cabinetmaker. I mean, I do everything, but I basically do it to fund traveling. I try to do six months here to make enough money to spend six months traveling and living abroad."

"Wow!" Holly raises her eyebrows. "You really are a commitaphobe."

"Oh don't you start." He grins. "You mean because I haven't settled down with a bachelor pad and a pension?"

"Well, isn't it opting out of real life a bit?" Holly can only say this because it's Will. Anyone else and she'd never dare say these things. "I mean, I could understand you doing this at twenty-five, but thirty-five?"

Will laughs. "I'm living the life that makes me happy, and wouldn't you say that's the most important thing of all? I can honestly say I love my life, and how many people do you know can say that?" There's a pause and he grins again. "Can *you*?"

"I have wonderful children," Holly says. "And a wonderful life. I adore my work, and the life I've created."

But even as she says it she knows it's not true, particularly after walking back into this house today.

For Holly always wanted *this*. She wanted crazy and chaotic, wanted the house filled with children and laughter and fun. But Marcus won't allow it, and it is just starting to dawn on Holly that she may never have the life she wants. Not with Marcus.

"But are you happy?" Will persists.

"Is *anyone?*" Holly tries to shrug it off. "As a concept it's great, but, honestly I think most of the time I'm just getting on with life. Sure, at times I'm happy, but happy all the time? I think that's unrealistic."

Will tilts his head. "That's the point. While I can't say I'm happy all the time, I can say I'm happy *most* of the time. I wake up in the morning and I love my life. I enjoy all of it. That's why I do it. If I wake up one day and decide that now's the time to settle down and buy a house, have 2.4 children and everything that comes with it, I'm sure I'll do it. But right now this is what makes me feel good."

Holly shakes her head with a resigned smile. "If it works for you, that's great. Really. I always think we can't question another person's choices—how can we judge unless we've walked in their shoes?"

"My philosophy exactly. So . . . have you seen Scary Sarah yet?"

Holly's mouth falls open. "How do you know I called her that?"

"Tom told me." Will's eyes sparkle with amusement. "He thought it was hysterical."

"Oh God, I'm so embarrassed," Holly groans, sinking her head in her hands. "And no, I haven't seen her yet. How is she?"

Will looks sad. "The truth is she's a complete mess. I would have expected her to be incredibly cool and stoic and to act as if she were handling it perfectly, but she keeps breaking down in tears, which none of us know quite how to handle. I was amazed she managed to pull it together for the service."

"Is she downstairs?"

"Probably. Or maybe in the guest room. I have to say I've warmed to her enormously these last couple of days. I always called her the Ice Queen, but I think I'm seeing the real Sarah now."

"Come on," Holly stands, "I have to find her, and we ought to go downstairs."

As they head out of the door they both turn to the other spontaneously and give each other a hug.

"It's so good to see you," Holly says into his ear. "Like rediscovering my long-lost little brother."

"Ouch." Will pulls away then smiles. "Did you know I used to have the most enormous crush on you?"

"You did?" Holly is stunned.

"I did. You were the first great love of my life."

"I was?" Holly's hand flies up to her heart that just fluttered in an unexpected way. "I never knew!"

"I never told you. Come on. Let's go and find Sarah." Will holds out his hand and guides Holly gently down the stairs.

"Come tomorrow," Maggie says as she hugs Holly good-bye. "Everyone will have gone and I'd love to spend some real time with you. How does the morning sound?"

"It sounds wonderful," Holly says. "Will Sarah be around, do you think? I'd love to talk to her."

"I hope so," Maggie says. "She just couldn't face talking to people after the service. All so draining for her, plus she's drugged up to the eyeballs. Her doctor's got her on all these pills. Zoloft and Xanax for depression and Ambien to sleep. I think she's taking pills pretty much all day."

"Sounds frightening."

"I rather think it is, but it seems this is what they do in America. Still. Hopefully she'll be up tomorrow. I'm sure she'd love to see you."

I'm not so sure, Holly thinks but doesn't say.

At three in the morning, as usual, Holly finds herself wide awake. She tries lying in bed for a while listening to Marcus snore, and eventually gets up, throws on a robe, and goes upstairs to her studio. Sitting down at her desk and turning on her computer, she slides the scrap of paper that Will had scribbled his details on from under her notebook and studies his e-mail address.

Opening her e-mail account she taps his address in and is smiling as she writes. A few sentences about how lovely it was to see him, how much she misses Tom, then she erases and starts again.

A few sentences about how good it was to be able to really talk to someone, how rare to reconnect so strongly with someone from your childhood, then she erases and starts again.

"If I was the first," she taps, a smile playing on her lips, "who was the second? From Curious Insomniac in Brondesbury." And she switches her computer off and goes downstairs to make herself some tea.

Marcus leans over to kiss her good-bye, as he always does at 5:30 in the morning. He leaves the house to drive to the tube station, briefly rousing Holly, who, if she isn't already awake, tries to go back to sleep for an hour until the kids come in to wake her up.

Today Holly lies in bed listening until the front door closes, hears his car start up and pull out of the driveway, and when she can no longer hear it she leaps out of bed and runs up to her studio, turning her computer back on, going straight to her inbox and smiling as she sees a reply from Will. Wow, she thinks. Sent at 4 A.M. He doesn't sleep either.

Dear Curious Insomniac in Brondesbury,

Interesting question. Am thinking that perhaps there has only been one great love of my life, however had a lesser love at Durham for Cynthia Fawley. Worshipped her from afar (seems to have been a pattern of my younger years) for a year, ended up going out with her for a year after she broke up with her muscular but dim-witted rugby-playing boyfriend. Have had several loves, unsurprisingly for a thirty-five-year-old, over the years but none quite as innocent or pain-searingly sweet as my prepubescent dreams. Do you remember we almost snogged once? You and Tom let me join in spin the bottle and I spun that thing, praying to God and promising that I'd never do anything bad again if I got you, and I did. And we went into the cupboard and you kissed me on the lips, and I was desperate to kiss you properly but I didn't know how. That kiss kept me going for years (may still be keeping me going even today) . . .

Is he flirting with me? Am I flirting with him? What is this? What am I doing? Isn't this how affairs start? Haven't I always said I would never have an affair, not after my father? Haven't I always said infidelity is the greatest betrayal a human being can make? Oh for heaven's sake, Holly, this isn't flirting. This is just having some fun. Who said anything about an affair?

And it can't *be flirting. This is Tom's brother, and Tom's not even cold in his grave. The last thing Will's going to be thinking about is this, and it's the last thing I would be thinking about. How entirely inappropriate would flirting be? There. Settled. This isn't flirting. This is friendship.*

Odd, perhaps, that these questions are even there, albeit not in the forefront of Holly Mac's mind, so Holly tells herself that she has rediscovered an old friend. That the reason she is sitting in front of her computer at

5:30 A.M., checking e-mails, is because she is excited at finding the Fitzgeralds again, excited at seeing Will again after all these years.

And so what if there is a touch of innocent flirting going on? How lovely, actually, to be flirted with after so many years of having no one look at her.

Holly used to feel gorgeous, but lately she feels harassed. In her running-around-with-kids clothes she feels like a stressed mum, and in her cashmere sweaters and pearls, out with Marcus in the evening, she feels like a fraud.

Rarely does she feel like Holly, the real Holly. The Holly that Will has known. Perhaps this is why she feels so comfortable, she muses, as she thinks about what to write back.

And if he is flirting gently, so what? Holly would never do anything, and how invigorating to have a gorgeous single man pay you attention. They will just be friends, she decides, and how lucky to have a male friend, how much she has missed male friendship since she and Tom drifted so far apart.

It doesn't occur to her that this is almost always how these things start.

Paul rings later that morning. "Maggie said you were going to their house today and I'd love to go too. I barely saw you yesterday, and Saffron disappeared early to take a call from P. I'm picking Olivia up at eleven, then heading over to the house. Want me to come and get you?"

"Thanks Paul, I'd love it," Holly says, replacing the phone and wondering how it is that you can go for twenty years not seeing people, then when you do, nothing has changed, it is instantly comfortable and familiar, as if all the years in between had been erased.

She takes extra-special care today before going to Maggie and Peter's. A little more makeup than usual, a little more blow-drying to ensure her hair is smooth and silky. A sexy shirt and navy trousers, high-heeled boots—thank God it's October!—and peridot flowers in her ears.

"Wow! Look at you!" Olivia grins as she gets in the car. "Are you off for a job interview later?"

Holly blushes, instantly self-conscious. Perhaps she should change, perhaps this was over the top. She had sent an e-mail back to Will telling him she was coming over today. As she showered she found herself thinking: *If he likes me, he'll be there.* And immediately reprimanded herself for being so childish.

"No, but a meeting at work," Holly lies. "I usually try to dress up a bit when I go in."

"You look great," Paul says. "Hey, both of you, if either of you want anything from Fashionista just let me know. You should look at the Web site because Anna said she'd give you anything wholesale."

"I'm not sure that Fashionista is my thing." Olivia laughs, gesturing at her old jeans and workman's boots. "I think my fashion days are long gone."

I wouldn't mind looking, Holly thinks. Although she said she bought from the Web site all the time, it isn't strictly true. She has bought from the Web site and does love it, but Marcus never seems to like anything from there—*too trendy,* he always says, *inappropriate,* he says, *just wrong.*

So it has been a while since Holly browsed Fashionista clothing online.

It's time I treated myself, she thinks, hearing Paul's offer. *Time I bought something for myself, something that I love, never mind about Marcus.*

Before Marcus, Holly had loved expressing herself through her clothes. She had spent hours at Portobello looking for the perfect vintage dress, had always known exactly what was in and what was out that season, and even though she couldn't afford it, she could make do between Miss Selfridge, Warehouse, and the markets.

And when she could afford it, when she married Marcus and he started to make serious money, she found that he hated the clothes she would bring home. Gorgeous shift dresses from Egg in Knightsbridge, beaded kaftans from little boutiques in Notting Hill, tumbling chandelier earrings of amethyst and quartz.

Eventually the trendy clothes were relegated to the back of her wardrobe, then given to her cleaning lady. Marcus would joke that Ester the Filipina cleaner had a more expensive wardrobe than most of their friends.

She learned to dress in clothes that Marcus approves of. Sensible, conservative, luxurious. Her jewelery is classic and unobtrusive, her hair sleek and usually pulled back because Marcus doesn't like it down.

Today she has put on the hoops that Marcus hates

and that she loves, and has slipped on the high-heeled boots that Marcus deemed cheap. She looked in the mirror before leaving and felt sexy, something she hasn't felt for years. And now, sitting in the car, Holly thinks she wouldn't mind having some fun, funky clothes.

She's fed up with the cashmere bloody jumpers and the Tod's bloody loafers. She will go to Fashionista, and she will see if they have anything she likes. She's not even forty yet, she muses. Too young to dress like a sixty-year-old, and so what if Marcus doesn't like it? She doesn't like his pretentious monogrammed Turnbull & Asser shirts, but that doesn't stop him from wearing them.

Sarah is sitting at the kitchen table as they walk in, pen in hand, writing letters to the hundreds of people who have written to her.

As Holly walks over she looks up and Holly is shocked at what she looks like. Sarah has only ever been immaculate. *Prissy* is the word Holly has always thought. Hair perfectly coiffed, makeup minimal but elegant. Today her face is puffy, her eyes red rimmed, deep shadows underneath. She is in an oversized sweatshirt that Holly immediately knows must have been Tom's, and her hair is frizzy, coming out of the messy ponytail.

Had you been at the service yesterday then saw Sarah right now, you would never know you were looking at the same person. Will was right. She had managed to pull it together yesterday. Quite how much, Holly didn't realize until now.

"Oh Sarah," Holly says, sympathy and sorrow washing over her. "I'm so sorry." And she puts her arms around Sarah, who leans into her shoulder and bursts into tears.

"I just miss him," Sarah sobs. "I just miss him so much."

"I know," Holly whispers, rubbing her back. "I know."

"I'm sorry," Sarah says after a while, pulling back and digging a shredded tissue from her jeans pocket. "I keep falling apart on people."

"I think that's what you're meant to do." Holly squeezes her hand.

"He loved you, Holly," Sarah says suddenly. Unexpectedly. "You always had a special place in his heart, and I was always jealous of you. I'm so sorry." And this time it is Holly's turn to cry, her carefully applied makeup running all the way down her face.

"No Will today?" Holly has waited an hour, hoping, each time the door opens, that Will will walk through, but nothing.

Maggie shakes her head. "Darling Will," she says. "We love him but he's hopeless. Responsibility has never been his strong point, and he's never been good at time keeping. He'll probably show up sometime this evening. Isn't he something? Can you believe our little Will has grown up?"

"Unbelievable," Holly agrees, wondering why her heart is sinking. This evening. *Could she come back?*

Would it be ridiculous? There are the kids to get to bed, Marcus to take care of. No. With a sigh she realizes she can't come back. *So much for "if he likes me, he'll come,"* she thinks, and when Paul comes over and asks her if she's ready to leave, she nods, amazed at how you can go from such a high to such a low in such a short space of time.

CHAPTER EIGHT

"Mummy, can you give me some cereal?" Daisy's plaintive little voice is inches away from Holly's face, as the sun streams through the wooden blinds on this bright Saturday morning.

"Yes, darling," Holly groans, opening one eye and squinting at the alarm clock. Six fourteen. Oh God. What she would give to have children who sleep in late. "Just give me a minute." Holly finds herself drifting back to sleep, when Daisy's voice intrudes again. "Mummy? When are you going to get out of bed? Are you stuck?" Holly has occasionally gotten away with Daisy believing she is stuck in bed, running into Frauke's room instead, allowing Holly to get back to sleep.

"No. Coming," she says, throwing the covers back and looking at the lump on the other side of the bed that is Marcus. In all their years together, Holly doesn't remember a time when Marcus got up to give the children breakfast. He is busy working all week, he says, and the weekends are the only time he gets to sleep. What about me? Holly once tried to argue. I work too, and I raise the children and I run the house and I pay the bills and I cook. When do *I* get a lie-in?

You have Frauke during the week, Marcus argued back. And then inferred that Holly's job was largely irrelevant. An indulgence, she thinks he called it, whereas his job was very important and he was tired and he *deserved* to sleep.

There are times when Holly looks at Marcus and hates him.

And there are times when Holly finds herself behaving like a teenager. "Oh yes," she has started muttering under her breath when Marcus finds he can't help wash the dishes or put up a curtain rod or give Holly a break by taking the children for half an hour. "I forgot you are a *very* busy and important man."

"You know my husband's a *very* busy and important man," she has started saying to Frauke, and the two of them snort with laughter, Frauke having lived with them long enough to recognize that Marcus would never deign to do anything helpful around the house when solitaire and backgammon are calling him from the privacy of his office.

Oliver is already curled up on the sofa at the far end of the kitchen, glued to some inappropriately violent cartoon, which he shouldn't be watching, but it stops him and Daisy from fighting, and it is Saturday morning after all.

Holly spent every Saturday morning during her childhood glued to *Multicolored Swap Shop*, occasionally switching over to *Tiswas* (which she didn't like nearly as much), and it didn't do *her* any harm.

"Morning, Olly," Holly calls, but gets no response. She tries again, and is rewarded with a flicker of eyes in her direction and a grunt.

"Who wants French toast?" she asks brightly, checking she has plenty of eggs, and Oliver finally rouses himself enough to say he does.

"Can I help, Mummy?" Daisy drags a chair across the kitchen and hauls herself up next to Holly. "I'll do the eggs," she says, and Holly smiles and watches as Daisy cracks both eggs and eggshells into the bowl.

"Watch me," Holly says, taking an egg and separating the shell carefully with her thumbs, the egg plopping into the bowl. "See? Now you try." Daisy does the next egg perfectly, her little chest puffing up with pride.

Holly changes the radio from Radio Four—Marcus's choice—to Radio One, and makes a strong cup of coffee for herself, opening the local paper on the counter to see if there is anything to do with the kids this weekend. Her weeks seem to zip by, she is busy flying from one thing to the next, with never enough hours in a day, but Saturdays and Sundays have started to crawl by, and she never thought she'd dread a weekend, but these last couple of years she has started to dread them more than anything.

They never seem to see anybody anymore. Despite Holly's—admittedly less—frequent entertaining, it is rare for them to be invited back. Perhaps it is that no one is doing dinner parties these days, for on the odd occasion their friends have a large party they always seem to be invited; but Holly has a sneaking suspicion that it may be more to do with Marcus.

Holly can't organize the playdates she organizes during the week because weekends are family time, and Marcus isn't usually up until lunchtime, so every weekend morning is now spent trying to find things for the children to do. She would be perfectly happy to stay at home with them and, frankly, let them watch CITV, but at some point a fight usually breaks out—who has the remote control, who has more space on the sofa, who pinched whom—and the couple of times they have woken Marcus he has emerged in a fury.

It's easier just to take them out, so very much easier just to find something out of the house to do. Olivia had left a message last night, saying she had her nephew for the day, and did Holly want to get together. Her sister's kids are older than Oliver and Daisy, but they're happy to play with younger ones occasionally, and she'd love to spend some time with Holly again. Holly calls her back, and a few minutes later the date is set, and she breathes a sigh of relief.

Because the easiest thing of all is to fill her life with distraction, with running around, with activity after activity, because if Holly ever stopped and took a breath, she might realize how lonely she is, and if she realized how lonely she is, the whole pack of cards might come tumbling down.

The park around the corner is Holly's favorite Saturday morning destination, especially on a crisp autumn day like today. The children can go leaf jumping, there's a great playground, both of them love seeing the dogs out on walks—several of whom they have come to know—and there's a sweet little café where Holly can get a cup of tea and occasionally a croissant or a pain au chocolat as a treat.

Oliver and Daisy both love the playground, although Oliver is professing to be slightly bored with it now that he's nearly seven, therefore nearly grown up, and it's really for children, but there are always other mothers for Holly to talk to, and she found most of her friends in the neighborhood at the park.

The au pairs all congregate here during the week, sitting on park benches as their charges run around, chatting nineteen to the dozen, all of them with cell phones in hand, texting furiously at the same time as talking. Holly has watched Frauke text, feeling very inadequate—she could never attain the same speed and ease. When Holly texts Frauke, it takes her about five minutes to bash out one sentence, and that makes her feel terribly old.

"Yay!" Oliver's face lights up as they walk through the park toward the playground, and he breaks into a run, tearing in front of them as he pushes the gate open. "They fixed the pirate ship!" He roars into the playground, closely followed by Daisy, both of them stumbling up the plank of a wooden pirate ship that has been cordoned off for a month while they've been sanding down the splinters and resealing it.

Holly sees Olivia sitting on a bench, and realizes that the only other boy in the playground must be Oscar. She walks over to Olivia, who grins widely as she finishes her phone call.

"Gotta go," she says on the phone. "I'll call you back

later. *Holly!* " She stands up and the two women hug. "God, so ridiculous how years can go by without seeing each other, and now I haven't seen you in a couple of weeks it feels like it's been years! How are you?"

"I'm great. It's good to see you. Thank God, actually." Holly sticks her hands in her pockets and shivers at the November sky. "I thought I'd die of boredom sitting in the park again by myself, it was a complete godsend when you called."

"I know." Olivia laughs. "Why do you think my phone is surgically attached to my right ear?"

"Where's your niece?"

"They've taken her to a girly birthday party. It's all makeovers and fashion shows, and Oscar pretty much said he'd kill himself if he had to go, hence his day with me. So what's up with Marcus, where's he today?"

Holly looks away.

"Uh-oh. If he's anything like my sister's husband I'd have to guess either working or sleeping. Hmm. I'm going to go with working."

"Nope, lazy arse is sleeping." Olivia rolls her eyes as Holly shrugs. "Why is it that they think they work harder than anything and deserve all this time off when they have no idea what we do? Christ, if Marcus had to look after the children and run the house for a week it would be a disaster."

"God, I know. When my sister went to Spain with the girls for five days she came back to find mountains of laundry and nothing had been done. And when Ruby ran out of underwear, Michael just went out to the Gap and bought her a ton more. Not to mention that their routine went out the window. He was giving them tubes of Smarties every night as a bribe to get them into bed, then wondered why they spent the next two hours thundering round the house on a sugar high."

Holly starts laughing. "At least he gave them Smarties. With Marcus it would be like bloody boot camp." She starts doing an impression of Marcus: "Oliver! Get your shoes off the sofa now! Daisy! Put those cushions back. Oliver! Upstairs to your homework now! Holly! Stop breathing! Now!" Holly sighs.

"Oh well," Olivia rubs Holly's arm, surprised at how much Holly is sharing. "These things are sent to try us. It's really great to see you, you know. There's just something about getting together with people who have always known you."

Holly smiles. "I know. It's like family."

"It is. And I've missed it. You and I ought to do lunch sometimes. Or a girls' night out. Something just to get away from it all and remember who we really are. God knows I could do with a few laughs now and then."

"I'd love to," Holly says truthfully, and Olivia's face lights up with inspiration.

"What are you doing tonight?" Olivia says. "Not a girls' night, but why don't you and Marcus come over for supper? I always feel horrible about not doing anything on a Saturday night."

"No babysitter," Holly says. "Frauke's going to Brighton for the weekend. But we're not doing anything, and anyway, you're the single girl, we ought to be cooking for you. Why don't you come over to us?"

"Are you sure? I feel like I've just invited myself."

"Well, you have. But that's okay. We weren't doing anything anyway. It will be lovely."

"I'm supposed to be dropping Oscar back at Jenny's at five. Unless you want to do it with kids." Olivia looks over at where Oscar and Oliver are bonding on the top of the ship, barricading it so Daisy can't get up, and as Daisy starts to wail, Holly looks back at Olivia with a wry smile.

"Oh, I think definitely without," she says.

Daisy stumbles over, her face dissolving in tears. "The boys are being mean to me," she says as Holly pulls her onto her lap and makes a face at Olivia.

"Yes," Olivia concurs. "Definitely without."

By the time they get back home—three pains au chocolat, two hot chocolates, and one cup of tea later— Marcus is sitting at the kitchen table with a *cafetière* full of coffee, classical music wafting softly from the speakers in the wall and the papers spread out in front of him.

"Hello, my darling children." He smiles, putting the paper down and opening his arms wide for his giggling, excited children to run into. "I've missed you this week. Oh my goodness, Daisy, have you grown two inches since Tuesday?"

"No!" She giggles. "Maybe just one inch."

"Well, you look much much taller. And Oliver, where did those muscles come from?" He squeezes Oliver's spindly little forearm gently.

"I've been practicing my push-ups," Oliver says proudly. "And I'm very good at gym at school. My gym teacher says I'm the best in class."

"Well, that is good news, isn't it? I can tell!" And Marcus looks over the children's heads at Holly and winks at her, and Holly can't help but smile.

At times like these, when Marcus is loving, and kind, and gentle, Holly knows that it will be fine. That she didn't make a wrong decision, that perhaps it is possible that she will spend the rest of her life with him. There are things missing, undoubtedly, but perhaps what they have is enough.

How could she possibly split up their family when he has the capacity to be such a good father? Yes, he is mostly an absent father, but nothing lasts forever and, perhaps, as the children get older, he will realize how important it is to be around for them, to leave work early to get to the children's shows at school or the PTA evenings or just home to put them to bed.

At times like these, Holly knows why she married him. He is a good man. He may want a different lifestyle than Holly, but she is such a good chameleon that it is not a huge hardship to step into the role he expects, and surely the payoff is worth it. He is a good husband, a good father, a good provider.

He is steady and reliable, the very opposite of her own parents. Everything about Holly's life is safe and stable, exactly what she had grown up craving, vowing she would have when she was married and had children.

But there's no passion, no excitement, no spark.

So what?

Doesn't that inevitably disappear after a while anyway? And so what if it wasn't there in the beginning? There are other things surely that make up for that . . .

"Oh, I met Olivia at the park," Holly says. "My old friend from school, remember? I've invited her over for supper." A pause, as she remembers how much he dislikes impromptu invitations unless they have been issued by him, and she tenses, her shoulders stiff as she prepares herself for his disapproval, prepares to phone Olivia and call it off.

"Is that okay?" she asks hopefully, the strain almost audible in her voice.

"It's fine!" he says, cheerfully, and Holly feels her shoulders sink with relief. "I could do with a good evening," he adds. "Anyone else we should invite?" This is when Marcus throws her, when he is unexpectedly generous, inclusive, warm. "It might be fun to have a proper dinner party. I could see if Richard and Caroline are around."

Holly's heart sinks. A boring old colleague of Marcus's.

"You'll like her," Marcus says. "She's a fashion journalist, very outgoing, interesting, I think."

"It's just that I don't think Olivia's expecting a proper dinner party," Holly says cautiously. "I think more of a kitchen supper, and it's very last minute so I doubt anyone will be around. But we could try . . . How about Paul and Anna, as well then, if your friend's wife is a fashion journalist?" Marcus looks confused.

"My other old school friends?" she reminds him.

"If you haven't seen them for twenty years, how come you suddenly want to leap back into being best friends with all these people?"

"I don't," Holly says defensively. "But if Caroline's a fashion journalist, Anna runs Fashionista so they'll probably have tons in common. I haven't even met her yet—she was on a business trip, so couldn't make Tom's memorial service—and I'd love to know what she's like. Paul's so easy, he gets on with everyone. They may not be able to come, but I'd love to ask them."

"Great idea!" Marcus says, having read a profile of Anna just last week, and deciding on the spot that she is just the sort of person he ought to be mixing with, and Holly picks up the phone to call Paul.

By six o'clock the children are bathed, fed, and mesmerized by *The Incredibles* on the DVD player in Holly and Marcus's bedroom. The braised lamb shank is bubbling merrily in the Le Creuset in the oven, and the tarte tatin is cooling off next to the stove. The table in the kitchen has been set with pretty Provençal-style blue and yellow linens, and Holly has checked her e-mail only eight times since waking up this morning.

On the eighth time of checking and finding nothing but dozens of junk e-mails offering to make her a fortune by investing in a Nigerian banking scam, provide her with Cialis, or enlarge her penis (this last she was tempted to forward on to Marcus with a note, *I believe this was meant for you,* except she didn't think he'd find it funny—but she used to forward them to Tom from time to time and he'd find similarly ridiculous e-mails on breast enlargement and natural Botox alternatives to send back to her), Holly puts her computer on standby.

I am being ridiculous, she tells herself. Of course Will isn't going to send me an e-mail. This isn't dating, for heaven's sake. I am a married mother of two, and just because he confessed he had a crush on me over twenty years ago, it means nothing today.

God, look at me, for starters. I have boobs that practically swing around my ankles when I walk, my stomach is covered in stretch marks, and if it weren't for my trusty tweezers I'd probably have a handlebar moustache. Of course he doesn't fancy me. He wasn't flirting, I was just reading too much into it, and isn't it just like me to think I have to fancy someone just because they fancy me?

Not that he does fancy me, which is perfectly clear, because if he did he would have responded to my last e-mail by now. I will not check this e-mail anymore. Will is lovely, but he's Tom's brother, which is probably what this whole thing is about. Less about Will than about having a connection to Tom. This isn't a real feeling and I know, I absolutely know, that this will pass.

These thoughts fly around Holly's head and, with a sigh of relief—now she understands—she turns her computer off firmly and walks downstairs to get ready for supper.

"She's gorgeous!" Holly whispers to Olivia as they emerge from the basement—or, as Marcus would call it, *the wine cellar*—with another couple of bottles. "I feel so dowdy next to her."

Holly colors immediately as they walk into Caroline, standing at the top of the stairs just outside the kitchen, but Caroline leans forward with a conspiratorial whisper. "She definitely has the whole winter look going on perfectly. Did you see her Chloe bag? That thing's impossible to get—waiting lists for months, unless you run Fashionista."

"I'm sorry, I'm sorry," Holly tries to get her foot out of her mouth. "You've never even met me before and here I am, gossiping."

"Don't worry about it in the slightest," Caroline says, and Holly and Olivia relax. "Fashion's all about gossip—what a boring world it would be without it."

"Well, then . . . I know this is a terrible thing to say, but I feel slightly embarrassed about my house." Holly winces. "I feel like she ought to be sitting on a Conran sofa in a beautiful stucco house in Regent's Park, not on my shabby old sofa that used to be my mum's in my Edwardian house in Brondesbury."

"Don't be silly," Olivia chides her firmly. "First of all your house is gorgeous—I'd kill for my house to look like this—and second of all they live in Crouch End, for God's sake. Hardly Regent's Park. Anyway, we mustn't judge a book by its cover. Everything Tom ever said about her was good. Caroline, you'll know her reputation, what have you heard?"

"She's a witch."

"No!" Both Holly and Olivia gasp simultaneously. Caroline starts laughing.

"Of course she's not a witch. She's delightful. One of the most down-to-earth people in the business. All I've ever heard about her is good. Let's go and talk to her properly."

Holly groans. "Oh, do I have to?"

"Stop it," Olivia grins. "I'll start and you can join in."

But she doesn't have to. As soon as they walk back into the kitchen, they find Anna with her shoes kicked off, sleeves rolled up, chopping the rest of the salad that Holly had abandoned to go and gossip with Olivia in the basement, and making a start on a salad dressing.

"Oh Anna, you don't have to do that!" Holly is horrified. "Let me."

"I do not mind in the slightest." Anna smiles. "I grew up in Sweden until I was eight, and my family always mucked in to help out with the meals. This is exactly how I grew up, everyone in the kitchen and everyone helping out."

"But . . . I don't want you to get your clothes dirty."

Anna leans toward her with a smile. "The beauty of having a fashion company is that you can always get a replacement for the clothes. Anyway, a bit of dirt never hurt anyone. I love this kitchen, Holly. I put in the white subway tile too, because I thought it would be clean and minimalist, but you know, it never feels cozy like this one does. This is the kind of kitchen where people just want to stay all day."

Holly's face lights up. "That's exactly what I always wanted."

"So where are the kids? Paul told me you had two. I would love to meet them."

"Upstairs, watching TV. Do you want to come up? I ought to get them into bed around now anyway."

"I would love to," Anna says, her language oddly stilted, even though there is barely a trace of a Scandinavian accent. "There. The dressing is done. Let us go and find those munchkins. Can I read the stories? I have three nieces who let me read the stories all the time. I'm particularly good at scary monsters."

"The kids would love it." Holly laughs. "Although Daisy's current favorite is *The Tiger Who Came to Tea*. Not sure your monster voice would work."

On the way upstairs, Anna continues to compliment Holly's taste, and Holly finds herself liking her more and more.

Flattery, as they say, will get you everywhere.

"You have created a real home." Anna turns on the landing to admire the antique game table, piled with books and knickknacks. "I always remember something I once read somewhere that said 'Houses are made of sticks and stone, but homes are made of love alone.' This is definitely a home. I am envious."

"Isn't yours a home, then?"

"It is beautiful but quiet. Too perfect. We need children running around to mess it up a bit, bring it to life."

Ah yes. There it is. The forbidden subject of children.

"Oh do not worry," Anna puts a hand on Holly's arm, "it is no secret that I am having IVF treatment. We keep telling ourselves that this will be the last time we try, and if we do not get pregnant, we will adopt, but then I keep thinking that perhaps the next time is the magic time."

"I hope it works for you," Holly says. "I really do."

Anna smiles. "Thank you." And they walk through the door and find Daisy and Oliver sprawled out on the bed, all the pillows scattered around them on the floor.

"She's amazing!" Holly whispers to Olivia, back downstairs.

"Told you!" Olivia smiles. "So it's true what they say."

"What are you two talking about?" Paul wanders over to get a refill of wine.

"Actually we were just saying how much we like your wife." Holly grins. "How did you end up snagging a gem like her?"

"God only knows. I ask myself the same question pretty much every day. I think most people see her and think she's going to be cold and condescending—that whole Swedish icy blonde thing—plus, of course, she always feels this enormous pressure to dress the part because people expect it of her, but she's not at all who you expect."

"How did you meet?" Caroline asks.

"You won't believe it, but I interviewed her for *The Sunday Times*."

"*No!*" both Olivia and Holly speak at the same time.

"*Yes!*" Paul imitates them as they laugh. "I interviewed her and instantly knew I had found someone special. I kept calling her on the pretext of having forgotten questions, and then, of course, I had to meet her for coffees to fact-check, and in the end she said she'd really just prefer it if I came clean and took her out for dinner."

"I hope you took her somewhere fabulously smart and trendy."

"Actually no." Paul grins. "I took her to Nando's."

"What!" Caroline is horrified. "You took her to a fast-food chicken place? Please tell me you're joking." Paul shakes his head. "Whatever for?"

"Because I wanted to see if she was really as down-to-earth as she seemed. It was great. She picked up that chicken with her fingers straight away and ate as if she hadn't eaten in months. If I remember, she went back for thirds of the frozen yogurt."

"I knew there was a reason I liked her!" Holly laughs.

Marcus raises his glass. "Here's to Anna. Holly would have been livid if I'd taken her somewhere like that on our first date." The others laugh, and Holly grits her teeth at the lie—she wouldn't have cared; it was Marcus who cared about things like that.

"Where is she anyway?" Paul frowns.

"Reading stories to Daisy, who realizes she's on to a good thing. First it was *The Tiger Who Came to Tea,* then a couple of Charlie and Lola books, and now she's got her reading *Cinderella,* which goes on forever. Not stupid, my daughter."

"Clearly," Paul says, smiling, but there is sadness in

his eyes. "She adores children. She'd stay up there all evening if she could."

"I'll go and get her in a minute," Holly says.

"No, don't. She's having a wonderful time," Paul says, and sure enough, when Anna walks back in the kitchen, half an hour later, her eyes are shining and she is beaming from ear to ear.

The meal is a huge success, and by the time the tarte tatin is brought to the table with vanilla ice cream, talk has turned to Tom.

"I can't imagine losing a son," Caroline says, shivering with horror. "There just can't be anything worse than losing a child."

"What about losing your partner?" Paul says. "Obviously I can't speak about losing children, not yet, but I can't think of anything worse than losing Anna."

Holly sits back in contemplation as the table continues to talk about the traumas of losing people you love. There is no question that there would be nothing more tragic, traumatizing and terrible for Holly than losing one of her children. But Marcus? How would she feel if she lost Marcus?

When the London bombings occurred, one of them was close to Marcus's office. Holly couldn't get hold of him all afternoon, and she didn't hear anything. She went through the motions of a wife in distress, but in truth there was only one emotion that she knew to be authentic if he had been one of the casualties.

Relief.

The talk turns to Sarah: how she has reacted so differently than they expected, how she will cope. And for a moment they all lapse into silence as they think about losing the person they love most in the world.

And Holly starts to cry. Not because she's thinking about Marcus.

Because she's thinking about Tom.

CHAPTER NINE

Saffron wheels her bag through LAX and waves hello to Samuel, P's driver. He's standing where he always stands, as reliable and discreet as ever, and Saffron has long got over the discomfort of Samuel knowing that she is the mistress. She is quite sure that she is not the first, and she tries not to think about whether she will be the last or whether, as she is hoping, P will eventually leave his wife and be where he belongs. With her.

Heads turn as she strides behind Samuel to the car park. A few Brits recognize her, but it is more likely that they are looking because she is beautiful. Beautiful and clever, but not so clever that she knew not to get involved with a married man. Not so clever that she was able to resist the demons that even now are hovering just above her shoulder.

Saffron was six years old when she met Holly. She was the new girl in school—a tiny, pretty blond thing who walked into Miss Simpson's classroom with a confidence and assurance immediately envied by Holly.

They didn't become friends. She fell in with one of the cool kids—how ridiculous it is now to think that even at that age there were cool kids, and that they all knew exactly who they were—and Holly sat with the clever kids on the other side of the classroom.

Saffron, it turned out, was clever as well. She crossed the bridge between the groups, and as they grew older she gravitated toward Holly and Olivia, and the three-some worked, rarely degenerating into the bitchy scenarios that so often occur with pubescent girls.

Saffron's parents lived in Hampstead. Her mother was an architect and her father was a magazine editor, and they lived in a house that was so avant-garde, so unconventional, that Holly and Olivia begged to go over there on a daily basis.

Saffron's bedroom was the converted attic. It was enormous, with huge windows that had no curtains, and in the middle of the room was a see-through acrylic tube, which was actually Saffron's shower.

At one end was a sunken living room, complete with fuchsia velvet cushions and, during the teen years, a bong that she never bothered hiding. In fact, Saffron claimed she smoked with her parents, and even though Holly and Olivia had never seen it happen, they were quite certain she was telling the truth.

Because Saffron's parents were the unlikeliest parents they had ever seen. They were . . . well, *exotic* is the only word that comes to mind. They were also hardly ever there. They still seemed to be madly in love and had no qualms about snogging in front of Saffron and her friends, none of whom had ever seen anything like it.

Saffron and Holly bonded over their shared freedom

although Saffron handled it differently. Where Holly was desperate for boundaries, for parents to be around, for someone to tell her what time to be home, Saffron thrived on the freedom, was enough of a free spirit to recognize that conventional parents would have suffocated her.

Conventional parents might also have stopped her drinking.

It seemed to be normal for all of them as teenagers. Perhaps Saffron had a little more than the others, but God knows most of them would get drunk or stoned when they went to parties.

The difference with Saffron was that she would drink on her own. Not much, but a beer, or a gin and tonic if she was feeling particularly grown-up. Not to get drunk, just because it felt good, and if she wasn't drinking, she'd have a joint; everyone was doing the same thing.

And then, at university, she didn't drink very much at all. Unlike her friends, most of whom were away from home for the first time and took advantage of the freedom by getting drunk every night, Saffron just made sure she had a steady supply of grass to help her wind down at the end of the day.

Back in London, having got a first in English and drama, she started working, one of the lucky few to get immediate castings in TV ads. Drinking seemed to become easier in London but, still, never enough to get drunk, just enough to unwind, and even if it took a little more alcohol to do the trick, nobody ever saw Saffron drunk.

She didn't eat much during these years. Got very thin, although no casting director ever told her she was too thin. Her mother admired her jutting hip bones—*very seventies, darling*—and her friends expressed concern, but Saffron waved them away. She liked being this thin. Liked not eating. She felt clean and in control when she climbed into bed knowing she had eaten just fruit and vegetables all day; and the less of them she ate, the better she felt.

Her career took off. A part in a TV series, and a cleverly concocted fake romance with one of the hot young stars in film pushed her into the public eye, and soon she was one of the bright young things in London. She was also drinking more and more.

Then the *Sun* printed an article about the celebs who were so thin they were disappearing in the public eye, and Saffron was the main focus. It still wasn't enough to make her change.

When Saffron moved to LA for a movie her agent insisted she go to rehab. She didn't want to, nor did she want to lose the part. Rehab followed, and then intensive twelve-step meetings. AA was her lifesaver. If ever she felt lonely, or insecure, or just needed some company, she could turn up at one of the hundreds of meetings on her doorstep, and instantly feel as if she were at home.

But it was more than just the company. She really lived the program. She would sit at night writing a daily inventory, would start each day with prayer and meditation, was working her way slowly through the steps.

She was doing what she was told to do: taking it a day at a time, learning to live and let live, learning that she couldn't do it alone.

It helped that the LA meetings were so glamorous. It made the work fun, and you never knew who you'd see at these meetings. Everyone in the industry, it seemed, whether they had a drinking problem or not, would turn up for the break in the middle—standing around the coffee machine, swapping business cards, handing out bios, talking shop, making deals.

One day Saffron was sitting in the corner, absent-mindedly doodling on the tiny notepad she always brought to the meetings, when she heard a wonderful voice. Rich and warm, she knew it was familiar but couldn't place it. She had tuned out when he introduced himself, but, when she looked up, she recognized him instantly. How could you not recognize him, three times voted Hollywood's sexiest man by *People* magazine, in one of those fairy-tale marriages with an equally famous film star wife, one of the biggest earners in the business.

But an alcoholic? She never knew. He shared that day about humility. About how, when he was drinking, he was an asshole. He was grandiose, pompous, thought he knew the answers to everything. He was a nightmare on film sets, he said, but this program had changed his life, had given him a second chance.

He had learned the gift of humility, had learned that he was one of God's children, no better and no worse than anyone else. He had spent years knowing he wasn't good enough, and so everyone was judged accordingly: are they better than me or worse than me, and, if they were better, he would automatically affect grandiosity. Now, he said, he treated everyone with kindness and respect and wasn't attached to results. If people were unpleasant, he assumed it was because they were having a bad day, no longer automatically jumping to the conclusion that it was all about him.

Saffron went up to him at the coffee break. He was standing in a corner looking at some leaflets on the literature table, and she could see a number of people ready to pounce, but she got to him first.

"I just want to tell you—" she said, her heart beating ever so slightly faster because, even though she wasn't intimidated by celebrity and had, in fact, acted with some of the world's finest, there was something about him that was different. "I just want to tell you that I loved your share. I loved everything you said. It is exactly what my experience has been, and I love that you were able to be so honest in these rooms, that despite your fame, you trust this program enough to do that."

He turned and really looked at her then. Intrigued by her English accent, her words, and the force behind them. "Thank you." He held out his hand. "I'm Pearce."

Their friendship took a while. Initially they'd see each other at meetings, smile hello, occasionally have a brief chat during the coffee break. When he won yet another sexiest man award on one of the entertainment shows,

Saffron had scribbled him a note taking the piss ever so gently, and she passed it to him during one of the meetings. He unfolded it with a frown, and she watched as he read it, then leaned his head back on the sofa as his shoulders shook with laughter. He snorted and looked at her, as if to say *you're incorrigible,* and she shrugged. He loved that she dared to take the piss. Everyone around him was so serious, only ever told him how wonderful he was, and he was intrigued by this English girl.

Her sharing was always startlingly honest and usually peppered with swear words, which made him smile. He always found himself commenting on something she had shared—whatever she said always seemed to speak directly to him—and he found that on the rare occasions she didn't turn up at a meeting, he missed her, would wonder where she was.

He had been married for seven years. Ah, the seven-year itch, people would joke, but in truth the itch had started at one. It had become a business arrangement. They didn't have children, and he would have divorced her years ago, but both their agents said their careers needed them to stay together, at least for now—so much mileage out of being Hollywood's golden couple.

For they loved his wife as much as they loved him. She wasn't, admittedly, in the same league, but she was beautiful and down-to-earth—at least in public—and they put on a great show of appearing to adore one another.

Both of them had flings on movie sets, but both learned to be discreet, and the truth was they were friends, they still liked each other, and they accepted that this was the way it had to be for now.

His agent strongly advised him against getting involved with anyone else. The press would get hold of it instantly, he said, and it would be disastrous, more so for him, who had such an image to protect. The alcoholism had been kept out of the papers, as should affairs of the heart. "Fuck who you want and be discreet," his agent said. "But don't fall in love."

It took about a year for him and Saffron to start having coffee after meetings. And then coffee became an occasional lunch, and soon they were chatting on the phone every day. Saffron had the glow of a woman in love, and P felt as if he were eighteen again—full of hope and excitement about the future.

He kissed her in her living room. Far too recognizable to take a chance of kissing her in public, he came in one day after dropping her off and, as soon as they walked in, they both knew things were different. Saffron knew that today something would happen.

She had stopped worrying about him being married, stopped worrying about his desire not to fall in love. All she could think about was him. Not because he was a movie star, not because of the fame or the money, but because she adored him. Because he made her laugh. Because he understood her like no one else in the world and because she understood him.

Their friendship was unlike any Saffron had ever had.

Perhaps because of the intimacy fostered in the safe confines of their meetings, they revealed things to each other that neither had ever told anyone else.

"I think I've fallen in love with you," P whispered just before he kissed her, and Saffron pretended she needed the loo immediately afterward. She had stood with her hands resting on the sink, weeping quietly with tears of joy.

Their affair progressed, always in private, often with other people around to throw the press off the scent. He even got her a part in his movie to legitimize their being seen together.

She, in turn, manufactured a romance with her costar, a lesser, but rising star, and they were regularly photographed kissing on beaches while walking their three rescue dogs. The costar was grateful that his lover—a male model—remained a secret and, of course, Saffron couldn't be linked to anyone else while so clearly in love with her costar.

Saffron learned to put her life on hold for P. He would phone her whenever he could, but when he was away filming, it was so hard. Saffron tried to bury herself in yoga, in seeing friends, but her friends had fallen away somewhat—it was hard to maintain a friendship with someone who canceled whenever her lover called—and even her meetings were suffering.

She found she wasn't getting quite as much out of them. When P was there, they would sit next to each other and surreptitiously touch—she cross-legged on the sofa, her knee gently touching his thigh as she closed her eyes and felt, she swore to God she actually felt it, the electricity.

She would tune out for most of the meeting, closing her eyes and thinking about him, opening them only to catch him looking at her, both of them smiling and looking away.

She wasn't focusing on the lessons of the program at all. Her sponsor—the only person who knew—was trying to be firm, trying to point out all the danger that came with her behavior, how ultimately it would be Saffron who was at risk by not working the principles of the program; but, in the end, she had sighed, knowing she had to be a loving witness. Knowing there was nothing she could do.

And it is true that Saffron hadn't found being around alcohol quite as easy as she used to. For years, while working the program, she found that alcohol didn't bother her. She could be at parties where everyone else was drinking copiously, and it would never occur to her to have a drink.

But lately, walking into her quiet little house at the end of the day, she found herself thinking, *Wouldn't it be nice to have one drink? Just one. Surely one wouldn't hurt?*

And last week, when she finished her grocery shopping, she found herself passing the liquor store, and she hesitated for longer than was comfortable before pushing her cart past and trying to think of other things.

She knew what this was called. She was white-knuckling it. She hadn't even told her sponsor she'd had these feelings, convinced, just like the old days, that she could do it on her own.

Saffron would look around her in restaurants and see people enjoying a glass of wine. *That could be me,* she would think. *I could have a glass of wine. I could be normal. If all those other people can do it, then surely I can too.*

"You need to start working the steps," her sponsor would say. "You haven't done any step work for ages."

"I know, I know," Saffron would groan. "It works if you work it." But she didn't seem to have the will to do anything other than turn up to meetings as an excuse to see P.

And last year has been the happiest of Saffron's life. She is convinced that P is her soul mate. That they belong together, that it is just his marriage of convenience that is keeping them apart, and that soon they will be able to stop sneaking around, and he will marry her: they will be together for the rest of their lives.

CHAPTER TEN

Sarah groans and rolls over in bed as the tapping on her door continues.

"Sarah, love," her mother-in-law's voice is soft as the door gently pushes open. "Paul and his wife, Anna, are here to see you. They're playing with the kids downstairs, and Paul brought some old photographs of Tom from school that he thought you'd like."

Sarah sits up and throws the duvet back. "Tell them I'll be down in a sec," she says, as she runs her fingers through her hair and sighs. *Why do people keep coming? Why do they keep arriving proffering gifts—food, photographs, stories? Do they think it's going to make her feel better? Is it going to bring Tom back?* All Sarah wants to do is crawl under the covers and sleep forever, waking up when the pain has disappeared.

It is easier to hide here in this house. Despite being surrounded by Tom—photographs, mementos, constant reminders—this is Tom's childhood home, not the home she and Tom created together.

Those first few days had been unbearable. Numb. Letters had started arriving, bills that needed to be paid, life insurance policies that needed to be dealt with, and

Sarah had taken everything and put it where she always put it—on Tom's desk in his office. She had never dealt with it, could not imagine dealing with it, and couldn't think about any alternative other than putting the mail where she had always put it.

She had tried to be normal for the sake of Dustin and Violet. Had even attempted to drive Violet to preschool one day despite the protestations of an appalled neighbor who had taken on that role. She had strapped Violet in the car, had climbed into the driver's seat in pajama bottoms, bare feet, and an old sweatshirt of Tom's, and had pulled out of the driveway.

An hour later she had found herself on I-95. No idea how she got there, what she was doing there, or where she was heading. Violet had been happily sucking her thumb in her car seat, listening to XMKids on the radio, and Sarah had started to shake before pulling to the side of the highway and bursting into tears.

Paul hovers in the doorway of the living room and watches Anna tickling Violet, whose peals of laughter ring throughout the house.

"I'm guessing it won't be long before you have children of your own," Maggie says, placing a hand on Paul's arm and smiling up at him.

"Fingers crossed," Paul says, and as Anna looks up and catches his eye, he feels a wave of sadness wash over him. Life never turns out to be the way you expect. How could Tom possibly be taken from them at such a young age, and how is it that he and Anna, Anna who would make the most wonderful mother in the world, have not been able to have children?

This morning they had been back to the hospital for egg collection. Egg collection. Sounds so innocuous. Paul remembers how they had laughed when they first heard the term, imagined themselves as country bumpkins, reaching under fat, happy hens to collect the eggs.

When Anna came out of sedation, the specialist told her they had released six eggs from the follicles. Better than last time, and they both left feeling a surge of optimism and hope.

Tomorrow, as always happens, they will receive a phone call to tell them how many of the eggs have been fertilized, or that, as happened before, no eggs have been fertilized, and there are no embryos to potentially carry their hopes and dreams into the future.

It seems inconceivable that out of six eggs, none should be fertilized, but that has been the case so many times already, and Anna doesn't think she has the emotional fortitude to go through it again, not to mention the financial ability.

Anna never minds being the breadwinner, never minds that the money that keeps the joint account afloat is almost exclusively provided by her. Paul puts the money he earns from freelancing into the same account, but it seems to be a drop in the ocean toward their lifestyle.

Not that it is particularly extravagant—heaven knows Anna could choose to live in a supersmart area of London—but they travel well and often, go to all the

best restaurants, and a couple of years ago, just before
finally deciding to go forward with IVF, they bought a
house in the country.

Well, not so much a house. More of a barn and one
that needed work; it hadn't been touched since the
early seventies. It is on the top of a hill with views for
miles over the Gloucestershire countryside, and even
though it was just about habitable, they brought their
friend Philip, an architect, to see it; and Phil's enthusi-
asm for the project was so infectious they found themselves, shortly afterward, the proud although slightly
apprehensive owners of White Barn Fields.

Plus the barn was a bargain. At the time, it seemed so
cheap they almost felt it would have been rude to say
no. So cheap they paid cash for the entire thing, planning on starting the work immediately. Phil designed an
incredible house. A modern stainless-steel-and-glazed-
concrete kitchen, huge windows to take in the views,
four bedrooms off a steel gallery upstairs: a huge master, a guest suite, and two bedrooms for the children
that were undoubtedly on their way.

A local landscape architect had designed a spectacular
garden. There would be a cobbled courtyard with huge
oversized terra-cotta pots that would hold olive trees in
the summer. Lavender and rosemary would spill out of
the raised beds on either side. The handful of old,
gnarled apple trees that sat at the bottom of the hill
would form the basis for an orchard—twenty fruit trees
were going to be added, and a raspberry patch. The
landscape architect added, "Your kids can spend hours
picking their own fruit."

It was Anna's idea of heaven, and Paul, who mostly thought of himself as an urban creature, was happy doing what made Anna happy. Plus even he had to admit that the plans were remarkable, and they would end up with an idyllic getaway. Anna made sure to include a study for Paul—all the way at the top of the barn, up a hidden staircase, the cupola would be open into his office, flooding it with light. "If you can't write the great British novel here," Phil joked when he showed the plans for the office to a breathless Paul and Anna, "I don't know where you can."

Now, over a year later, they can hardly bear to think about it. People assume that Paul and Anna are rolling in it, they assume that Anna makes a fortune; but the truth is that although the company is thriving, Anna only takes out a salary. And what used to be a comfortable salary has been eaten up by buying the barn, followed by back-to-back IVF treatments.

White Barn Fields is jokingly referred to by everyone they know, themselves included, as the Money Pit. Except it doesn't feel quite so funny anymore, not since finding out they weren't getting pregnant, and they weren't going to take no for an answer.

Anna's stubbornness is something Paul has loved about her from day one. So tough she is referred to by her father as a ball breaker. Said lovingly, of course. She knows exactly what she wants and how she is going to get it, and nobody ever says no to Anna. She is charming and down-to-earth and persuasive, and she somehow always manages to get her own way.

She cannot understand why having children hasn't come to her as easily as everything else in her life. She will tell the various journalists who interview her about Fashionista that she is stunned by its success, but in truth she is not stunned. It is exactly what she expected to happen. Too many fashion Web sites had fallen by the wayside because they didn't keep their stock on site, had to ship it from afar, running the risk of delivery being far later than their instant-gratification-obsessed customers would accept. And then when the clothing did arrive, it was badly packaged, in ugly plastic envelopes or badly wrapped in wrapping paper.

Anna designed shocking-pink boxes, layers of delicate orange tissue paper carefully enfolding the purchases, all tied up with animal-print velvet ribbon. The boxes and the ribbon are a fortune, but worth it. They are always voted best packaging on the Internet, and the boxes are so beautiful her clients regularly write to her to say they can't throw them away. Many is the time Anna has opened an interiors magazine to see someone's dressing-room shelves piled with Fashionista boxes in assorted shapes and sizes.

And shipping is twenty-four hours. No matter where in the world you are, if you order an item on a business day, you will have it the next. Customer service is everything in Anna's book. It is one of the reasons she loves having an Internet company—she is fed up with going into trendy boutiques and having young, imperious sales assistants ignore her as they chat on the phone, only perking up when she hands over her credit card and they realize who she is.

So the fact that Fashionista is now the third most successful Internet company in the UK is no surprise to Anna whatsoever, although she would never admit that in public. The truth is that Anna has always felt blessed, always felt that her guardian angels were looking after her. Where others see adversity and hardship, Anna has only ever seen a challenge that she will inevitably overcome. She always believes the glass is half full, even when everyone else is convinced it is empty, and because she has always believed her life is charmed, her life has always been charmed.

When she met Paul, she knew he was perfect for her. After she left him on the very first day he interviewed her and well before he started pestering her about things he had forgotten to ask, she phoned her mother. "Mum? I've met the man I'm going to marry," she said, and her mother knew that she had, because when Anna stated something, it always happened.

So when Anna announced they were trying for children, everyone knew that Anna would have a baby within the year. It was partly why they bought the barn: what a wonderful place for children, how perfect to spend summers out here with the kids, or come down on winter weekends for leaf stomping and hot chocolate in front of a roaring fire in the huge stone fireplace at one end of the enormous great room.

Anna's obstinacy is why they cannot give up on IVF. Why Anna refuses to believe there will be a last time.

She cannot believe that this will not work when everything else in her life has gone according to plan.

So far they've spent around fifty thousand pounds on IVF, a huge chunk of the savings they had put aside. The work on the barn has started. The walls that were rotten have been replaced with reclaimed barn siding they found at an auction, and the roof has been done. Kitchen and bathrooms were ordered and then canceled. The house is half done. Piles of sawdust everywhere, dust sheets on half-sanded floors, unpainted window frames. The last time they went up to have a look, Anna burst into tears.

"This was our dream," she said to Paul. "And now we cannot even afford to finish it."

"We will one day," Paul said, so sorry that he wasn't able to pull out a magic wand and make it happen, so sorry that his work didn't provide him with enough money to take over when the going got tough. "I promise you one day this will be finished."

They left that night and stayed at a local B&B—a few hundred steps down from the Relais & Chateaux along the road where they used to stay before starting IVF, but a lot of things have changed since the treatment began.

"If they could see me now," Anna sang, picking her way gingerly down the hallway, having run lukewarm water into a cracked bath in the bathroom at the other end of the hall, and Paul shrugged.

"We have to stop the treatment, you know," he attempted carefully. "This is ridiculous that we can't afford anything anymore. We can't keep going like this."

"Hopefully we will not have to." Anna had squeezed his arm. "I have a feeling this one is going to work," and Paul sighed. She said that every time. But having to watch every penny was stressful, to say the least, particularly when it had never been an issue before.

Although if you didn't know, you'd never know. Anna still looks the part—she has to for her job, and no one was a better PR for Fashionista than Anna herself—but watch her carefully and you'll see that she isn't frivolous in the way she used to be.

Her makeup is always from work. No longer does she run to Space NK to replenish the jar of Eve Lom that's almost finished. Now, if she can't get it sent to her through Fashionista, she'll change brands. Her finances have dictated that her brand loyalty is no longer important.

Her hair is no longer cut and colored at Bumble & Bumble. For cuts she goes to the local hairdresser on the high street, and she has discovered that Sun In, thanks to her natural fair Swedish locks, does almost as good a job of highlighting her hair as Enzo used to.

They don't go out to the expensive restaurants anymore unless it is for work and either Anna is expensing it or someone else is paying, and frankly there is always more than enough to eat and drink at the hundreds of fashion parties that are going on all around London on practically any given night.

Not that they can't afford to feed themselves—heavens, no! But where Anna used to absentmindedly put whatever she wanted in a shopping trolley with no thought to the price, now she will look at the price and, if it is too much, she will think about whether they really need it.

She will no longer wander round Graham and Green on a Saturday afternoon, filling her arms with throws and candles and interesting statuettes and lovely linens that she certainly doesn't need, just because it's there and because she can.

You would never know any of it. Looking at Anna right now, sitting cross-legged on the floor as Violet— who, like all children who come into contact with Anna, has fallen completely in love with her—hangs around her neck squealing, you would think that she is beautiful, poised, and perfect. You would think that nothing in her life could ever go wrong.

"Hi." Sarah's voice is listless as she comes into the room and sits on the sofa, dark shadows under her eyes, her hair still mussed.

"We brought some photos of Tom." Paul thinks about going across the room to hug her, but something about her is so shut down he knows he'll be rejected, and he stays where he is, unsure of what to say.

"I know. Maggie said so."

"Would you like to see them?"

"Sure," she says. Paul hands them to her and she starts to sift through the photographs. A ghost of a smile hovers over her lips as she stops at a picture of Paul, Holly, and Tom, all of them with braces on their teeth, at Paul's fifteenth birthday party.

"God, look at that hair!" Sarah says. "I never knew Tom had long hair. He looks awful!"

"We all looked awful," Paul says, grateful that Sarah finally seems to be engaged. "Look at Holly's shocking pink lipstick. I think she thought it was sophisticated."

"Tom was so skinny," Sarah muses, tracing his arm in the photo with her forefinger. "You'd never think he'd become so buff."

"Buff?" Paul asks.

"Fit. He was forever in the gym. He got this thing about Ironman contests. Crazy stuff where you bike 112 miles, swim 2.4 miles, then run 26.2 miles. He did one in Florida and was training for another." She shakes her head. "He was so fit. So strong. That's what I find so hard to believe. I mean, I could understand almost anyone else not surviving, but Tom? How could Tom not have got himself out of there? How could anything take Tom down?"

There's an awkward silence, neither Paul nor Anna knowing what to say, and after a while Sarah turns to the next picture and bursts out laughing. "Tom was in the army?" she splutters.

"TA," Paul says sheepishly. "Was the thing to do at the time."

In the kitchen, getting a tray of tea ready to take inside, Maggie sits down heavily at the table.

"Thank you," she looks up at a concerned Anna, "this is the first time Sarah has sounded anything like herself. Those photos are what she needed right now."

"What about you?" Anna says gently. "What do you need right now?"

"Oh I'll be fine," Maggie says with a false brightness.

"I'll just finish making this tea and I'll be right out. If you could just take Pippa outside to pee that would be wonderful."

Anna leaves, but she turns just as she reaches the doorway to see Maggie collapsing in her chair. Anna hovers, unsure of whether to go back, but she knows Maggie thinks she is alone, thinks Anna has left the room; she knows Maggie would never allow herself to drop her composure in front of anyone.

It is absolutely quiet. There are no more tears, there surely can't be a drop of water left in her body, but Anna watches as Maggie leans her head on her arms on the kitchen table and groans softly as she rocks back and forth.

And Anna sees this matriarch of what is left of her family, this strong, stoic, wonderful woman is finding the pain may be too much for a human being to bear.

As she listens to Maggie's quiet groans, she understands that Maggie honestly doesn't know how she can get through the rest of her life knowing she will never see her beloved son, her firstborn, again.

CHAPTER ELEVEN

"What's the matter with you today?" The receptionist at the animal shelter walks into the sitting room with a sandwich at lunchtime and collapses on the sofa as Olivia looks up in surprise.

"What do you mean? Nothing's the matter. Why?"

"You're acting like you've got ants in your pants," Yvonne says. "We think it must be a man."

"What?" Olivia attempts a laugh, then rolls her eyes. "Good Lord, Yvonne. I'm the bloody director, haven't you got anything better to do than gossip about my love life?"

Yvonne purses her lips. "Actually we all wish you had a love life for us to gossip about. Lovely girl like you, you deserve someone much better than that awful George."

Olivia's mouth falls open. "But you all said you loved George."

"Yes, well. That was before he dumped you for that American bimbo."

"Yvonne! How do you know all this?"

"Know what? I don't know anything. I'm just saying. You ought to have a lovely man who makes you happy."

"I'm not going to talk about it anymore," Olivia says, picking up her coffee and walking out through the door. "But just for info, I do have a date tonight," and as Yvonne's face lights up and she prepares to shower Olivia with questions, Olivia shuts the door and walks off toward her office, giggling.

She is meeting Fred tonight. He is finally here. She shouldn't be excited, sees no reason to be excited, particularly given that this is a five-day business trip, and she'll probably hate him once she meets him anyway, but this is the first time she has felt there is something to look forward to. She has arranged to pick him up from the Dorchester at seven o'clock.

At three, she does something she never does. Pulls on her coat, picks up her bag, and announces to Sophie, her assistant, that if there's anything urgent, she'll be on her mobile. "But only call if it's an emergency," she says, and Sophie, who has inadvertently seen a couple of e-mails from Fred, winks her approval and shoos her away, knowing that nothing, bar the shelter burning down, would cause her to interrupt Olivia on her date.

Her first stop is the hairdresser. "I need to cover the gray," she tells Rob the colorist, "and then I need a trim."

Rob purses his lips as he examines Olivia's never-been-touched hair, "God, you've got a lot of gray," he murmurs, almost to himself as he picks up her hair. "Natural color, or can I throw in a few lowlights just to add a bit of depth?"

"Whatever you want." Olivia shrugs. "I'm in your hands now. Knock yourself out."

Two hours later, Olivia stares at herself in the mirror in awe. Chestnut and copper streak her hair; and Kim, the junior stylist, has cut long layers into her bob that sweep her cheeks and make her look years younger.

Kim and Rob stand behind her, arms crossed, waiting for Olivia's reaction. They have dealt with women like her before—women who come in, wearing jeans and boots, who don't possess a scrap of makeup, and believe that natural is better. They have performed makeovers on these women before, and are never quite sure what the outcome will be. Some have cried with joy at how much younger, how much better they look; and others have spat in fury and refused to pay, demanding they strip the color off the hair immediately, somehow put it back the way it was.

Olivia, thank God, is one of the good ones. She started smiling halfway through the blow-dry when her new color emerged, and is now clearly delighted.

"I love it," she squeals. "I love, love, love it," and they hand her a mirror to see the back, laughing as she stares with obvious delight at herself and her new swinging, shiny hair.

"Now just remember what I said," Rob says as he walks her to reception to pay. "Lipstick and blush, little black dress and a lot of confidence."

Olivia turns to him. "Thank you so much," she says, spontaneously reaching out and giving him a hug. "Wish me luck!" And with that she's off.

Her Beetle zips through the London traffic, and at every traffic light Olivia stretches up and checks herself in the rearview mirror. It's not that she's vain, it's that she can't believe how different she looks. She is, just as Rob suggested, wearing a black wrap dress that she got on sale last winter, and wore to George's office Christmas bash. She felt beautiful that night and loved feeling George's pride as he introduced her to his colleagues at work. She tried not to think about it tonight as she pulled the dress from the back of the wardrobe, tried not to think how that pride and love that she was so sure was in his eyes could turn so quickly to dust.

The dress should have swamped her, given how much weight she has lost, but she merely wraps it tighter and it's perfect. She has added black tights, low kitten heels, and a chunky amber necklace that used to be her mother's, and resisted the urge to pull everything off and start again with her usual comfortable uniform of jeans and boots.

In the old days, she would have phoned Tom and they would have laughed about it together. "Wear the black dress for God's sake," he would have said. "Make an effort. Show him what great legs you've got."

"I hope you're watching, Tom." She had looked up at the sky just before she climbed into the car. "And I hope you like the outfit." Olivia had performed a small twirl in the driveway of her house and had blown a kiss toward the sky. "Wish me luck," she'd whispered, and then she was off, navigating the Edgware Road once more.

There are pools of men huddled at the bar, and Olivia's first instinct is to turn around and run home. She can't do this. Has never been any good at this. Admittedly she became well versed in navigating blind dates pre-George, but she was so much younger and had so much more confidence.

Some of the men turn and look at her, a couple of them approvingly, and she takes a deep breath and looks around, hoping to see Fred, hoping to know instantly which one he is after having seen only an old, corporate picture. Sitting at a table in the corner is a man reading the *Financial Times*. Olivia squints at him as he looks up and catches her eye, his face breaking into a huge grin.

Please, God, she whispers a silent prayer in her mind as this tall, broad-shouldered athlete of a man comes over, displaying a perfect American smile—huge white teeth, and boy-next-door good looks. Please, God, she whispers, let this be him, because God knows they don't make them like that over here.

"Olivia!" There's no question in his voice but, of course, she had sent him a picture of herself, of course he would know what she looks like.

"Hi!" she says shyly, gratitude and delight in her eyes as he envelops her in a bear hug, making her feel very small and delicate and feminine. How ridiculous, she tells herself, turning her head to the side and resting it for a second against a muscled shoulder. How silly I am being, but oh how lovely, what a spectacular specimen of a man. Fred steps back to grin at her, then ushers her over, a large, strong hand resting in the small of her back as he guides her to her chair.

"Wow!" he says, holding out the chair for her to sit down. "You look great," and as he looks around for a waiter to take their order for drinks, Olivia finds herself smiling. This is going to be a good evening after all.

"Tom was right," Fred says, as the waiter places one Cosmopolitan and one vodka martini on the table.

"Right about what?"

"Right about the fact that I should meet you." He smiles, raising his glass for a toast. "To new friendships, and to Tom, wherever he may be."

Olivia smiles even as the tears well up in her eyes. "To Tom," she echoes, and Fred passes her a napkin, which she dabs against her eyes, looking up and blinking furiously until the tears go away.

"I'm so sorry." She smiles again. "It still gets me at the most unexpected times."

"Of course it does," Fred says. "It gets me, too, and I was just a work colleague. I know how hard it must be for his friends."

"So hard." Olivia nods. "You think that time must be the great healer, that people wouldn't say it all the time if it weren't true, but I'm still waiting for time to kick in."

"You know, when it happened, it was all I could think about for days. I became, like, addicted to the news. I'm serious! I was watching everything, reading everything about the attacks, the survivors, the families of those who had been lost, and still now I think about it every day, but not all day, not the way I did, like, immediately afterward."

"That's true," Olivia says. "I do think about it too, but not all day, not anymore. Still, Tom wouldn't want us to sit here and cry over him, so let's talk about dinner. What do you feel like eating? There's a wonderful restaurant here in the hotel."

"I know, I already checked it out, but I feel like something more fun, something different. Apparently there's a great noodle place round the corner, which sounds great."

Olivia grins. "Wagamama. It's one of my favorites, and much more my speed. Let's go," and with that they drink up and leave.

As soon as they walk in Olivia feels at home. All dressed up in the bar of the Dorchester is about as far removed from Olivia's life as you can get. Not that those places are altogether unfamiliar to her—a large part of her childhood was spent in the smartest of London restaurants—but she had never felt entirely comfortable as a child, and was relieved, upon reaching adulthood, that she actually had a choice and didn't have to frequent those places unless absolutely necessary.

She realizes as she sinks down on the bench opposite Fred, squeezed between strangers busy slurping noodles, that she has been playing a role tonight, something she is never comfortable doing.

"You know what?" Fred looks around the room, taking it all in. "I wish I wasn't in this damn suit. I'd much rather be in jeans and sneakers."

Olivia starts to laugh. "Thank you for saying that. I was just thinking I wish I was in my jeans and boots.

When I'm all dressed up, I feel like I act differently, that I'm more formal and trying to be someone I'm not."

Fred grins at her. "Same here. Tell you what," he looks at his watch, "how long would it take you to run home and throw on jeans, then get back here?"

"About half an hour if I rush." Olivia smiles.

"Okay. Done. I'll run back to the hotel, and I'll see you back here in thirty minutes."

"Are you sure you're not going to do a runner on me?" Olivia asks quickly, a hint of nervousness in her voice. "This isn't another way of saying you think this is going to be an awful evening so let's end it now."

Fred looks shocked. "Are you kidding me? This is going to be a great evening. Let's just get it started on the right foot. Hey, maybe we can catch a movie after we eat."

"That's the best idea I've heard all week." Olivia laughs, and when they stand up and thread their way through the restaurant to the door, she doesn't mind in the slightest that Fred again places a hand gently on her back to guide her.

In fact, if she has to be honest, she'd say the shiver that runs up and down her spine is something she hasn't felt in a very long time.

Olivia wakes up early, as she always does, and lies in bed for a while replaying the events of last night. She turns her head slightly to see Fred, face squashed into the pillow, snoring gently, still sound asleep. Yes. It was real. Yes. She did bring him home to her flat. Yes. She had sex for the first time since George. And yes. It was fan-fuckingtastic. Oh shit.

What now?

Not that Olivia has ever had any firm or fast rules when it comes to dating but she's never been the sort of girl who engaged in one-night stands, and given that her mother utters phrases like "Why buy the cow . . ." it's hardly surprising that she doesn't exactly go around jumping into bed with near strangers.

But Fred doesn't feel like a stranger. If anything, he feels like an old friend. Their e-mail exchanges have been so frank, so honest, and in the days leading up to their meeting, so intimate, they seem to have propelled this . . . what, friendship? Relationship? Fling? . . . into a space that Olivia isn't sure she is ready for.

Not to mention how strange it is to have someone in her bed who isn't George. How odd to feel Fred's body, how delicious to have someone so young, so strong, and so very eager to please her.

She was the one, last night, who invited him back, ostensibly to see "how real people live in London, not like the tourists stuck in your posh hotels," but in fact she knew exactly how it would play out, had been ready from the beginning of the evening, although she would never admit it.

Why else would she have ensured there were fresh sheets on the bed, candles scattered around the room, no dirty laundry visible anywhere in the bathroom?

She was making coffee when Fred kissed her. He came up behind her and put his arms around her—such strong arms, so very different from George—and she tensed slightly, unsure of what to do, how to stand in this unfamiliar position, when he took the decision out of her hands by turning her to face him and leaning down to kiss her.

What a wonderful night it was. And now . . . what? Morning. Isn't this when it is supposed to be awkward, difficult? Isn't he supposed to wake up and be cold, regret what happened, get out of the flat as quickly as possible?

Olivia gets up and goes to make coffee in the kitchen. Under normal circumstances it would be Nescafé Gold Blend, instant of course, but—and yet another clue that this outcome isn't altogether unexpected—she has fresh ground coffee to put in the *cafetière* and huge buttery croissants in the fridge.

"Morning." Olivia jumps, turning to see a disheveled Fred sleepily padding through the kitchen in his boxer shorts. God, she thinks, taking in his chest, the muscles in his legs. He is just so completely delicious.

"Morning," she says, a touch frostily, but only because she is not sure where this is going and doesn't want to be humiliated by coming on too strong when he may be getting ready to cold-shoulder her and walk out the door, never to be heard from again.

"So, Saturday morning, huh? What do we have planned today?" And he comes up to her and wraps her in his arms, bending down to kiss her on the lips, and Olivia folds into him feeling warm and secure and oh so very, very good. She has forgotten, in fact, quite how good this can feel.

"Thank you, God," she whispers, as she hands Fred a towel to take a shower. "And thank you, Tom," she grins at the ceiling. "He's pretty great, after all. You did good," and when Fred hollers at her to join him, she slips her robe off her shoulders and opens the steamed-up door.

CHAPTER TWELVE

"Hellooooo?" Olivia pushes open the front door and her niece and nephew trip in behind her. "Holly? Anyone here?" She follows the sound of a television and walks through to the living room where Daisy and Oliver are comatose in front of a cartoon.

"Hey, guys," Olivia says, as her niece and nephew move like zombies toward the sofa, planting themselves next to the other kids without taking their eyes off the screen for a second, without even saying hello.

"Where's Mum?"

No answer.

"Where's Mum? Oliver?"

"Upstairs." He gestures feebly with a hand, and Olivia sighs and goes to find Holly.

The problem with grief is that it doesn't go away. As time ticks on, the rawness dissipates somewhat, and you find yourself settling into the pain, becoming accustomed to it, wearing it around your shoulders like an old, heavy scarf.

And life has to go on. There are children to look after, meals to cook, cards to illustrate, playdates to

arrange. Grief has to be filed away, compartmental-
ized, allowed out only when the rest of your life is
sufficiently organized, when you can have time to
yourself to give in to the pain.

Both Holly and Olivia allow themselves that time for
grief, but as the weeks go by they are finding they are
bound less by their shared grief, or indeed their shared
history, but more, in fact by a true friendship, by
respect, admiration, and a delight in each other's company. A delight that led them to find each other, and to
swear they would be best friends forever, all those years
ago.

Holly hears the footsteps on the stairs and quickly min-
imizes the e mail she was writing, so what is left on the
screen is an innocuous picture of a ladybird.

"Hey, you!" Olivia walks over and gives her a hug.
"What are you doing?"

"Oh I just had some bills to pay online," Holly says.
"I know, I'm a horrible mother sticking my kids in front
of the TV, but it's the only way I can get anything
done."

"Do you not think Jen does that about a million
times a day?" Olivia laughs. "And she says she also feels
horrible but, frankly, when the au pair is at language
school, what else is she supposed to do? I'm far bloody
worse. I stick them in front of the box and I'm only
their aunt who babysits from time to time."

"Just time to time?"

"Okay. Most weekends. Still, do you think we ought

to turn it off now that we're here? Probably best that they all play, don't you think?"

Holly flushes a bright, guilty, red. "Oh God, of course. You should have just switched it off. Come on, let's go downstairs," and the two of them head down to the silence of the ground floor.

Twenty minutes later Oscar and Oliver are racing around the house shouting, waving light sabers, and Ruby and Daisy are behind closed doors in Daisy's bedroom, Ruby helping Daisy draw pictures, much to Daisy's delight, although Daisy periodically opens her door and roars at the boys, in a very ungirly fashion, to stay away from her bedroom, or to get out.

Olivia sips her tea and recounts, blow by blow, the events of her glorious few days with Fred.

"He sounds completely delicious." Holly laughs.

"He is." Olivia blushes. "He's practically perfect in every way."

"So . . . how are you going to navigate it?"

"Navigate what?"

"A long-distance relationship."

"I'm not." Olivia frowns at Holly. "I'm pretty certain that isn't what this is. The truth is he was, he is, gorgeous, but he's in his early thirties, and he's still a boy, not someone I could see myself with at all."

"Really? So it was just mad sex?"

"Pretty much."

"Oh God." Holly sighs heavily as gets up from the table. "How I miss those days of mad sex."

Olivia laughs, thinks nothing of it as Holly bends

over to get the carrot sticks and hummus out of the fridge for the kids' snack.

"Okay, so come on then, 'fess up," Olivia says finally. "What have you been doing?"

Holly straightens up and looks at Olivia in confusion, and ever such a tiny touch of guilt. "What are you talking about?"

"You look fantastic, that's what. You look like you've lost about a stone since I last saw you, which was, what, about two weeks ago? And you're all glowy and gorgeous. What are you doing? Hang on, let me guess . . . Pilates? No, it's probably Bikram yoga or something and the GI diet . . . am I right?"

Holly starts laughing. "God, no, I'm far too lazy to do exercise, are you mad? Running around after the kids is more than enough exercise for me, and the three times I tried yoga I almost died of boredom."

"God, I know!" Olivia groans. "Every now and then I feel horrible about not doing any exercise, so some well-meaning friend drags me off to a yoga class telling me I'll love it, and I'm always bored stupid."

"But you look insanely fit."

"It's just running an animal shelter, not to mention walking the dogs. That's about all the exercise I need."

"I don't even walk dogs," Holly laughs, "and definitely no yoga for me. I'm not sure that chocolate digestive biscuits are on the GI diet . . . what do you think?" Holly jams a whole biscuit in her mouth and Olivia starts to laugh.

"How old are you, Holly? Six?"

"No," Holly mumbles, crumbs flying out of her mouth. "I'm four," and the two women grin at one another.

"So . . ." Olivia muses, refusing to let it go. "Are you and Marcus having lots of fantastic sex all of a sudden? Is that what it is? I mean, I'd always heard that once you get married you stop having sex altogether, but there's clearly something going on."

"Christ, no." Holly swallows quickly. "Can't think of anything worse. I've just been feeling really happy recently and haven't been very hungry. You know how it is, sometimes you're hungry and sometimes you just seem to have no appetite, and the last few weeks I just haven't had much of an appetite."

"Well, whatever it is you're doing, don't stop. You look completely fantastic," Olivia says, reaching out for a chocolate digestive of her own.

"Don't stop," is what she said. Does that mean I have permission to carry on doing what I'm doing? But what am I doing? I'm not doing anything. We're just friends. That's all.

Holly had forgotten all about Will. She had written him off as one of those silly crushes you have when there has been emotional turmoil in your life. She had been to Maggie and Peter's house many times since the day after the service and was grateful to have them back in her life; and she'd known that if she ran into Will there, she would have been polite but cool.

Heaven forbid she would have given him the slightest indication that she was the least bit interested.

Life had gone back to normal very quickly. She had written a long letter to Sarah. A letter filled with memories of Tom. Of the things she had loved about him, of stories she hoped would bring some solace to Sarah. She'd known she couldn't send the usual condolence card. The I'm-so-sorry-to-hear-of-your-loss card, of which she'd seen hundreds on tables around Peter and Maggie's house. Holly hadn't planned to write the nine pages she did, but she'd been glad when she finished, knowing that even if it wasn't received in the spirit in which it was sent, it had somehow comforted her to write it all down, and that had been enough for the moment.

One morning she had just got back from taking the kids to school and had dashed upstairs to get her portfolio before running into the office for a meeting about next year's line of Christmas cards—the theme was going to be angels, and Holly had spent a week researching and coming up with ideas for illustrations.

She had put together a presentation that was incredibly beautiful in its simplicity: thick vellum card, rough edged, almost as if it had been torn, and a halo of tiny white feathers. On others, tiny Christmas trees of the same delicate feathers, some with a small sprinkling of glitter. Another had a single sprig of miniature mistletoe and another a tiny holly leaf. In small handblocked letters beneath were individual words: peace, love, faith, trust, joy. They were exactly the type of Christmas cards Holly likes to receive herself.

Holly loves Christmas, probably, she has always joked, because of her name. Her memories of childhood Christmases are nothing but good, and she still feels a flutter of childlike excitement when she finishes decorating the Christmas tree and stands back, turning on the lights for the first time.

As a little girl she would make car journeys pass more quickly by leaning her head on the window and counting how many trees she saw in windows. Each one was exciting, each one a promise of more glorious things to come.

Marcus has never quite been able to see the point of Christmas, so although Holly still does all the things she has always done—a huge tree glistening with lights, holly wreaths over the fireplace and around the front door, fat red candles nestling among gleaming cranberries in glass vases—sharing Christmas with her family isn't ever infused with the joy that Holly had always anticipated.

The kids love it, though. They make paper snowflakes and stick them to all the windows, string multicolored paper lanterns throughout the playroom and kitchen, and bake gingerbread men and mince pies—which they adore although they both refuse point-blank to take even one bite of them once they are baked.

Holly had been completely consumed by this presentation for the past few days, and turned back to check her e-mails before she left, just to be sure there wasn't, as there so frequently was, a last-minute e-mail from work saying the meeting had been canceled.

And there it was. An e-mail from Will. Holly, as usual, was in a hurry, but she leaned over her chair and clicked it open, the rush of receiving the previous e-mails he had sent disappearing completely, simply curious to know what he might have written after what feels like weeks of radio silence.

To: Holly
From: Will
11/26/06 4:56:09 AM
Subject: Apology

Dear Holly,

I meant to write earlier but life suddenly seemed to become very difficult. Losing Tom felt like I was living in a dream sequence for a while. A part of me kept expecting to wake up and hear that it was a joke, that someone had played an enormous trick on me, and that the next time the phone rang it would be Tom at the other end.

But at some point after the service, it hit me. He's dead. And I just couldn't handle speaking to anyone at all. I think it hit Mum and Dad at the same time. It's almost as if having a house full of visitors, people dropping in all day and night to pay their respects, allows you to not think about the terrible thing that's happened to you, and you spend each day thinking that although it's horribly painful, it's not unbearable, and you are relieved that you are able to function, to smile when you see people you haven't seen for years, and even to joke with them. You feel a bit guilty, particularly because you sense that there are those who want to see you fall apart on them, expect you to break down on their shoulders, and resent you for not doing so, but then there are the others who are relieved you're normal, who turn away from you and whisper to their friends that you are doing fantastically, and they're so grateful they haven't been the ones to kneel down on the floor and pick up the pieces they once knew as you.

And of course there are Mum and Dad to think of. I've been going over every day, and they're fantastic when people come over—they can sit and chat about nothing and everything and listen to stories about Tom without falling apart, but then as soon as everyone leaves, as soon as the house is quiet, I hear Mum sobbing in the bathroom, or Dad goes out to his greenhouse and I see him there, shoulders heaving as he buries his head in his hands, sitting on a plastic milk crate, thinking that no one can see him from the house. I have a bird's-eye view from my bedroom window, though.

So I have to be the strong one, particularly now. So strange to find yourself taking care of your parents. I didn't expect to be doing this until they were old, although even then I suppose I had thought Tom would be the caretaker. It's a role I've never played. Tom was the strong, responsible one. Tom was the one who always bailed me out of trouble when I was younger, whom I turned to even as an adult if ever I wanted sensible advice or words of wisdom.

We'd grown apart the last couple of years. Mostly because I always sensed Sarah didn't approve of me, and I had been out to Boston to stay with them, but it didn't feel comfortable, and so I'd see Tom when he came to England, and we'd talk on the phone every couple of weeks.

Of course now I feel so guilty. So much I wish I'd said, so many things I wish I'd told him. I imagine he knew that I loved him, but I'm not sure I ever told him, and I wish I had. And even though we weren't as close as when we were kids, I still can't believe it.

I think one of the biggest surprises is how alone I feel. Even though he lived in America, and I barely saw him, I feel completely alone in the world, and the grief sometimes does seem harder than I can bear, after all. And I suppose with that loneliness comes fear—not an emotion I'm used to, and I still can't figure out exactly what it is I'm fearful of—my own mortality, perhaps?

So, I digress. The point of this is twofold: somehow I feel that I can talk to you and not be judged, and coming out of the abyss, I so desperately need someone to talk to right now; and I wanted to apologize for not being in touch sooner. I just couldn't talk to anyone for a while.

I hope you understand and hope you're still willing to play the role of big sister—God knows I could do with someone like that now.

Thinking of you and sending my love,

Will

To: Will
From: Holly
11/27/06 9:56:24 AM
Subject: Re: Apology

Will—

What an amazing letter. Thank you for being so honest and so brave—clearly you're writing to the right person, since I am someone who finds it far easier to express herself on the page than in person. Mostly, though, I feel honored that you've chosen to reveal yourself to me, and I'm relieved that this is a way for you to get at least some of it out.

I think I do know what it feels like to be that alone. In many ways, I feel like I've been alone for years. I'm not sure whether you'll understand, but when I was younger, I suppose when Tom and I were closest, I never did feel alone. Tom was always my closest friend, my ally, but since I've been married I haven't really felt like I've had an ally. Of course Marcus is my partner, but he is away so much for work—I realize as I'm writing this that I do understand loneliness far better than I think I'd like to admit (God, big step for me even writing this down . . . and I apologize if I'm gabbling).

As for fear, it doesn't come naturally to me—I tend to rush in guns a'blazing—but I can relate to the fear of our own mortality. Somehow we are not supposed to lose people we love—we're too young. I remember friends of my parents dying when I was a child, but even though I am now the same age as they were, I don't feel old enough to lose people, and if people I love can die in a flash, then so can I.

So clichéd to say that when someone dies, it forces you to reexamine everything about your life, and I'm not sure I'm ready to reexamine it all now (I think I may not like what I find . . . joke!), but it does definitely make me aware that my time here is finite, and there are still things I want to do, to achieve, still so much about my life that hasn't turned out to be the way I expected.

Or perhaps this is just a midlife crisis?

So . . . sigh . . . (gabbling again) . . . the point is, I think, that you are entitled to feel exactly what you're feeling. Tom's death has forced all of us to reevaluate, and perhaps in your case, you are having to step into a role that you weren't prepared for. BUT—and so important for you to hear this, Will—it's a role I know you can do. I have such wonderful memories of you when we were younger—you were always so sweet and so caring even when you were, as usual, getting into trouble (of course, I didn't know then you had a crush on me and, admittedly, perhaps I am being naive. Perhaps you were actually a monster who did a very good line in pulling his big brother's friends . . .). I think this is going to be such a difficult time for all of you, but you can get through it, and just as you said yourself at the memorial service, Tom wouldn't have wanted you all to give up your lives. Tom's probably looking down on each of us now, shaking his head, sighing and saying, "Pull your finger out, you silly arse." (Can't you just hear him now??!!!)

I'm also so glad you felt able to write as honestly as you did, and so eloquently as well—who knew the annoying little brother would grow up to be so emotionally aware? Seriously, though, many kudos to you for being able to express yourself in this way—I think if there is any outlet at all for the kind of grief you must be feeling, the kind of grief we are all feeling, writing is probably one of the best.

And I'm sure you know this, I'm sure I don't have to tell you this, but you can absolutely trust me. Strange, I know, given we haven't seen each other properly in about twenty years, but I would love to become friends, and mostly would love to be there for you if ever you need to talk.

Holly x

Friends. They can be friends, can't they? Naturally she can't deny a slight hint of attraction, but weren't all her old friendships with men based on a hint of attraction? Didn't those crushes almost always disappear, leaving in their places friendships that were fun and strong and solid?

And Holly has been so lonely. She never thought it was possible to be this lonely in a relationship. But until rediscovering friendships with these old friends, she hadn't thought about what she was missing.

But aside from Olivia, Saffron, and Paul, who better to be friends with now than Will? Not a replacement for Tom, never a replacement for Tom, but someone else who loved Tom as much as she did, someone else who has a shared history with her, someone else perhaps she could talk to.

For Holly misses having a man to talk to. She and Marcus have become, she realizes with horror, the couple she has always pitied in restaurants. The couple who look bored to be with each other, who spend the evening eating a delicious meal and exchanging less than a handful of comments. They sit in silence and observe people around them, both looking as if they wish they were anywhere but where they are, anywhere but with the person they are with.

For the last year, Holly has tried very hard to talk to Marcus. She has even—and, oh God, how like a teenager she felt—made a list of subjects to talk about over dinner just to ensure they don't sit in silence.

She stores up stories about the children and about her work, but she tails off when she realizes Marcus isn't paying much attention. So unlike her dinners with Tom, the two of them talking so quickly because there never seemed to be enough time to say everything they wanted to say.

She remembers one time when they went for a Chinese meal in Queensway. Out of nowhere Tom brought up her time as a nightclub hostess, complete with fake French accent, in a smart French club in a basement in Piccadilly. Holly started laughing, and something about the night sent the laughter spinning out of control, both Tom and Holly laughing so hard they were leaning over the table clutching their stomachs, tears running down their faces. The neighboring tables had started laughing too, just at the sight of Tom and Holly together.

Has Marcus ever made Holly laugh like that? Well, yes. In truth there are a couple of times he has. But they seem so very long ago, a lifetime ago. Holly can't remember the last time they really laughed together, just the two of them, nor the last time they even had fun.

"One person can't give you everything," she said to Saffron just the other night when Saffron had phoned her from LA to bemoan the fact that P, who was supposed to be coming over, had just canceled, and she wished he'd just hurry up and realize they were soul mates, made for each other, perfect together.

So odd, Holly thought in the beginning, *to have fallen*

straight back into these friendships as if no time had gone by at all, and perhaps more odd that it wasn't odd, but so normal, and so easy.

"You must think I'm mad," Saffron sniffed dramatically, "phoning you when I hadn't spoken to you for about twenty years before Tom died, but Holly, you're the only girlfriend I have who is happily-ish married, and I need your advice."

"Happily-ish?" Holly had laughed. "I'm the very last person you should be coming to for advice. Plus I don't believe in that whole soul-mate theory."

"Probably because you haven't met him yet," Saffron said. "Oh God, Holly, I'm sorry, I didn't mean that to come out the way it sounded, and maybe Marcus is the one."

"Don't worry." Holly chose to ignore it. "But I really don't believe there's one perfect person, I think there are any number of people who could make you happy. And I also think it's completely unrealistic to place so many expectations on one person. No one person can fulfill all your needs." And as she said it, she thought about Will. *It is innocent,* she thought. *It's just having a man she can talk to, a man with whom she can be friends.*

"I know that," Saffron said. "I do, really, but I love this man. I just never expected life to be this hard."

Me neither, Holly thought, but she didn't say anything at all.

CHAPTER THIRTEEN

To: Holly
From: Will
11/30/06 10:23:38 PM
Subject: Friends

Dear Holly,

I liked getting your e-mail. It made me smile, and it made me think. All the things you said about questioning your life are absolutely right. I hadn't thought of it as a midlife crisis—in fact, I don't feel old enough to actually be having a midlife crisis, but I started to think about what would happen if I were to die tomorrow (more apologies for the morbidity), and I realize I wouldn't leave much behind.

Tom had created so much. Scary Sarah. She may not be entirely my cup of tea either, but there is no doubt in my mind that they loved each other, and although I couldn't ever imagine myself with anyone that rigid, I know it worked for Tom, and I believe that, against all our better judgment, they had an exceptionally strong marriage.

And of course the children. Dustin and Violet, Dustin like a little Tom, serious and gentle, always preferring to hang out with the grown-ups just as Tom did when he was little. But both of them so incredible—these little people that Tom created, who will take his spirit into their world.

Then there was his success in business. Not that I ever wanted what Tom had—the suits and the business meetings and the ties . . . the conventional life, which fills me with horror, but I always felt safe with Tom, always trusted his advice because he always seemed to know where he was going, and I have less than no idea what I am doing from one day to the next, let alone for the rest of my life.

So I have wondered what I would leave, and the answer is not much. I never thought that bothered me, but all of a sudden it does. Not that I'm going to do anything stupid like get married to the first girl who captures my heart (although if you're interested in divorcing Marcus and making an honest man out of me, do let me know!), but Tom's death has made me think, for the first time, that maybe I should settle down a bit. Get a mortgage. Find a girl I could love. Maybe have a couple of kids.

I can't even believe I'm writing this! It does feel good, being able to "talk" to someone about this. I suppose it is true what they say after all—so much easier to write your feelings down than talk about them. I think if I ever said any of this stuff out loud, they'd put me in the loony bin.

Hope you are having a peaceful day and that you have got your little monkeys to bed. I'd love to see photos of them—do they look like you? I'm imagining Daisy as, naturally, a mini-Holly—I know she's younger than you were when I first met you, but I still remember you as this exotic bohemian creature, and I am hoping Daisy has inherited that. Unfairly I see Oliver as being a mini-Marcus, and I only say unfairly because I hope he isn't as serious or as stuffy as I've heard Marcus is.

Love,
Will

To: Will
From: Holly
12/01/06 04:09:28 AM
Subject: Re: Friends

Will—

I have always wondered who "they" are. "They" do seem to say an awful lot, and they do seem to be right a lot of the time, so if you ever come across "them," do let me know—would love to say hello . . .

I ought to be fast asleep, but find these days that I wake up in the middle of the night and I'm done for. Recently I've been coming up to my studio—a quiet place to read, have a cup of tea or surf around reading inane gossip on the Internet, but how lovely to have received your e-mail and lovelier still to have some peace and quiet to send back a proper response.

My day yesterday was quite peaceful, since you asked. The monkeys went to bed early, and I was able to sink into a hot bath with a glass of wine, then crawl into bed. As far as I'm concerned, a good night is going to bed by nine, and a great night is going to bed by eight. Tonight was a great night. I have to say I do love it when Marcus travels around the country for trials—I can do whatever I want whenever I want, although it occurs to me, writing to a young, energetic, childless whippersnapper such as yourself, that you probably think I am deeply boring, going to bed at such an unseasonably and unreasonably early hour.

Yes, well. You're probably right.

And you made me laugh saying I was exotic and bohemian. I never saw myself like that at all. I'm thinking it was those cheap Camden Lock Indian fringed skirts with little mirrors all over them that must have made me look bohemian. I have a very hard time picturing myself as anything other than a mum and wife these days. I like the word exotic too.

Am going to forward a joke after this—don't normally forward those things and hope you don't find the levity inappropriate, but this one made me laugh and I figure you could do with smiling a bit these days. I love that you felt able to unload to me—truly. I feel enormously honored, happy that you said such sweet things and that I feel I have rediscovered a friend I didn't know I had, and sad that this is all the result of such a tragedy.

To: Will
From: Holly
12/01/06 04:42:56 AM
Fw: Cowboys (Friends Part II)

An old cowboy sat down at the Starbucks and ordered a cup of coffee. As he sat sipping his coffee, a young woman sat down next to him.

She turned to the cowboy and asked, "Are you a real cowboy?"

He replied, "Well, I've spent my whole life breaking colts, working cows, going to rodeos, fixing fences, pulling calves, bailing hay, doctoring calves, cleaning my barn, fixing flats, working on tractors, and feeding my dogs, so I guess I am a cowboy."

She said, "I'm a lesbian. I spend my whole day thinking about women. As soon as I get up in the morning, I think about women. When I shower,

I think about women. When I watch TV, I think about women. I even think about women when I eat. It seems that everything makes me think of women."

The two sat sipping in silence.

A little while later, a man sat down on the other side of the old cowboy and asked, "Are you a real cowboy?"

He replied, "I always thought I was, but I just found out that I'm a lesbian."

To: Holly
From: Will
12/01/06 10:33:25 AM
Re: Fw: Cowboys (Friends Part II)

So not only am I a whippersnapper, but I'm a lesbian too???!!!!!!!!

Holly bursts into laughter reading Will's e-mail. She files it away and goes back to reread his previous e-mails. She's not sure why she does this, but she has reread them every day. They make her feel happy. Free. Young. She even stole away one night when Marcus was asleep, just to check if another e-mail had arrived. It had. It seems Will is as obsessive as she.

There is nothing quite as exciting as sitting at her desk, clicking on the inbox, and seeing his e-mail address, the anticipation so sweet at times she can hardly stand it. For the first time in years, Holly has something to look forward to, a reason to get up in the mornings.

She alternates between being giddy with happiness when the e-mails arrive and riddled with insecurity and doubt when they don't. A lot of the time, she feels as if she is sixteen.

She is fun and playful with the children but far too distracted to give them her full attention, and her distraction is affecting her relationship with Marcus. She doesn't care anymore that he's never at home or that he doesn't seem particularly interested in her life.

One night Marcus comes home so much earlier than usual and announces that he has booked a table at Petrus as a special treat. Holly runs upstairs and changes, and Marcus frowns at her as she walks back into the hallway.

"New clothes?"

"Yup." Holly twirled. "You like?" She was wearing a brightly colored print dress, huge splashy flowers, and a long, retro necklace of enamel daisies. She fell in love with all of it when she took Daisy to Petit Bateau, Westbourne Grove the other day. And of course Daisy ended up with underwear and Holly ended up with four bags stuffed with the type of gorgeous, funky, hell— *bohemian*—clothes that she had tried to pretend she would never wear anymore because she knows they don't fit her role as Marcus's wife.

"It's fun," Marcus says eventually, and they leave, Holly not feeling the slightest bit upset by Marcus's clear disapproval. When it comes to Marcus she doesn't feel much of anything these days. Not love. Not hate. Nothing. Sheer indifference.

Marcus's wife, it seems, has left the building.

At the restaurant Marcus says, "You seem miles away." Tonight Holly hadn't done what she so often does—chatter away about inane things, nineteen to the dozen, so all he has to do is smile and nod every now and then and look interested while he is actually thinking about work. Tonight Holly seems happy but not altogether there. And she looks different. Her hair is not pulled back in a sleek ponytail tonight, the way he likes it. It is messy, even a little curly. As it happens, it is actually quite sexy.

When they get home, Marcus comes up behind Holly in the bathroom and puts his arms around her. She turns round and kisses him back, and fifteen minutes later, when he rolls off her with a kiss and a smile, he watches her get up to go to the bathroom and says, "Holly, that was fantastic."

"It was rather, wasn't it?" She shoots him a smile as she disappears through the doorway. What she doesn't tell him is that she had closed her eyes—just twice, and only for seconds at a time—and imagined it was Will. Not that she is planning an affair—God, no!—but she just wanted to see what would happen if she did it. What the hell.

Isn't everyone entitled to a little fantasy now and then?

Across the pond Saffron is indulging in a little fantasy of her own. P's wife is away filming, and he's staying with Saffron while she's away, at least for tonight.

Saffron has ordered his favorite from Wolfgang Puck, currently being picked up by Samuel, to be dropped off at Saffron's and heated up when P arrives. Alcohol-free beer is in the fridge, the logs have been stacked in the fireplace ready to be lit just before his arrival. Jack Jones is emanating softly from the Bose speakers—a gift from P when he realized all she had were tiny iPod speakers that made everything sound tinny.

Her legs are newly waxed, her nails newly painted, and her hair newly highlighted. She hasn't seen P for two weeks and, as always, is almost dizzy with excitement at the prospect of seeing him, and not just for the evening but for the whole night.

No makeup, though. P loves her natural. He tells her frequently he loves her best first thing in the morning when her hair is messed up and her face scrubbed clean. He loves her in old sweats, baseball caps, and his oversized sweatshirts. That's how she looked when he fell in love with her, he tells her, seeing her at meetings looking as if she had just fallen out of bed.

She wonders sometimes whether their incredibly intense attraction for each other would wane if they were together all the time. She suspects it would not. They have shared so much together on such an intimate level in the meetings, how could it possibly wane when she knows him better than anyone else in the world, and he, her?

Her fantasy tonight is much the same as it is every night. That he realizes the futility of staying in a marriage just for the sake of his career and finally decides to leave. That he moves into this little house—and it would be this little house, Saffron has no desire to step in and take over from his wife as lady of the manor—and that they fall asleep every night, wrapped around one another.

The fire is lit, the food warming gently in the oven, the setting is perfect. When P rings the doorbell, Saffron runs down the stairs like an overexcited teenager, flinging her arms around him in the hallway and kissing him for hours.

She cannot believe how much she loves kissing him. Her previous relationships, previous flings, have wanted to move straight on to the main course, but P, so starved of affection in his marriage, loves nothing more than lying in her arms on the sofa, just kissing, well into the small hours.

He loves being loved. Of course, he is one of the most-loved stars of this generation, but that is not love. When he married his wife, he loved her and, naively he now thinks, he thought that she loved him.

He married her because she made him feel safe, because he thought they would be a good team, and because wherever he was weak, she seemed to be strong.

Where he could be, particularly in those drinking days, self-important and pompous, she seemed grounded and down-to-earth. She had an amazing perception and wisdom, and he loved taking her to business meetings with him, listening to what she thought afterward, knowing that she invariably had insights that were spot on, that he would never have thought about.

He loved her business mind. That she set up her own production company and immediately set about buying scripts. That she would lie in bed for hours, reading glasses perched on the end of her nose, pencil in hand as she made scrawling remarks on the manuscripts she would read endlessly.

In those early days, he would often reach out for her, slide a hand up her thigh, and lean over and kiss her neck, but she would shake her head distractedly and move away from him, telling him she had to read this by tomorrow or she had to get up early or not tonight, darling, too much work.

He doesn't blame her for making him turn to alcohol, but certainly alcohol made the rejection easier to bear. It excused his bad behavior, when he started looking elsewhere for the love and affection he craved. It made him feel strong and invincible; that it didn't matter that the one person in the world he wanted didn't seem to want him in return.

Now he thinks bitterly that it was a marriage orchestrated by their agents. He wishes he'd known it at the time. It would have saved him a lifetime of pain if he'd known she had always seen it as a business arrangement.

So he turned to other women, but what he had never found before Saffron was love. He had never found intimacy and had never trusted that anyone loved him for him rather than for being a rich and famous actor.

LA abounded with young gorgeous women who would drop their knickers at the bat of an eyelid and, for a while, that was enough, but when he found Saffron and got to know her slowly in the safety of their shared AA meetings, he knew what he had missed.

He has spoken to his manager more times than he cares to think about of leaving his wife and being with Saffron. His manager, his agent, and his publicist all agree: it will be career death. He can't do it. He doesn't tell Saffron he thinks about this all the time, doesn't want to give her false hope, but he thinks that at some point in his career, he will be able to stop, buy a ranch in Montana, leave his old life behind and create a new one with Saffron.

For Saffron is not the only one with fantasies. P has fantasies of family life. He has fantasies of a wife who loves him, who sleeps cuddled up to him at night, who supports him unequivocally in the choices he makes. He has dreams of children—a pack of kids running around laughing—and of his wife showering them all with kisses and fun. He dreams of wide open spaces, of horses, of owning land. And he still can't quite believe the choice he made when he married his wife.

A good friend though she may be, she doesn't want children. She doesn't like animals. Her idea of a perfect house is the mansion they are currently in, in Bel Air, expertly decorated by the top decorators in town, beautiful to look at but nothing about it spells home.

In the beginning, he vaguely recalls, they would talk about their vision for their lives. He remembers her saying she wanted a production company, but she also said she wanted kids. He told her of his vision of the ranch, and she said it sounded wonderful. She said a lot of things in those days, he realizes now. A lot of things he wanted to hear, very few of them true.

When he first came into AA, he hated her. He resented her for trapping him in a loveless marriage, hated her for lying to him, could barely bring himself to talk to her. They would sit in limos on the way to premieres, arguing fiercely, then step into the flash of light bulbs with equal megawatt smiles on their faces, stopping for the film crews to demonstrate how much they loved one another.

They gave interviews about the strength of their marriage, the things that they loved about each other, and with every one he believed he was giving the performance of his life, easily Oscar-winning, if faking undying affection were ever to be added as a category.

The twelve-step program gave him the gift of acceptance. He learned to accept her rather than hate her because she wasn't who he wanted her to be. It was never going to be the marriage he wanted, he realized, but he also realized he had a choice: he could stay in a slump of self-pity and resentment, and stay a victim for the rest of his life, or he could change the way he looked at his life and embrace it exactly as it was.

And just as he had learned to accept it, to accept that his marriage was a great friendship and a wonderful working arrangement, Saffron had walked into the meeting and captured his heart.

There is no such thing as coincidence. There is no doubt in his mind that he and Saffron were in that particular meeting that particular day for a reason, and however much he tells his manager he is committed to perpetuating the lie of the golden couple that is his marriage, he knows that there is only so long that he can live not being true to himself, and the longer he stays in AA, this program that demands nothing less than rigorous honesty, the harder it becomes.

And so much harder on nights such as these when Saffron is so clearly everything his wife is not.

"Confession time," Saffron says, as P helps her stack the dishes in the dishwasher. "But first," she says, grinning, "can I just say how much I love that you, hottest sex god in America, are stacking dishes in a tiny kitchen in this apartment? If your fans could see you now. . . ."

"What? You don't think this is sexy?" P places a hand on his hip and poses with a plate. "Isn't this what every woman wants? A man who helps out?"

"Sort of, but I think if they were with you they'd expect to be waited on hand and foot by a butler, no?"

"They'd be waiting a very long time for that." P laughs. "So, back to confession time. What's the confession?"

Saffron blushes. "Okay. I lied."

"About what?"

"I didn't cook this. I really want you to think I'm a great cook, so I lied."

P roars with laughter. "I know you lied. Only Wolfgang Puck makes this as well as this. Plus I was with Samuel when he picked it up. I'm not stupid, my darling."

Saffron breathes a sigh of relief. "I know you're not stupid, but I wanted you to think I'm a great cook."

"Honey, cooking is the last thing I care about."

"Oh yes?" She raises an eyebrow and P closes the dishwasher and puts his arms round her waist, pulling her in for a kiss.

"Do you know something?" He pulls back and gazes into her eyes as she smiles at him. "I love you, Saffron."

"I love you too," she says, and taking him by the hand she leads him out of the kitchen and upstairs to bed.

CHAPTER FOURTEEN

Frauke looks up from where she's scrubbing down the counter after Daisy's lunch and whistles, low and slow. "Wow! You look fantastic!"

"Really?" Holly does a delighted twirl in the kitchen. "You don't think it's a bit . . . young?"

"Holly, you are young. I am always telling my other au pair friends that I am lucky because I have such a young host mother. I even say that you should dress more like this. Younger. The clothes you wear are beautiful, but they make you look older. If I didn't know I would think you were in your mid-forties."

"Frauke!" Holly says indignantly, even as she laughs. "Talk about knowing how to ruin a good mood."

Frauke looks confused. "Why? Today, Holly, I think you look maybe thirty. No, twenty-eight."

"Really?"

"Yes, and I love your hair like this. It is very sexy. Where are you going?"

"Oh just lunch with an old friend. Daisy!" She shouts up the stairs. "Come and give Mummy a kiss good-bye!"

Holly climbs into her car and takes the CD from her bag. She has made it herself, a series of songs that somehow speak to her, tell her about her life, fill her with optimism about what her future holds.

She had forgotten music could be this powerful. As a teenager, her life was music. She would leave her mother's house with her Walkman in hand, and spend hours traipsing, depressed, around Hampstead Heath, being the lonely misunderstood teenager who needed to be rescued by a knight in shining armor.

She listens to the radio now, but hasn't actually bought a CD for years unless it was something for the children. Two weeks ago, on Will's advice, she went out and bought an iPod, bringing it home and spending the next two days uploading CDs, buying songs, creating playlists. This one she called "Happy," filled with music that lifts her up.

Van Morrison's "Brown-Eyed Girl"; "I'll Take You There," by the Staples Singers; then Corinne Bailey Rae. Holly shakes her hair out, curls that she expertly worked in using the curling iron this morning, and she sings along at the top of her voice, feeling sixteen, feeling young and free and as if anything is possible.

Which it is.

She is first to arrive. Damn. She hates being first. She had deliberately timed it so she would be five minutes late, but when she walks into Nicole's, she doesn't see him.

"How many?" The maître d' asks politely and leads her to a table at the back for two. Holly resists the temptation to run to the loo to check her makeup. She knows it's fine—she checked it at every red light on the way here and several times while driving somewhat erratically along the winding London streets.

She taps her boot impatiently on the floor and catches sight of herself in the mirror on the other side of the room. God, if she didn't know better she'd never recognize herself. Skinny jeans tucked into knee-high, buttery leather boots, high enough to be sexy as hell, not so high she can't walk. A cotton shirt, classic, but slim and long, and a chunky wide belt.

She realizes, as she gazes around at the rest of the clientele, that she looks as if she belongs. She looks no different from the other young mothers sipping cappuccinos with their strollers parked next to the tables, and even though she is childless today, strollerless and child-accoutrement-less, she is what she is, and, how funny, she thinks that she has exchanged one uniform for another.

Her uniform of cashmere and pearls, so befitting a lawyer's wife, has today been swapped for a uniform of Notting Hill trendiness, and although still a uniform, Holly notices how much better she feels in what she is wearing today. She does feel young, and, let's face it, she is only thirty-nine. No need to pretend to be forty-five.

"You look amazing!" Will's eyes widen in surprise and, she hopes, delight. No. She doesn't hope that. No point in hoping that. Or is there? Isn't it fine, surely, to want to be attractive to other men? Isn't it fine to enjoy someone appreciating you? It doesn't mean you're going to have an affair, for heaven's sake. Holly would never have an affair. She isn't the type.

You're married, my darling. Not dead!

"Oh this? Wow. Thanks." Holly blushes slightly as she stands up to step into Will's hug, to receive his air kisses on either cheek, except they are not air kisses, his lips land softly on each cheek, even as hers skim the air on either side of his. *Stop it!* she tells herself as her heart flutters ever so quickly, and she sits down quickly, spending rather more seconds than are altogether necessary smoothing the napkin on her lap in a bid to calm down.

"Now you look like the Holly I remember." Will grins, and as he does, she thinks with a jolt how much like Tom he looks.

"This is a bit weird, isn't it?" Holly finds herself saying.

"What? You and I having lunch? Frankly I think it's about time we took our e-mail correspondence to a proper friendship, and you can't be friends if you never see one another. As the dating service says, it's only lunch."

"No, not that. You just looked exactly like Tom when you smiled." Holly picks up the napkin and holds it to her eyes. "I'm so sorry, Will," she says, attempting a smile. "So stupid that I'm the one sitting here with tears in my eyes when he's your brother. I feel I don't have a right to this display of emotion in front of you."

Will leans over and places a hand on Holly's, squeezing it ever so gently. "Holly, you loved him too. Just for the record, you do have a right to display any emotion you want, and I know, God knows I know, how it reaches up and grabs you at the most unexpected times."

"I'm sorry," Holly says as a tear slides its way down her nose.

"It's okay," Will says, and he keeps holding her hand, not saying anything, and after a few seconds it is okay, and Holly smiles through her sniffs.

"I'm pathetic," she says. "I'm sorry."

"The only thing that's pathetic is that you keep apologizing. Will you stop? Please?"

"Okay." She smiles. "Sor . . . oh fuck off."

"That's better!" Will grins. "When was the last time you told a friend to fuck off?"

"Probably yesterday," Holly says. "I think I may have told Saffron to fuck off over the phone."

"That's nice," Will says in mock horror. "Can't imagine why she's friends with you."

"Because I'm kind and funny and loyal."

"And pretty damn sexy with that hair, if I may say so."

"I . . ." Holly flushes bright red and Will starts to laugh.

"Are you going to turn scarlet every time I compliment you? Because if you are that's fantastic. I can start pouring them on. Those jeans and boots make your arse . . ."

"Will!" Holly stops him, even as she's laughing.

"What? Can't I say arse?"

"No you bloody can't. You don't know me nearly well enough to make comments about my . . . well. You know."

Will leans back in his chair and crosses his arms, studying Holly with a smile. "Well, well, well," he says. "Holly Mac, a prude. Who knew?"

"I am not a prude," she says indignantly.

"Tell me you have a great arse, then."

"No! I absolutely do not have to tell you I have a great arse to prove to you that I'm not a prude."

"Go on. I won't believe you unless you tell me."

"Fine. I have a great arse. Happy now?"

"Very, thank you. And yes, I agree. So. Shall we get menus?" The waiter appears immediately, and Holly hides her embarrassment—her secret thrill—behind choosing what to have for lunch.

"You're not used to being complimented are you?" Will muses, gazing at Holly over the rim of his cappuccino at the end of the meal, each of them reluctant to end what has been a lunch filled with laughter and teasing.

"No," Holly says cautiously. "Although I don't think that's me, particularly. I can't imagine being in a situation where I would be complimented these days. My life as a mother and freelance illustrator is very dull. You see the same people, and run around in the same clothes, so why would anyone compliment you on your looks? Surely it's the same for you, no? When was the last time you were complimented?"

"Well, I did get a compliment at Tom's memorial service. Not particularly appropriate, but there was a girl who came up to me and told me she and her friends had always fancied me when we were young. Remember when I worked at the chemist's for that summer? Apparently they'd watch me play football on the weekends, then make excuses to come into the chemist's and buy stuff. They even had a name for me. The lusty leg man."

Holly bursts out laughing. "Is that because of your thick footballer legs?"

"Nothing wrong with having thick footballer legs."

"Didn't say there was. But that's funny. The lusty leg man. I like it."

"Yes, well. I didn't make it up. Holly?" Will's face turns serious for a second. "Can I ask you something?"

"Yes, but I'm not altogether sure I'll answer."

"In one of your e-mails you said something about a good night meant being in bed by nine and a great night meant being in bed by eight. You didn't really mean that, did you?"

Holly smiles and leans forward. "Will, my darling, one day hopefully you will have small children, and then you will understand exactly what I mean, and why, sadly, it is the truth."

"But I have tons of friends with kids, and I don't know anyone besides you who actually goes to bed that early."

Holly shrugs. "I just get tired."

"Are you sure you're not just checking out of life?"

"What?" Holly sits up straight, shocked.

"I'm sorry, Holly. I don't meant to say anything to offend you. It's just that you're so vibrant, you always were, but today, sitting here now, is the first time I've seen the old Holly. When I saw you after the memorial service I couldn't believe how, well, how old you seemed. Obviously it wasn't ideal circumstances, but even the way you were dressed was so staid and proper. Like a shadow of who you used to be, who I always dreamed you'd become. And I'm not saying this to upset you, but I think it's heartbreaking that you're in bed every night by eight or nine. That's not living. That's running away from life. That sounds to me like you're burying your head under the covers, literally, and checking out of your life."

Holly doesn't say anything for a while. Can't say anything for a while. When she looks up and meets Will's eyes, she just shrugs sadly.

"Maybe you're right. A little," she says. "Maybe going to bed keeps me from examining my life more closely, and maybe things would be different if Marcus were around more. You have to understand that he works so incredibly hard; it's not like he's around and I'm canceling stuff to go to bed. There is nothing else for me to do. Admittedly I could stay up and watch TV until he got home, but I'd rather climb into bed with a good book."

"But that's ridiculous that there's nothing else for you to do. You could be out with friends, having fun. You could be going to the movies, having a drink. Something. Anything. Just engaging in life." He is horrified and making no effort to hide it.

"Okay," Will says. "I'm throwing down the gauntlet. I'm going out on Friday night with some friends to see a band. It's very casual, just live music at a bar. If Marcus isn't around, I want you to come. Just do it. Say yes. Get a babysitter and come."

"I can't." Holly shakes her head, but even as she shakes her head she knows she can. She knows she will.

"Why not? I bet Marcus will be working and, think, you have a choice of going to bed at eight o'clock or having a fun night with interesting people, doing something different, something that might make you grow as a person." Will sighs. "I just hate this concept, this belief that so many married people seem to buy into that if you're married you have to behave a certain way; your world has to revolve around the children; it has to shrink and shrink until there's almost nothing left of who you used to be before you had kids."

"I have tons of married friends," Will continues. "And what they all have in common is that they still retain a really strong sense of who they are. They still go out drinking, still have fun, still retain enough of their identity that they never feel as if a part of them died when they walked down the aisle."

"God!" Holly sucks in a sharp intake of breath. "That is exactly how I felt when I walked down the aisle. I've never even realized it before now."

"See? And here's your chance to change. Go on. Say you'll come. I'd love you to meet my friends and I think you'll enjoy them. Will you?"

"Okay." Holly leans back and relaxes. "I'll come," and as the thought, *What am I doing?*, enters her head, she shouts it back down.

I'm not going to think about this, she tells herself. *I'm just going to be in the moment and see what happens.*

In a quiet restaurant in Highgate Village, Paul and Anna sit in a corner, nursing their wine, trying to find the words.

"I'm so sorry, Anna," Paul says again as he puts his arm around her and pulls her close for a hug. "I'm just so sorry."

"We can try again, no?" Anna looks up at Paul hopefully, but she already knows the answer.

"I just don't see how we can," Paul says. "I know we both want a baby more than anything, but I just think that physically and emotionally this is going to destroy us. I don't know how many times we can continue to go through it. And the financial burden is just so big. We need to start building our savings again, putting aside money for a rainy day, not to mention the barn that we're not even using because we haven't put a penny into it. I think . . ." He pauses. "I don't know if you're ready to find out about this yet, but I think that now might be the time for us to start investigating adoption."

Anna sighs as a tear drips onto the table. "I did not honestly believe this would happen," she whispers. "I just kept thinking that the next time it would happen, the next time I would get pregnant. I still cannot believe it. I know we've always said we would look at adoption, but it's so final. Adoption means I have failed. We have failed. Adoption means we've admitted that this is it. No more Clomid, no more Synarel, no more injections. And no more hope. I just do not know how I can bear it, how I can accept it."

"I know," Paul says. "I feel the same way. And perhaps at some point in the future we can revisit IVF, but even if you're not ready to actually start whatever the adoption process is, I feel like we've reached a time when we have to explore it, have to find out what it involves. Maybe that will help us, help us see things more clearly."

"Why me?" Anna leans her head into Paul's shoulder as he cradles her gently. "Why us?"

He loves her vulnerability, he thinks, as he strokes her back gently and kisses the top of her head, shushing her like a baby, rocking her to make it okay. He loves that she can run meetings with cutthroat skill, has held her own against the toughest names in the business, and has created herself and her business out of nothing. And he loves most that it is not all of who she is.

The Anna he loves has so many sides. She can be tough, unyielding, fierce, soft, gentle, and vulnerable all in the same breath. He loves that she is never frightened to show him who she is, like tonight.

He continues to rock her until she calms down. As for her questions, *Why me? Why us?* There is only one answer he can think of.

Why not?

"Shall we go away this weekend?" Paul says as they gather their coats and thread their way through the tightly packed tables.

"White Barn Fields?" Anna smiles grimly. "Go and see all the work we have not been able to afford to do?"

"We could always do it ourselves." Paul shrugs. "On some level I'm sure it would be a hell of a lot of fun."

"Do you think they have the *Idiot's Guide to Renovating Houses*?" Anna smiles, the first genuine smile of the evening.

"If not, I could always write it and make ourselves a fortune."

"Now that is the best idea of the night." Anna smiles up at him. "I do love you, you know."

"Even though I can't afford to keep you in IVF?" Paul is joking, but Anna sees the doubt in his eyes.

"Yes, even though you cannot afford to keep me in IVF. At least they will never say I married you for your money."

"No, it was my good looks and charm."

"Actually I think you hypnotized me sometime during that interview. The good news is I am still waiting to wake up."

"I love you too," Paul says, kissing her on the forehead as he closes his arms around her for a hug, both of them swaying gently on the pavement outside the restaurant, their breath blowing soft clouds in the air. "Really, I feel so lucky to have you, to have us."

"So are we going to White Barn Fields this weekend with our toolbox in the back of the car?"

"Let's do it," Paul nods as they start walking toward the car, "let's go down there and get busy. And can I start looking into what's involved in adoption."

"I cannot promise anything," Anna says, "but yes. I am fine with you starting to look into it."

"So what do you think?" Will leans over and whispers in Holly's ear so she can hear him, and Holly grins at him.

"I think your friends are great. The music's great. I'm having a great time."

"So it's all great?" Will laughs.

"It's all great," Holly says, as Will orders another round of beers.

They are sitting in the Jazz Café in Camden. To Holly's surprise, it is not crowded with people a decade younger than herself as she had feared. Nor is it ghastly loud music that gives her a headache.

Nor is it an awful evening. She wasn't sure why she'd said yes. She knew that she would hate it, but she was proving a point. Proving to herself that there was a reason she went to bed at eight and that there was nothing to be gained from pretending to be in her twenties and going to bars to listen to live music and drink with people she didn't know.

But Will's friends have been lovely. An electrician who works with Will from time to time, a chiropractor and her journalist husband, and an Australian couple who, like Will, work to fund their traveling. The chiropractor couple—Jan and Charlie—have four children, and Holly spent the early part of the evening, before the band came on, bonding over shared child-related stories, catching eyes with Will, on the other side of their crowd, chatting to the Australians.

The band is a jazz trio. Not too soft, not too loud. The music is wonderful, and Holly is stunned at how much she is enjoying this: sitting at the bar listening to music, a beer in hand—and God knows when was the last time she sat and enjoyed a beer—a beer! Vodka and tonic is more her speed these days.

She is surrounded by good people. Easy people. People who don't need to impress, who aren't judging her but are just happy to be where they are and who they're with.

So different from her life with Marcus, and her role as Marcus's wife.

Ah. Marcus.

She told Marcus she was going out, just wasn't entirely truthful in telling him who with. She mentioned Will, couldn't lie completely, but told him that there was a group of them going out: Paul and Anna, Olivia, a couple of others. "It's such a shame you're not here," she lied to Marcus on the phone. "We'll miss you."

"Have fun," he said distractedly, and she hadn't felt guilty about telling him a lie.

Hugs all around at the end of the evening, and Will turns to Holly. "I'm going to pop in to drop some stuff off to Mum and Dad tomorrow, and I'm planning on staying for lunch. Do you want to come? They'd love to see you."

"Tomorrow?" Holly looks at her watch, stalling for time. Tomorrow. Marcus is still in Manchester and not expected home before late afternoon. She doesn't have any plans for tomorrow other than the usual Saturday with the kids.

"I have the kids," Holly says, not sure what Will is saying. Although he is not saying anything other than come and see my parents who know and love you.

"So bring them." Will grins. "I'd love to meet them."

"Do you want to check with your mum and dad? Make sure it's okay?"

"Oh come on, Holly, this is Mum and Dad. You know Mum will have cooked enough to feed an army and, as far as she's concerned, you're family anyway."

"Will you tell them we're coming? Make sure it's okay?"

"If it makes you happier, I'll tell her you're coming. Does that mean you're coming?"

"Yes."

"Great!" Will says, and with that they have one last hug good-bye and Holly climbs into her car. She turns the music up and smiles all the way home. She smiles as she gets undressed, smiles as she brushes her teeth, smiles as she falls into bed. It takes her two hours to get to sleep, two hours and an eventual Valium, but even as she lies there replaying every minute of her evening, the smile never leaves her face.

CHAPTER FIFTEEN

"Do they have children?" Oliver bounces up and down in his booster seat as Holly winds her way through the quiet streets.

"Yes, darling," Holly says, "but not your age. Remember Mummy's friend Tom? He was their son, and also Will, who you'll meet today."

"Mum?"

"*Mummy*. Yes, darling?" She hates that Oliver has started shortening her name to Mum. Every time she hears a *Mum*, she feels his childhood slipping through her fingers like sand. Such a small thing to try to grasp on to, being a *Mummy* rather than a *Mum*, but one that Holly refuses to give up.

"Mummy." Oliver rolls his eyes, unseen in the back-seat. "Mummy, do you think that Tom can see us from heaven? Do you think he's watching us now?"

"I think he probably is, darling. Sometimes I talk to him, and I feel that he's here with us even though he's not. I dream about him too." Holly has had precisely two dreams about Tom since his death. Both times, Tom just appeared out of nowhere, and Holly, shocked, flung her arms around him saying, *I thought you were dead*. Tom hugged her and reassured her that he was fine. That he was happy where he was and that he wanted her to be happy too.

She awoke confused but with a sense of peace each time, and although Holly never thought she was one to buy into contact with your loved ones in the afterlife, she is now certain that Tom is watching her, that he is fine and this is his way of reassuring her.

Daisy's high voice pipes up from the back seat. "Mummy, I want to go to heaven. Can I go to heaven?"

Holly shudders. "Not for many years, darling."

"Silly," Oliver reprimands her. "Heaven is where you go when you die. You don't want to die."

"I do!" Daisy insists. "I want to die and go to heaven, and there are beautiful princesses there and ponies, and I do! I want to die!"

"Daisy!" Holly's voice is harsher than she intends. Even though Daisy can have no idea what she is saying, she cannot bear Daisy saying that. "You mustn't say you want to die. I would miss you terribly if you died, and you have too much to do on this earth first."

"See?" Oliver is triumphant. "Told ya." And Holly slips in the audio CD of *Harry Potter* in a bid to keep them quiet.

"Oh look at her!" Maggie stands back and watches Daisy with a delighted smile on her face. "She's a little *you*, Holly! She's exactly like you. Gorgeous!"

"And this is Oliver. Oliver, say how do you do to Mrs. Fitzgerald."

"Mrs.? Don't be ridiculous, Holly. Mrs. Fitzgerald is my mother-in-law. I'm Maggie to everyone, children included."

Of course she's Maggie, Holly thinks. *How could she possibly be anything else?* Holly has never been comfortable instructing her children to call her friends Mr. and Mrs., but Marcus insists. Insists that all children are to call all adults Mr. and Mrs., irrespective of how good friends they might be.

It is, she realizes, part of Marcus's pomposity, part of his behaving how he thinks he is supposed to behave if people are to believe that he is from the upper-crust background he so desperately wants to come from. In line with his behavior, Marcus had very clear rules about how the children ought to behave.

They are to shake adults by the hand, look them in the eye and say how do you do. They are to sit at the table and not speak unless they are spoken to. They are not to watch television during the week and only an hour on each day of the weekend. Daisy is to wear smocked dresses and patent-leather Mary Janes, and Oliver is to wear corduroy trousers and woolen sweaters.

Never mind that Daisy has a will stronger than anyone Holly has ever met and getting her into *anything* that isn't pink, purple, and sparkly is a battle Holly doesn't have the energy for.

Never mind that Oliver is nearly seven and wants to be a supercool skateboarding dude, dressed in Gap Kids like all the other children in his class. Marcus seems to want the children to belong to another era and is bewildered and not terribly happy that Holly is clearly not following his instructions when he is out of the house.

"They're children, for God's sake!" Holly actually moaned to Marcus's mother one day when Joanie was on a rare visit from Bristol.

"They're only little," Joanie agreed with Holly. "And we're living in 2006, not 1886." Holly burst into laughter. "You just keep on doing what you're doing and they'll turn out great." Joanie nodded. "I think you're a wonderful mother."

"Thank you, Joanie." Holly smiled at her, wondering how such a down-to-earth woman had produced a son like Marcus.

Holly stands at the kitchen sink, peeling potatoes, and stops for a few seconds, smiling as she gazes across the garden to the large old oak tree at the bottom, where Peter and Oliver are looking very industrious as Peter—rather bravely, Holly thinks—holds a nail and Oliver bangs it very carefully.

Peter came into the kitchen when they arrived and squatted down on his haunches so he was the same height as the kids.

"You look like you're very strong," he said to Oliver. "Do you have big muscles?"

Oliver nodded cautiously.

"Oh good, because I need some help building a treehouse. Do you think you'd be any good at building a treehouse?"

Oliver almost squealed his answer, jiggling up and down with excitement.

"Well actually it is built, but the ladder is broken, and there's no point in having a treehouse if you can't climb up to it, is there? How are you with a hammer and nails?"

"I'm really good with a hammer," Oliver said, although, as far as Holly knows, he's never picked up a hammer in his life.

"Come on, then. I'll be the builder and you can be my second in command. Sound good?" He extended a hand to Oliver who immediately slipped his hand into it and nodded as he walked out to the garden, Peter stopping in the doorway and turning around to wink at Holly.

She watches Oliver chat away to Peter, nineteen to the dozen, and echo Peter's pose, hands on his hips as he surveys his work, in a bid to be just like him.

"He's lovely with kids, isn't he?" Maggie slides up next to Holly and smiles as she watches them. "He misses Dustin and Violet so very much. We both do. Nothing like the relationship between a grandchild and a grandparent, and so difficult when they live so far away."

"Have you spoken to them? How are they? How's Sarah?"

Maggie lets out a long sigh. "Mostly distraught. I expected her to be fabulously stoic, to get on with her life and keep her grief contained, but it seems grief gets us in unexpected ways. Her sister is living with her for a while, helping out enormously with the kids. We offered to have the kids for Christmas, give her a break, time to grieve properly, but of course she rightly pointed out that the kids are the only thing keeping her going at the moment."

"And the kids?"

"I think a lot of it is over their heads, particularly Dustin, the little one. Violet is struggling with it. She understands that her daddy isn't coming back and just misses him hugely. She draws him pictures every day . . ." Maggie's voice tails off and she wipes her eyes, biting her lip to suppress the tears, willing them to go away.

Holly puts her arm around Maggie, and Maggie rests her head on Holly's shoulder. Together they stand at the window until Daisy, sitting at the kitchen table making doll's houses out of cereal boxes, demands some help with the tissue "sheets."

At one fifteen, there's still no sign of Will. The roast lamb is "relaxing" on the counter, the fresh garden mint has been chopped into a sauce with vinegar and sugar, the vegetables are steaming, and the potatoes are crisping in the oven.

Holly has been surreptitiously looking at her watch for the last hour. She is dying to ask when he is coming—whether he is, in fact, coming—but she does not want to give Maggie any indication of what she might be feeling.

Hell, she doesn't even know herself what she might be feeling.

She does know that she got home last night on a

high, which continued this morning when she woke up knowing that she had something to look forward to today. Marcus phoned after breakfast, and even he commented on how happy she sounded.

"I just woke up on the right side of the bed," she said.

"How was last night?" he asked miraculously, for most of the time he never asked her anything about her days.

"It was great. Great band. Lovely evening."

"That's nice," he said distractedly, and didn't ask anything else. He would be due home late afternoon. What plans did she have? She told him lunch at Peter and Maggie's and that she'd see him at home later.

She didn't tell him that she'd spent the last hour trying on clothes to come up with the perfect combination for Saturday lunch. Not to look as if she tried too hard, not too mumsy, but comfortably casual. She'd settled on skin-tight cords, a long-sleeved striped T-shirt and baseball shoes, another recent purchase.

But with every minute that passes, the high is starting to leave, and at one fifteen Holly is moments away from sinking into a depression. *Stop it,* she tries to tell herself. *You are here with your children, here for Peter and Maggie, not here to see Will. So what if he doesn't come, you'll still have a lovely time. You're* having *a lovely time.*

But she knows it's not true.

Maggie calls everyone to the table, and Holly promises herself she will not ask about the empty setting at one end.

She doesn't have to.

"Where's Will?" Peter says.

Maggie shrugs. "You know our Will. Saying he'll come at twelve means he could come any time between ten in the morning and ten at night, if he comes at all."

Peter shakes his head. "Sometimes that boy is so infuriating."

"We've learned not to rely on Will very much. Although . . ." she shoots a cautious look at Daisy and Oliver, both engaged in teasing Pippa with a green dental chew that has to taste better than it looks, given Pippa's overexcited reaction, "he has been fantastic through all . . . this. I never thought we could rely on Will the way we have, but he's come through."

"Yes he has." Peter nods somberly. "And now I suppose it's back to business."

"Well, I don't know about you, but I'm starving," Maggie says, even though she has eaten almost nothing since the day she heard about Tom and has dropped over a stone, which, at her age, makes her look haggard and old. "Let me serve the kiddies first."

Holly clears up the dishes, then excuses herself to go to the loo. She feels like crying. From the heights of exhilaration to the depths of depression in the space of an hour. *Grow up,* she hisses at her reflection in the mirror. *You are a married woman,* she tells herself. *Stop behaving like a teenager.*

But that is exactly how she feels. Like a teenager who has no control over her emotions. Whose emotions and mood can be changed in a heartbeat by external influences.

She still has no idea where this is leading, still thinks of herself as someone who would never have an affair; and the truth is she hasn't contemplated anything happening between her and Will, hasn't thought about what the end result of all this . . . friendship . . . might be.

She knows she is attracted to him, but he's gorgeous, how could *anyone* not be attracted to him? She is still waiting, wishing, hoping that at some point in the foreseeable future, the attraction will wane and they will have a true friendship.

That doesn't mean she's going to act upon the attraction, doesn't mean anything's going to happen. And yes, so there have been a couple of times when she has closed her eyes while having sex with Marcus and has pictured Will there, but only out of curiosity, only to spice up their sex life a bit, and God knows it worked.

What is clear to her is how much she has missed having a man in her life who is a friend. Marcus has never been her friend, she realizes now. Has never been her partner. She would tell people in the beginning that Marcus was her best friend, but she knows now that was to make up for never feeling physically attracted to him, as if somehow being her best friend would be enough.

Where Marcus puts her down—subtly, always so subtly—Will will listen. Their e-mails are still fun, still funny, but now Holly finds she is revealing more about herself, letting him in to how she really feels.

The one subject they haven't discussed, not in any great depth, is her marriage, and why she feels the need to seek out a male confidant, someone to offer her a man's point of view, someone to make her feel beautiful again, when she has a perfectly good husband sitting at home.

Or not. As the case may be.

The front door slams shut and Holly tenses as she hears the familiar jangling of keys. She can picture exactly what Marcus is doing. He is fishing his BlackBerry out of his pocket, scrolling down quickly to see if any e-mails have come in during the last ten seconds that absolutely must be taken care of now. He's putting his keys in the ashtray and emptying the coins from his pocket into the same ashtray before taking his briefcase into his office on the ground floor and unpacking it quickly.

While unpacking his briefcase, he will pick up the post that arrived yesterday and skim through just to check there's nothing that cannot wait, and at the same time he will listen to the messages on his office answer phone. Inevitably there will be issues that cannot wait, and he will spend the next hour tapping out e-mails, making calls, and hissing at any family members that appear in the doorway desperate to see their dad because they've missed him.

As usual, Holly gets a perfunctory kiss on the way to his office, and the kids get a perfunctory ruffle of the hair.

"Off Daddy now," he says sternly to Daisy, who has

entwined herself around his legs. "Daddy needs to work." He looks up at Holly, gesturing impatiently at his daughter, and Holly gets up and attempts to disentangle Daisy, who immediately starts crying. "Will you keep them away from the office while I just check messages," he says. "I'll be out in a sec."

"Fine," Holly says, carrying a now-screaming Daisy into the kitchen and shutting the door behind her, slightly harder than she had planned. She sits down at the kitchen counter and sinks her head in her hands. "Jesus Christ," she whispers, "is this all there is?"

An hour later Marcus is still locked in his office, the kids are bathed and happily playing with Play-Doh in the playroom. Marcus would have a fit if he saw them playing with Play-Doh after their baths, but frankly it was a toss-up between that and TV, and Holly figured that in Marcus's mind Play-Doh would be the lesser of the two evils.

She runs up to her studio and clicks on her inbox. Just to see. *If he loves me, he'll have sent me a message,* she finds herself thinking, reprimanding herself sharply. *Grow up,* she thinks, but she can't help the flutter when she sees the e-mail waiting for her.

In another room, a few miles away, Olivia is also checking her e-mail. *Stupid, stupid me,* she thinks, battling the hope that there will be an e-mail from Fred. *Stupid, stupid me for jumping into bed with him, for allowing myself to feel that this might be something special, that he would have gotten back home to America and thought*

*that he missed me. That perhaps there was enough here for
us both to want to work at it.*

But the truth is, Olivia doesn't really want to work
at it. Deep in her heart she knows that Fred was, exactly
as Tom had said, just a fling. A lovely, sweet, gorgeous
boy, but nowhere near settling down and having a
relationship.

Olivia doesn't want a walk down the aisle, but she is
old enough and wise enough to acknowledge that her
time for mere flings is over; and if she were to get
involved with someone, it would be with a view to a
long-term commitment.

For a couple of days there, as she and Fred had the
most blissful time, she allowed herself to think, what
if . . . but even then she knew that what ifs were unrealistic. And it wasn't so much that she wanted Fred, it
was more that she wanted him to want her, that even
though their good-bye was mutual, her ego wanted
him to have got back to America and found that he
had fallen madly in love with her.

She even planned the conversation she would have
with him. "Fred, darling," she would say in her best
Katharine Hepburn voice, "You're the most delicious
boy, but you need to play the field. I know you think
you're in love with me, but it's really not real. Go and
enjoy yourself, get on with your life, and we'll always
have London."

And yet every night before she goes to bed, she
checks her e-mail to see if he's written. There were a
couple of exchanges when he first got back, a thank-you

for the most wonderful time in London, for being such a special friend, and wishes of luck and happiness in the future.

She wished him the same and was then astonished when all e-mail correspondence stopped. Was that it? She let the gray start poking its roots back into her hair, sadly relegated her black dress to the back of the wardrobe. It had been, she decided, a lovely holiday but not one to be repeated. The confusion and uncertainty of a relationship or fling, or whatever it was you called it, was something that Olivia was quite certain she could do without.

So when Sophie told her that a sexy, single man had come in asking about one of the dogs, and she passed his number on to Olivia, telling her she had to call him, Olivia shook her head. "Not this time," she said. "I'm done with men," and she handed the phone number back to Sophie.

CHAPTER SIXTEEN

To: Holly
From: Will
01/23/07 7:52:32 PM
Subject: No-shows and Apology

Holly, Holly, Holly. Am SO very sorry I wasn't there today. Had far too much to drink last night it seems and was horribly hungover this morning. Didn't wake up until lunchtime and just blanked about going to Mum and Dad's until Mum phoned after you'd gone. I feel awful about letting you down. Not to mention what a treat it would have been to see you twice in two days and meet your kids. (Mum says they're fantastic, by the way.) Please, please say you'll forgive me . . . would like to buy you lunch this week to apologize properly. On another note, fantastic night last night (what I can remember). Do remember you looking rather sexy (am I allowed to say that now that we're becoming friends?), good music, good people. Hoping you're not furious with me, Will x

Holly reads the e-mail five times until Daisy starts
screaming at Oliver. She walks down the stairs smiling,
every disappointment forgotten, back on the cloud of
exhilaration.

*He thinks I'm sexy! He thinks I'm sexy! I'm seeing him
this week!*

And floating into the playroom, she dives on the children and covers them with kisses, both of them so
shocked they dissolve into uncontrollable giggles.

To: Will
From: Holly
01/23/07 9:11:23 PM
Subject: Apology

Hello, my lusty leg man friend . . .

I'm sorry, I'm sorry. I just can't resist calling
you that, it makes me laugh so much. Have to say
I'm deeply impressed at your ability to unwittingly seduce young girls. I feel like any looks I
had were wasted on me when young—I didn't
have the confidence to know what to do with
them, and then, of course, getting married at
twenty-five I never had to think about it.

Still, I'm hoping that somewhere down the line
I'll become a MILF (I KNOW you know what that
means . . .). I suspect I'm probably a little young,
no? I think you don't get to attain MILF-hood until
you're forty, but perhaps I'm wrong, in which case I
ought to start making a bit more of an effort.

And thank you for your apology about not turning up at your parents'. We had an amazing time anyway, but it would have been fun if you'd been there. (Tom was right when he talked about how unreliable you are . . .)

So, am off to have supper downstairs, kids finally asleep. LOVE getting your e-mails, especially the long ones. I missed you.

Me xx

To: Holly
From: Will
01/23/07 11:35:11 PM
Subject: Re: Apology

To my favorite MILF,

How can you even question your status as a MILF? You are, by far, the sexiest mother I know, and infinitely more qualified than most to reign as queen of the MILFs.

I really am sorry about yesterday. I am trying in so many ways to turn over a new leaf, to be reliable and consistent, and mostly not to forget to do the important things in my life, and then yesterday I blew it royally.

Yet you're so forgiving. Is this what you are like with Marcus? I just keep thinking about all the things you've told me: that he doesn't help with the kids, isn't around much, and I wonder if perhaps you acquiesce too easily? This isn't a criticism, never a criticism, but you are so sweet and loving and good, and Marcus just seems to take advantage of all of that.

But, what's important is that you're happy, and maybe there's a way for you to do the things you need to do for you and find yourself again. Anyway, enough gabbling, as you would say. I am just happy this is the start of a new year, and to have you in my life. I look forward to seeing you this week . . .

Me2 xx

CHAPTER SEVENTEEN

"Where have you been?" Olivia sets the box she's carrying on the kitchen counter and turns to Holly, hands on hips. "I've left you two messages and haven't heard back, and now I've decided I must have inadvertently done something to upset you so I've brought you cakes, figuring that I must owe you an apology for something. Come on, then, what's been going on?"

"I'm so sorry, Olivia. Life's just been so busy recently. This project for work, and the kids, and you know how it is."

"No, not really," Olivia harrumphs. "I think you're just being a completely crap friend."

"Okay, you're right. I am being a completely crap friend and I'm sorry, and I cannot believe you brought cakes over . . . yum!" She opens the box and licks her lips at the sight of the tiny fruit tartlets and chocolate éclairs. "Oh my God, this is the most decadent thing I've ever seen—did you get them at that new patisserie on the high street?"

"Yup. It's amazing. How about you put on the kettle and I'll get plates?"

"Done."

Half an hour, two fruit tarts and two éclairs later, Holly takes a deep breath and looks at Olivia. She doesn't want to tell her. Doesn't want to tell anyone. Not that there's anything to tell. It's not as if anything has happened, not as if her friendship with Will is anything more than that—a friendship—but the urge to tell someone, to share what is happening in her life with someone, is more than she can bear.

She has thought about telling Saffron because, given that Saffron is having an affair, she would understand all about temptation, but Holly trusts Olivia more, and trusts that Olivia will be discreet, will perhaps give her the counsel she needs to hear.

Does she need counsel? She isn't sure. What she does know is that her feelings are all over the place. All she thinks about from the moment she wakes up in the morning until the moment she goes to bed, is Will. Nothing bothers her about Marcus anymore. She finds that she is able to switch off, to float away to a daydream about Will, a memory of something he said, something they did, and the less she focuses on Marcus, the less of a problem he becomes.

She is still convinced this is innocent. Convinced that she and Will are just friends. Sure, there is a little harmless flirting, but that is all it is: harmless. Holly is not the sort of woman who would ever have an affair. Of this she is certain.

Not least because of her father, Holly has never been unfaithful in her life, has always thought of infidelity as the one transgression she would never commit. And even now, when she looks at Will and thinks he is quite possibly the most handsome man she has ever seen in her life, even now she knows she will not have an affair.

What has crossed her mind, what is crossing her mind more and more frequently these days is that perhaps she married the wrong man. She never felt this attracted to Marcus, took it for granted that physical attraction was not part of the equation, but this friendship with Will has reawakened feelings, wants, needs she had forgotten she had. Wants and needs she pushed away into a compartment in her mind, telling herself she could live without them, telling herself they didn't matter.

They matter.

It matters that she is not, as she presumed, dead from the waist down. And now that those feelings have been reawakened, she's not sure if she can ignore them. Not sure she can spend the rest of her life sleeping with a man who makes her feel . . . nothing.

And the thought that she can't seem to push away, the thought that wakes her up in the middle of each night and prevents her from going back to sleep is this: I think I married the wrong man.

This is why she needs to talk, this is why she's sitting at her kitchen table, swallowing hard and taking a deep breath.

"I have a friendship," she says awkwardly, unable to look Olivia in the eye, but knowing she needs to say something, knowing that Olivia *is* the right person to be talking to about this.

"Great," Olivia says nonchalantly, alerted to something else when Holly finally looks up and meets her eyes. "Oh *no!* You mean, a *'friendship'*. . ."

Holly nods.

Olivia's eyes widen. "Are you having an *affair*?" Her voice drops to a whisper on the last word.

"No!" Holly says loudly. "Sssh. Frauke's upstairs, I don't want her to hear any of this. But no, I swear to you, I'm not having an affair. Though I am having a friendship with a man, and I just feel . . . incredibly confused."

"Confused because you want to be having an affair?"

"No! Well . . . maybe. No, I don't think so, I don't think that's what this is about."

"So what is it about?"

Holly sighs deeply. "Oh God, Olivia, I don't even know. I just know that my marriage feels . . . I don't know. Just nothing. It doesn't feel anything. I don't feel anything at all, and when I'm with this man I just feel alive. I feel young and free and as if anything were possible, and this awful thought just keeps coming back to me: what if I married the wrong man?"

"Wow!" Olivia exhales and sits back in her chair. "That's pretty bloody huge."

"I know." Holly looks at her sadly. "It's awful, and hearing the words out loud makes it more awful because it makes it real. But I had to talk to someone. I had to know what you think."

"What I think? I have no idea what I think. What do I think about what? Should you have an affair?"

"No," Holly shakes her head, "I'm not going to have an affair, but the fact is I have this friend, yes, I'll admit it, I am attracted to him, but more than that he listens to me. He's interested in what I have to say, he thinks I'm funny and clever, and he makes me feel important."

"And Marcus doesn't?"

Holly snorts. "What do you think?"

"Well, yes, okay. I see your point."

"What do *you* think of Marcus?" Holly asks suddenly. "I mean, I know you hardly know him, but what impression did he make on you? Could you see us together? Do you think he's the right man for me?"

"No way, Holly," Olivia laughs and shakes her head. "That's one road I won't be going down. The last time this happened, my friend Lauren had left her husband, who was the biggest jerk you'd ever met, and I spent weeks telling her how much better off she was and how awful he was, not to mention how all her friends completely hated him, and the next thing you know she's back with him and she cut me off entirely, has never spoken a word to me since."

"So you think he's a complete jerk?"

"No! I didn't say that. I'm not saying anything."

"Yes, well, if you thought he was wonderful and that he and I were made for each other, you'd have no problem saying it, would you? So I think I can read between the lines."

"All I'll say is that I don't quite understand the two

of you together. You just seem like very different personalities; but hey, opposites attract and all that, and I've certainly come across other couples who are like chalk and cheese, but they're madly in love and that seems to overcome everything."

"So you think he's a pompous arse?" Holly offers a wry smile, knowing it's true.

"What about the other one?" Olivia shakes her head, refusing to comment. "Does he have a name? Could it, in fact, be someone I might know?"

Holly turns bright red.

"I know." Olivia sighs. "I knew there was something with you and Will. Every time you mention him, which, by the way, you do an awful lot, just in case you hadn't realized and were doing it with Marcus, but every time you mention him you go all sort of dreamy."

"So what do you think about it?"

"I think Freud would have a thing or two to say about that. We lost one of our best friends, and you're obviously feeling unhappy or unfulfilled by other things in your life, so I wonder if it's a possibility that you might be transferring that, projecting it or whatever the hell it's called, onto his brother."

"Does that mean you don't think it's real? And if it were just that, how come you're not feeling anything for him?"

Olivia burst out laughing. "Your logic seems a little off-kilter, my love. Will's not my type in the slightest, but I'm just worried that it's a crush that has emerged because of losing Tom, or at least is perhaps stronger because of Tom, and I wonder whether it's actually something that should be causing you to question your marriage."

"Freud or no Freud, though, what if I'd be much happier with Will, or someone like him? What if I did marry the wrong man?"

"Do you think you'd be happier with someone like him?"

"Well . . . no."

"Why not?"

"Well, he'd probably drive me mad. You know him, for heaven's sake. He's thirty-five years old and doesn't have a proper job—he's a carpenter slash beach bum. He travels abroad for six months, sleeping on beaches, or camping out on friends' sofas. He's clever and funny and amazingly sexy, but you couldn't find a worse proposition for a husband if you tried."

"So husband-material aside, what makes you think you might be happier with someone like him?"

Holly is quiet for a while as she thinks. Then eventually she looks up at Olivia, her voice small, almost breaking. "I just miss having a friend. I miss having a partner. I feel like Marcus and I are two ships that pass in the night. And more than that, I worry that we are just so completely incompatible and that I've spent my married life trying to be this . . . this *wife* he wants me to be, but that it isn't me, it's not the life I wanted, it's not how I want to spend the rest of my life."

"So what do you want? What do you want that's different from what you have? Because, Holly, from where

I'm sitting, what you have is pretty damn amazing," Olivia gestures at the house, and Holly sighs.

"I know, I feel like I'm so ungrateful. I have my gorgeous children. And this gorgeous house, and a wardrobe full of beautiful designer clothes, but you know what? I don't care about all the *stuff*. I feel like the only time this house comes alive, the only time the children and I can laugh and be free, is when Marcus isn't here because when he is here these days all he does is bark at everyone to behave differently, to do something differently, to somehow be other than who we are.

"I feel like I'm trapped in a prison when he's around. Tiptoeing about, walking on eggshells in case something displeases him. You know, when we were first married I thought I could change him. I thought I could knock some of that ridiculous pomposity out of him, but it's got worse. And all he cares about is work. All he thinks about is work. Even when I try to have a conversation with him, I can see that he's not even listening, he's thinking about some bloody case."

"Couldn't you tell him?" Olivia says gently. "Couldn't you sit down with him and tell him that? Surely he'd understand, surely the two of you could work it out."

"Maybe." Holly shrugs, but what she doesn't say is that the will just isn't there for her.

"Would you ever leave him?" Olivia asks after a while.

"I think I'd be too frightened to," Holly says with a sigh. "I mean, he's a divorce lawyer, for God's sake. I think it would be a nightmare."

"Well, then, you'll have to find a way to make it work. Talk to him, Holly. It's not too late, you just have to communicate."

Saffron opens the door as everyone looks up to see who is coming in. She waves at the handful of people she has grown to know and love during the years she has been coming to this room, and pulls a folding chair from a cupboard in the corner, sitting down as quietly as possible at the back.

She is thirty minutes late but knows it is better to hear thirty minutes of a meeting than not to come at all.

As she sits down someone hands her a notebook and she scribbles her name and number, the best time to call, and thinks for a second about what to write under the heading "feeling." *Irritated,* she finally writes, leaning forward to put the book on the table, then pulling her Big Book out of her purse and quickly skimming the step they read earlier: *Step Three: We made a decision to turn our will and our lives over to the care of God as we understood him.*

No P today. He's flown to New York for a preproduction meeting of his new movie, and although he wanted her to come, she has a meeting of her own tomorrow—the uber-successful producers of the biggest hit of last year have shortlisted her as the love interest for their new film. If she gets it, it will be the biggest break of her career and will catapult her onto a whole new level. They want to see if she can pull off an authentic Southern accent, and, according to her agent, if so, she's the lady of the hour.

The last week has been spent working with her voice coach 24/7, paid for by her agent, whom she will reimburse from her next job, hopefully this one.

P sent flowers and a good luck card this morning, phoned to tell her he was missing her, then made her laugh by describing quite how much she was missing in his suite at the Carlyle.

She needed a meeting today, and a meeting in which she wasn't distracted by P's presence was always welcome. She found that P tended to be a distraction to everyone, not least the number of bimbette actresses who, she was certain, showed up only to try to get noticed, and who spent their time making eyes at him or cornering him during coffee break.

"Hi, I'm Saffron and I'm a grateful recovering alcoholic." Funny how smoothly those words roll from her lips. The first time she ever said them, she couldn't say them. She said, "Hi, I'm Saffron, and I suppose I'm here because I drink." She couldn't say the word *alcoholic*, her denial and shame so strong that the words were physically unable to leave her mouth.

And now it's so easy for her to say those words even though, of late, she has been doubting their veracity.

"I'm sorry I'm late," she continues, "but I'm so happy to be here. I missed the reading of the step, obviously, and I skimmed it a bit, but I really need to talk about where I am today." She takes a deep breath. "You know, for years I've had really good, clean sobriety. I swore I'd never go back to the place I came from when I first came into these rooms and, for so long, it's been so easy for me to be surrounded by alcohol without giving it a second thought.

"And I suppose I've grown complacent about it. You always hear in these rooms that this is a simple program but it isn't easy, and that it works if you work it, and I suppose that sitting here today I realize how utterly true that is. Because I haven't been working it lately. I've been like that man who says, 'Thanks for the ride, God, I can take it from here.' " The group laughs in recognition, and Saffron pauses for a while before continuing. "So I think that recently I've been trying to do it by myself, and it's not working.

"I find myself sitting in meetings fairly regularly, talking about what I'm not doing, no stepwork, barely calling my sponsor, occasionally reading literature when I'm desperate, but I don't seem to have the will to do anything more. And even though I'm not drinking, recently I've found myself watching people in restaurants with, say, a glass of wine, and thinking, *I could do that. Why couldn't I have just one glass of wine with dinner in a restaurant? I'm sure I could do that.*' " The group laughs again. "And even though on some level I know I can't, on another I think I can, and I have to tell you, I'm completely white-knuckling it."

She takes a breath. "And then there's my relationship." She doesn't say his name, remembers her sponsor's advice from a long time ago: *Don't talk about him in rooms unless it's in very general terms. Despite the principle of anonymity, everyone loves to talk, loves to gossip, and this is too big a secret for people to keep to themselves. Be careful,* she said. *Very careful.*

Still. There were people who knew, or thought they knew. No one had proof, but a few had seen the way they looked at each other, a few had noticed the closeness between them even when they were sitting on opposite sides of the room and even when they took great pains to avoid each other during the coffee break and after the meeting.

"I'm struggling with it at the moment. I know that I have to learn acceptance. That it is what it is, and I have to accept that he can't be with me all the time, but it's just so bloody hard. And then I've got this huge audition tomorrow that I feel a bit sick about, and . . ." She heaves a big sigh. "You see? This is what happens to me when I don't work my program. I just get completely overwhelmed with my life. But I'm here, and I heard what I needed to. I need to pray for the willingness to turn my will and my life over to the care of my higher power. Because ultimately I'm not in control, and everything will work out the way it's supposed to, and I have to remember that. And I'm making a commitment to the group today to go home and start working on my step one again. I've been promising my sponsor for ages that I will do it, and this is my commitment to you. Anyway," she glances down at the timer in her hand, "time's up. Thank you, everyone, for sharing, and I'm just so damned grateful I have a place that's home and I have a place where people listen and understand."

Afterward, a girl Saffron has seen only a couple of times comes up to her. She's pretty, dressed like every other actress in LA, and something in her eyes gives the impression that she may not be entirely trustworthy.

"Hi, I'm Alex," she says, putting her arms around Saffron and giving her a giant hug, which is still something Saffron is not entirely comfortable with, although she thinks perhaps this is her English reserve. She will happily accept hugs from friends, from colleagues in the program whom she has known well and for years, but to have a stranger hug you so intimately never feels quite genuine to her.

"I just wanted to thank you." Alex pulls back, but keeps hold of her hands, looking Saffron in the eye. "Everything you said spoke to me. It was like hearing my story, and I got so much out of your share."

"Thank you," Saffron says, willing herself not to judge, to find the part in Alex she could love or, at the very least, like.

"So you have an audition tomorrow? That's so exciting. What's it for?"

Saffron's heart sinks. Of course. As if she expected anything different.

"A movie," she says.

"I have an audition tomorrow for a movie!" Alex lies smoothly. "I bet it's the same one. Which one are you auditioning for?"

As if I'm stupid, Saffron thinks; but she smiles pleasantly. "It's the remake of *The Wizard of Oz*," she says. "Spielberg's producing it and I'm up for Dorothy."

"Me too! Well, good luck, maybe I'll see you there," Alex says, and practically runs out of the door, clearly about to phone her agent to find a way of getting in on the audition. Saffron smiles to herself as she picks up her bag. Shame there is no remake of *The Wizard of Oz*. Feeling very unrecovered, she sniggers as she imagines Alex phoning Dreamworks, demanding to be seen.

At home Saffron finds a message from Paul. Nothing much, he says, just caught a rerun of one of her movies on cable TV and he is thinking about her and wondering how she is. She smiles as she hears his voice and calls him back, leaving a message on his machine; then she dials Holly, and leaves a message on hers.

She loves LA. Loves the life she has built out here, but meeting up with this huge chunk of her past has made her homesick in a way she didn't expect. And not homesick for London, God knows she spends enough time there as it is, but homesick for friends. For real friends. Friends who aren't rivals, aren't pretending to be friendly to find work, aren't judging you for how famous you are.

She is homesick for the people who knew her when it all began. Who loved her when she was a gangly teenager with railway tracks. Who held her hair back on those nights when she had more to drink than even she could handle, spending hours with her as she knelt down with her head down the toilet bowl. Those are the friends she misses. Friends like Paul, Olivia, and Holly.

Ringing Olivia, Saffron readies herself to leave another message, when Olivia picks up.

" 'lo?"

"Olive Oil? Saffron here."

Olivia starts laughing. "God, I'd completely forgotten you ever called me Olive Oil. That's hysterical. Where are you?"

"LA. Bored. Missing England and my old friends. What are you up to?"

"Actually it's not very pleasant. I've picked up a stomach bug and I've been throwing up for days."

"Food poisoning or a bug?"

"I think a bug. Doesn't food poisoning end after about a day?"

"I think it depends on how severe it is. You should go and see a doctor. Unless, of course . . ." Saffron allows a dramatic pause, "you could be pregnant."

"Hardly." Olivia laughs, and then the color drains from her face.

CHAPTER EIGHTEEN

"Such a treat." Maggie smiles over at Holly and covers Holly's hand lightly with her own. "All these years of not seeing you, and now it's just like you're my daughter again, back in the family, and seeing you with your own children, a mother yourself," she laughs, "it's just lovely, Holly. And I love that you invited me out for lunch. I haven't been out anywhere since we lost Tom, and I'm glad I'm able to be out with you."

"I'm glad you're here with me too." Holly's smile is tinged with sadness. "It is lovely to see you and to be with you. I hadn't realized, all these years, how much I missed talking to you. Do you remember how you would sit with me at the kitchen table for hours, talking through my problems, giving me advice while Tom rolled his eyes and went upstairs in a huff to plug in his headphones and drown out our laughter with Pink Floyd?"

Maggie nods and closes her eyes as she remembers, the pleasure and pain burning a tear down her cheek even through her smile.

"I think he was always a bit jealous of our relationship," Maggie says, "of how easy it was for you to turn to me. Tom was never much good at asking for help."

"That's because he never needed any," Holly says, and they both laugh. "It is so good to see you. It makes me wonder how I managed without you all these years. You know you've always felt more like my mother than my own mother."

"Your other mother, you used to call me." Maggie smiles. "Do you remember?"

Holly nods and laughs.

"My heart always went out to you, Holly," Maggie says, her face now serious. "You seemed so lost in those days. So unhappy."

"I did?" Holly is shocked. Of course, it was how she'd felt inside, but she'd seemed so at home at Maggie and Peter's, she hadn't expected them to see it too, had thought she masked it so well.

"Peter always used to say that you would grow up to be a great beauty." Maggie's eyes grow distant as she reminisces. "And although I could see the possibility, I was never sure you were going to fulfill your potential because you were so very awkward in your skin as a teenager. You never looked as if you were comfortable, as if you liked who you were; and I was never certain you were going to be able to claim your self, sit in your skin and be proud of who you are."

There is a long pause as Maggie enfolds Holly in the warmth of her smile. "And of course," she continues, "look at you. So utterly beautiful and lovely, and finally so very sure of who you are."

"Oh God, Maggie. How can you say that? How can you believe that, have so much faith in me when I don't even have it in myself?"

"You don't?" Maggie frowns. "But you do, my darling. I see it all over you."

"Maybe in some respects, but there are times when I wake up and have no idea who I am or what I want. Whether this is the life I'm supposed to be living."

Maggie leans back in her chair and nods. "Aaah." She smiles finally. "This sounds like a midlife crisis."

And Holly sits forward, leans toward her, her face now alert. A midlife crisis. She was joking when she mentioned it to Will. How can she be having a midlife crisis at thirty-nine? Isn't it supposed to happen at forty? But a midlife crisis doesn't sound wrong. Something about it sounds very right, and if it is, in fact, a midlife crisis, then there are ways to get beyond it, surely, ways to move on without blowing your life up and watching the pieces land where they may.

"Do you really think that's what it might be?"

"I had one when I was thirty-nine." Maggie smiles. "Just where you are now. In fact, you were around then. I'm surprised you weren't aware of something and didn't pick up on anything, given how perceptive you were."

"I was? How old were we?"

"You and Tom were fifteen. It was soon after you came into the family. An awful time. The things I put poor Peter through, but I understand why I did it, just as I understood it then, although I was in a slightly different situation."

"How so?"

"Remember, I married Peter when I was twenty-three. A child. I married him because I was desperate to be a grown-up, to have a house of my own, children of my own, and it was the only way I could see to do it."

"So you weren't in love with him?" Holly is hoping to hear her own story, that Maggie will mirror her and Marcus's story, will give her hope for redemption, for a happy ever after, which she is so certain Maggie has had with Peter.

Maggie frowns. "Oh darling, of course I was in love with him. I was madly, hopelessly in love with him. Even when he had those ghastly leg-of-mutton side-burns I thought he was the most handsome, devilish, delicious man I'd ever come across. Don't ever tell him this, but sometimes my butterflies would be so bad before he'd come to pick me up at my parents' house, I'd actually throw up."

Holly makes a face as she laughs.

"I adored him. But I married him too young. He was my first serious boyfriend, and we married a year after we met; and I thought I'd never look at another man again for the rest of my life."

Holly draws a sharp intake of breath. "You mean you did?" Her voice drops to a whisper. "Did you have an affair?"

Maggie smiles. "No, my sweet girl. I didn't. It wasn't about someone else. It was about wanting to be young again, not wanting to be a mother of teenagers, not wanting to be up to my elbows in laundry and cooking and cleaning."

"But you love cooking . . . you always seemed so happy when I was over. I never saw any dissatisfaction."

"I do love cooking, but I had joined a life-drawing

class at the local art school, and all my friends were young and hip. Even the ones who were the same age as I was had carved out very different lives for themselves, lives that didn't involve boisterous teenagers and entertaining the husband's boss at home. I didn't want to be me. I wanted to be them; I wanted to walk in someone else's shoes."

"So what happened?"

"I was going to leave, not because I didn't love Peter anymore, but because I needed some space to figure out what I wanted." Maggie sighs as she remembers. "Good lord, Holly, I haven't thought about this for years. Hard even now to remember how much pain I put Peter through."

"How did he react?" As she speaks, Holly is thinking about Marcus. How would he react? Would he care? Did he even love her anymore? Did he ever?

"He put his foot down and said no. Absolutely not. He wasn't having it. He said it simply wasn't acceptable. He said he wouldn't tolerate the damage it would do to Tom, Will, and him, and that everyone had whims from time to time, and if I thought he didn't sometimes think about going off and spending night after night at the Playboy club chasing after blond models, I'd better think again. He said that marriage was for life and that this was what commitment meant. It meant riding the ups and downs, recognizing that marriage wasn't always champagne and roses. Nor was it always dull or awful. That everything passes and that love, real love, means weathering the storms and emerging stronger as a result."

Holly's eyes are wide as she takes it all in. "So you stayed."

"Of course I stayed." Maggie smiles. "Reluctantly at first, but honestly, that bit about him seducing models gave me a bit of a start. It was one thing for me to fantasize about being single, but quite another to think of Peter going off with some blond totty. Also," she leans forward with a conspiratorial smile, "I actually completely fancied him when he got all stern."

Holly breaks into peals of laughter.

"It's true."

"And you've never regretted it?" The laughter disappears as Holly grows pensive.

"No, my darling. I never have. We've been married over forty years, and it is just exactly as he said." She pauses for a while then smiles gently at Holly. "So that, Holly my darling, is my story and my story alone. If my experience can help you in any way, so be it, but whatever the journey that awaits you, it will be yours and no one can tell you what to do."

Holly sighs as she looks at the table. "That doesn't help, Maggie."

"I know, darling. It's not supposed to. Your answers will come, just trust that time and experience will tell you what you need to do."

"You really are my other mother, aren't you?" Holly smiles.

"Meaning?"

"Meaning my real mother would sit here and tell me exactly what I was doing wrong and what I have to do to fix it."

"It's not my job to judge you, Holly."

"Now you sound like Tom."

"That's what Will always says."

At the mention of his name, Holly feels herself flush ever so slightly. She has wanted to speak his name with Maggie, find out . . . what? Something. Anything. Does Maggie know anything? Has he spoken about Holly to Maggie? Would Maggie feel differently about Holly's impending journey and the outcome if she knew that Will, her own beloved son Will, was the catalyst for this storm of emotions and feelings?

Maggie watches Holly color, and she is not sure what to say, whether to say anything at all. For just as Tom was the caretaker, her reliable, wonderful, consistent son, Will has always been her ne'er-do-well, her irresponsible, frustrating, but oh-so-beloved baby of the family.

As a mother you are not supposed to have favorites. If anyone ever asked Maggie—before this, of course, before Tom—whether she had a favorite, she would shake her head in horror and say she loved them the same, loved them differently, but not one more, or less, than the other.

But that is not quite true. Tom always had a special place in her heart as her firstborn, a bond that could never be replicated; but something in her heart shifted the moment Will was born—a love that was so overwhelming, so overpowering in its purity that she didn't actually know before that moment that love that strong could exist.

When he was a toddler she would follow Will around with her eyes, watch his face crease up with laughter. And he was always laughing, was the happiest, funniest, cheekiest toddler she had ever seen.

And he loved his mother. Oh *how* he loved his mother. Maggie would say, for years, that he would crawl back into her stomach if he could. And it was true. Wherever she was, whatever she was doing, Will was next to her or on top of her, flinging his arms around her and covering her with kisses.

"I lub you Mummy," he would say at age two, almost the only thing he could say.

"I lub you, too," she'd say; and he'd parrot it back, over and over. The two of them could go on for hours.

And when she got cross with him or found herself raising her voice at him, he would look at her, his eyes wide, stricken, and say, "Mummy, why are you being mean to me?" And all would be instantly forgiven.

Perhaps, she has often thought, this is why she has a special spot in her heart for him; perhaps because he loved her so much, he gave her little choice. Tom had always been stoic, independent. Tom had loved her, of course, but he hadn't *needed* her; and Will has always needed her. Still does.

Even now, at thirty-five, independent (allegedly), when he should be getting on with his life. Maggie knew she would do anything for Will.

And the worst thing—the thing she tries very hard not to think about, has never even whispered out loud to another living soul—is that in the dead of night, when she is lying awake, hurting with the pain of losing Tom, the thought that so often comes to her is: At least it wasn't Will. At least Will is still here.

Will, who leaves a trail of broken hearts wherever he goes, who she prays will find happiness eventually, who is so clearly involved with dear, lovely Holly. Will, who is so clearly, and oh so frustratingly, the force behind whatever crisis Holly imagines herself to be going through in her marriage.

Oh Lord, she thinks. *What am I supposed to say?* But the words come out without her even thinking about them for she has sat here too many times with women who are not Holly but who are heartsick over Will, heartsick over his lack of commitment and his inability to love them in the way they love him, heartsick that he isn't able to be the man they want him to be. And now she finds herself sitting opposite Holly.

Dear, lovely Holly, who is married and has children, must not pin her hopes or anything else on lovely, incorrigible Will.

"Be careful," Maggie says softly. Suddenly.

And Holly's faint flush deepens to a rich burgundy.

"What do you mean?" Holly says quietly.

"I mean Will, my darling."

Holly attempts a laugh. "Maggie, there's nothing going on with Will. We're just friends. He's certainly not the reason for this . . . midlife crisis."

"Darling girl, it is not mine to judge, and, if I am mistaken, then I so hope you will forgive me." She takes a deep breath. "If Will has anything to do with whatever you are going through, and it is quite possible that he has not, but if he has, please, my darling, don't make any changes, don't do anything with the belief that Will is the man for you."

Holly is mortified. Humiliated. Wishing a hole could open beneath them and swallow her up.

"I haven't . . ." she starts. "I wouldn't . . . I mean . . ." And she can't say anything else because the lie is written all over her face.

Maggie leans forward, holds Holly's chin in her hand, and forces Holly to meet her eyes. "My darling girl, I love you, and I want you to be happy. And I love my one remaining son more than anything else in the world; and yet I, as his mother, can absolutely vouch that he is a bad bet. He is devastatingly handsome and funny and exciting, and a worse possible proposition for a relationship you couldn't wish to find. If he is the reason for your dissatisfaction, and you leave your marriage because you think there will be a future with Will, it will not end well."

There is a silence as Holly looks away, and Maggie drops her hand with a sigh.

"What if you're wrong?" Holly says with all the truculence of a sixteen-year-old. "What if Will and I are supposed to be together?"

"Oh darling." Maggie's voice is now sad. "Do you really think that?"

"No!" Holly is insistent. "No, I don't. I don't even know why I said it. I just . . . I don't know. I don't seem to know anything anymore other than I feel hot and bothered and as if there are big changes afoot and I just don't know what to do about anything. Anyway," she peers at Maggie sullenly, "I thought you said you wouldn't judge me."

Maggie grins. "I would never judge you, sweet Holly. But as Will's mother I'm afraid I have to judge him. It's my job."

"So I shouldn't leave Marcus and run away to the Bahamas or wherever the hell Will is going next winter?" Holly is attempting humor.

"I'd say by all means leave Marcus if that is the right thing for you to do, but do it for the right reasons. Not because of Will, or anyone else for that matter. Don't do it to fall into another's arms; do it, if indeed you end up doing it, because you are absolutely certain that you are not happy, that you will never be happy if you stay in this situation. That, to me, seems the only justifiable reason."

"So when you were ready to leave Peter, how did you know you could be happy again?"

Maggie shrugs. "I think because I'd been so happy before. This felt like a temporary blip. I still loved him, I just needed to make myself fall in love with him again."

There is a long silence as the waiter brings them cappuccinos. Holly raises hers to her lips and sips thoughtfully.

"What if . . ." she begins, setting the cup down quietly on the table. "What if you were never in love in the first place?"

Have I ever loved you? Holly wonders later that evening as they sit in the Automat, having dinner with a couple from Daisy's school, a mother who has clearly been going out of her way to befriend Holly the last couple of months, who has invited Daisy to play with her daughter on a weekly basis, and who has now suggested they get together with husbands.

Holly sits and talks to the mother—Jo—about Mrs. Phillips, the form teacher. They talk about nannies and about other mothers in the class. About where they might consider sending the girls for junior school. Marcus and Edward talk about work—Edward is a barrister—and when their main courses are served, the four of them finally talk in a group. Jo keeps them amused with funny stories about how she and Edward met, and Marcus offers his own version of events of when he and Holly first got together.

She watches him talk, is aware that when she tries to interject to correct him or add something of her own, he subtly puts her down or ridicules her or waves her comments aside as if they are completely irrelevant. And eventually she finds herself doing what she always does—withdrawing.

So instead of engaging in the conversation this evening, she watches Marcus and wonders whether she ever loved him.

What is love anyway? she finds herself thinking. Maggie talked today of loving Peter, of being in love with him, of losing it temporarily and then being able to fall in love again. But how are you supposed to fall in love again when you have never had anything there to begin with?

Holly knows she wasn't in love with Marcus, not even in the beginning, but she thought she would grow to love him and that would be enough. She knew she didn't have passion, didn't have the excitement, but thought those things spelled pain and discomfort, and life seemed safer without.

But her life is so safe now as to be deeply dull. And there is nothing about Marcus that she loves, little that she even likes. She realizes that those words she spoke to Olivia about her marriage are so true. They are not partners. They are not friends.

And if they are not partners, if they are not friends, if they are not lovers—although she does have sex, reluctantly when she has to, when Marcus refuses to take no for an answer—then what are they?

And what, after all, could possibly be the point?

Olivia stands in line at Boots and clutches the pregnancy test to her chest. She's convinced someone she knows is going to walk in and see her, convinced someone will catch her in this miserable, awful situation—a situation that she already knows can lead to only one possible outcome.

This test is merely a formality.

She hadn't used protection, hadn't known quite how to bring it up. Being in a relationship for seven years, she had forgotten the rules, forgotten how to play them. Plus she had been on the pill with George, never had to think about contraception. And somehow bringing up condoms at the point of entry hadn't seemed quite, well, appropriate.

And it had been the day after her period ended so she'd been pretty damn sure it would be fine. Who gets pregnant on day eight, for heaven's sake? A physical impossibility, surely . . .

But she now knows that it's not. Heading home with a sinking heart, she pees on the stick and attempts to read a magazine for a minute while she waits for the test to take hold, but she can wait only a few seconds, and already, as she stares, she sees the beginning of a blue line.

Oh God. Please let this be a mistake. Please let this be a false positive, let there be such a thing. She rips the other packet open, pees on the stick, and again, there it is. No doubt about it. Olivia, who has never wanted children, who is single and doesn't have enough money to raise a child even if she wanted to, is pregnant. There it is in blue and white. Undeniable.

With child.

CHAPTER NINETEEN

Saffron reaches for the phone, bleary-eyed, knocks it out of the cradle, curses as she reaches down by the side of the bed and finally finds it.

"Hello?" She is still half asleep, and half opens one eye to see the time flickering on the digital clock on her bedside table. Five-thirty-six. Who in the hell is calling at this ungodly hour of the morning?

"Saffron Armitage?"

"Yes?"

"I'm calling from the *National Enquirer*. We're running a story in the next edition about your affair with Pearce Webster and wondered if you'd like to make a comment."

"What?" Saffron sits bolt upright in bed and shrieks, then slams down the phone, shaking.

The phone rings again seconds later.

"Hello, this is Jonathan Baker from *E! Online*. We'll be running a story in this morning's edition about your relationship with Pearce Webster. Would you give us a . . ."

Saffron slams down the phone again and huddles in bed, under the covers, as the phone rings. And rings. And rings.

Each time she hears the machine pick up and journalists leaving messages, and then, horrifyingly, ten minutes later her doorbell rings. She gingerly opens one wooden slat of her blinds and gasps in horror as she sees news crews parked all the way up her street, journalists huddled together with microphones tucked under their arms, drinking Starbucks, waiting for her to emerge.

"Oh fuck," she whispers, sinking into a corner of the room and rocking back and forth. She grabs her cell phone and dials the only person she can think of to get her out of this mess.

P.

"Do you know how lucky I am to have a husband who is like you?" Anna opens her arms as Paul carefully sets her tea down on the bedside table, then sinks into her, planting a great, squashy kiss on her lips.

"And do you know how lucky I am to have you?" he says, turning his head to lick the marmalade off his fingers.

"So, oh lucky man of mine, how do you feel about White Barn Fields?" Anna has been lying in bed waiting for Paul to come home with fresh croissants and the Sunday papers, entertaining thoughts of how they could do up the house using the little money they have left.

"You're thinking it's a project, aren't you?" Paul smiles at her knowingly.

"I am thinking, my darling, that I want to take a break from thinking about pregnancy and adoption and babies. I just want to live for a little while without thinking about how incomplete our lives are, when they are not really so incomplete at all, so yes, in that respect, I am thinking it would be a great project. Do you understand, my love? I need to center myself again before diving back into Babyville, and focusing on this house could be just what I—we—need."

"I'm glad," Paul says after a long pause. "And I think you're right. I feel like everything in our lives has revolved around possible pregnancies for months, and we need a break. The question is, can we do it ourselves?"

Anna props herself up on the pillows and spreads butter and marmalade thickly on a croissant. "Here is the thing," she says, chewing slowly. "There is no way we could do what we originally intended. As lovely as Phil's plans are, we have not got the money to spare now after the treatments, and I do not know if I think that now is the time to do a big renovation anyway. But," she pauses, "it would not take that much to make it livable, and just because it will not look like it is out of the pages of *House and Garden* does not mean it will not make a wonderful retreat for us."

"What do you think it would take?"

Anna counts off the list on her fingers. "The one thing that we do need to spend money on is the bathroom."

"You mean you don't want to move in and use the outhouse?" Paul grins.

"Exactly. So if we could find a plumber to do the

plumbing in that useless bedroom next to the master bedroom, we could have a bathroom; and we could also put one in downstairs. If a plumber does the work and installs the stuff, we could tile and paint it and put new floors down.

"The kitchen needs more of a face-lift than anything else. I would love to replace everything, but we do not have the money, so for now we could paint the kitchen cabinets and replace that horrible Formica work top with butcher block, then put simple white subway tiles on the backsplash. New hardware on the cabinets would transform them. And I found this place online that sells industrial stainless-steel worktables for nothing, which would be perfect.

"After that," she continues, almost breathless with excitement, "we pretty much could get away with sanding and painting the floors, maybe staining them a lovely ebony.".

"What 'we' is this?" Paul looks at her in amazement. "All this talk about sanding and tiling and staining. Since when have you ever tiled anything in your life?"

"Since before I started Fashionista, my darling. I used to do everything myself. I did my first flat in London with Bob the builder."

Paul laughs. "Tell me that wasn't really his name."

"It actually was." She grins. "He did everything and I would watch and help out, and by the time I bought my next flat I could do everything myself. I have just never had the time since starting the business. Plus there has never been anything here really that needs doing."

"So given that time has always been a problem, when could we do it?"

"That is what I have been thinking about. I think a plumber could do the bathrooms in a flash; and once they are ready, you and I could go down for a couple of weeks and get most of it done, I think. The biggest key is having everything ordered and there so we are not waiting for anything."

"I know you," Paul says slowly. "You've already ordered everything, haven't you?"

Anna shrugs and looks away. "Um . . . actually, I am not quite sure how to tell you this, my darling, but . . ."

Paul rolls his eyes. "You're going to tell me it's done, aren't you?"

"Well . . . not *all* of it. But I did get a plumber in, and the bathroom stuff has been done, well, the big stuff anyway. Not the tiling, which means we could actually stay there now and get the rest of the work done."

"God, Anna. Don't you think you might have discussed it with me? I suppose you've bought everything else too?"

"Well . . . Oh Paul. Please do not be angry with me. I only went ahead with the bathrooms because everything was on sale, and there were only two days left, and it was all very cheap. I thought I would surprise you." She pouts. "I thought you would be pleased."

Paul shakes his head. "I'm just surprised that you'd make such a big decision without talking to me."

"Are you angry at me?" A little girl voice.

Paul shakes his head. "No. Not angry. I'm just upset you didn't tell me. It feels dishonest."

Anna looks aghast, then hangs her head. "You are right. You are absolutely right. I am so sorry. I did not mean to deceive you, I just got carried away with the excitement."

"It's okay," Paul says. "I suppose it's good that we can use it now."

"So can I show you the rest of the stuff I've chosen?"

"So it's a fait accompli? Where is all the stuff?"

"Hopefully sitting in the barn, waiting for me to confess so we can plan a trip down there to start the work."

And with that she reaches into the drawer of her bedside table and pulls out a stack of catalogues earmarked with Post-it notes.

Half an hour later Paul is having a shower while Anna lazily flicks through what she jokingly refers to as her "secret shame"—the *News of the World*.

As she turns to the center pages, she gasps in disbelief. "Paul! Quick! Come here . . . it's *Saffron!*"

The story is everywhere. First broken in America, every news channel has picked up on it, everybody is talking about it, everyone wants to know everything they possibly can about Saffron Armitage, Pearce Webster, and how the two of them got together.

Saffron has spent a horrified couple of days holed up in a hotel—whisked there by Pearce's manager as soon as the news broke—flicking through every TV station, feeling more and more sick as she hears what they were saying.

A lot of it is false. She froze in horror when one of the entertainment shows had as their guest that bitch Alex from the meeting, introduced as a "close friend" of the couple. The more she listened to Alex, the more she suspected that she was the one who gave the story away.

But enough of it is true. Enough of it makes her shrink with horror at the people coming out of the closet to talk about her, to give their opinions, to share some minor piece of information about Saffron that she hasn't thought about for years.

Her parents have offered her refuge at their house, but given that they too were surrounded by the press, as is her flat, there seems to be little point. Nowhere feels safe. Never has she felt so exposed. The only thing she wants to do is bury her head under the ground and come out when it has all been forgotten.

Pearce rings and says, "I love you. And it will all be fine. This will pass."

"Are you saying anything?"

"Nope. My managers have advised me to keep quiet. Marjie and I are doing this ridiculous fake romantic dinner tonight to try to calm things down." Saffron feels her heart sink as he says this—the last thing she expected was for him to pretend to the world that everything was normal, that Saffron didn't matter, that his marriage was far stronger than the public now believed.

"Are you okay?" Pearce can tell from her silence that she is not.

Saffron takes a deep breath. This is what she's learned in recovery. Not to say I'm fine, I'm fine. But to explain how she feels. Clearly and kindly.

Say what you mean, mean what you say, don't say it mean.

It's still hard, though. Even after all these years, it's still so hard to tell someone how she really feels, especially someone she loves. The fear has always been, still is, that they won't like her. That somehow she will end up being abandoned for expressing her needs.

"To be honest," she says quietly, "I'm hurt that you're telling the world that you and Marjie are fine. I feel . . ." She stops to think about how she does feel. "Well, apart from feeling frightened and overwhelmed and upset, I feel completely irrelevant in your eyes."

Pearce sighs. "I'm so sorry, Saff. I never want you to feel that way, and it has never been my intention to hurt you."

Saffron lets out a bitter laugh. "Even though this is such an awful thing to happen, there's a part of me that thinks this will allow you to leave and be with me."

There's a long silence. "Saff," Pearce says eventually, "I do want to be with you. More than anything in the world. I also have my career to think of, and my life. I believe you and I will be together, but my managers say there will be nothing more destructive than me leaving Marjie now to be with you."

Saffron forces her voice to stay calm, light, unemotional. "So where does that leave us?"

"The same place we've always been. I love you and I want to be with you, but you need patience, my darling. The one thing I'm certain of is that we can't be seen together until all this blows over."

Saffron pouts in silence. He's right. Of course he's right. It's just not what she wants to hear.

"So how is Marjie taking it?" she asks finally, curiosity getting the better of her.

"She couldn't care less about you and me, but she feels she's been publicly humiliated, and she's pretty damn furious about that."

"I'm sorry," Saffron says sadly.

"So am I. But I'm most sorry I can't be with you now, making you feel better. Did someone from my management team talk to you about England?"

"Yes. They're putting me on a plane in the morning and I'm going to hole up there for a bit until it dies down. Mum and Dad have been besieged by the press, but I just left messages for old friends. Hopefully one of them will come through."

"Just make sure you stay in touch and let me know where you are. I'll call you later, my darling, and remember whatever happens, I love you."

"Saffron? Are you okay? We've left messages, we tried to call. We just read . . . Well, we were a little bit worried about you." Anna bites her tongue quickly, stunned to have picked up the phone to find Saffron on the other end.

"I'm sort of okay if being holed up at the Beverly Hills Hotel with bloody bodyguards outside the door while millions of press try and break into my room by pretending to be room service counts as okay. It's pretty fucking horrific, that much I will say."

"Oh you poor thing. And you must want to speak to Paul, but he has gone out and he has left his mobile behind. I can get him to call as soon as he is home."

"So are there no press outside your house?"

Anna snorts with laughter. "No! Should there be?"

"They've managed to infiltrate pretty much everyone else. Look, Anna, I know you and I don't know each other very well, but I'm desperate for somewhere quiet to stay until this blows over. Is there any chance I could come and stay with you and Paul? I know it's a huge imposition, and I promise I wouldn't ask unless I was completely desperate, but I don't know where else to go."

"Of course you can come and stay. As it happens, you could even stay in the country if you wanted some serious peace and quiet. We have got an old barn we are doing up in the middle of nowhere in Gloucestershire, which would be much better for you, although at the moment it is a bit of a dump. We are just starting to do it up, but at least there is now a nice bathroom. If you stayed with us here, the press would find you very quickly—north London is not exactly the easiest place to hide, but Gloucestershire, I think, would be perfect."

"Oh Anna! I don't know you but I love you already. Thank you, thank you, thank you!"

"So when are you coming?"

Now it's Saffron's turn to sound sheepish. "Actually I'm hiding in the first-class lounge at LAX about to get on a flight."

"You mean you were flying over here with nowhere to stay?"

"I didn't know what else to do."

"Well, of course you are welcome here! Do you need anyone to pick you up from the airport?"

"No. Pearce has organized a driver. Should I go

straight down to the country? I just feel a bit weird about going somewhere I've never been before, by myself."

"You know, you will be fine. We will take you down there to start you off, show you where everything is, and you will be perfect. I am sure long walks in the country and roaring log fires will do you the world of good."

"You have roaring log fires?"

"Ah. Well. No, actually. Not until we get someone up to check the flue, but he swears blind that that will be within the next couple of days. But they do at the pub at the end of the road, and there is no better place to curl up with a good book. No one will bother you there, and we will come down on the weekend, if you would like, come and bring you bottles of wine and delicious food."

"No wine for me, thanks," Saffron says, knowing that at some point she will have to explain. She always does, but not yet. "But if you wouldn't mind coming down with me that would be lovely."

"Oh by the way," Anna says slowly. "How do you feel about sleeping bags and floors?"

"It doesn't look like I have much of a choice." Saffron laughs. "I'll pick up one of those inflatable mattresses on the way." And promising to call as soon as she lands, she puts the phone down.

The first-class lounge is quiet, but, even with few people there, Saffron is aware that everyone is staring at her. The staff have been whispering nonstop behind the bar, shooting surreptitious glances over at her, and free newspapers are scattered around for everyone to read the latest installment.

She supposes a part of her ought to be grateful. Who was it said there's no such thing as bad publicity? But being famous has never been her motivation. Acting, for Saffron, is a craft, and the only reason she would want to be famous would be to get better roles in movies. This sort of publicity is not what she has ever wanted although she knows there are many—Alex, for one—who would kill for this kind of attention, however badly they may come across.

For that is what is so hard. Nobody is reading about the wonderful love story that Saffron has with Pearce. They are painting Saffron as a marriage wrecker, a cheap harlot who set her sights on Pearce and is determined to break him up with his wife. Ghastly men she has dated once or twice have emerged to say that Saffron is the most ambitious woman they have ever met, that she has always said she would do anything to go out with a Pearce or Mel or Tom, that nothing could stand in the way of her drive.

None of it is true.

An hour to go before her flight is called, Saffron finds herself walking past the bar. A wall of free drinks. In the old days, she would have perched on a stool and ordered one after another just because it was free and because she could.

But she doesn't do that anymore.

"God grant me the serenity . . ." she starts to recite in her mind, but the serenity prayer is drowned out by a buzz. A buzz she hasn't felt for a long time, a buzz that seems to drown out everything else, all sane thoughts, any mechanisms she may have used to stop herself.

She should call her sponsor. Call someone in the program. Anyone who could talk her down from this.

But the buzz has propelled her to the bar.

Fuck it. After what I've been through, I deserve a drink. Just one, just to calm me down, and who wouldn't deserve a drink after this? What normal person wouldn't be entitled to one drink after this?

And what harm could it do? I mean, really. What harm could it possibly do?

CHAPTER TWENTY

Holly phoned Marcus that morning and asked if they could go out for dinner that night. It's been a long time since they have properly talked, and there are some things Holly wants to talk about.

And this time Holly really does want to talk. Her conversation with Maggie has stayed with her, and although, as time progresses, she is becoming more and more unhappy, she knows that she can't just let things slide without involving Marcus. She's never told him anything about how she feels about him or their marriage, other than the perfunctory "I love you" after they have sex, or occasionally on the phone.

They never talk about what each of them wants, where they are going, or whether they are continuing to grow in the same direction. This, particularly given her growing friendship with Will, bothers Holly the most.

What if Marcus could be a different man? she keeps thinking. *Would I love him then? Would I be happier?* The devil on her shoulder repeatedly whispers that people don't change and that Marcus isn't a different man. She will have to accept it. But the angel persuades her to give him a chance, to at least let him know how she feels.

And yet . . . it is so very hard for her to find the will-ingness given that she has switched off, has, almost without realizing it, absented herself emotionally and mentally from her marriage. The only move left to make is physical.

And it is so hard given that the only person occupy-ing her thoughts, twenty-four hours a day, is Will.

Their e-mails and occasional lunches have progressed to phone calls. When things happen to Holly during the day, if the children make her laugh, or she reads some-thing interesting, or she is thrilled with herself for a new card design, the very first person she calls—the only person, in fact—is Will.

Her initial discomfort at her attraction to him has waned somewhat. She still thinks he is the most hand-some man she has ever seen, but she has grown com-fortable with him. They are able to tease each other, she is able to reveal things to him she has never told anyone else, and certainly not Marcus.

There are things in her past that Marcus would find abhorrent, shameful, or disgusting. Stories he could never enjoy. He never enjoys hearing about who Holly was before she became his wife. Who the real Holly is.

"What's the most embarrassing thing that's ever hap-pened to you?" Will asked her one day when they were having lunch. Lunch has become a somewhat regular occurrence these days. It feels safe to her: friends meet for lunch all the time, and there is nothing that needs to be read into lunch.

She is also mindful of Maggie's advice. As humiliated as she was at having been "caught," she did hear Maggie when she told her to be careful. Not that she can help the way she feels, but she certainly doesn't have to act upon it.

"I hate those questions." Holly rolled her eyes. "Why would I possibly tell you something that's completely embarrassing? And anyway, I can never remember things like that."

"Oh go on. I'll tell you mine if you tell me yours." He grinned at her, knowing she was going to talk.

Holly groaned. "Oh God. I can't believe you're going to make me tell you something embarrassing. Okay. One time I was in Jamaica on holiday . . ."

"How old were you?"

"Sadly, old enough to know better. I was twenty, I think. Maybe twenty-one. I was in a bar with some guys we'd met at the beach that day who seemed really nice. I ordered a rum and Coke, and instead I got a huge glass of every conceivable alcoholic drink you can imagine with Coke splashed in for coloring."

"So you didn't drink it, right?"

"Yes, I bloody drank it. I've never been a big drinker, and I've always hated rum. I was just drinking it because everyone else seemed to drink rum and Coke, and it never occurred to me that it was particularly disgusting because of the mix."

"So let me guess, you passed out?"

"Well, yes, but not before jumping up on stage to take part in a wet T-shirt competition, snogging about eight men in the club, then projectile vomiting from the stage onto the entire front row."

"Wow!" Will leaned back, his whole body shaking with laughter. "Holly. That's really disgusting."

"Yeah, well. Told you."

"Quite like the idea of the wet T-shirt contest, though . . . Fancy a rum and Coke?" As he said it, he started to gesture the waiter over, and Holly yelped and smacked him on the arm.

"Ha bloody ha." She grinned. "Your turn."

Will looked all wide-eyed and innocent. "I don't have one." He shrugged. "Seriously. I'm a bloke. There's very little that embarrasses me."

"You big old liar. There must be something."

"Okay. Not the most embarrassing, but last year my friend Nick got married and we all went down to Brighton for a stag weekend. Bear in mind, we were all rugby players at school, and this was all the old team, so we knew we were in for a weekend of heavy drinking. So . . . we spent the afternoon doing a pub crawl, and then someone had the brilliant idea of playing rugby on the beach wearing just underwear."

"So far it's not very embarrassing."

"Yes, well. Some bright spark had thoughtfully pro-vided pink furry thongs from Ann Summers as the underwear."

A smile spread wide on Holly's face. "Now I'm start-ing to enjoy this story."

"So here we are, nine great big rugby players, pretty pissed, wearing nothing but a piece of pink fur over our crotches, tackling one another on the beach when this guy comes over—completely normal-looking guy—and says he's a photographer and would we mind if he took a few pictures."

"Uh-oh." Holly leaned forward, chin on her hands.

"Had we been sober, we might have thought the same thing, but as it was we all basically said, sure, mate, take whatever you want. So we're all showing off, flexing our muscles and being supermacho as this guy's snapping away; and then, just as he leaves, Nick calls him back and asks him if he's going to use the photos anywhere. 'Yep, they're for *Boyz*, a gay lifestyle magazine. Thanks so much, guys,' " he says and disappears, leaving us all completely mortified."

Holly burst out laughing. "Ha! Serves you right, appearing in a public place with nothing but women's pink furry thongs on."

There was the time she went to a Police concert when she was nineteen. She and Saffron had slept the night before at Saffron's house, got stoned beforehand, and had excitedly approached Wembley Stadium with the determination to get backstage, meet Sting, and have him fall madly in love with them. They didn't particularly care which one he would fall in love with. Hell, he could have had both for all they cared. The important thing was to get backstage.

And backstage they got, but only by virtue of turning themselves into classic rock star groupies and delivering blow jobs to a couple of roadies who couldn't believe their luck. Incidentally, Sting did say hello, asked them if they enjoyed the show, and that was it. Much to their consternation, he didn't fall in love with either of them.

"So from Sting to Marcus," Will mused. "Can't say I can quite see the similarity there."

Holly still doesn't talk much about Marcus with Will. Can't talk about Marcus with Will. They touch upon it, upon Holly's unhappiness, but she doesn't go into the details, doesn't share the intimacies of their life.

And she hasn't shared that tonight she's asked to go out for dinner with Marcus. She's going to take a deep breath and tell her husband that she's not happy. She's going to ask him to spend more time at home, to pay more attention to the kids. To pay more attention to her. She doesn't particularly want him at home more, but perhaps, she thinks, it would all be better if they were together more, if they had more of a partnership.

He is coming home at seven, and they have a table at E&O for eight.

At a quarter to seven, just as Holly is stepping out of the shower, Marcus phones. "I'm sorry, darling," he says. "I've just had a call from a client who needs me to do some urgent case-history research on child support. It won't take too long, but I'll never get home and get back into town. Can I meet you at the restaurant?"

Holly shakes her head in dismay. What can she say? What, other than it's not exactly a great start.

Holly is sitting at the table, nursing a Cosmopolitan, and smiling broadly as she reads a text from Will.

These days, Holly goes nowhere without her phone.

The Holly of old would forget her phone daily, forget mostly that she even had a phone, but today's Holly has her phone clutched in her hand twenty-four hours a day. Even when she is out shopping or picking the kids up from school or sitting on a bus on her way to the office, she can text Will. Not as good as e-mail, but not far behind.

And their e-mails, texts, and phone calls flow thick and fast. Her eyes light up when she gets a text from him; she will excuse herself from the table, from dinner with Marcus and the children, and escape into the loo to read the latest message, tap out something quick and witty before rejoining her family or her friends.

"Hello." Marcus swoops down and pecks her on the cheek. "I'm so sorry I'm late. What are you drinking?"

"A Cosmopolitan," she says, leaning back and watching him as if watching a stranger. *Dutch courage* is what she thinks. This is her second. She was early, Marcus was late, and she has been sitting here for twenty-three minutes. The first Cosmopolitan took the edge off her nerves; the second is making tonight's mission—the business of telling Marcus she is unhappy—almost ridiculously easy.

"How was your day?" Marcus smiles across the table at her as he accepts a menu, his thin fingers opening it up, and as he glances down, Holly thinks about Will's fingers. She loves his fingers. Loves his hands. Loves watching him move them, could spend hours fixating on his forearms. She has become used to Marcus's lanky, pale body, the hair on his arms black against the whiteness of his skin, his fingers elegant and expressive but not strong. Not sexy.

Will has large hands. Thick fingers. Holly can see the muscles move under the skin when he moves his wrists. His skin is dark, almost olive. He looks as if he has been sunbathing even in the middle of winter, although, as he points out, he usually *is* sunbathing in the middle of winter, on some exotic island with some exotic woman. Holly tries not to think of the woman.

But how different from Marcus. Holly suppresses a slight shiver—lust? Revulsion? She doesn't know, but she moves her gaze away from Marcus's fingers to meet his eyes.

"Everything all right, darling?" he says, but he is not asking because he suspects anything; it is just one of his stock phrases.

"Let's order." Holly forces a smile and swigs another gulp of her drink as the waiter comes over, taking a deep breath when he finally leaves.

"Marcus," she starts, "we need to talk. I . . ." She pauses. How does she say this? What are the words she should use? It felt so easy earlier today, practicing in front of the bathroom mirror, having a one-way conversation with herself in the car after she'd dropped the kids off at school.

"I feel so disconnected from you," she says slowly, barely able to look him in the eye. "You seem to be at work all the time, and uninterested in us, and I'm not happy." There. She said it. She raises her eyes to meet his, almost scared of his reaction. "This just isn't what I expected marriage to be."

"What?" Marcus looks dumbstruck. "What on earth are you talking about? I don't understand. What are you trying to say?" He looks hurt and angry, exactly the reaction Holly expected. Exactly the reaction she doesn't want.

Because Marcus's anger scares her. Has always scared her. It is why she has never confronted him before. His temper is not something she sees often, but when it emerges it is explosive. He shouts and stamps, much like a little boy, and he can be both cutting and cruel.

He has said many a thing in anger that has wounded Holly deeply, and she has retreated from him for a few days to lick her wounds and attempt to heal. He is always contrite eventually and she has always forgiven him and has tried hard not to do or say anything that will set him off again.

She has thought, she realizes tonight, many times of what her life would be like if she were single, if she were to leave Marcus and raise her children herself. She has lain in bed and planned it many times, but the plan always starts with her telling Marcus she is leaving, and she can almost predict what he will say. "Me, leave?" he would shout, his voice fierce with anger, causing Holly to shrink. "Me? You're the one who wants to leave. *You* leave. I'm staying in the house with the kids." And he is a divorce lawyer, after all, and knows what he's entitled to. He knows how to fight the dirty fight, and Holly has always been just too damned scared.

"I'm not saying anything," Holly speaks calmly, trying to smooth things over, and she reaches over and takes his hand. "Marcus, listen to me. I'm saying that

I'm not happy. That I'm sure this is just a phase in our marriage, but that something needs to change, I can't go on like this."

"Like what?" His voice is icy cold.

"Like this!" Her voice rises with anger, and she consciously takes a deep breath. "Like you being late for everything. Like you being away all the time, canceling our plans, not seeing the children. Daisy cries almost every night wanting to see you. We don't have any friends left because nobody bothers making plans with us anymore, and I never see you. When I do see you, it feels like we're two ships passing in the night. We barely even talk anymore. Perfunctory questions about what our days are like, but that's it. I don't feel married, Marcus. I don't see the point."

"So what are you saying?" Marcus leans forward, his voice dangerously soft. "You want me to leave work so you can see me more? You want me to leave my job so I can spend more time with the children? Fine." His voice starts to rise, and as people sitting around them turn to stare, Holly wishes she could disappear.

"You want me to be a stay-at-home husband or dad, fine, but who's going to pay the mortgage? Who's going to put food on the table? Who's going to put the children through school? Your illustrating work doesn't exactly contribute to anything; but fine, if that's what you want, I'll give my notice in tomorrow."

"Oh for God's sake," Holly whispers, rolling her eyes. "I'm not saying that, I'm just saying that we have to find a different way of doing things."

"Fine." Marcus sits back and crosses his arms, waiting. "How?"

"I don't know, Marcus!" Holly is almost in tears. "I'm trying to talk to you about this, to tell you how I feel. I'm not attacking you. I don't know why you're jumping on the defensive."

"I'll tell you why," Marcus hisses. "Because I work like a dog to keep you happy. Do you think I'm doing it for me? I couldn't care less about work. All I care about is my family, you and the kids, and I'm doing this so you can live in your big, beautiful house in Brondesbury. I'm doing this so you can wear your cashmere sweaters and not worry about anything. You can't have it both ways, Holly. That's not how it works."

Holly sits back and looks at him, four words going through her head. Over and over and over.

You big fucking liar.

He's not doing this for her. Or the children. The truth is Holly doesn't give a damn about the big, beautiful house or the cashmere fucking sweaters. She never has.

She doesn't give a damn about any of the stuff that Marcus deems so necessary in order for people to look at him and think he is someone important, someone special. A big shot.

You big fucking liar.

He's doing exactly what he always does. He doesn't hear her, can't hear anything he might be able to interpret as criticism. He throws it right back at Holly, making it her fault, painting himself as the victim, sending Holly retreating with the force of his denial.

Their hors d'oeuvres arrive. Holly looks miserably at her parsnip and apple soup—her appetite long since disappeared—and back at Marcus, who has now fished his buzzing BlackBerry out of his pocket and is punching an e-mail into the phone.

"So what do you want me to do?" Marcus says, when he finishes his correspondence, placing the BlackBerry on the table next to his plate. "What am I supposed to do?"

"I don't know." Holly shrugs. "I wanted you to know how unhappy I am. I wanted you to care."

"I do care, Holly." His voice is gentle now, now that he no longer feels attacked. "Of course I care if you're unhappy, but darling, I don't think it's anything to do with me. I have no idea why you're so unhappy . . . Do you have your period?"

Holly shakes her head, resisting the urge to leap across the table and throttle him.

"Maybe you should go to see a doctor," Marcus says gently. "It could be depression, and perhaps you could look at medication. I do understand you're unhappy, but I also know it's nothing to do with me."

Holly shrugs again and goes back to playing with her food.

She tried, she thinks. At least she tried.

The phone shrills, waking Holly out of the most bizarre dream. She and Will are at the theater. The actress on stage is supposed to be Saffron but in fact it is Olivia, and Holly keeps wondering why Olivia is on stage when she can't act and why she and Will seem to be a couple, but she knows it is just pretend.

"Holly? Are you awake?"

"Only just. Who is it?"

"Oh God, sorry. Holly, it's Paul."

"Hey, Paul, how are you?"

"Well, I'm fine. But the thing is, you've seen the papers, right?"

"About Saffron? I know! Isn't it awful? Poor darling. I've left her a ton of messages and I've had a couple from her, but we haven't managed to catch up. Have you spoken to her?"

"Well, that's the thing. You know we've got this place in the country? We offered it to her as a hideout because it's in the middle of nowhere, and she was coming over to stay. But basically her driver called us this morning from Heathrow, asking for help because she's . . . well . . . she's completely shit-faced."

Holly sits bolt upright. "What do you mean, shit-faced?"

Paul starts laughing. "What do you think I mean? Here, I'll pass you over. She wants to talk."

"Holly Mac? Is that my darling Holly Mac?"

And of course Holly hears instantly that Saffron is drunk. And she knows instantly what this means. She knows all about Saffron's drinking, her drinking years of old, and she knows about her long-standing sobriety since walking into AA. She isn't supposed to know but Tom told her, swore her to secrecy, although Paul clearly hasn't heard about it. Paul thinks Saffron is just drunk. A one-off. An amusing incident.

"Where are you, Saff?"

"About to get in a car, darling. Where are you? Why aren't you here? I want us to be all together again."

"Let me talk to Paul a sec, Saff. I'll talk to you in a minute." The phone is passed back. "Where are you, Paul?"

"Driving down to Gloucestershire to deposit her. Except she can't be on her own. I think we're going to stay with her just until she sobers up."

"Paul," Holly whispers, "do you know she's in AA?"

"What? You're not serious!"

"Desperately. This is huge, Paul. She's fallen off the wagon. This is terrible."

"Oh shit," he mutters. "I had no idea. I thought it was just funny she was . . . Oh God. Now what do we do? Don't we have to stage an"—he drops his voice to a whisper—"intervention or something?"

"I have no idea."

"Oh God, Holly. Here we are again, getting Saff out of trouble. Listen, I'm completely out of my depth here. Can you come? Please?"

"Come where? Gloucestershire?"

"Yes. Bring the kids. Bring Marcus. Whatever. But she needs us all now, Holly. Please come."

Holly takes a deep breath. "Okay," she says. "I'll need to rearrange some stuff but I'll come. I'll ring you later and tell you the plan."

Oh God. Falling off the wagon. Holly gets straight on the Internet to read about interventions, to read what she should do, and as the page uploads, she starts to think about the dream that Paul interrupted.

And she realizes something.

In fourteen years, she has never dreamed about Marcus. She has dreamed about her children, about her friends, about her parents. She has dreamed about partners who have been nameless or faceless, and more recently her dreams have been populated with Tom, and now Will.

But in fourteen years she has never dreamed about Marcus. He has never once set foot in her subconscious.

She's not sure what this means, but she's pretty damn sure it isn't good.

CHAPTER TWENTY-ONE

Paul had escaped later that morning to phone Holly and provide her with an update. "She fell asleep in the car and now she's awake and pretty hungover," he said gravely. "She said that was it, she'd never drink again."

"Do you think she means it?" Holly asked dubiously.

"I think so. She seemed pretty low-key and said she had a splitting headache. I think she feels awful about what happened, but God only knows whether she'll drink again. We didn't bring any wine with us, so I suppose we'll just keep an eye on her. What time are you thinking of coming?"

"After school. The au pair will get the kids, then I'll pack them up and come down."

"Great. Saffron's put in a request for sushi. Any chance you could stop somewhere and bring some down?"

Holly laughed and rolled her eyes. "God, you can take the girl out of LA, but you can't take LA out of the girl. Sushi, indeed. Where does she think she is?"

"Not Gloucestershire, that's for sure." Paul laughed. "We popped into the corner shop but mayonnaise and baked beans didn't seem to quite do it for her."

"Can't make any promises but I'll do my best."

"Oh, and one more thing. It's bloody freezing. The plumber's supposed to be coming tomorrow morning, and we're waiting for the chimney guy, but bring tons of clothes. We may have to sleep in our coats tonight."

"Oh great." Holly affected a dramatic sigh. "First you tell me there's nothing to eat except mayonnaise and baked beans, and now you tell me it's the North Pole. Anything else I ought to know before I climb in the car?"

"Shit! Yes! Can you pick Olivia up? I know it's a bit out of the way for you, but Saffron insisted that Olivia come too. Is that okay?"

"Sounds great. A proper reunion. I imagine we'll be there around five or six. See you later, and thanks for the directions." And Holly took her cup of coffee up to her studio to phone Marcus.

"What? You're what?" Marcus spits with anger. "Taking the children and going where? Just a little bit of a coincidence, isn't it? You tell me you're unhappy and now you're leaving with no notice? Do you really think I believe this is about Saffron? Christ, Holly, you barely even know these people, you haven't seen them in, what, twenty years? And now all of a sudden you're dropping everything for them?"

And then his voice dips to a familiar calm. "No," he says. "I will not tolerate this. You're not going."

"I am, Marcus," Holly says quietly. "I'm sorry, but I have to."

"If you go," Marcus is still eerily calm, "if you go and take the children, Holly, don't bother coming back. I'm warning you, Holly, if you carry on and do this, I won't be here when you come back. I will not have my wife deliberately defy me in this way. This is not acceptable. This is your last chance, Holly. It's me or these people you think are your friends. Your choice, Holly. Your choice."

Holly stares blankly at her computer screen, listening to all the familiar noises in her house. The slight tapping of the pipes, the buzz of the washing machine downstairs, the tinny music, barely audible, from the radio in the kitchen. Everything sounds exactly the same, but everything is suddenly completely different.

Here it is. As if God has reached down and opened up a window of opportunity for her, a window of opportunity she has only fantasized about, but has never been certain she would actually pass through if it were offered.

Here it is.

And there is no doubt in her heart, no second thoughts, barely a thought at all. Freedom is being offered to her on a plate, and feeling the weight being lifted off her heart, she speaks.

"I'm sorry you feel that way, Marcus. I'm sorry you're giving me a choice, but I can't let my friends down. I'm going."

"Fine," he shouts. "I'll get your stuff packed while you're away, because let me tell you this, you're not getting the bloody house, and you're not getting a penny out of me."

"Fine," Holly echoes, and feeling she is in a dream, and not a particularly bad one, by the way, she hangs up the phone and immediately calls Will.

She leaves him a message on his cell, a message at home, and sends him a brief e-mail explaining what just happened. She isn't sure how she feels, and part of her knows she should be scared, but why then is there a smile on her face? Why does she skip downstairs to pack, and to pack way more than she would have done had they not just had this conversation?

Already, a few minutes in, she knows this is it. There is no going back. Think. Think. What does Marcus do when he is hurt? When he is angry? She is not sure how far he will go, but this is the ultimate humiliation for him, and when Marcus is hurt, Marcus strikes out.

She has to take everything that is important to her, she realizes. She doesn't know whether he'll have changed the locks by the time she gets back. She doesn't much care, but there are paintings she wants. Books. Things she has collected over the years that have no financial value, but all the value in the world to her.

She checks her watch. There isn't that much time. She goes from room to room, picking up the things she really wants, the things she will miss if Marcus does indeed act as disgustingly as some of his clients.

The smaller paintings she takes, stacking them in the car, and her collection of antique porcelain pill boxes. The books she leaves, aside from a few she has had since she was a little girl, a few she was hoping to pass on to Daisy.

Her mother's pearls, her grandmother's ring. Some favorite bags and scarves. It doesn't look as if she has moved out, and she's hoping she hasn't, hoping too that few judges would look well on a man shutting the door on his wife and children, but preparing herself for the worst-case scenario.

The children's rooms are harder. How is she going to explain this to them? How will they take it? Particularly Oliver, Oliver who adores his father even though he hardly ever sees him.

Holly sinks down on Oliver's bed clutching his old blanket, and shivers. She can't cry. She doesn't feel the slightest hint of sadness about Marcus, but what about her children? Her beloved children. How can she do this to them?

But how can she do it to herself? All these years, unhappy. All these years knowing she had made a mistake and waiting for it to get better, thinking that perhaps she could make it work until the children go off to university when she could leave to rediscover herself.

She never expected this to happen. Not so quickly nor so simply. One minute she was married, and the next, it feels, not. She shakes her head and gets on with the business of picking the important things for the children.

A necklace Daisy has been given by her great-grandmother. Her teddies and favorite dresses. Her coloring pads and crayons. Oliver's *Star Wars* transformers collection. His Darth Vader speaking mask that long ago stopped speaking but is still one of his prized possessions. Uppy, the threadbare stuffed dog, once brown and white, now mostly gray with his fur loved off, that Oliver sleeps with every night.

Holly gathers them up and crams them into the boot of the car. She is hoping she will be able to get the rest of her stuff when she gets back, but there are no guarantees and, at the end of the day, it's just stuff. She has her children with her, and she has the things that are important to her.

The rest is just furniture.

"But where are we going, Mummy?" Oliver asks again as Holly hauls their suitcases downstairs and squeezes them in the back of the car. "Whose house is it?"

"My friends Paul and Anna, darling. Our friend Saffron is here and she hasn't been very well, so she needs all of us to go and look after her."

"What's the matter with her?" Daisy asks, sitting on the front step cuddling lambie. "Does she have flu?"

"Sort of." Holly smiles, crossing her fingers that they won't arrive to find Saffron drunk.

They say there are seven stages of divorce: breakdown, shock, anger, pain, hatred, grief, and acceptance.

What they don't tell you is that in cases like this, cases like Holly's, there are actually eight. They don't tell you of the very first stage, the stage that comes before breakdown. The stage that is enabling Holly to drive over to Olivia's house with *High School Musical* blaring out of the radio as she and the kids sing along at the tops of their voices, a huge grin on her face.

The first stage?

Exhilaration.

"You look good!" Olivia climbs in the car and wedges her rucksack under Daisy's feet on the floor of the back-seat.

"Thanks!" Holly smiles. "I think my marriage is over." She keeps her voice low so the kids don't hear, and she turns around to check, but because she cleverly brought her computer and armfuls of DVDs, they're currently engrossed in *The Ant Bully*.

"What?" Olivia's mouth drops open. "What do you mean? I thought you weren't going to do anything."

"I mean I just had the mother of all arguments with Marcus, and he told me that if I went to Gloucestershire, my marriage would be over." Holly feels completely stupid because she can't stop smiling. Hasn't been able to stop smiling for hours.

"Well, he obviously doesn't mean it." Olivia is con-fused. How can Holly be giving her such terrible news with such a huge grin?

"No, no. I think he does."

"So how do you feel, or is that a stupid question?"

"Honestly?" Holly turns her head to look at Olivia. "I feel free. For the last three hours, once the total shock had passed, I haven't been able to stop smiling."

"God, Holly, I had no idea you'd be so impulsive . . . Oh no. Stop the car!"

Holly turns again to look at Olivia, who is now as white as a sheet.

"Seriously, Holly. Now. Please."

Holly pulls over and watches, concerned, as Olivia jumps out the car and reaches over to vomit into the gutter. She leaps out and rubs Olivia's back, and when Olivia has finished and is wiping the tears from her eyes, Holly asks gently if she's okay.

"I'm okay," Olivia says, suddenly leaning over and vomiting violently into the gutter again.

"No you're not," Holly says. "We ought to get you to the doctor."

"Really, I don't need the doctor," Olivia says flatly. "But I could do with some crackers."

Holly looks at her carefully as it dawns on her. "Are you . . . ?"

Olivia nods.

"But . . . who? The American guy? I mean, congratulations . . . No?"

"No." Olivia shakes her head. "I don't think I'm going to keep it. I'm pretty certain I'm going to have an abortion. It is Fred, the American, but he's very definitely no longer in the picture."

"Look, you get back in the car if you're feeling up to it, and I'll run into that shop and get you some ginger ale and crackers. The one thing I know about is morning sickness."

Half an hour later, Olivia starts laughing. By this time *Barnyard* is the movie du jour, and the two women haven't stopped talking since Holly got back in the car with the ginger ale, crackers, and snacks for the kids.

"What are you laughing at?" Holly sneaks a sideways glance as she zips across to the fast lane to overtake a white van.

"I'm laughing at how much of a mess we all are. You may have just left your husband, I'm pregnant, Saffron's been exposed. God, what else could there possibly be? I feel like Tom's death has propelled all of us into these huge midlife crises."

Holly snorts and peers through the windshield up at the gray sky. "Thanks a lot, Tom—interesting way to keep us all together."

"Isn't that weird, though?" Olivia shifts in her seat so she's looking at Holly. "It is keeping us all together. I mean, I loved seeing everybody for Tom's memorial service, even though it was obviously under such awful circumstances, but then after, I intended to stay in touch more but forgot to phone people, other than you, of course. Life just became so busy, and yet here we are, together again. It does feel that this is Tom's doing," and with that she peers through the windscreen herself, looking up at the sky. "Nice one, Tom. I ought to be pissed off with you for the pregnancy, but I am grateful for seeing everyone again."

"Do you do that too?" Holly asks quietly.

"What? Talk to Tom?"

"Yes, but look up at the sky when you do it. I do that a lot. Still. I have little chats with him."

"I know. It feels a lot of the time that he is watching and, corny as it sounds, I feel like he's become my protector a bit, sort of a guardian angel."

"It's not corny." Holly can feel the tears well up. "It's exactly how I feel."

"Oh God." Olivia reaches around in her bag for a tissue. "Don't set me off. I cry at everything these days."

"You're supposed to." Holly smiles through her tears as Olivia hands her a tissue. "Your hormones are all out of whack."

The phone starts ringing, and Holly picks it up, plugging the earpiece in as she looks at the screen to see who it is.

Will.

"Hey," she says softly. "Did you get my message?"

"Oh Holls," he says. "I was so shocked. I can't believe he did that. I can't believe you left. How do you feel? Are you okay?"

"Yes. Better than, actually. But I can't really talk. I'm on my way down to the country. Long story. I'll tell you another time. Is everything okay with you?"

"Everything's great. I'm just worried about you."

"Don't be. I'll call you when I can."

She hangs up to find Olivia looking at her with raised eyebrows.

"What?" Holly says although she is flushing with guilt.

"Sounds like there's more to the story."

"What? The phone call?" Holly attempts to laugh it off. "That was just a friend. Oh God. Okay. It was Will."

Olivia tilts her head. "Oh I didn't realize. Thought it might have been some other dangerously sexy, single, completely gorgeous man."

Holly laughs. "I thought he wasn't your type?"

"Only because men that perfect terrify me."

"There's nothing going on. I promise you. We're not having an affair."

"Holly," Olivia says, "I couldn't care less whether there's anything going on. And I'm hardly in a position to judge, given that I'm pregnant after what was basically a four-night stand."

"But there really isn't anything going on."

"You don't have to explain anything to me. Anyway, Will is lovely, and Tom was never very keen on Marcus so I know he'd approve."

Holly is stunned. Tom not keen on Marcus? He never said anything, never gave her any indication he didn't like him.

"What did Tom say about Marcus?"

Olivia groans. "Oh God. Here I go again, putting my foot in it." She sighs. "Oh well, in for a penny, in for a pound. Do you remember that time Tom and Sarah met you and Marcus for a drink, somewhere in the West End, I think, one of the bars?"

"Yes. It was the Blue Bar at the Berkeley. Marcus's idea."

"I don't know if I should tell you this . . ."

"You can't not." Holly flashes her a look, the anticipation almost too much for her to bear.

"Okay, so Tom apparently made it clear that the drinks were on him, and Marcus looked at the menu, and when the waiter came he looked at Tom with a raised eyebrow and asked, 'Do you mind?' "

"Do you mind what?" Holly tries to remember that night but can't.

"Well, that's exactly what Tom thought, so he said no, not at all. And then, when the bill came . . ." Olivia tails off, wincing at having to tell Holly, who clearly has no idea. "He'd ordered a glass of cognac."

"I vaguely remember."

"It cost a hundred and twenty-five pounds."

"What?" Holly almost chokes. "What?" She is aghast.

"I know." Olivia's face is pained. "Tom was completely horrified."

"But, but . . . ," Holly splutters. "Who does that? Who in the hell does that?"

"Marcus, it would seem."

Holly shakes her head. "Oh my God, that's the most disgusting thing I've ever heard. He knew Tom was paying so he ordered that. I don't even know what to say. It's just so fucking Marcus, and . . ." She groans. "I'm so embarrassed."

"After that," Olivia continues, "it was pretty much all downhill. He just never got it. He never understood why you got together, what you saw in him. He said that Marcus was pompous beyond belief. He always said that you hadn't changed, that you were still as down-to-earth as you'd been at school, and he never understood how you put up with Marcus. So, bottom line is, I would think Tom would be delighted if there was something going on with you and Will."

At that they both lean forward and look up at the sky, then look back at one another and burst out laughing.

It's dark by the time they bump over the old gravel driveway that leads up to the barn. The children are fast asleep in the back, and Holly and Olivia haven't stopped talking for a second, discussing everything from how they feel about the things in their lives, to whether they are where they expected to be, and where were the forks that might have led them down a different path.

And Holly realizes that given the events of the morning, she is exactly where she is supposed to be.

With friends that feel more like family, not because of her closeness to them now, but because of the strength of a shared history. They know her mother, she knows theirs. She knows their brothers and sisters, who they were before they adopted the mantle of adulthood, the mantle of who they thought they were supposed to be.

And it may only have been a few hours, may be, as Holly suspects, the vaguest separation in the history of separations, but in her mind it is real. It is undeniable. And there is no going back.

She no longer has to be Mrs. Marcus Carter, wife of a successful lawyer, mother of two, sometime illustrator of greeting cards. She no longer has to walk in unfamiliar, uncomfortable shoes. Since around eleven forty-four this morning, Holly has remembered who she is.

Holly Mac.

No more, and no less.

"Hello!" Paul comes out of the house and tramps over the driveway to help them in. "Good God, Holly. Are you moving here permanently?" He peers nervously into the back, where the bags and possessions reach the roof.

Holly starts to laugh, and then finds herself suddenly, unexpectedly, sobbing.

"I didn't mean anything," Paul says nervously, hopping from one foot to the other and wishing he'd said nothing. "I'm really sorry."

Olivia walks over to Holly and puts her arms around her, and Holly leans her head on her shoulder and lets the sobs come.

"Mummy?" A small voice from the back of the car. "Mummy? Are we there yet? Why are you crying?" And Holly gently disengages and plants a bright smile on her face as she tries to think of an excuse to tell Oliver.

"Wow . . . this place is . . . unfinished." Holly and Olivia stand in the living room and look around at the piles of paint in one corner, the dust sheets in another, the sawdust, and the lack of furniture.

"I thought I warned you we were redoing it." Paul grins.

"I thought . . . well, I didn't think you were *building* it," Olivia says. "Is this part of your evil plan?"

Anna walks in from the garden. "You mean, get you down here and get you working? Absolutely. Do you think we are idiots or something like that? What is that expression . . . there's no such thing as a free lunch?" And with a laugh she comes over and gives them both hugs.

"So where is she?" Holly says. "Where's Saffron?"

"She couldn't get any reception on her cell phone," Anna explains. "She went to the top of the driveway to try to make a call. Didn't you pass her?"

"You probably did," Paul says. "It's pitch-black out there, though. Which reminds me, can we see if we can rig up some sort of outside light? Seriously, I think it's a bit bloody dangerous."

"I'll add it to the list." Anna rolls her eyes. "I have to warn you, the beds are a bit funky."

"Beds? I thought we were on the floor with sleeping bags."

"We were, but we're starting to look at doing furniture on Fashionista, and we found this company that makes wild and wonderful blow-up beds in these seventies retro patterns, so we've brought a load down."

"Excellent—have to say I wasn't particularly looking forward to a sleeping bag. Lots of fun approaching twenty, not so much approaching forty." Olivia laughs.

"I'd say lots of fun approaching ten, myself," Holly says. "Not too much fun at any point after that."

"Does anyone realize it's been around half an hour? Do you think we should check on Saffron?"

"I'll go," Paul says, jumping off the kitchen counter.

"You should all go," Holly says. "I'll stay here with the kids, but I'm jealous. I love smelling this clean country air at night."

"Wait until morning," Anna says. "The views are to die for. At least walk up the driveway with us, sample what I'm talking about."

"Saff!" they all chorus as they walk up the driveway, then more urgently as they reach the end. "Saff? Saff!"

"Oh fuck," Paul says suddenly. "I know exactly where she is."

"I don't suppose there's a pub nearby, is there?" Holly looks at Paul with eyebrow raised.

"Funny you should mention it. I'll go."

"I'll come with you," Anna says, concern written all over her face. "God, you don't really think she's drinking? She said this morning that this was it, she wouldn't drink again."

"From what I read this morning online," Holly says, "those statements are pretty much par for the course."

"You mean they don't mean anything?"

"Coming from an alcoholic in relapse? I'd say not worth the paper they're written on."

"Great," Anna groans as she makes her way gingerly back to the house to get the car keys. "Can you perhaps put the kettle on for coffee?"

CHAPTER TWENTY-TWO

Saffron has passed out on a pink and orange inflatable bed in one of the bedrooms off the gallery upstairs. The children are fast asleep, Anna and Holly are in the kitchen making coffee, and Olivia is helping Paul bring logs in from the shed outside to keep the fire going.

It is almost as cold inside the house as it is outside. Holly leans back on the counter as Anna puts the kettle on the stove and practices blowing smoke rings with her breath.

"I am really sorry," Anna mutters, rubbing her hands together over the gas flame of the stove. "I think the pipes must have frozen or burst or something. I cannot say I expected to have a load of friends down just yet."

"I think we're probably all much hardier than we look," Holly says. "Anyway, I for one certainly feel spoiled by the way we live. It seems ridiculous to have all the stuff we have, and this feels sort of like getting back to basics. This barn is gorgeous, and it just makes you realize that you only need a few things to make it perfect—a sofa, a table . . ."

". . . beds." Anna laughs.

"Well, yes, but not all the things that we all tend to

collect. I just feel like I have so much, and all of it's so unnecessary. I just don't need all of this *stuff*."

"Paul said you'd brought most of the stuff with you . . ." Anna turns to give Holly a questioning look. "Is everything okay?"

"Well, I feel like saying it's a long story, but it really isn't." She takes a deep breath. "I think I've left Marcus."

"I should say I'm surprised, but I am not." Anna frowns.

"I have a feeling that nobody is. The truth is, Anna, I haven't been happy for ages. Years, I think. Not that there haven't been happy moments within that time, and obviously I've got my wonderful children, but I think it just dawned on me really recently that the thing that's making me so unhappy is the one thing I haven't been able to face."

"Your marriage."

"My marriage. For so many reasons. I never see Marcus, I don't feel that we have a marriage, or a partnership of any kind." Holly sighs deeply. It is good to finally talk about this, to say all these hidden thoughts out loud, the thoughts that have kept her awake night after night for months. The thoughts she was too frightened to face.

"I don't feel that we're nice to each other," she continues. "There's no kindness or respect or love. And by the way, I'm just as bad to him. It feels like we're in a constant war of words and wits, our humor always at the other's expense."

"Do you think he loves you?" Anna asks.

Holly sighs. "I think he loves who he wants me to be, which isn't who I am. I don't think he's the slightest bit interested in any parts of Holly that don't fit the picture he has of me in his mind, so I've become someone else, a Holly I don't recognize. And although it's fun to step into somebody else's shoes, to play a part for a while, it's finite. It's not something you can do forever."

"To thine own self be true," Anna says. "My grandfather always used to say that, except in Swedish, obviously."

"It's so true." Holly nods. "I haven't been true to myself at all. I understand the reasons why I married him. On paper he seemed to be everything I thought I should want. I was completely on the rebound, and he appeared to offer such a glamorous, steady, wonderful life. I thought . . . well . . . I suppose I knew I wasn't in love with him, but I thought we'd have a different kind of love. I thought it would grow, and I kept telling myself that passion always dies, so it didn't matter if you didn't have it there in the beginning, and that the important thing is that you're best friends."

Anna tilts her head. "It sounds like you never thought it was possible to have passion and a best friend."

Tears suddenly fill Holly's eyes. "I didn't. I didn't think I could do better than Marcus, and he seemed to adore me, and, honestly, I'd never been adored and I thought that was enough."

"I hope you do not take this the wrong way," Anna says carefully, "but that night we all came over for dinner, when Paul and I left, he asked me if I thought the marriage was okay."

"He did? But how could he have known anything when I didn't even know myself?"

"For exactly the reasons you just gave to me. There did not seem to be any kindness between you. You were funny together and obviously something worked, but he seemed to take every opportunity to put you down, pretending to be funny except it was not funny. It was horribly uncomfortable. I think he put down everyone. It would seem to be a habit of his."

"I know." Holly winces. "He isn't bad, he's just incredibly insecure with an enormous superiority complex that disguises an even bigger inferiority complex. He thinks he's being funny, but it's a way to subtly keep everyone beneath him."

"That is exactly what we saw that night. And he controlled you so much, Holly. Every time you opened your mouth, he would stop talking to hear what you were saying, and you became quieter and quieter all evening until you seemed to have disappeared. I was not even the one who noticed, not that I would have known you were different, but Paul was surprised. He said it felt like Marcus was the puppeteer, pulling your strings until you were absolutely under his control."

Holly shakes her head in amazement. "Not exactly a healthy relationship, right?"

Anna laughs. "Would not seem so."

"So . . . do you and Paul have both? Do you have passion and friendship?"

"After as much IVF treatment as we've had, let me

tell you, there is not a lot of passion left," Anna rolls her eyes, "but even now, even after all this, I still look at him sometimes and want to rip his clothes off and jump him in the bed."

Holly laughs at Anna's English. "Are you serious?"

"Yup. And he is my best friend. Most of the time, quite honestly, I am in bed by nine and the last thing I want to do is even think about sex, much less do it, but there are those times when I remember, when I feel exactly the same way about him as I did in the beginning. But you must have fancied Marcus at some point, no? . . . Not even a bit?"

Holly continues to shake her head sadly.

"But you were married for, what, thirteen years? Fourteen? You had two children. How did you . . . *why* did you? Why would you stay with a man for that long, given everything you've said?"

Holly shrugs as she tips coffee into the *cafetière*. "I think fear," she says slowly. "I think I was just too frightened to leave. I was always so strong, so independent. But I suppose I lost myself in the marriage, was just beaten down to the point where I couldn't do it. And then, of course, the children. I still feel horrible. How can I have done this to the children?"

"They will be happy if the mother is happy," Anna says gently. "There is nothing worse for children than to grow up in an unhappy marriage. Are you sure it is over, though? Would you give it another chance?"

"I don't know," Holly says. "I feel sure it's over, but then I think about supporting myself and the kids, and I'll admit that it's terrifying. It's been only a few hours, as well. God knows how I'll feel in the morning."

"I think you are very brave," Anna says, setting the coffee on a tray. "And I believe that whatever decision you ultimately make will be the right one. Take it a day at a time and know that everything happens for a reason. Come on, let's try and warm ourselves up."

"Is Saffron definitely asleep?" Paul says, prodding the logs so the flames shoot up to the top of the fireplace.

"Asleep? Unconscious I think would be a better term," Holly suggests, coming down from checking on the children and Saffron. "I feel like I'm back at school. I turned her on her side and stuck a broom down the bed to stop her lying on her back, in case she throws up, and I put a bucket on the floor next to her."

"How are the kids?"

"Cold. I piled everything I could find on top of them, but they're fast asleep so presumably they're okay. I'm a bit worried, though."

"Why don't we all sleep in here by the fire tonight?" Anna says suddenly. "The plumber's coming tomorrow so we should have heat then, and this is the warmest room. We can carry the kids down."

"And Saffron?"

"I think we should leave her," Paul says. "The cold will probably help her hangover. Anyway, speaking of cold . . ." He reaches into his jacket pocket to pull out a small bottle. "God knows, this is probably stupidly risky given we have Saffron here, but does anyone want some brandy in their coffee?"

A muted cheer goes up as three mugs approach Paul,

who pours copious amounts into each. "Probably better to finish it," he muses, tipping the last drops in. "I'll take it outside when we're done so she doesn't find it."

"I have to say I was stunned at how drunk she was," Olivia says quietly. "I remember her partying at school and getting drunk then, but somehow you sort of expect that from teenagers. It's been years since I've seen someone sway and slur their words."

"I think what stunned me most was how drunk she was in so short a time," Holly says. "Wasn't she gone only about forty minutes? How much do you have to drink in forty minutes to get that drunk? Did she have an IV of vodka or something?"

"Pretty much, apparently. The barman said she was drinking vodka martinis like they were water. And through a straw."

"Oh great. How to get shit-faced in five easy minutes." Holly rolls her eyes. "A straw? Who drinks martinis through a straw?"

"Someone who wants to get shit-faced in five easy minutes." Paul grins.

"I do feel a little out of my depth here," Anna says quietly. "I thought it was funny when she first showed up, and understandable after what she's been through, but I had no idea she's an alcoholic. I'm really worried about how she's going to cope. I for one certainly don't know what to do or how to help her."

"I was reading up about interventions," Holly says. "When you tell the alcoholic what it's like living with them and what they're like when they're drunk, but the thing is none of us really know, so it seems a bit pointless. It's not like we're present in her life and see the difference. I feel a bit helpless too."

Paul unbuttons his jacket, followed by the others as the fire starts to give off some serious heat. "Isn't the first step of these programs to learn that you're powerless over alcohol? I think there's something about being powerless over the alcoholic. I think there's probably nothing we can actually do to stop her drinking, but perhaps she'll want to stop herself. She's done it before so I'm sure she can do it again."

"You mean just sit here and watch her get shit-faced all the time?"

"No. I think we should all do our best to keep her away from alcohol as much as we can, but I also think we shouldn't judge her if she slips. We should support her as much as we can."

"What about keeping her busy?" Anna pipes up. "I think we should get her working on the house."

Olivia bursts out laughing. "What? 'Saffron? Would you just climb up and retile the roof while you're here? Saffron, I see you sitting around with nothing to do, would you mind just building some kitchen cabinets?' "

They all laugh, but Holly says, "Actually I think it's a brilliant idea. I know we were joking about your evil plan to recruit your friends for slave labor, but I think the best thing we could do for Saffron *is* to keep her busy, and I wouldn't mind keeping busy myself. The worst thing for me right now is to have hours and hours of time to think about the state of my life."

Paul looks at her quizzically.

"Long story, Paul. Short version is I think my marriage

is over, which is probably a huge blessing in disguise.
Anna can give you the details later. I'm a bit talked out
for today, if that's okay."

"That's okay," Paul says, sympathy in his eyes. "I'm
sorry."

"Liar!" Anna kicks him and Holly laughs.

"I mean, I'm sorry if Holly's in pain."

"I'm very much not in pain, and don't be sorry.
Right now I still feel liberated. Ask me again in the
morning."

"Speaking of morning," Olivia stretches, "I'm completely exhausted. Would anyone mind if we brought
the beds down now? I don't think I can keep my eyes
open for another second."

At five in the morning Holly is wide awake. It takes her
a while to orient herself—too many people breathing,
too cold, where is she? She slips out of bed, bundles the
duvet around her and puts some more logs on the fire,
poking and blowing until the flames catch, for it is now
freezing in the room, whatever heat there was earlier
having risen to the top of the vaulted ceiling.

The flames catch and Holly sits for a while staring
into them, thinking about her life. She had vaguely
thought she would wake up in a panic, terrified of the
future and knowing she had made a huge mistake, but
what she feels at this moment, sitting wrapped in a
duvet as the flames start to lick up the stones, is peace.

For the first time in years, Holly feels at peace.

She kisses Daisy and Oliver, holding her breath as

Daisy stirs and settles back down with a light snore, then takes her cell phone and a deep breath as she braves the outside to stomp up to the top of the driveway. It's still dark, and absolutely quiet. Frost is on the ground, and the grass crunches satisfyingly under her boots as she makes her way to the road.

This is the longest Holly has gone without speaking to Will in weeks. Their brief conversation in the car didn't count, not when she was used to sharing the innermost workings of her mind, and to have not spoken to him after this, the most momentous thing to have happened to her since Tom's death, seems inconceivable.

She can't call him, not at five-thirty in the morning, but she is hoping, praying, there will be a text from him; and turning on her phone she walks around until she gets the briefest of signals. One line, but enough.

> Miss talking. Am thinking of u & worrying.
> R u ok? Where r u? lunch? Wxx

She smiles. Why do his messages, his texts, his e-mails, his phone calls make her instantly happy?

> am v. ok. In country. Miss u 2. can't do lunch.
> Will try 2 talk later. Me XX

A minute later, shockingly, her phone rings.

"What are you doing awake?" Her smile stretches from ear to ear.

"Couldn't sleep," Will says. "I was up at my computer reading some of your e-mails, when, boom! your text arrived. I was worried I wouldn't get you. Where are you?"

"What a gorgeous surprise," Holly says. "I'm in Gloucestershire. At Paul and Anna's place."

"How come?"

Should she tell him? They are trying to keep Saffron's situation as quiet as possible—it's not called Alcoholics Anonymous for nothing—but she doesn't have to tell him everything, and God knows she trusts him, she has trusted him with almost all her private thoughts and fears for weeks now. Weeks that have felt like months.

"We've got Saffron," she says. "We're hiding her. You've seen the papers, right?"

"Seen them? I was reading all about it yesterday online. Sounds pretty evil, and most of what they're saying seems to be untrue. Mum called last night and she's the most naive person in the world, but even she can see that most of these worms crawling out of the woodwork to give their shocking love stories about Saffron are money-grabbers."

"Oh God!" Holly groans. "You're not serious? More stories?"

"It seems they're obsessed. Brad and Angelina have been relegated to page four thanks to Saffron and Pearce Webster. Have to say it's pretty damn impressive, though. Pearce Webster! He's only about the most famous man in the world."

"God, you're shallow." Holly starts to laugh. "You're impressed, aren't you?"

"Well, have to say I am slightly. Not bad for a girl from northwest London."

"More LA-influenced now I'd say." Holly snorts. "I had to do a sushi run on the way up here to keep her happy."

"You're not serious?" Will laughs.

"Sadly, yes."

"You can take the girl out of LA . . ."

"That's exactly what I said!" and they both laugh. "I'm so glad you called," Holly says, after a comfortable silence. "It's really good to hear your voice."

"It's really good to hear yours," Will says, his smile audible down the phone.

"Don't you think it's odd," Holly starts haltingly, "that we've become such good friends after such a short space of time? I . . . well, I don't want to embarrass you or anything, but I missed having a male friend. The only male friend I had was Tom, and once he and Scary Sarah started it wasn't ever quite the same. I really don't know what I would do without you." She stops, flushing. Has she gone too far? She didn't mean to say it even though it's quite patently true. She didn't mean to get soppy, sentimental, serious.

"I feel the same way," Will says. "Sometimes I find it hard to believe that we didn't really know each other four months ago. I feel like I've become so reliant on our friendship, on filling you in on everything that's happening in my life. I do actually feel that I finally have a best friend."

A pang. Pleasure or pain? Holly doesn't know whether she wants to hear this or not. Does being a best friend preclude anything else? And why did that thought suddenly make its way into her head? Hadn't she accepted that they were friends? And despite her marriage possibly being over, now would be the worst time in the world to get involved with someone else?

Although the someone else just called her a best friend. What does that *mean*?

"But I want to hear about you," Will moves swiftly on. "It sounds like Marcus took it really badly, are you okay?"

"I am," Holly says, sitting carefully on a large stone as she checks her signal, desperate not to lose Will, comforted so much by his voice. "I know this sounds bizarre, but I feel at peace. I mean, obviously, a bit scared and apprehensive about the future, and I fully expect Marcus to be a prick, but I feel . . . free. Peaceful. Like me."

"Your voice sounds lighter," Will says after a silence. "I know that sounds mad, but it really does sound lighter."

"I *feel* lighter." Holly laughs.

"Do you think this is it, though?"

"I think so," Holly says. "It turns out, of course, that no one seems to be surprised. Everyone, it appears could see that our marriage wasn't great. The thing that scares me most is that I'll go back because I'm too scared to do it on my own."

"Do you really think that would happen? Because, Holly, I think you're much stronger than you give yourself credit for. I think you've allowed yourself to live in a place of fear because you've been pretty much forced there. You don't have to live there anymore, and you certainly don't have to worry about doing it on your own—you have a huge support system."

"Marcus hissed that I wouldn't get the house or a penny out of him."

"Sounds just about typical from someone like Marcus. He's just reacting because, as far as he's concerned, you've just destroyed his life and humiliated him royally."

"You know what's weird? I was sitting in front of the fire just now thinking about him, and I suddenly had this really strong feeling that he will look back and know that this marriage was wrong. I don't love him, and everybody deserves to be loved. I feel horrible that I wasn't able to love him. I've never been able to give him the attention or affection that he wanted. Maybe that's why he disappeared off to work all the time."

"I think that's incredibly noble of you," Will says quietly. "And you're right, everyone does deserve to be loved. Including you. Haven't you always said that you felt that Marcus didn't love you, but that he loved who he wanted you to be? Don't you deserve to be loved as well? Loved for who you are, not for dressing up and entertaining and being a perfect trophy wife?"

"Yes. Thank you for saying that."

"My pleasure. So how long are you up there for?"

"I have no idea. Saffron will be here until it all blows over, I suppose, and the rest of us will just have to see. Maybe we could do some sort of a rota."

"Is Saffron not capable of being alone?" Will laughs. "Has she turned into that much of a diva?"

"God, no. Not what you think. She's just . . . fragile right now. She needs her friends."

"I was joking," Will says. "I think you're all amazing being there for her. It's exactly what Tom would have done."

"I know. That's just what Olivia and I were saying." She shivers, standing up and pacing in the cold. "I'm bloody freezing, Will. I have to get inside and there's no reception."

"Can I call you out there?"

"You probably won't get me but text or leave a message and I'll call you back when I get a signal. Thank you, Will. It means so much to me that you called." And Holly goes back inside to curl up by the fire and think about her life as she waits for the house to wake up.

"Bacon, eggs, bread, orange juice . . ." Paul turns to Olivia. "Was there anything else?"

Olivia looks at her list. "Milk. Papers."

"Okay. I'll get the papers and start paying, you get the milk."

Paul grabs a handful and stops in his tracks as he looks at the front page of the *Mirror*.

"Got the milk!" Olivia calls as she comes back up the aisle, weighted down by a giant bottle of semi-skimmed milk. "What's the matter?" And she sidles next to him, her hand flying up to her mouth as she sees the front page.

SAFFY DAFFY AND DRUNK.

Brit actress bonking Pearce flies into Heathrow, smashed! Do you know her mystery new man? Call this number and tell us who he is!

"Oh shit!" she whispers. "It's you, isn't it? I mean, you can't see that clearly, given that you're carrying Saffron, but it is you."

"Oh fuck," he whispers. "Let's just hope to Christ nobody phones them. The last thing we need is for the press to bring Anna into it and then find out where we are. This is just horrific."

"What a bloody nightmare." Olivia sighs. "Don't bring it home, let's check the rest for Saffron-free papers, and we'll bring those instead."

"What? No tabloids? What kind of a man goes out to get the papers and comes back without the rags, for God's sake?"

"The kind of man who wants to protect his friends from seeing yet more stories," Paul leans down and whispers in Holly's ear.

"Oh God. Is it bad?"

"Let's just say it's not good. Sssh. I think Saffron's coming. Don't say anything, and I'll tell you later. Here, you whisk the eggs," and he hands Holly the box of eggs and a large blue bowl.

CHAPTER TWENTY-THREE

Saffron has never done anything by halves. When she smoked, she smoked two packs a day. When she quit, she never looked at a cigarette again . . . until she started again. When she exercises, she does so obsessively, two hours a day with a personal trainer, every day, lying in bed exercising in her mind, thinking of little else until she misses a day or two and then does nothing at all for months.

She can go for weeks without spending a penny, then goes on spending sprees, buying armfuls of stuff she neither wants nor needs, unable to see clearly, so excited by the buzz of shopping, like a drug addict getting high.

Or an alcoholic getting drunk.

So when Saffron falls off the wagon, she doesn't do so slowly and gracefully. She does it in the way she does everything else in her life. Spectacularly. At great speed and to great excess.

She hadn't meant to lose her sobriety. When she was sitting in the airport bar, her intention truly was to have one drink. Perhaps two, just to help her relax, just to take the edge off the enormous stress that she was suddenly under. Other people were able to have one or two drinks, why not her? She'd been sober for years, had been to countless parties where alcohol was being served, and hadn't been tempted once. Of course she could handle one or two drinks, why was she so different?

Then there was the plane. First class. Champagne on tap. Why not? Just this once. Such a warm, familiar feeling. So lovely to relax as the buzz started up. She felt loose and giggly and happy. Happy again for the first time in days. She wasn't a noisy drunk, just snuggled up quietly under her blanket downing glass after glass as the rest of the cabin fell asleep or watched movies.

She doesn't remember much about arriving. Stewards and stewardesses seemed to be muttering in their walkie-talkies, and she was able to remember to cover her head with a scarf, push huge Jackie-O-style sunglasses onto her face. She remembers being hustled through noise, her name being called, flashes of light on her face as she giggled woozily, and then—bliss—being picked up and falling asleep on someone's shoulder as she was carried out to a car.

Again, last night, she hadn't meant to drink. Had absolutely meant every word when she told Anna and Paul—oh sweet Anna and Paul who had come to her rescue—that she would never drink again. She felt horrible when she finally woke up. Her head was pounding, waves of nausea kept coming over her, and she knew that it was a brief slip. That she never wanted to feel this way again, the way she felt for so many years before coming into AA.

But then late yesterday afternoon, all she could think about was having a drink. Just one. Not to get drunk, just . . . just because she could. The thought became an obsession, and no one would know if she disappeared for a quick drink. Just one. Why not?

"Saff!" Holly looks up from whisking the eggs and grimaces at the sight of Saffron, bleary-eyed, hungover, skin an odd shade of gray. "Oh if they could see you now." She shakes her head in amazement, thinking of all the publicity shots of Saffron over the years, gorgeous and glamorous, posing on red carpets all over the world in floor-length beaded gowns.

A world away from this creature now. Not a scrap of makeup, old gray sweats and a baggy jumper, long glossy locks held back messily in a clip.

"Oh don't," Saffron groans, coming over to give Holly a kiss. "I feel horrible. If they could see me now they'd have a field day." Paul and Olivia exchange a glance—thank God they didn't bring that paper home.

"Oh look at your chickens!" Saffron says, seeing Daisy and Oliver, bundled up in hats and gloves, playing outside the kitchen window. "Aren't they gorgeous!"

"I'm surprised you can see them under all those layers." Holly smiles. "But thank you. I think they're pretty damn gorgeous, even though I'm ever so slightly biased."

"Coffee?" Paul says brightly, placing a mug in front of a grateful Saffron.

"Mmm." She takes a sip, looking sheepishly around the table. "I think I owe you all an apology," she says quietly. "I'm so sorry about last night. I didn't mean to . . ." She stops, sighing. "It won't happen again. Honestly. I don't know what came over me, but I won't let it happen again."

The others just look at her, not saying anything, and Saffron raises her hand, dipping her head in contrition. "I know, I know I've said that before, but this time I mean it."

"In actual fact," Anna starts setting the plates around the table as Paul brings the eggs over, "you'll probably be too busy to think about sneaking off to the pub again."

"Busy? How?"

"We've decided to try to get this house finished." Paul sits down and helps himself to bacon. "We've assigned everyone jobs, and you and Anna are starting with tiling the bathroom."

Saffron starts to laugh. "Ow," she groans again, holding her head. "Shit, that hurts. You have to be kidding . . . me? Tiling a bathroom?"

Olivia's mouth opens in amazement. "Tell me you haven't seriously become that much of a diva."

"No!" Saffron exclaims in horror. "It's just that I'm hopeless at anything like that. I've never tiled a thing in my life. I mean, fine, I'll do it, just as long as you don't mind wonky tiles."

"You'll be fine," Anna brushes her off. "I'm doing it with you and I'll show you what to do. It's easy. Of course you could do the floor sanding instead if you want."

"No, no," Saffron shakes her head, looking at the vast expanse of rough, stained wood in the living room, "tiling's fine." She starts to laugh.

"What's so funny?" Paul looks up.

"Just that I never expected to be here tiling a bathroom. Life seemed so settled, and then . . . It's just so bizarre how everything in life can change in a heartbeat."

"Tell me about it." Holly snorts. "Just so you know, I think I've left Marcus."

"You have? Good girl!" Saffron exclaims.

"Why good girl?" Although it's not as if Holly doesn't know.

"Because he's a pompous, stuck-up arse, that's why."

"Saffron!" Olivia admonishes her.

"Why? It's true, isn't it?" And at this, Holly starts to laugh.

"You haven't changed at all." Holly grins. "You still say exactly what's on your mind."

Saffron shrugs. "I'd rather be honest, although I apologize if I upset you. I could have been less mean."

"Don't worry," Holly says. "He is a pompous arse. I'm just not used to people coming out and saying it. Do me a favor, though, and don't say anything in front of the children."

"I imagine that once people know you're definitely separated, you'll be hearing that from pretty much everyone, but of course I won't say anything in front of the kids. Can I meet them?"

"Is breakfast ready?" Saffron looks over at Paul who nods. "Let's get them in."

"Mummy," Daisy has put down her fork and is staring at Saffron, "I thought you said your friend was a beautiful famous actress."

Paul shouts with laughter and Saffron gives him an exaggerated evil eye.

"Daisy!" Oliver says loudly. "That's very rude."

"No it's not!" she says, her voice rising toward tears. "It's not rude, it's true."

"It is rude. Isn't it rude, Mummy? To make comments about people when they're sitting in front of you?"

"I wasn't making comments." Daisy pouts. "I was just saying she's not beautiful."

"It's okay, Oliver." Saffron smiles. "I don't mind. Usually I am beautiful and famous, but today I'm just ordinary. I change, a bit like Cinderella."

"You forgot to say modest." Paul grins.

"Ah yes. That too. Olivia?" Saffron suddenly looks over at Olivia. "You look horrible. Are you okay?"

"Back in a sec," Olivia gulps, standing up and rushing from the table, hand over her mouth.

Seconds later the unmistakable sound of retching and heaving comes from the upstairs bathroom.

"Oh God." Paul stops chewing and lays his knife and fork down. "Just what I need to hear in the middle of breakfast."

Saffron reaches over and steals a piece of bacon off his plate, chewing on it thoughtfully. "Doesn't bother me. Is she ill or is she pregnant?"

Paul starts to laugh. "Olivia, pregnant? Hardly," and then he sees Holly's face. "Oh God. Is she?"

Holly tries to feign ignorance, but she has always been a terrible liar.

"Don't ask me," she says eventually. "It's got nothing to do with me."

Olivia comes back into the room, breathing newly brushed minty breath, looking more than a little uncomfortable.

"So . . . are you preg?" Saffron looks straight at her.

"God, Saff." Paul rolls his eyes. "Subtlety would take you a long way, you know." Olivia shoots a look at Holly, who shakes her head vigorously. *It wasn't me,* she wants to say.

"What's preg?" Oliver pipes up loudly. "What does that mean?"

"Sssh, Oliver," Holly says. "I'll tell you later."

"It's okay, Oliver." Olivia sinks down at the table, and shrugs. "It means I'm having a baby. It also means it's a bloody nightmare. Whoops, excuse my language. But, yes. It would seem that despite being resolutely single and having never wanted children my entire life, I am now pregnant."

"So who's the lucky man?" Saffron says.

"No one worth talking about. Nice guy, American, we're no longer in touch."

"Not the guy Tom introduced you to?" Saffron says, and Olivia nods miserably.

"Does he know?" Anna asks. Olivia shakes her head.

"I can't see the point," Olivia says quietly. "I haven't decided whether or not I'll keep it."

Holly is looking at Anna as Olivia talks and sees the shock on Anna's face. The shock and dismay that Olivia could so casually get rid of a baby, when she and Paul would give anything in the world to have one.

"You would have an abortion?" Anna asks softly, attempting to keep the emotion out of her voice, attempting not to judge, or at least not to let her judgment show.

Olivia, suddenly remembering Paul and Anna talking about IVF, starts to backtrack furiously. "I don't know . . ." she says quickly. "I mean, I haven't decided. I just don't know what to do, haven't really made any decision . . ."

"It's okay," Paul says, taking Anna's hand under the table and squeezing it. "You don't have to censor yourself because of us."

"I'm so sorry." Olivia looks directly at Anna, who looks as if she's going to cry. "I didn't want to say anything. I wasn't going to say anything. I thought I could just quietly go and have a termination and nobody would ever know."

"It's fine," Paul says as a tear rolls slowly down Anna's face. "Don't worry. What's important is how you feel."

"Mummy?" Oliver again, looking confused. "What's a bortion?"

Holly rolls her eyes and leans toward him. "Ask your father," she says with a sigh, reaching over to pour herself more coffee.

"How are you?" Paul crunches over the field to an old tree stump where Anna is sitting, gazing out at the view, a crumpled damp tissue clenched in her hand. Her eyes are red-rimmed, and at the sight of Paul a few more tears squeeze their way out.

"It just does not seem so fair," Anna starts to talk; it comes out as a sob. "We have tried so hard and for so long, and then someone like Olivia just falls pregnant at the drop of a hat, and she is going to have an abortion. How does this happen? How could she do that?"

"I never realized you were anti-abortion," Paul says gently, surprised.

"I'm not. I mean, I was not. I never had any feeling about it at all, but now, I . . . just do not understand how someone could do that when there are so many people in the world who are desperate to have children and who cannot have them."

Paul puts his arm around Anna and hugs her as she settles in, leaning her head on his chest. Safe. Loved. Exhausted. No more sobs for now, too tired, just a blankness as she whispers over and over again, "It's just not fair. It's just not fair."

They keep to their separate corners of the house for the morning, waiting for the emotions to die down.

Anna and Saffron in the bathroom, Paul sanding the floors of the living room, Olivia painting the window frames. Holly and the children are sanding down the kitchen cupboards, the children delighted to be taking part in grown-up work, each clutching sandpaper and working on their own cupboard doors.

Saffron doesn't ask Anna about the IVF, or how she feels, or if she's okay, for which Anna is grateful. There are times when talking about things is exactly what you need, and there are other times, times like today, when no amount of talking will make you feel better. When all you can do is breathe, put one foot in front of the other, get through the day until you can sink into unconsciousness, hoping that tomorrow things will be easier. Tomorrow you will be fine.

"Paul!" Holly walks into the living room, yelling over the noise of the industrial sander, coughing as a cloud of dust settles over her.

"Hang on." He switches the machine off and pulls the mask off his face. "Yup?"

"You need to come and look at the kitchen cupboards. I think all the wood might be rotten."

"Oh God," he groans. "Let's get Anna down here; she'll know more than me."

Anna crouches down, stroking a finger down the wood, then looks up at Paul with a frown. "Yes. They are rotten all right. If one is, then they probably all are. We need new kitchen cupboard doors."

Paul sighs. "That's the problem with these bloody renovations. You think you know exactly what you're going to be doing, but the more work you do, the more you uncover that needs doing. Great. I don't suppose any of us knows anything about building kitchen cupboard doors . . ." They all look blankly at him and shrug. "So now it will probably cost a small fortune to get this done. Just what we need." His irritation is obvious, and Anna shifts uncomfortably, guilty at having initiated this project at a time when clearly they couldn't really afford it.

Holly's face lights up. "We could ask Will!" she says, and Olivia suppresses a smile, raising an eyebrow instead as she turns to look at Holly. "No, seriously." The others look blank. "Will. Tom's brother. He's a cabinet-maker. He'd come in a heartbeat."

"Oh my God!" Anna starts leaping in delight. "What an excellent idea! I did not know Tom's brother is a carpenter. Does anyone have his number?"

This time, Holly avoids catching Olivia's knowing eye. "I think I do," she says, happiness lifting her up and floating her toward the door. "I'll go outside to get a signal and call him."

A beaming Holly comes back twenty minutes later.

"What took you so long?" A still-disgruntled Paul asks, convinced Will won't come, convinced Holly won't even have his number.

Holly blushes. "It took me a while to get through," she lies unconvincingly. "But he's coming. He's taking the train this afternoon. I'll go and pick him up at the station with the kids."

"Yay!" Anna shouts with joy, turning to Paul. "See? I told you everything would be all right."

"We don't know how much he's going to charge us," Paul grumbles. "It might still be more money than we can afford to spend. Even this plumber coming out to fix the heating is yet another unexpected expense."

"Will said he'd do it for cost," Holly says, unable to wipe the smile off her face—and not because he's doing it for cost. "He's bringing all his tools. Apparently lumber is much cheaper out here, and he's not going to charge anything for his time."

Anna plants her hands on her hips and shoots Paul an I-told-you-so look as Paul shrugs. "If that is true, that is amazing."

"Of course, it's true," Holly says. "Remember, he's Tom's brother. Tom would never have promised something he wasn't going to deliver. Think his brother's going to be any different?"

"Let's just hope you're right," Paul says, and donning his face mask he goes back into the living room to finish sanding the floor.

Holly hasn't thought much about Marcus. Hasn't thought much about her marriage ending or about the fact that she probably isn't going home to the same life she left behind. Marcus has left two messages. The first furious, the second sad, asking if they could talk.

She responded not by calling him, but by phoning Frauke. She left details of where she was with Frauke, in case of emergency only, and told Frauke to tell Marcus they'd talk when she got home.

The rest of the time, she hasn't thought about him.

Partly, she is burying her head in the sand. Just as she

did throughout her marriage. When her unhappiness became almost too much to bear, she would bury her head in the sand and pretend that everything was fine. If she didn't think about it, it wasn't happening.

There is only one thought filling her head today. One thought that is keeping her going, keeping her as dizzy as a teenager.

Will.

Saffron, when sober, is as perceptive as she is direct. She has learned to become an expert people watcher for her acting profession, and as soon as Holly mentioned Will, Saffron saw how her eyes lit up, how she couldn't stop smiling when she came back from having phoned him, how it would appear that she is practically bubbling over with happiness since that phone call.

Saffron would have to be stupid if she really believed that Holly is bursting with joy over the fact that the kitchen cupboards will be done at cost.

Hmmm, she thinks. *Interesting.* Not that she can see Holly and Will together—Will, though sexy and charming, is definitely not ready to settle down, but doesn't Holly deserve a bit of fun after being married to that awful bloody Marcus? And Holly may not have the strength to stay separated—Saffron could see how Marcus might talk her back—so maybe it's a good thing there's someone else around to help Holly see she's made the right decision.

Maybe it's a very good thing indeed.

CHAPTER TWENTY-FOUR

Holly pulls in to the tiny little station and zooms right into one of the parking spaces next to the tracks. She is nervous, jittery, keeps pulling the mirror down to see what she looks like, so lost in her own world she tunes out of the constant questions from Daisy in the backseat.

"I'll be back in a second," she says to the kids as she sees the distant lights of the train, and she jumps out of the car and up the steps onto the platform, feeling dizzy with excitement and nerves.

It feels like an age since she last saw Will but it is only, what, a few days? She is used to speaking to him all day; and somehow, now that she has left (for in her mind, over the last few hours, she has not been thinking that her marriage may be over, but she has rewritten history as her having left Marcus, as it being signed, sealed, and delivered), something has shifted. She no longer feels guilt at the amount of time she spends thinking about Will or the thrill she feels at the prospect of seeing him.

She paces nervously as the train doors sigh their way open and squints as she sees him—one of three to get off the train—walking up toward her from the far end of the platform, waving an acknowledgment.

There is no mistaking Will. Could never be any mistaking Will for Holly, and her heart leaps as she takes in his familiar face, his familiar stride. In old Levis, leather boots, and a beaten-up old jacket that can't possibly be keeping out the February chill, Will looks, as far as Holly is concerned, perfect.

His hair is no longer as short as Tom's. It's growing longer again, messy brown hair that doesn't seem to be in any style other than tousled, his green eyes sparkling as he gets closer, his grin widening. Holly's heart skips another beat.

He is quite simply the most gorgeous man she has ever seen—the most perfect specimen of maleness Holly could possibly imagine, oozing testosterone out of every pore. His legs are long and strong, his shoulders broad, his neck thick. His hands are large and clean but calloused from the work, and that smile—oh that smile! Dimples and unbearably cute, it is a smile that could launch a thousand love songs.

Holly smiles. Cannot stop smiling.

If you were an observer, perhaps sitting in your car waiting to catch the next London train, you might think, watching how Holly and Will both speed up and fly into one another's arms, that they are like magnets. The force of mutual attraction pulls them together with such speed and such intensity that when they stick together in a tight hug that lasts and lasts, you might think that it would take greater strength than you or I have to prise them apart.

It is their first serious physical contact. Holly didn't plan a hug like this. Didn't think about how she would say hello, far too busy attempting to calm her nerves to worry about whether to kiss him, hug him, whether there might be any awkwardness.

Her arms automatically wind themselves around his back, his around hers as they squeeze one another tight and he rests his head on the top of hers, pulling away after what feels like hours to reach down and plant a kiss on her cheek, all the while grinning like a schoolboy.

They pull apart reluctantly, and for a few seconds it does feel awkward. Holly is shaking, hadn't realized the effect it would have, to rest in his arms, to feel so secure, so looked after, so loved.

She hasn't realized until exactly this moment how much she has missed this, how much she has missed affection. But she knows now that even if Marcus were to give this to her, were to put his arms round her and hug her close, resting his cheek on her head, she wouldn't want it, not from him.

But Will? With Will, she could stay in his arms all day. She has been fighting these feelings for so long now, so guilty at feeling this way about a man other than her husband, knowing how wrong it is, knowing she would never be unfaithful, would never have an affair, that now she no longer has to hide her feelings, they are overwhelming.

"God, it's good to see you." Will grins down at her as he picks up his bag and toolbox and they start walking toward the car.

"I look a complete mess," Holly says, stupidly, feeling like a nervous sixteen-year-old.

"No. You look lovely. I know it's ridiculous to say

this, but you look happier. Already," Will says. "I was sort of hoping I might get an invitation down here, and then there you were on the phone, my damsel in distress."

Holly blushes. "Not quite. If anyone's the damsel in distress, it's Paul. He's being a bit of an old woman about the kitchen cupboards, although I think money is a much bigger issue than any of us realized. He really seemed to panic when Anna said they needed replacing."

"Glad to be the knight in shining armor," Will says as they reach the car. "Hi, you two." He pauses before climbing in, looking into the backseat.

"I'm Will. You must be Oliver." He leans into the back and shakes Oliver by the hand. "And this cute little thing must be Daisy." Daisy smiles flirtatiously up at him and Will laughs, turning to Holly. "Good lord, Holly. She's exactly like you. She's gorgeous."

"Thank you," Holly turns the ignition on. "A bit of a handful but we love her."

"So—" Will turns in his seat so he's leaning back against the door, facing Holly, who feels horribly self-conscious as she drives—"how's everyone getting on? Any exciting bits of gossip?"

Holly barks with laughter. "God, Will. This is about the most dramatic gathering you could ever imagine. First, you have to swear not to tell anyone. If you're staying, I should fill you in on everything."

"I swear," he says solemnly, placing his hand over his heart, and Holly tells him the whole story.

"Tea?" Will hollers up from the kitchen and the gang gratefully lay down their tools and come, one by one, into the kitchen, to be met with a tray of steaming mugs and chocolate digestives.

Anna looks at the tea, then at Will admiringly. "You are really good," she says. "Any chance you would be interested in being a second husband?"

"Not the slightest bit interested even in being your first husband, thank you," Will says looking aghast when Paul shouts with laughter. "Sorry." He backtracks furiously. "I didn't mean that to come out the way it sounded. Not because of you, it's just that marriage isn't my bag."

Holly hears this and turns away quickly, busying herself with getting more milk from the fridge. She feels uncomfortable hearing him say marriage isn't his bag, which is absurd. What was she expecting? That he would say he's desperate to get married, and his idea of the perfect woman is Holly?

And more to the point, why is she even thinking about it? She's not out of her own marriage, and already she's looking to the next? *Ridiculous,* she shakes her head. *Don't be so childish,* she tells herself. A vision floats into her mind of herself sitting at the kitchen table, doodling. Holly Fitzgerald, Mrs. Will Fitzgerald. She shudders at the stupidity of it all, at how this obsession that she no longer seems to be able to pretend isn't real is turning her into a teenager.

There is no doubt about it being an obsession. There is no doubt that she has allowed herself to give in to it, to focus on Will instead of on her own unhappiness. To think only of him, to dream the dreams that have been lingering on the outer edges of her subconscious for months now.

The handful of times that she allowed herself to close her eyes and picture Will when Marcus was pounding away on top of her, led to yet more guilt, and she promised herself she wouldn't do it again.

But last night, lying in bed upstairs—the plumber had come and the defective pipe had been replaced so the house was finally warm—Holly had allowed herself to give in to the fantasies she had always been too frightened to invite in before.

She had lain in bed and thought of undressing Will. Imagined stroking his forearms, his chest. Imagined him kissing her, moving slowly down her body. She had come quickly and quietly and had fallen deeply asleep, waking up again in the early hours, this time with a different fantasy. Could Will in fact be the right man for her? If Marcus was—as he so clearly was—the wrong one, could Will be her soul mate? Could he be the one that she is destined to be with?

Holly has never particularly believed in soul mates. Perhaps for a while, when she was a dreamy-eyed teenager, but once she met Marcus she stopped believing in them. Until now. She looks across the kitchen table at Will, who is so real and seems so very right.

"So come on, be honest with us." Anna ribs Will. "You must get millions of passes made at you by bored horny housewives."

Will looks slightly sheepish. "Not millions, but I've had a few."

"A few what? Passes made or horny housewives?" Saffron laughs.

"Both," Will says. "In all seriousness, though, I haven't taken anyone up on those particular kinds of offers for a while. I had the misfortune to get caught by a husband who was supposed to be away on a business trip. His flight got canceled so he came home."

"Could it be more clichéd?" Saffron rolls her eyes.

"I know." Will laughs. "Wasn't bloody funny at the time, though. I fell down the stairs, pulling up my trousers, with this raving madman roaring he was going to kill me. Honestly, I was lucky to get out of that one alive. I retired from the business of mixing work with pleasure about a second later."

"Doesn't that make you think of Tom?" Paul looks around the table with a grin.

"What do you mean?" Olivia looks confused.

"Don't you remember that time he was upstairs in a bedroom with that girl, oh God, what was her name . . . pretty, blond, year above you. Kate something . . ."

"Oh *God!*" Saffron barks. "Kate Barrowman! I'd completely forgotten that!"

Holly and Olivia start to laugh as Paul continues telling the story to Will. "He was getting up to no good . . ."

"Almost to fourth base from what I remember," Holly adds, rolling her eyes.

"Yes, well, everyone was supposed to be out of the

house but her dad apparently had his workshop or something in the attic, and he came down and caught Tom and Kate, half naked, writhing around on the parents' bed. I think Tom had a similar thing—falling down the stairs as the father threatened to kill him."

There's a silence as they all sit, remembering Tom, remembering being sixteen, snuggled under coats in dark bedrooms on the top floors of unfamiliar houses, making out with strangers and swigging planters punch as they pretended to be sophisticated.

"This is very weird," Saffron breaks the silence softly, her voice in a half whisper.

"What?" The others look at her questioningly.

"*This*. That we're sitting here talking about Tom with Tom's brother, and Tom's not here. It's just . . ." She blinks hard two or three times, willing the tears that have suddenly welled up not to fall.

"It's just that Will looks exactly like Tom used to now that he's had his hair cut, and I keep catching myself wanting to call him Tom, or about to remind him of something he did or something we all did, and then I remember that it's not Tom because Tom is dead, and I just feel this enormous sense of loss." Saffron wipes a tear from her eye.

Nobody feels differently. They have all been sitting there thinking exactly the same thing, but no one has dared say it, no one has dared to admit their own grief or their own loss when Tom's brother is sitting in the room. *Tom's brother.* How could they possibly have a right to feel this way when his own brother seems to be managing fine?

"I'm so sorry I'm not Tom," Will says quietly, his voice breaking. "I'm sorry for all of you that it's not Tom sitting here, and mostly I'm sorry for me. I'm sorry that it wasn't me that was on that train. Tom was so good. Just all good, through and through. He was loved by everyone. He had a wife and children. He never deserved to be blown apart. I keep thinking that his absence has left such a gaping hole in so many people's lives when it could have been me, and I wouldn't have been missed. It should have been me," he says, as his own tears start to fall.

"That's not true, Will." Saffron turns to him. "It shouldn't have been you. You would be missed by a tremendous number of people and I'm so sorry, Will. I never meant to upset you or to make you feel unwanted."

Will stands up and allows Saffron to give him a hug before he walks quietly out of the back door. They all watch through the window as he walks across the field to the tree stump, where he sits down and buries his face in his hands.

"I feel horrible," Saffron says. "I didn't mean to make him feel bad."

"You did not," Anna says. "I have a sense this may have been . . . cathartic . . . for him. I imagine he has just been able to say the thing he has been carrying around with him for months, that he has never before been able to say. Can't you just see it all over his face? Poor man, the guilt he is carrying must be terrible."

Holly stands up with a start. "Keep an eye on the kids," she says quickly. "I'm just going to see if he's okay," and she disappears out of the door. She hasn't been able to take her eyes off Will, and knowing he was sitting there crying was tearing her heart apart. How can she not go to him? How can she let him feel these terrible feelings all by himself?

She tramples over the grass and stands behind him, resting a hand on his shoulder to let him know she's there, and when he turns, his eyes red, his face streaked with tears, she sinks down and puts her arms round him just as she would her own children, and they stay there, with Holly crouching, wrapped tightly in her arms as she rocks him gently and whispers in his ear, "It's okay. It's okay. It's all going to be okay."

When they come back in, everyone is still drinking tea around the table. Saffron goes straight up to Will and offers another apology. "I do owe you an amends," she says. "I want to tell you that I'm glad you're here. That I'm not expecting you to replace Tom, but that I'm glad you're with us. It helps and, in a funny way, as odd as it feels, it also feels very right that you're here."

"Hear, hear!" Paul raises his empty mug in a silent toast as the others join in.

"Not a replacement for Tom," Olivia says, munching her way through the rest of the biscuits that are rapidly disappearing from the plate. "Know that we're not saying that, but you fit in, in your own right. It's lovely having you here."

"And to Tom." Holly raises her mug and looks up at the ceiling. "For in his own twisted way, he's brought us all back together again. Thank you, Tom." The others look up and raise their own mugs. "To Tom," they say, and as they sip their tea there are tears in all of their eyes.

"Mummy?" Daisy and Oliver come in, their hands and faces covered with purple felt-tip ink. "We've finished coloring and now we don't know what to do." They scan the table, spying the biscuits and both faces light up.

"Go on." Holly laughs and pushes the plate toward them. "Just one. How would you like to watch a film?"

"Yay!" Both kids jump up and down.

"Can we watch *Ice Age 2*?" Oliver asks.

"No!" Daisy squeals. "I want to watch *The Little Mermaid*."

"No way," Oliver says. "I'm not watching a girl film. *Ice Age 2*, Mummy."

Daisy starts to cry.

"Enough!" Holly looks at both of them sternly. "I'm choosing the film." And she goes out to the car, bringing back *Shrek*.

"Oh not again," Oliver groans, but he follows them quietly as Holly sets the computer up in their room and puts the DVD on.

"You know what we should do?" Anna breaks the silence that descends. "We should cook a wonderful dinner tonight. Fancy clothes. Candlelight. Delicious food."

Paul bursts out laughing. "There's just one problem, my darling wife: we haven't got a table big enough for all of us to fit around at the same time."

"Not yet, but there's a filthy old trestle table in the barn. We could grab a tablecloth from the supermarket in Gloucester."

"Chairs?" Paul persists.

"Don't be such a killjoy." Anna tuts. "We could drag the benches in from the garden."

"Great idea!" Holly echoes. "Let's do it. God knows all of us could do with a bit of fun, and God knows I could do with a few drinks. Oh shit . . ." Her face falls and she looks nervously at Saffron. "I forgot. Obviously no drinks." She tries hard to hide her disappointment.

"I'll be fine," Saffron lays a hand on her arm. "I know I've had a couple of slips, but remember, guys, I've spent years surrounded by alcohol without wanting to have any. I don't mind if you have alcohol. Especially if it's red wine." She grimaces. "I've always hated red wine."

"Done!" Anna says, excitement sweeping her up, sweeping all of them up, removing all sensible thought. "Why don't we pack up and hit the shops now? We should make it there and back by six."

The iPod is plugged into Paul's speakers and KT Tunstall's sweet voice fills the room. Holly has made a deliciously retro coq au vin, Olivia is tackling the salad, and Anna is finishing off a gingerbread trifle. Saffron is whipping up some disgusting-looking fat-free, sugar-free concoction that is masquerading as some sort of butterscotch pudding, which she swears is delicious.

Paul walks past and swipes a finger around the top of her mixing bowl. "Mmm," he looks at Saffron in surprise, "that's pretty good. Sugar-free, fat-free, eh? What's in it?"

Saffron looks at him coolly. "Chemicals," she says, and as he recoils in horror Anna starts to laugh.

"Seriously," Anna says as she comes over. "What is in it?"

"Seriously," Saffron proffers the box proudly, "chemicals—additives and preservatives. Disgusting things that are probably making my insides melt. There ain't nothing natural about this gig."

"At least you'll die thin." Olivia doesn't get it, has never gotten this whole obsession with supposedly "healthy" eating, preferring to have a teaspoon of double cream than a gallon of fat-free milk.

"Exactly, my love." Saffron laughs, licking the spoon with rapturous, put-on joy. "I vill be sin and bee-yoo-tee-ful even ven I am ded."

Holly laughs and walks into the living room to finish setting the table. She stands back, delighted with how cozy it looks. The fire is blazing, there are candles filling the room with a warm glow; and the table, complete with place settings designed and executed by the kids, looks gorgeous.

"Come on, kids." Holly holds her hands out for Daisy and Oliver. "Bedtime."

"But Mummy . . ." Oliver starts to whine.

"No buts." She smiles. "It's already half an hour later than your usual bedtime. Come on. Up we go."

Holly kisses Daisy on the top of her head, standing back and watching her for a few seconds as she snores quietly, already fast asleep. "Good night," she whispers, "I love you," and as she tiptoes out of the room, she bumps into Will, who leans back on the wall, arms crossed, smiling down at her.

Holly's heart misses a beat.

There is a chemistry in the air, a static that is almost palpable. She looks expectantly up at Will, and he shakes his head as he continues smiling.

"It's really weird, seeing you as a mother," he says softly.

"Weird, how? Weird bad?"

"No, no. God, no. You seem to have a really warm, loving relationship with the kids. But weird because I've never thought of you as a mother, never known you as a mother. I mean, obviously I knew you had kids, but to see you so . . . I don't know . . . so grown-up, I suppose. I just always think of you as being young and, well, like me."

Holly raises an eyebrow. "You mean young and irresponsible?"

He shrugs. "I'm afraid so. I think I just never thought about the responsibilities you actually have. I mean, you're a grown-up. A proper one."

"So . . . does that mean you think of me differently now you've seen me with my kids?"

"A bit," he says.

"Uh-oh. Different good or different bad?"

"I could never think of you as anything bad," he whispers.

Neither of them is smiling anymore, and Holly's heart is beating very fast.

"So what are you thinking?" Her voice almost catching with apprehension.

"I'm thinking," he leans forward ever so slightly, "I'm thinking about what it would be like to kiss you."

If you had asked Holly what it was like to kiss someone for the first time, she would laugh and say she couldn't remember. She would say that she would be terrified to kiss someone now, that at approaching forty she has pretty much forgotten how it is done.

But she hasn't forgotten. Had forgotten perhaps how gorgeous it feels to kiss the man you've been longing for, to kiss the man who has occupied all your thoughts and fantasies for the best part of every day, to kiss the man who may be the one to save you from yourself, or at least, save you from your marriage.

She had forgotten the sweetness of a first kiss. Had forgotten how you lean your foreheads on one another's, looking into each other's eyes with a sweet smile when it is over, cupping each other's faces with your hands, wanting to drink the other in, wanting to just eat them up with a spoon.

She had forgotten.

Now she remembers.

CHAPTER TWENTY-FIVE

Each time Olivia leaves the table, Anna feels as if someone were twisting a knife in her heart. There is no mistaking why Olivia leaves—her face turns that peculiar shade of gray, and she runs to the bathroom, hand over her mouth.

This time Saffron follows her to see if she's okay, Anna going into the kitchen to bring out the salad.

It has been a wonderful meal. A meal filled with laughter. It is almost as if the tears they all cried earlier were extraordinarily cathartic, as if they were all able to shed—perhaps temporarily, perhaps not—the mantle of grief they have carried since arriving, with Tom's absence being so very noticeable.

But not Anna. Anna who never really knew Tom. Anna is carrying her grief for a different reason. Anna is trying so hard to focus on getting on with her life, trying to accept that perhaps she and Paul are not destined to have children but will have to adopt instead.

She is trying so hard not to resent Olivia, but as the evening wears on, with Olivia rushing off to the bathroom all the time, she is finding the sadness settling on her shoulders once again, her bravado slowly melting away.

Anna leans her hands on the counter for a second, breathing deeply. The bathroom is directly above the kitchen, and she realizes that she is able to hear everything from upstairs.

She hears Olivia retch into the toilet bowl, then a soft knocking before Saffron walks in. She can picture Saffron rubbing Olivia's back and hears her gently asking if she's okay.

"Why do they call it morning sickness?" she hears Olivia groan. "It lasts *all* bloody day."

"I had a friend who had this during the entire pregnancy," Saffron says. "Can you imagine? Her gynecologist told her it would be over at three months, but it went on for nine. Ghastly. They had her on all sorts of drugs, but nothing worked."

"Oh God, that's horrific," Olivia says. "Thank God this is going to be over soon."

"You're definitely not having it?"

There's a silence. "I can't," Olivia says in a soft voice. "What would I do with a baby? There's no room in my life, and frankly I've never been one of those women whose biological clock started ticking. Either mine wasn't working or I didn't have one."

"What about adoption?" Saffron asks. "Would you ever consider that?"

"I don't know. I've never thought about it."

Everyone looks up as Anna rushes into the dining room.

"Paul," she blurts out urgently. "I have an idea! We could adopt Olivia's baby!"

"What?" Paul shakes his head. Did he understand her correctly?

"No, no, I am serious! She does not want a baby and we do. Doesn't it make perfect sense?"

"Oh Anna," Paul says sadly. "I don't think she wants to have a baby at all. Listen to her, she's been throwing up for days. The last thing she wants is to go through a pregnancy. It's a wonderful idea, but I don't think it's ever going to happen."

"Why not ask?" Holly interrupts. "It is a wonderful idea, and you won't know unless you ask."

"Do you think?" Paul says doubtfully. "I think it's incredibly presumptuous."

"It's not!" Anna insists. "Imagine if she said yes! This could be the answer to everything. I swear, Paul, do you not think it is too much of a coincidence that Olivia is pregnant and does not want a child? And here she is, staying with us, when we have been trying for a baby for two years and now we are talking about adoption? I think God brought us all together for a reason, and I think this is it. I swear to you, I really do."

"God brought us together for what reason?" Saffron and Olivia have come down the stairs.

Paul looks down at his plate, not wanting to be the one to ask.

Anna waits until Olivia sits down, then looks straight at her. "Olivia . . ." She is suddenly nervous. "You know Paul and I have been trying IVF, and it has not worked. Well, we were thinking that, um, maybe, now you are pregnant and you do not want the baby . . . we were thinking that if you would consider having the baby, perhaps we could adopt it."

It is far more difficult for Anna to say this than she realized. She has always been impulsive, has never had any problems with asking for what she wants—you don't get to run the third most successful Internet company in the UK without knowing how to ask for what you want, but this is so important to her, something she wants *so* badly, she is uncharacteristically nervous, terrified the answer will be no.

"God . . . I . . . I don't know what to say." Olivia is shocked. Has never truly considered adoption as an option. For it's not simply that she doesn't want a baby, it's that she doesn't want to be pregnant, doesn't want to be any place other than where she was a few short weeks ago. She wants to pretend this never happened.

She doesn't want to have a growing bump, to have everyone ask her when the baby is due, only to turn up after nine months with no baby. She doesn't want to— oh horror—throw up for the next seven months.

But can she deal with an abortion? She has never had any particularly strong feelings about abortion. It's never been an issue that she's had to consider. Of course, she must know people who have had them, but if they have, they have never turned to her for help. It has never been a fact of her life until two weeks ago.

She has tried not to think about it. Not to think about what she will be doing—that there is a life growing inside her, which she has the ability to end. She hasn't thought about that but has merely thought of the one thing she wants, and the quickest way to achieve it—to turn the clock back.

"I don't know," she repeats, thinking for the first time about carrying a baby to term, what that would mean, giving birth and then giving a child away. "I didn't seriously think . . . hadn't thought . . ."

"We realize you'll need to think about it. Obviously," Paul interjects. "And we don't want you to feel any pressure or to do anything you don't want to do, but if you did decide to go through with the pregnancy and put the baby up for adoption, we would love to adopt your child."

"And think," Anna knows she is too eager, too excited, but she can't help herself, "you would still be around, still be part of the child's life."

"I need some time." Olivia looks first at Paul, then at Anna. "I think it's an incredible offer, but I need some time to think about it."

"Of course," Anna says. "Take as much time as you need."

Under the table, Will strokes Holly's hand. They are sitting next to each other. They have barely been able to function throughout this meal, have certainly not been able to keep their hands to themselves.

Their hands have been clasped the entire time. Will lays down his knife and reaches down to where no one can see, resting his hand on Holly's leg, or running a finger stealthily around her wrist, sending shivers of electricity up and down her spine, an electricity she hasn't felt in years.

An electricity she never expected to feel again.

The others may not see, but they know. The air around Holly and Will is fizzing. Holly may think she is being subtle by not looking at Will, not giving any indication that anything has happened, but there is now a thread joining them, a thread that may not be visible but can clearly be felt.

Saffron sees. She clears the plates, and on the way back from the kitchen her eyes are drawn to Will's hand drawing quickly back from Holly's lap. She already knew, of course, but she is too caught up in her own troubles to give it much thought.

For Saffron did think she could handle the alcohol. She thought tonight would be like all those other nights when she could happily sip her water or her juice and not feel the taste of alcohol on her tongue, not feel the happy buzz as the vodka loosens her up, makes her warm and silly.

But as the evening progresses it is becoming harder and harder to think about anything other than alcohol. Her mind is barely focused on the conversation, she loses herself in a fantasy of everybody leaving the room so she can grab the bottles of wine, tip her head back, and pour them down.

It is so real, she has to physically stop herself from reaching for a bottle, grabbing it and drinking the contents, there and then, in front of everyone.

She can't sit still. She keeps jumping up from the table, her body suffused with an itch for which there seems to be only one cure. And yet there is the part of her that doesn't want to and knows she shouldn't, but she's pretty certain she doesn't have the strength or the willingness to fight.

When Saffron stepped into her first AA meeting, she knew she didn't have a choice. Her meager earnings from various advertisements were all being spent on alcohol, and she was beginning to lose jobs. She was becoming known for being unreliable, turning up hungover, or worse, drunk.

At first, she would just drink at night. Like everybody else, she told herself. She was young, in her twenties, and that's what they did at night. When she hit thirty, she tried telling herself the same thing while the drinking progressed and her career stopped rising to the heights that all the press had predicted.

By her early thirties, she stopped being the next big thing, had started being a has-been. It was her agent who brought her into AA, and she was been sober from her very first meeting, knowing there wasn't another choice.

Ninety in ninety. Ninety meetings in ninety days. For the first time since arriving in America, she felt she had a home, had a fellowship of people who truly understood her, who listened without judgment, supported her with what felt like, extraordinarily enough, unconditional love.

She vowed, back then, never to drink again. She did exactly what she was told to do: don't drink; get a sponsor; work the steps. She thought she was fine.

Recovered? Perhaps. Others described themselves as recover*ing* alcoholics, a process that never stopped. They talked, Saffron included, of having a progressive disease, one that didn't go away or get better, one that would inevitably lead to death if they gave in to it.

"I'm Saffron and I'm a grateful recovering alcoholic," she got used to saying. Yet at some time over the last few months, she stopped thinking of herself as recovering and started thinking of herself as recovered. Which is when the problems started.

And now, just like those days of old, Saffron finds herself wishing the evening was over so she could drink in peace. Wishing she could escape to run down to that lovely cozy pub and settle in a corner, drinking herself into oblivion.

She misses Pearce. Misses him so very much. She misses her life—the simplicity of it all. And as lovely as it should be here in the country with the friends who have known her forever, she'd rather be somewhere else.

She'd rather be drinking.

They get to bed by midnight. Saffron kisses everyone good night, distracted as she plans her return to the kitchen for a drink. She goes upstairs and listens to the sounds of the house, waiting for absolute quiet, waiting until she can sneak downstairs in secrecy and drink the bottle of wine she surreptitiously hid behind the cleaning stuff under the kitchen sink.

Every time she hears a footstep, a door creak, a toilet

flushing, she wants to scream with irritation, cast a spell to send everyone into a dreamless sleep.

Eventually, at one o'clock, she is certain the house is quiet. She pads out and downstairs to the kitchen, opening the cupboard door under the kitchen sink, reaching toward the back.

"Fuck!" she hisses as a bottle of bleach falls over, the crash shockingly loud in the stillness.

"What are you doing?" Saffron jumps as Olivia stands in the doorway, rubbing the back of her neck with a cold, wet flannel.

"I'm . . ." Saffron, so good at excuses, has nothing to say, nothing to explain why she is rooting around under the sink at one o'clock in the morning. She shuts the cupboard door quickly, but Olivia moves her out of the way and sinks down herself, reaching behind the bleach and Fairy Liquid to pull the wine bottle out.

She shakes her head, disappointed, resigned, and uncorks the bottle, both of them watching in silence as the wine glugs its way slowly down the drain.

"Why?" Olivia turns to look at Saffron, who is torn between wanting to either slap Olivia or burst into tears.

"Why do you think?" she snaps, anger getting the better of her. "Because I needed a drink, for God's sake. I'm an alcoholic, aren't I? Isn't that what we do?" She snorts derisively. "Why? What a stupid bloody question. Why *not*?"

"Saffron!" Olivia is shocked, upset, her voice rising. "I'm trying to help you. We're all trying to help you.

Do you think any of us would be here if it weren't for you? We've all bent over backward trying to make you better, keeping the press away from you, keeping you away from alcohol. How are we supposed to help you if you're not willing to help yourself?"

"But don't you see?" Saffron hisses. "I'm not willing to help myself. That's exactly the problem. I wish I was. I'm praying for the willingness to help myself, but it isn't there. All I want to do is drink."

"Sssh!" Olivia is suddenly distracted. "What's that?"

"What?"

"Listen. That . . . Oh my God, is that groaning?"

Saffron stops in her tracks and both of them move toward the door, listening to the unmistakable sound of a couple making love.

"Is that Paul and Anna?" Olivia is confused, the sound coming from somewhere else.

Saffron starts to laugh and, for a minute, her urge to drink recedes. "No!" she whispers. "It's Holly and Will."

"No!" Olivia starts to smile.

"I know." Saffron rolls her eyes. "Could you believe the electricity between them over dinner?"

"Wow. Do you think she's sleeping with him? Already?"

"Oh God, I can't listen." Saffron covers her ears as they hear a soft moan, a louder, distinctly male, groan.

Olivia giggles. "I feel like I'm back at university. Jesus. I haven't listened to noises like that in years."

Saffron nods. "Come on. Let's go back in the kitchen. I feel like a voyeur."

They walk back and Saffron sits down at the table, sinking her head on her arms as Olivia fills the kettle then turns to look at her. "I don't suppose a cup of tea is enough to stop you wanting to drink?"

"Hardly. But it's better than nothing. Oh God, Olive," Saffron looks up at Olivia pleadingly, "what am I going to do?"

"Oh darling." Olivia reaches down and puts her arms around her, hugging her tight. "We'll help you. Just don't drink. Not today."

"I know," Saffron whispers. "Just for today. A day at a time."

"Anyway," Olivia says, smiling, "the pubs are all closed and that wine was the last of the bottles we bought. You couldn't drink right now even if you wanted to."

And I want to, Saffron thinks. Still. I want to.

Holly lies snuggled up against Will, his arm wrapped tightly around her shoulders as he lies on his back, snoring gently.

She turns her head to look at him, wanting to trace his profile with her fingers, but she doesn't, too scared she'll wake him. What she wants to do is exactly what she's doing right now—drinking him in, watching him breathing, marveling at the feeling of wanting to snuggle up with someone, wanting to stroke her fingers over his chest, rest her fist gently in his clavicle, cover his shoulders with kisses.

She knew, from the second he kissed her, that something more would happen. She had wanted to have sex, wanted to make love, but she found that she couldn't go further than foreplay, couldn't allow penetration, even though it seemed to be the one thing she wanted more than anything else.

It was a bridge she wasn't prepared to cross, not yet. But oh how lovely the rest of it was. How lovely kissing was.

With Marcus, she always tried very hard not to kiss him, would close her eyes as Marcus was thrusting into her, and lose herself in a fantasy, knowing that should she open her eyes and see Marcus's face looming above her, any pleasure there was would disappear in a flash.

She and Will may not have had sex, but she made him come, came herself—oh how she came . . . And after she came, Will lay there and cuddled her, and he talked. And talked. And talked.

She was stunned. Was so used to that perfunctory kiss, rolling over to her side of the bed for a Marcus-free dream, she had forgotten that people did this, that they cuddled up and talked softly.

This is intimacy. This is what she has missed.

Perhaps tomorrow they will be able to make love, she thinks. Perhaps tomorrow she will not feel guilty. Perhaps tomorrow she will trust him enough, trust herself enough. For tonight this is all she needs. She plans on getting out of bed in a minute, going back to her own room; but before she knows it, she has fallen into a peaceful sleep.

At five in the morning, Holly wakes up. She swims into consciousness, aware that she is squeezed up against Will in the middle of the bed. She can feel his body the length of hers, and she lies for a minute trying to get used to the sensation.

She and Marcus never touched in their sleep. How odd, then, that unconsciously she would allow Will to get so close. Holly slips out of bed and pads down the hallway to her own room, grateful that the children haven't awakened, haven't found her with Will—how stupid, she shakes her head. Not worth the risk, even though it was an accident, even though she never meant to fall asleep in his arms.

Holly lies in bed replaying every second of the night before. From that first kiss to the stolen hand-holding under the table, to lying naked with this man she has desired more than she has ever desired anyone.

She lies in bed smiling, and when Daisy wakes up and climbs into bed with her "for a snuggle," she strokes Daisy's face and gazes into her eyes with love. How lucky I am, she thinks, to have my children, to have all these people I love right here with me. And lying in her bed, with Daisy's arms wrapped around her neck, Holly feels, for the first time in years, entirely and unreservedly happy.

CHAPTER TWENTY-SIX

"I'm exhausted," Olivia announces over breakfast. "We've all been working like dogs, and I haven't seen anything of the area. Would it be awful if we took the afternoon off?"

"I think that is a great idea," Anna says. "God knows you all deserve it. I am going to stay, I think. We are so close to finishing those bloody floors. I will help Paul, but you could go into Gloucester, do some shopping. And Holly, if you want to leave those yummy children with me, I would love to babysit."

"You would?" Holly's face lights up. "That would be amazing!"

"So you'll come?" Olivia turns to her. "And Saff? Will?" They all nod.

"I wouldn't mind seeing what the shops are like." Saffron gets up and pours herself some more coffee. "I feel a bit of a spending spree coming on."

"You won't find many designer labels in Gloucester." Paul laughs.

"She doesn't need any with me here." Anna pouts. "Seriously, Saff, if ever you need anything you know you just have to ask me."

"I do know that, and thank you, darling. I will. I just want to get presents for friends back home."

"Home as in LA?" Holly asks.

Saffron nods.

"Friends as in Pearce?" she asks again. Saffron shrugs.

"I would like to get something for Pearce. Not that I even know if I'll see him anymore."

"Have you been in touch?" Olivia says gently.

"He's been texting me, but it's obviously not the same as talking to him every day."

"What is he like?" Anna ventures curiously, the question all of them have been dying to ask but none of them wanting to bring him up. None of them wanting to appear too uncool, too impressed, too keen.

So Saffron tells them. She tells them first about most of the actors in Hollywood. She tells them of people who have struggled from humble beginnings, who have then made it big, have not known how to deal with the sudden fame and fortune.

She tells them of young starlets, featured in every gossip magazine, every week, who get swept up in the Hollywood party life of drink, drugs, and sex with a small coterie of wealthy playboys who seem to shuffle the women among them. She talks of how these same starlets are desperate to stay famous, yet none seem to know how to treat people nicely, to be kind, gracious, warm. None of them seem to remember that if you are not nice to people on the way up, these same people will not treat you well on the way down, for there is always a way down.

She tells them of huge Hollywood names leading secret double lives. Some involving substance abuse; most involving affairs with partners of the same sex, signing secret contracts with naive young actors and actresses to date them, and sometimes marry them, while carrying on the front for years as they sleep their way through the grips and handlers on the sets of their movies.

She tells them of how lost she felt when she first got there. That she thought she was a good judge of people, knew how people worked, trusted that when someone said something was black, it was black.

But she learned that in Los Angeles nothing and no one is quite what they seem. She learned that she would be called back to audition again and again, promised a part, told she was the perfect fit, that they had wanted her and only her, were thrilled she would be in the movie, only to open *Variety* a few days later and find Drew Barrymore had the part. No one ever bothered to tell her; they had clearly been lying through their teeth, which came as naturally to them as waking up in the morning.

She learned never to get excited about a movie until the contracts arrived at her agent's office and were signed. She learned not to trust anyone, not the actress friends she thought she had, who would have dropped her friendship in a second for a part, and not the good-looking producers and directors, who subtly—oh so subtly—offered to make her huge if she would just do something for *them*.

She tells them that integrity is something she has found to be in short supply and that when she went to that first AA meeting, it wasn't just that it stopped her from drinking, saved her life, it was that for the first time in LA she found *real* people. People who may have been in the same business as she was, but were living honestly, had the humility to know they were no better nor worse than anyone else they met, were able to say what they meant and to do so lovingly and kindly.

Not everyone, she says. AA meetings are filled with wannabe actors and actresses who heard that this is the place to get work, the place to make contacts, to see and be seen. But you quickly learned who is real and who is not; and the wannabes, the fake alcoholics, are quietly left alone by the members who needed this program.

She tells them about Pearce. About how honest he is in the meetings and how brave she thinks he is when everyone knows him, anyone could go to the press.

"But it's Alcoholics *Anonymous*," Anna says. "Who would go to the press?"

"It happens," Saffron says. "There are breaches all the time."

She tells them that one of the traditions is not to gossip, and yet she has lost count of the times she has overheard members gossiping about others, even gossiping about Pearce.

She tells them that he is a kind man, that he genuinely thinks of others, treats others as he himself wants to be treated. The money he makes—the millions from his movies—he describes as a blessing. He gives a huge proportion away each year to charities he supports, but quietly, often anonymously.

She describes him as funny. Gentle. Sweet. She says he is the wisest man she has ever known, with a sensitivity and perceptiveness that is almost female, and yet he is also the most male man she has ever known.

She says that above all else, she considers him her best friend. That whatever he is doing or wherever he may be in the world, he has always been there for her when she needs him.

And finally there is his marriage. A business arrangement, Saffron explains. He has too much to lose if he leaves. They have been waiting for the right time.

"Wouldn't now be the right time?" Paul ventures.

"One would think so, right?" Saffron snorts to hide her fear. Because, of course, that is exactly what she thinks and has always thought, what a secret part of her has often fantasized about: if their relationship were to come out in the press, what reason could there possibly be for him to stay?

"Who wants to play Monopoly?" Anna pulls Daisy's hat off as they all stomp inside after their nature walk, Oliver swinging a plastic bag half full with feathers, stones, and pebbles they found down by the creek.

"So much for you helping me," Paul says, coming into the kitchen and smiling as he watches Anna crouch down to help Daisy off with her coat. So lovely to see her with children, so clear that she is one of those women whose maternal instinct is just so entirely natural.

What a horrible irony it is that she is not able to have her own children.

Paul doesn't realize that it is easier to be the perfect mother with children who are not your own. That children you have temporarily do not push your buttons in the way your own children do. That when those children aren't actually yours, you are not exhausted or stressed or distracted when you are with them.

Holly is a good mother, but she rarely does what Anna is doing with the children this afternoon. She rarely gets down on her hands and knees and plays with them. That is Frauke's job, she tries to tell herself. Surely. She is around for her children all the time, but rarely this past year, struggling with the depths of her unhappiness, has she been truly present.

Everyone agrees that Holly is a wonderful mother, but Holly carries around a burden of guilt because this past year she has not been the mother she could be nor the mother she once was.

In withdrawing from life, and from her marriage, she has also, she realizes now, withdrawn from her children at a time when they needed her most. She has realized this since being here. She is already feeling lighter, happier, having nothing to worry about other than the mindless jobs of painting or sanding or tiling, her children delighted to be working away with her, by her side.

And lucky Daisy and Oliver have Anna today, who is present in every way. Who has decided she has nothing else to do except play with Daisy and Oliver. If Daisy wants to make beds out of twigs she has found, Anna will help her. If Oliver wants to crack open a geode he thinks he has found, she will help him. She will not run up to her computer to check her e-mails every few minutes. Nor will she shush them while she's on the phone. She will not stick them in front of the television while she makes supper, to get some peace and quiet, nor will she shout at them to stop fighting.

Because they don't fight. They have a grown-up's undivided attention. Why on earth would they fight?

Holly and Will, Olivia and Saffron are standing at the edge of the pedestrian section in town, cobbled streets beckoning invitingly. Will needs to find new head-phones for his iPod, and Saffron wants to look at the touristy shops on the other side.

"Let's split up," Saffron suggests, a smile twitching at the corners of her mouth. "Holly, why don't you go with Will, and Olivia can come with me?"

"Great!" Will says. "Let's meet back here in an hour."

Olivia laughs as they walk off. "That was very nice of you, but you know they have absolutely no idea that we know."

"I figure a young couple in lurrve need a little time together." Saffron laughs too.

"Do you think they're in love?"

"They're definitely in lust. Does that count? Did you see, in the car, she kept touching him when she thought no one was looking. Oh God," says Saffron with a sigh. "I miss that. I miss Pearce."

"It sounds like you have something very special."

Saffron stops and turns to look at Olivia. "Thank you." She smiles as she blinks back tears. "Thank you for saying that. I think we do." Turning back, she links her arm through Olivia's as they walk. "And what about you, Olive? So far you've said little about the father. Isn't there more to the story now? Can't you make things work?"

"God, I just don't know. Sometimes I lie in bed and I think that maybe there's a way. But, Saff, this was a fling, nothing more. I heard from him once, and honestly, even if I thought there was a smidgen of a chance he might be interested, I just can't see how it could work."

"I still can't quite believe you managed to get yourself pregnant. Aren't you, aren't we all, old enough to know better?"

Olivia shakes her head, almost in disbelief at her stupidity. "I know. In this day and age I can't believe it either, but it was about a minute after my period stopped. I know this sounds ridiculous but I didn't even think it could happen then."

"Hmmm. I seem to recall human biology never was your best subject."

"Oh thanks. That was largely due to you looking at me and making me giggle every time they talked about the human reproductive system."

"That wasn't me. That was Holly!" Saffron is indignant.

"It was both of you. I hadn't thought about that for years. That dragon Mrs. Steener, who used to tower over us and bellow . . ."

"Mrs. Steener came to see me in a play I was in after I left university. She was really nice actually. It was the first time I realized that teachers were human beings too."

Olivia gives her a sideways look. "At St. *Catherine's*? Are you *sure*?"

"Oh yes, I'm sure. I kept in touch with Jane Fellowes for years, although I haven't actually spoken to her for about a year."

"Miss Fellowes? The music teacher? That's completely mad. Why would you do that?"

"I really liked her. She was having a raging affair with Martin Hanover, you know. For years."

"You're kidding!" Olivia is truly shocked. "Miss Fellowes and Mr. Hanover? How did we not know that?"

"They had to be enormously discreet. The headmistress would have had both their heads on a platter if she'd known."

"God. But Mr. Hanover! I had a bit of a crush on him myself."

"I think everyone did. Not that he was exactly crushworthy, but as the only man in a sea of young females with raging hormones . . ."

". . . beggars can't be choosers and all that." Olivia laughs.

"I know. You do see how these mad affairs happen,

with male teachers jumping into bed with dangerous adolescents. All-girl schools are just hotbeds of yearning and lustful fantasies. Anyway, back to the subject in hand . . ."

"You were the one who digressed."

"I did." Saffron nods. "And I apologize. So, no protection even in these dangerous days of STDs and all kinds of nastiness, but tell me more about this Fred. And more to the point, *where* is Fred?"

"He's in Boston. Back home. He's gorgeous, Saffron. Exactly the kind of man I would have fallen in love with when I was younger, but he's young. Thirty-three, and it really was just a fling. There's no reason for him to know."

"You don't think he has a right to know, given that it is his child?"

"Saffron, I don't see the point in freaking him out. I'm never going to see him again. Why ruin his life or give him this information when I'm not going to have this child? Why bother giving him the heartache? My child, my body." She sighs deeply. "My decision."

"So . . . you haven't thought about Paul and Anna's offer, then?"

"I have. It's about all I have been thinking about. I just don't know. One minute, I feel I have to do what's right for me, however selfish, and I can't face going through a pregnancy, particularly feeling as awful as this, and for what? Then the next minute, I think about Paul and Anna and how hard they've been trying, how desperately they want a baby, and the most wonderful thing in the world would be for me to give them mine. I keep jumping from one to the other. I don't know. I honestly don't know what I'm going to do."

Saffron puts an arm around her shoulders and squeezes for a second. "Whatever decision you make it will be the right one for you. It has to be the right one for you. I understand you wanting to make Paul and Anna happy, and I think it's probably the most selfless, giving thing you can do for a friend, but you would have to be fine with it, have to be fully reconciled, I would think; and, if you're not, then you know what your decision is."

They walk for a while in silence until they reach a gift shop that is obviously doing a brisk trade in catering to American tourists. The window is filled with a miniature village, tiny thatched Cotswold cottages, some of which light up, a couple of which play music.

Saffron yelps with laughter. "Oh joy!" She stands outside the shop, smiling with delight. "Aren't they the most ghastly things you've ever seen? My American friends will love them!"

Olivia turns to look at her in horror. "Because they're ghastly?"

"Absolutely. No one I know back in Los Angeles has any taste. They assume they can buy it by employing the best decorators, so all their houses look exactly the same, and they're all mad Anglophiles—they'd go crazy over this shit."

They go inside and Saffron quickly sweeps almost a dozen assorted houses onto the counter. The young girl smiling shyly and serving them keeps stealing looks at Saffron. At first she thinks she must be someone she knows, there is something so familiar about her, but she doesn't know anyone that posh, has never known anyone that posh, and as she watches the two women walk around the shop, she realizes who it is.

Saffron Armitage! The film star! For the publicity has served to elevate Saffron's status enormously in the eyes of the world at large, particularly naive shop girls in the Cotswolds.

"You'll never guess what!" she whispers on the phone to her best friend when they have gone. "You'll never guess who just came into the shop! Saffron Armitage!"

"You're joking!" her friend says. "You should call the papers! The *Sun* is printing a number asking for her whereabouts! Go on! You could make yourself some money."

The girl laughs. "Nah," she says. "I'm too shy. Anyway, she was nice. I don't want to mess up her life. Still, a bit bloody exciting. Not too often we get a film star in the shop. I wish I'd asked for her autograph."

On the other side of town, Holly and Will sit in a tea shop. They are surrounded by elderly women with blue and pink rinses, sipping English breakfast tea out of delicate floral-printed, mismatched china cups, a few chips here and there, which nobody seems to mind, slightly tarnished silver trays on each table, piled high with tea sandwiches, tiny cakes, and lopsided scones studded with dried-out raisins.

Will ordered the tea, but neither of them is eating anything, neither of them having the slightest appetite today, too high on each other to do anything other than gaze, kiss, touch.

Even now, tucked away at a table in the corner, they are kissing. Like teenagers, utterly oblivious to the rest of the people in the tea shop, some of whom are openly staring at them with envy, big smiles on their faces, others tutting disapprovingly and trying not to look.

Holly and Will don't care. Their passion doesn't have to be hidden anymore. This is the first time since last night they have been able to touch each other openly, kiss each other openly, lay heads on shoulders, no holds barred.

"I can't believe this has happened to me," Holly says, unable to stop smiling. Unable to stop taking Will's face in her hands and planting soft kisses all over it—on his forehead, his eyes, his nose, his cheeks.

Will is adoring being adored. As the apple of his mother's eye, he has always adored being adored. But he'd be lying if he said he wasn't a little apprehensive about this. Holly isn't just anyone, she's *Holly*. Holly Mac! Almost family, not to mention the fact that she's married.

He got involved, seriously involved—the flings through work don't count—with a married woman once before. He had thought she was on the verge of finalizing a divorce but, in fact, she had only recently separated, was still in couple's counseling, had a husband who thought they were going to be mending the marriage.

Will found himself involved in the divorce. He was named in the petition, had to deal with a woman who wasn't, as he had thought, fun and clever and independent, but one who coped with the stress of the divorce by crying and screaming and clinging. He wanted to leave, but he felt he was in too deep, didn't know how to extricate himself.

He swore he'd never go down that road again.

Yet here he is with Holly. Object of his teenage fantasies, a fantasy he never dreamed he'd fulfill.

Although isn't it true that you should never fulfill your fantasies because the reality rarely measures up? As much as he adores Holly, as much as he has loved this friendship they have built, he is unprepared for this outpouring of affection, unprepared for the way the floodgates of adoration seemed to burst open in Holly last night.

Anyone who has known Holly from when she was young would describe her as passionate. Holly, much like Saffron, would love or she would hate. She, much like Saffron, saw the world in black and white. She was luckier than Saffron in that she didn't have the addictive gene. Or perhaps she wasn't luckier. Perhaps that would have helped.

In marrying Marcus, Holly tried to change who she was. *Passion hadn't ever served me well*, she decided. She wasn't going to be black and white anymore. She was going to live in shades of gray. *So much healthier,* she thought. *Now,* she decided, *I am thinking like a grown-up.* So she suppressed her passion. Neither loved nor hated. Mostly she just existed.

And now, since last night, she feels as if Will has awoken feelings in her she didn't know she still had. She trusts him enough to be honest with him about those feelings, never thinking that he might not feel the same way. Never thinking that Maggie didn't tell her to be careful with Will because Maggie doesn't love her son, but because Maggie knows that the one thing guaranteed to send Will running for the hills, quite literally for that matter—Thailand, New Zealand, Vietnam—is adoration.

Maggie remembers who Holly was. She knows who Holly is. She still sees the stream of passion bubbling away underneath and knows full well that if anyone could bring it to the surface, it would be Will.

Maggie is the one person who knows about the night that Tom and Holly slept together. Maggie had held her breath with anticipation, fighting the excitement that made her shiver inside, for she had always hoped that Tom and Holly would get together, had always thought they had the ability to bring out the best in each other, to be one of those couples that could change the world.

Tom was too young then. He wasn't ready. Maggie always hoped that time would work its magic, that they would find their way back to being lovers again through their friendship, but then Marcus had come along, then Sarah, and she knew that was one wish she would have to set aside.

And now Will. *That* she had never imagined. Although naturally, she is not surprised. But her fear is that, once Will has unleashed a passion in Holly, he will not be able to deal with it.

She doesn't know what she has done wrong, but Will has always been frightened of commitment.

Others say he just hasn't met the right woman, and she is willing to accept that may be so. But there are those other times when she knows she has babied him too much, given him unrealistic expectations that have taken away any responsibility he may have had to deal with, in case it caused him discomfort or pain.

If she were to walk past the tea shop today, look inside and see Holly and Will, Holly gazing adoringly up at Will, resting her head on his shoulder as she strokes his hand and turns his head toward hers for a kiss, Maggie would groan.

"Oh God," she would whisper. "Not again. Please not Holly." Other people might look at Will and think he feels the same way, but not Maggie. And she is, after all, his mother. She is the woman who knows him better than anyone else in the whole world.

CHAPTER TWENTY-SEVEN

The old Land Rover bumps over the driveway as Holly, Saffron, Olivia, and Will head back home with the trunk filled with food for tonight's dinner and, of course, Saffron's prized Cotswold cottages.

There is another car in the driveway as they pull up to the house. From afar, Holly catches her breath, but it couldn't be . . . could it? A black Mercedes, a recognizable number plate.

"Whose car is that?" Saffron wonders out loud. "Doesn't look like the plumber."

"No." Holly's heart sinks to her knees. "It's Marcus."

Her first instinct is to hide. Childish, she knows, but she doesn't want to see him, doesn't want to face him, wants to continue to pretend, as she has been pretending these last few days, that she has no husband, that she is as free and single as Will.

Oh God. *Will.* How difficult this will be. How uncomfortable. Is it possible that Marcus will be able to see the guilt in her eyes? Is it possible he will look at her and know—*sense*—that she has been unfaithful?

Although she is still telling herself she has not been unfaithful. If ever she were impeached, she thinks wryly, she knows what she would say: "I did not have sex with that man."

She turns her head, aware that Will is looking at her.

"You okay?" he mouths, and she nods, swallowing hard. She is shocked but not surprised that Marcus is here. Marcus is a man who believes he must get what he wants.

Memories flood into her head as they drove closer. The countless times Marcus decided he wasn't being treated importantly enough. In restaurants, hotels, airports. Marcus demanding to see the manager, never introducing himself as Marcus Carter, always insisting on being called Mr. Carter—even when he was in his twenties—to men who were far more important and senior than he, then explaining imperiously why their behavior wasn't acceptable.

He usually bullied them into submission. He got upgrades, freebies, and letters of apology. It didn't matter that all of them disappeared into their offices thinking he was a pompous arse, rolling their eyes when their secretaries buzzed through to inform them that Mr. Carter was on the phone. What mattered to Marcus was that he got what he wanted.

He always got what he wanted.

He was treated as important because he demanded it. People kowtowed to him, pretending to be happy to see him because he expected it and because he made too much of a scene if they didn't.

Holly has always been embarrassed by the way Marcus treats people. Holly treated everybody exactly the same. She doesn't judge them by what they look like or how important they are; and there have been times, so many times, when she has been mortified by Marcus's behavior and wanted the ground to open up and swallow her whole as she listened to him rant and rave about someone's unacceptable behavior.

These last few days have been the happiest days she's had in years. Fourteen years, to be precise. She has barely given Marcus a second thought, and—oh God, why?—now he's here, and as Holly climbs reluctantly out of the car, she doesn't even realize that the veil of unhappiness, the veil that has always protected her from Marcus, has kept her both withdrawn from the rest of the world and safe from harm, has silently and stealthily slipped over her head.

Marcus is sitting at the kitchen table with Daisy on his lap. Her arms are wound tightly around his neck, and she has a huge grin on her face as she says over and over again, "Daddy! I love my daddy! I love my daddy!" Oliver is running excitedly around the kitchen table, holding the bag of things he collected on the nature walk, explaining what each thing is as Marcus tries to divide his attention between the two.

Holly stands in the doorway watching for a while, everybody too immersed in what they are doing to notice her, when someone taps her on the arm. She turns to see Anna, a look of apology on her face.

"I'm sorry," she mouths. "I didn't know what else to do."

Holly places a reassuring hand on her arm. "It's okay," she whispers back. "I'm a little shocked, but I'm glad he's with the kids."

Daisy looks up and sees Holly. "Mummy!" she squeals, wriggling off Marcus's lap and running over to her, wrapping her arms this time around Holly's legs.

"Hi, darling," Holly kneels down to give her a kiss, grateful she doesn't have to meet Marcus's eye, grateful she can busy herself with Daisy, win just a few more seconds of time before she has to confront the inevitable.

"Holly?" She hears something—anger? Hurt? Dismay?—in his voice and finally looks up.

"Hi, Marcus."

"Holly, we need to talk. Anna said she would look after the children. I thought maybe we could go for a walk."

Holly nods. She knew this moment would come. She just wishes she was a little more prepared for it.

The others stay away. They are huddling together upstairs in one of the bedrooms, clearly talking about Marcus. An uncomfortable silence falls as Holly walks in.

"Okay, okay!" Saffron puts guilty hands up in the air and Holly raises an eyebrow. "We're sorry. We were talking about you. Are you okay?"

"Depends on your definition of okay. Listen, Anna, can you take the kids again? Marcus and I are going for a walk."

They don't say anything for a while. Holly is hunched up, hands tucked firmly in her pockets, shoulders raised to protect her from the wind. And Marcus.

The sun is dipping slowly behind the bare branches of the trees lining the edge of the field, and Holly looks over at the sky, thinking that under different circumstances the peace and beauty of this scene would redeem her soul.

Holly loves walking. Loves exploring. Was in heaven in Gloucester with Will, not just because she was with Will, but because they were wandering around, chatting, going into shops that caught their eye, exploring narrow lanes that were off the beaten track, finding unexpected tea shops and making the time to go in and have tea.

This was how she lived her life before Marcus. She loved nothing better than exploring or going for long walks in the country with or without friends. She always dreamed of having someone to share this with, someone who would happily meander through the streets with her, explore, be her partner and companion in everything she did.

But Marcus hates walking. Hates doing anything much other than working and occasionally shopping, but only in expensive shops where he is treated as he deems appropriate. Bond Street became their regular Saturday outing, not for any reason other than it kept Marcus happy.

They would go on holiday, and Holly would ask him if he wanted to go for a walk, and his answer was always no. Last summer they went to Key West, and Marcus sulked the entire time because Little Palm Island was fully booked, and they'd ended up staying at the Ocean Cottages, which Marcus thought was beneath him. He complained bitterly to the front desk manager about their room and was upgraded to a suite, which he still thought was horrendous. It ruined their trip.

He walked up Duval Street with her, hurrying her along each time she wanted to stop at a bar where live music was pouring out and scores of people milled around, looking as if they were having fun. All except Holly and Marcus.

She peered longingly into those bars. "Can't we just sit at the bar and have a beer?" she pleaded, but Marcus sniffed disdainfully. "The music's much too loud, Holly. You think you'd enjoy it but, trust me, you'd be asking to leave in two minutes."

He didn't want to go on the tour of Hemingway's house. Nor did he want to explore the hidden gardens or the beautiful old houses tucked away. So she went on her own while he stayed in the hotel and worked on the computer.

And now, strolling across the field, Holly thinks about how different they are. How different they have always been. And she wonders why she never admitted it to herself sooner.

"We have to talk," Marcus says eventually, his voice still strained. Gruff and tough. The Marcus she has always known.

"Okay," Holly says slowly. She doesn't want to be the

one to talk. She wants to listen first, to hear what he has to say.

Marcus takes a deep breath. "I didn't mean what I said on the phone," he says quickly. "I thought I meant it at the time, but I . . ." He tails off, then looks over at her for a second, showing his distress. "I never thought you would still go."

Holly knows this. Knows that Marcus was employing the same bullying tactics he always has, fully expecting Holly to back down the way she always has. This time, though, for the first time, it didn't work.

There is a long silence as Marcus waits for Holly to respond. She doesn't. She doesn't yet know what to say.

"Holly," he says again, and this time he places a hand on her arm to stop her, to force her to look up at him. "I love you," he says pleadingly. "I don't understand what's happening to us. I don't understand why you came here when you knew how important it was to me that you didn't."

I know, thinks Holly. *I have always known how important it is that I obey you.*

"But that doesn't matter now," Marcus says. "I've forgiven you. And I want you to come home now. I want us to be together again."

"You don't get it, do you, Marcus?" Holly is incredulous. "This isn't about me coming down here or disobeying you. This is what I was trying to tell you that night we went for dinner."

"What night we went for dinner?" Marcus genuinely doesn't remember. He doesn't know what she is talking about. For this is what he always does with things he doesn't want to hear. If you rewrite history enough times, it's as if it never happened. If you can pretend for long enough, eventually history will be rewritten.

"When I told you how unhappy I am!" Holly whirls on him. "When I said I didn't feel that I had a marriage, or a partnership. I told you I never see you anymore and that I'm not happy. That I can't carry on like this."

"How can you say that?" Marcus says, and she thinks he has finally heard. "How can you seriously say that? We have an amazing marriage. I love you, Holly. I mean I *really* love you. I love you more than I love anyone, and we have two beautiful children and a wonderful life together. I don't understand. It just doesn't make sense to me, how you can even think of throwing all this away."

"I know it doesn't make sense to you," Holly says. "It doesn't make sense to you because you never listen. You refuse to hear anything you don't want to hear. I'm tired, Marcus. I'm tired of trying to explain to you why I'm not happy in this marriage and why I need some space. I just—" fear dwindles her voice away to almost nothing—"I just don't think I can do it anymore," she whispers.

And Marcus starts to cry.

Holly stands awkwardly, watching him. She has seen him cry only a few times before, and she doesn't know quite what to do. It would feel wrong to reach out to him, to try to comfort him when she is the cause of this pain, yet it feels more wrong and more awkward to stand here doing nothing.

She reaches up and puts her arms around him. He buries his head in her shoulder, sobbing, and she strokes his back, feeling his pain, suddenly realizing how hard this is going to be. How hard to see someone in so much pain and to be the one who has caused it, knowing that you're not able to do anything about it, not if you are to be able to live your life and be happy.

Not if you are to be true to yourself.

Marcus has let go. His defenses are well and truly down. So rarely has Holly seen this side of Marcus, seen him vulnerable, and when she has in the past, those were the times she tried to convince herself that everything would be fine.

Marcus, so caught up in being a big shot, being important, needing to be seen as someone who is worthy of respect, is suddenly, alone in this field as the sun goes down, a little boy.

No more arrogance and pretense, just a scared little boy, terrified of the future, of his life being turned upside down, of not being the one in control.

And even as Holly attempts to comfort him somewhat with her hug, she knows there is no going back. If, at points during the last few days, even for a split second, she has ever thought of staying married to Marcus for the sake of the children, perhaps until they go to college, as she stands here with him right now, she knows she cannot.

She feels the strangest mix of emotions: sorrow, grief, relief. She feels Marcus's pain almost as if it were her own, and despite seeing the real Marcus, seeing the frightened little boy, she meant what she said.

She is done.

"Please think about it," Marcus sobs, pulling away to look her in the eye. "Please come back. I miss you. I miss *us*. We have so much to look forward to, you'd be throwing away so much." He stops, unable to go on, and takes a few deep breaths before continuing. "I'm a divorce lawyer," he tries again, a different tack. "I see what this does to children and I see what it does to families. Our children don't deserve this. *I* don't deserve this. Whatever the problems are in our marriage, none of them is insurmountable. I can be home more, maybe work from home on Fridays. We can do marriage guidance counseling. I mean it, Holly. I'll do whatever you ask me to do. I'll do whatever it takes."

"Okay," Holly whispers, nodding, not knowing what else to say, hating causing him so much pain, hating that she knows she will only cause him more. "I need to think about it." Not true, but she is buying time, knowing she can only hurt him so much at a time.

"I've booked a room," Marcus says. "I'm staying in a hotel, if that's okay with you. Can I take you all out tomorrow morning? With the kids? Is that okay?"

Holly shakes her head. "I . . . can't, Marcus. I just can't. Not yet. But if you want to come and take the kids out, that's fine. They'd love it. They've missed you."

He gulps and swallows hard. "Okay," he says. "I'll come and get the children early. Maybe I could take them out for supper tonight, though? Would that be okay?"

"Sure."

"There's a film on in town as well, *Night at the Museum*. I know they'd love it, but it's a bit late. Would it be okay if I brought them back around nine?"

A film. Holly doesn't remember Marcus ever taking them to a film before. She doesn't remember him spending any time with them unless she was present. Other fathers took their kids on the weekend, let the mothers have a lie-in, have a rest. Not Marcus. Marcus has never done anything with just the kids.

But she can't dwell on that. Thank heavens, he's thinking of doing something now.

"That sounds lovely," she says. "Hopefully they'll sleep in, in the morning, and Daisy can always have a nap tomorrow if she needs it. They need to spend time with you. Thank you."

Holly turns her head, gesturing back toward the house, and Marcus falls into step beside her as they cross the field, the sun now streaking the sky with pink and orange.

"Where are you staying?" Holly asks, not because she wants to know, but because she's struggling to make small talk.

"Le Manoir." He grins and, in a flash, his humility disappears. "It's fantastic!" he enthuses, back on familiar territory. "I've got the Lavande suite, which you'd love."

In her mind's eye, Holly rolls her eyes. Here at last is the Marcus she has known. As he describes Le Manoir—the food, the service, the expense, and luxury of it all—Holly knows that, without question, she is doing the right thing.

Poor Marcus. Perhaps if he had booked into the local B&B in the village or an old inn on the outskirts of Gloucester, it might have been a different story. Unlikely, but possible. Perhaps if he had shown Holly that he wasn't obsessed with needing to live the high life, she might have been able to glimpse a way forward.

But the minute he starts to describe Le Manoir is the minute Holly switches off for good. He may think she would love it because she has always accompanied him to the Four Seasons, the Peninsulas, the best hotels in the world, but Holly couldn't care less. It just isn't what she's about, and she's finally realizing that their worlds are so different, there isn't a way to meet in the middle.

There never was.

"Fuck!" Holly screams when Marcus has pulled out of the driveway, the kids bouncing happily in their car seats in the back of the car, thrilled to be with their daddy.

The others come running.

"Fuck!" she shouts again, stamping her feet, getting the frustration out. *"Fuck! Fuck! Fuck!"*

"I take it the children are gone?" Paul asks wryly as Holly stamps around for a few seconds until she is calm again and able to take a deep breath.

"Why are you so angry?" Anna's voice is filled with sympathy. "Was he awful to you?"

"No," Holly shakes her head and starts to laugh. "It's so stupid. I don't even know why I'm angry.

Because he's an arse. Because I was just starting to feel sorry for him, for how much pain he is in, when he started banging on about Le Manoir and how fucking fantastic it is, and in that moment I just knew that he's never going to change. He's such a pompous fucking arse, I can't stand him." She takes a sharp intake of breath and looks around the room. "Shit," she whispers. "I can't believe I just said that."

"So tell us how you really feel?" Saffron grins.

"Oh God," Holly groans. "It's true. I just looked at him today and realized I can't stand him."

"I wouldn't think that's a great way to feel about your husband," Olivia says. "Not that I would know, admittedly, but I'm sure it's not good."

"You didn't feel even a little bit of love?" Anna asks. "Nothing?" Holly shakes her head. "What about in the beginning? You must have done then."

"I didn't," Holly says sadly. "I mean, a sort of love, perhaps. He is, after all, the father of my children, but not a love you're supposed to feel, not the kind of love you have with Paul."

"So you're not going back, then?" Will has, until this point, been quiet, not wanting to get too involved.

"No." Holly raises her eyes to meet Will's. "I'm not going back. I just can't face telling him that yet."

CHAPTER TWENTY-EIGHT

The thrill and excitement of commune living is beginning to pall somewhat. No arguments, not yet, but Olivia is starting to miss her flat, miss her animals, and is wondering exactly how long she will have to stay here. Saffron seems . . . fine. Not as fragile as she had expected, certainly not fragile enough to need to be surrounded by five people looking after her.

Saffron always was strong, Olivia realizes. Stronger, perhaps, than all of them. They ought to have changed so very much, she thinks, since school. Ought, as they approach forty, to feel grown-up, surely, but Olivia certainly doesn't. She doesn't feel much different at all. Just older, more tired, and, with this pregnancy, sicker.

Holly *feels* different, which is not to say she is. Holly always thinks that if she were to pass people from her class on the street, they would not recognize her. She is surely better looking now, her hair sleeker, her cheekbones more pronounced. But in fact Holly, like all of them, has barely changed. Look just slightly below the surface and they are all exactly the same.

In so many ways, Holly is slowly coming back to

herself. In just a few days, she has stopped acting like Marcus's wife, is rediscovering who she is.

But it's a Holly she doesn't quite remember, a Holly she has to get used to. And this Holly has a different life than the one she has lived these past fourteen years. She no longer has a home to go back to, no longer has the safety and familiarity of her old life.

This stay in the country is like a time out, a break from her real life, a holiday that she doesn't want to end, because whatever the changes going on in her life, she is trying to stay focused on the present and not think about the future.

She lost herself for a while this evening. The kids had just left with Marcus, Will was finishing off the kitchen cupboards, and Paul and Anna, Olivia and Saffron were reading the papers in front of the fire. Holly poured herself a vodka and went to sit outside.

It was cold. Too cold really to be outside, but she kept her hat and gloves on, and snuggled down in one of the beaten-up wooden chairs that Anna found in a junk shop on their last trip up here.

At first everything was pitch-black. As her eyes adjusted, she started to see the outline of the trees. The noises of the country seemed so loud, yet so calming. For a while she was just . . . being. Listening to the noises, no thoughts at all.

After a few minutes, as the vodka warmed her up and her body started relaxing, her mind started wandering. She thought back to a girl she had done the NCT childbirth classes with when she was pregnant with Oliver.

Her name was Julia. They had become friends through their shared experiences, not a friendship that would otherwise have happened but one born of having children within a week of each other, of being neighbors and in a similar plight. Not that Holly admitted it at the time.

Julia had married Dave, she said, because she thought that no one else would marry her. She had married him, she said, because he seemed to be everything she ought to be looking for in a husband. He had a good job, was kind, treated her like a princess, and he loved her.

"So are you happy?" Holly remembers asking her, trying not to compare her own marriage, trying not to go to a place from which there was no return.

Julia had shrugged. "I'm . . . fine," she'd said. "And now there's Felix." She had jiggled her baby on her knee and covered his chubby cheeks with adoring kisses. "We're a family. It is what it is. I think," and she had looked up at that point and met Holly's eyes, "I think there are many different kinds of marriages. I think there are some people who are lucky enough to find a soul mate, to find the person with whom they are destined to be, but I think those people are few and far between. I think most of us just make a choice and get on with it. Do I love Dave? Sure. Could I be happier with someone else?" She had shrugged. "Probably. But this is my choice, and it's enough."

Enough. Holly had shivered when she heard this, knowing that she felt the same way but refusing to dwell on it. Refusing to consider that while it may have been enough for Julia, it may not be enough for Holly.

Last year she bumped into Julia at the bookshop. It was one of those dull, drizzly London afternoons. Daisy was at a playdate and Oliver was bored, Holly more so. He couldn't amuse himself at home, none of his friends were around. Holly felt too guilty about planting him in front of the television for a further two hours.

She stuck him in the car and went to the local Barnes & Noble. Admittedly he was a little old for the Thomas the tank engine train set, but she promised him a hot chocolate in the café, and he settled himself in a corner with a *Star Wars* book as she went up to join the queue of mothers who all had the same idea.

"Holly?" It was Julia. They exchanged a hug, both of them genuinely delighted to see one another.

"How *are* you?" Holly pulled back, looking at her. "You look *great!*" And it was true. Julia did look great. Holly had only known her pregnant and then for the three years or so after the birth when Julia didn't seem able to lose her pregnancy weight, always what Holly would describe as "a big girl."

Yet now she was skinny. Like a gazelle. Tall and graceful, there was nothing of her. And her whole face had changed—was it Holly's imagination or was she . . . glowing?

"I *am* great." Julia beamed. "Have you time to sit down? Can we have a coffee together."

"So what's your secret?" Holly insisted, stunned by the change.

"I'm getting divorced," Julia said, and Holly's mouth fell open.

"What? How? Why?"

"Oh God." Julia rolled her eyes. "I was so unhappy. I've been so unhappy for such a long time. Don't get me wrong, Dave isn't a bad guy, he's just entirely wrong for me, and we never should have gotten married." She shrugged, used to telling her story, used to sitting opposite women like Holly who quiz her for the answers to their own unhappiness.

"I knew, walking down the aisle, that I was making a terrible mistake," she said, "but I didn't know how to stop it, I just let myself get pulled along, caught up in the momentum and excitement of planning a wedding, and I thought I'd make it work. I knew things were missing but I thought it would be enough."

Holly had so many questions she wanted to ask. And so many questions she didn't. Questions that she already knew the answers to because she had been there herself, was just trying for a different outcome.

"But the divorce . . . isn't it awful? Everyone says going through a divorce is ghastly, and yet here you are looking amazing and seeming so . . . happy."

"I am happy." Julia laughed. "Everyone says they're so sorry I'm getting divorced and I always tell them not to be. And then, of course, there are the people who tell me I haven't got a right to feel this happy, that I need to give myself time to grieve for my marriage, that I won't get out of this scot-free, that something will come back to bite me."

"And will it?"

"I doubt it. Frankly I did my grieving for my marriage while I was in it. Since the moment I left him, I've felt nothing but relief. Sure, there are moments when I am down, when I wonder how I'm going to do it, but I've been liberated. I feel like I've discovered myself, I'm being true to myself again."

She looked at Holly intently, and Holly shivered.

"How are you?" Julia then asked gently, "How is Marcus?"

And Holly raised her eyes to meet Julia's and shook her head. "I can't," she whispered, "I can't go there, Julia. Not yet. I'm not ready. Let's talk about something else. Tell me about Felix, he must be enormous now, how's school?"

She hasn't seen Julia since then, she realizes. They left, saying they would get the boys together, would get together themselves, and Julia phoned, but Holly wasn't able to return her call. She was too scared to see her.

For this, she realizes, is why you lose friends when you get a divorce. Not because, as she had always assumed, you are suddenly a threat, a glamorous divorcee who may steal all your friends' husbands, but because in getting divorced you force people to question their own marriages. And we never know what goes on behind closed doors. We may assume that our friends' marriages are strong and sacred, but when people listen to the reasons why you left and how you knew it was wrong, they realize that their own marriages aren't so strong. And if it can happen to you, then certainly it can happen to them too.

It is so much easier to bury our heads in the sand, to pretend that everything is fine. Even when things are crumbling all around us.

What about grief? Holly thinks, swishing the vodka gently in her glass as she shivers, the cold starting to seep in through her winter coat. Will *she* grieve? She doesn't think so, is sure she will feel the same as Julia, that she has done enough grieving during her marriage. As for loneliness, she couldn't possibly feel any lonelier than she has felt the last few years.

Not that she'll get out of it scot-free, of course not, but there is no denying that at her very core she feels the same thing Julia felt: relief.

Even Will doesn't seem quite as relevant now. It is as if, by finally giving in to this attraction, her eyes have cleared again; she is able to see him for who he is, rather than as her savior.

And who is he? Handsome, wonderful, sweet brother of Tom. The man who, she realizes, gave her the strength to get out; for in her obsession, she didn't stop to think of the fear or stop to consider how frightened she was to live life on her own. She wasn't scared of being bullied into submission as she always had been in the past.

Marcus stopped having power over Holly because she was too distracted to give it to him. And in detaching from her fear, she was able to detach from her marriage.

But all this obsessive thinking that Will might be the man for her, getting through these last few months only because she was lost in thoughts of Will, now seems unrealistic. He's already talking about his next trip. He can't wait for the sun, for Thai beaches and fat joints at sunset.

It's a world she left behind many years ago, not a world she wants to be in now, not even to dabble in for a second. While it might be tempting to pretend to be a teenager again, the fact is she has children of her own, she is now a grown-up. There is no place in her world for Thai beaches and fat joints at sunset.

Holly sighs and tips the dregs of the vodka back, standing up and going inside to see what's happening for dinner.

"So what can I do to help?" Saffron walks into the kitchen and leans over Olivia's shoulder, reaching down to steal a carrot.

"Are you . . . ?" Olivia turns around and looks at Saffron, then, with panic in her eyes, at Anna and Holly.

"Oh God." Holly shakes her head. "You're drunk, aren't you?"

"I am not!" Saffron says, and were it not for the tiny weave as she sat down, the slight misfocus of her eyes, you might not notice.

"You bloody are," Holly says. "Where did you get it? How much have you had?"

Saffron sighs and leans her head on her arms. "Not much," she mumbles into her arms. "Just a tiny bit."

"I'll go," Olivia says, leaving to hunt for the source of the alcohol. She comes back, a couple of minutes later, a nearly empty bottle of vodka in hand.

"But we still *have* all the vodka." Holly frowns and opens the cupboard to prove it and, sure enough, the bottle of vodka that she and Will bought in town is still there.

Olivia groans. "Jesus," she says. "I can't believe how sneaky she is. I'm just realizing that she said she left her purse in that gift shop and ran back to get it when we got to the car. She must have . . ."

"Oh stop being such a killjoy," Saffron snaps. "Yes, that's exactly when I got the vodka. So what? I'll start my sobriety again in the morning. At least let me enjoy it tonight."

"I just do not know what to do," Anna says helplessly, looking to Olivia and Holly for help. "I am completely out of my depth here."

"Me too," they say in unison.

"Good!" Saffron laughs, getting up to pour herself a glass of wine. "In for a penny, in for a pound. Cheers!" And oblivious to the worried looks of everyone around her, she takes a large sip. "Oh relax." She puts the glass on the table with a laugh. "At least I'm a fun drunk. You should just enjoy me while it lasts."

It's true. Saffron is fun while she's drunk. Still the center of attention, perhaps more so. She is the one who remembers all the funny stories from school, helps them all remember things they hadn't thought about for years.

"Who is that?" Anna frowns at the headlights shining brightly through the window. "Oh Marcus, I forgot."

"Ah, my number-one fan, Marcus." Saffron grins. "I'll go," and before anyone can stop her she is up and out the door to greet Marcus.

"Guess what?" She reappears in the doorway. "He's staying for a drink!"

And Holly's heart plummets as she scoops the children up and upstairs to bed, wondering if she can stay up there until he's gone, not wanting to spend a minute in his company, furious with Saffron for inviting him to stay.

What the hell was she thinking?

Marcus is clearly not comfortable. He is staying for a drink because he wants to spend time with Holly. He is convinced that given a chance he will prove to her how much he loves her, how much she needs him. He does not accept for a moment that this is it. He may have made his threats, but he didn't mean them, doesn't think for a moment that this hiccup will end in divorce.

And he should know. He has seen exactly how these stories play out, has heard about every trick in the book, and he will not let that happen to his marriage. He will not let Holly throw this all away.

So he is not comfortable, but he is here. He is here with Holly, and give him some time alone with her that is relaxed, give her a couple of glasses of wine, and he will make her see; he will win.

There is no doubt in his mind that he will win.

But this is not a Holly he is used to. This is not a quiet, pliant Holly. A Holly he has always been able to control. This Holly is stiff and uncomfortable. This Holly is unyielding, not giving him anything to work with, and he sits and gazes at her across the table, sad puppy-dog eyes wanting her to be normal, wanting everything to be as it was.

"More wine?" Paul is passing the bottle to Holly, and Marcus is about to interject, as he always would. *I think she's had enough,* he is about to say, but Holly doesn't look at him for permission as she always has, and he finds himself biting his tongue, watching in silent disapproval as she pours herself yet another glass.

He can see she is drinking her discomfort away. Oh hell. Perhaps this will work in his favor. Perhaps she will soften as she drinks. Who knows, perhaps the left side of the bed in his suite at Le Manoir will stay uncreased tonight. Perhaps he will be back where he is so certain he belongs—in Holly's bed, by her side.

"So, Marcus," Paul is desperate to dissolve the tension. "How's the hotel? I hear you're staying at Le Manoir. Meant to be amazing."

"Really nice," Marcus says, back on familiar ground at last. "I'm always a bit nervous about new hotels. Frankly, unless it's the Four Seasons, you just never know what you're going to get, but I was telling Raymond this morning that he's done a really wonderful job."

Anna exchanges a look with Olivia and quickly looks down, suppressing a small smile.

"Who's Raymond?" Olivia asks.

"Raymond Blanc," Paul fills in the blank. "The owner and chef."

"He must be thrilled you're staying with him," Will pipes up, and as Holly looks at him in amazement—is he joking? Is he serious? Will Marcus explode?

Marcus chooses to take Will's words at face value. "I

think he's just thrilled to have anyone staying there," he says. "It's apparently one of the quietest times of the year."

"You obviously know him well, socializing in London," Will persists.

"Oh you know," Marcus shifts around in his chair. "We know some of the same people, go to the same parties, that kind of thing."

"Who do we know?" Holly asks, no longer willing to play his pretentious game.

"Sally and Greg in my office. I don't think you know them. They're great friends, they stay at Le Manoir all the time."

Holly catches Will's eye and he winks at her. She smiles and looks down.

"So . . . Marcus." Saffron drags her chair over to Marcus and gives him her most killer smile. "I'm playing a lawyer in a new film. Tell me some of your best tricks for winning clients."

Marcus loves it. A famous beautiful actress is sitting next to him, hanging on to his every word, treating him as if he were the most important man in the world, as if everything he says were the word of God, and he forgets that he is a man who is at risk of losing his life. Right now he is not Marcus Carter, potential divorced father. He is Marcus Carter, world-renowned lawyer, omnipotent and omniscient. Master of his universe.

"Oh this must be so boring for the rest of you," Saffron says, looking up after a few minutes. "Marcus, I'm dying to hear more. Let's you and I sit in the kitchen," and a mesmerized Marcus follows her out to the kitchen.

"Shit," Olivia says. "She grabbed a bottle of wine. Did you see that?"

"There's nothing we can do," Paul says. "I'm telling you. If she chooses to drink, we can't stop her."

"I can't believe we brought alcohol into the house with an alcoholic who's fallen off the wagon," Holly says. "I just can't believe how stupid we've been in believing her when she said she wouldn't drink again."

"Me especially," Olivia agrees. "I was the one who managed to talk her out of it the other night, and I thought . . . I suppose I just hoped that every day it might get easier. I definitely never expected her to get shit-faced so quickly."

"She is pretty shit-faced," Paul says. "Earlier on I thought she was going to pass out, but now she seems to have gotten her second wind. Actually, what's so scary is how normal she seems. She's been drinking like a fish all evening, and now she seems sober."

"She's not," Olivia says. "Trust me."

"Do you think I should maybe go and grab the wine or something?" Anna says. "I know you keep saying we can't do anything but it just feels wrong to leave it in there."

Holly sighs. "Don't worry. I'll get it. I'm going to try to get rid of Marcus too. I mean, Jesus! What's he doing here? Why is he still here, for God's sake? Why did she invite him to stay?" She pushes her chair back and, shaking her head, she walks into the kitchen.

It is a sight she can't quite believe. Saffron is sitting on the lap of her husband with her arms wrapped around his neck, kissing him passionately. Marcus's hands are running up and down her back, and were it not for Holly's sharp intake of breath, they would have continued.

"Oh God," Marcus groans, standing up and dislodging Saffron, who lands in a heap on the floor.

"What the hell?" Holly says to no one in particular, then looks at Marcus. "Get out," she says coldly.

"It's not what . . . you don't understand . . . it wasn't . . ." But he can't quite find the words.

"Out!" Holly fumes, no longer scared of him, her arm extended, pointing to the door. "Just go. Now."

The others come in, unaware of what happened, aware only that Holly's voice has carried, that she is furious, and that Marcus has gone. They gather Saffron up and take her upstairs—she is in no fit state for anything other than bed—and Will sits downstairs with Holly, a fuming, shocked, disgusted Holly.

"How could he?" she keeps saying, more upset by the betrayal than the actual fact of what happened. She didn't feel jealous but bemused and betrayed. "How could he, so soon? What the hell? And how could *she*? What was Saffron thinking?"

"Holly," Will puts his hand gently on hers after a while. "Saffron was drunk, she probably didn't even know what she was doing, and as for how he could . . . Think of where you were last night, think of how it can happen."

"But that's different," she explodes.

"How?" he says softly. "Because we're friends? Because I'm Tom's brother? How is Marcus kissing Saffron different from you kissing me? Oh Holly." He sighs, looking intently at her, sorrow in his eyes as he shakes his head sadly. "I don't think you're ready for this. I don't think you know what you want, do you?"

As she raises her eyes to look at Will, she knows that he is right. She is not ready for this, but not for what Will is talking about. Not that she's not ready to let Marcus go.

She's not ready for a relationship. She's not ready for Will. For anyone.

She is furious, but not with Marcus. With Saffron. Saffron who is supposed to be her friend, who has no reason to seduce Marcus. And she isn't buying the drunk card. What Saffron did tonight showed Holly that their friendship is a house of cards. It's a friendship based on a shared history, on the past, not on what is today.

As Holly sighs and looks at Will, she knows it's time to go, to leave this house and get on to whatever her new life will be.

Upstairs, Anna gently pulls Saffron's cell phone out of her bag, tiptoes down the stairs, and walks to the end of the driveway. She taps on the screen of the Treo, pulling up her address book, and she scrolls through until she finds it. P.

The phone is picked up on the first ring.

"Pearce? I am so very sorry to bother you. This is Anna Johanssen, I am a friend of Saffron's. I would not be calling if this were not urgent, but she is drinking again, big time, and none of us know what to do. We need your help, and I do not know who else to call."

"Give me your number, Anna," says the voice that Anna knows so well, the voice of one of the most famous men in the world. "I'll get back to you in twenty minutes."

Anna clicks off the phone and goes back to the house where the others are. She doesn't know if she's done the right thing, but she doesn't have a choice. They really are out of their depth here, and calling Pearce seems the only thing left to do.

Holly goes upstairs slowly, her feet feeling almost as heavy as her heart. Everything about her life has changed, and it's a terrible feeling to be this vulnerable, to not have a clue where you will end up, nor even, it seems, who your friends are.

She checks on the children, then gets undressed, switching off the light and climbing gratefully into bed, longing to forget everything even for a while, in her sleep, when her door creaks open.

"I can't, Will," she whispers, irritated that even after their chat earlier he presumes she still wants him in her bed. "I'm sorry but I just can't."

"It's not Will," slurs Saffron, sliding over to the bed and half sitting, half falling onto the pillows.

Holly groans. The very last person she wants to see.

"Go to bed, Saffron." She sighs. "Just go. Please. I've got nothing to say to you."

"Oh Holly," Saffron pouts, still clearly drunk as a skunk. "Don't you see, darling? I did it on purpose. Your pompous awful husband can't accuse you of anything now. You caught him kissing another woman! How could you ever trust him again? Never mind what Marcus comes up with, *you* caught him with someone else—what's the judge going to think about that?"

"What?" Holly sits up and switches on the light. There is a drunken, triumphant smile on Saffron's face. "You mean you did this for me?"

"Course!" Saffron giggles. "You don't seriously think I fancied him, do you? Yuck yuck yuck!" She starts sputtering all over the duvet as Holly's mouth falls open.

"You're crazy," Holly says, not knowing what else to say. "I can't believe you seduced him."

"Yup." Saffron grins in delight. "I've known men like Marcus before and he would wipe the floor with you. Can't do much now, though. I know it was only a kiss, but how do you know he hasn't done this countless times? How could you possibly stay married to a man who does this?"

"But, Saffron, if this went to court I'd have to name you."

"As if my reputation could get any worse. Fuck it." Saff flings her arms in the air. "If you believe everything you read in the papers, I'm Scarlet Saffron, superslut and destroyer of marriages."

"You're amazing." Holly shakes her head, unable to

resist a smile. "Even though you're shit-faced, you're just . . . I don't know whether to thank you or never talk to you again."

"Trust me," Saffron falls into Holly's hug, "I had to be shit-faced to do what I just did," and she snorts with laughter, knowing she will be forgiven, before snuggling down next to Holly and falling into a deep, drunken sleep.

CHAPTER TWENTY-NINE

Holly leaves the house early, doesn't want to talk to anyone this morning. Marcus has canceled seeing the children—an urgent work thing—so she takes them down to the riding stables they had passed down the road, and spends an hour there, pretending to be normal, pretending to be happy as they feed the ponies Polo mints and let them nuzzle in their pockets.

She doesn't want to see anyone. Not Will. And not Saffron. What she really wants to do is climb back into bed, pull the covers over her head and not come out again until she remembers what normal is.

How stupid she was, she realizes, to think that she, like Julia, would have done her grieving in the marriage. How naive to think the hardest part was over, that everything from here on in would be hearts and flowers.

"Mummy?" Oliver asks on the way back to the house, going via the bakery for cinnamon rolls and hot chocolate. Holly would have left this morning, knowing it's time to get back to London, but she is bringing Olivia back in the car, and Olivia's morning sickness tends to abate somewhat by midafternoon, hence this wait.

"Yes, darling?"

"Are you and Daddy going to divorce?"

Holly almost jumps with shock. "What do you mean, darling? Why are you asking that?"

"Well, there's a girl in my class, Jessica, and her parents are divorcing, and if we're here with you and Daddy's not, then I was thinking that maybe you'll be in a divorce."

Holly crouches down so she's on eye level with Oliver. "Oliver, did Daddy say something to you?"

Oliver shrugs and looks away.

"Oliver, it's okay. You can tell me anything." Holly tries to keep the anger out of her voice.

"Well . . . Daddy did say that he wanted to be here with us but you wouldn't let him and that it was up to you if we came home. So is it, Mummy? Will you let Daddy stay?"

Holly stands up and tries to take a deep breath. She thought Marcus was bigger than this, thought that they would both try to protect the children, put them first, not involve them in a game of he said, she said. Clearly she was wrong.

Bastard. Fucking bastard.

"Oliver," she crouches down again, looking him straight in the eye, "sometimes mummies and daddies need to have a little time apart. It's like when you have an argument with Jonny, and both of you decide you're not talking, but everything's always fine after a few days." Oliver nods. "Well that's like Daddy and me. We're all taking a holiday and Daddy could stay here but he has to go back to work, and the most important thing is that Daddy and I both love you very much, and, if we are taking a little holiday from Daddy, it's not because of anything you've done, okay?"

Oliver nods, not really understanding, but wanting now to move on to something else.

"Okay, darling? I love you."

"I love you too, Mummy." His voice is muffled as Holly wraps him in a tight hug, opening her arms to include Daisy. "I think we probably ought to go back," she says, not knowing what will be waiting but knowing the time is up.

Her phone rings on the way home. Marcus.

"Yes?" Her voice is terse.

"Holly, I need to explain. I didn't do anything last night, Saffron just jumped on me and started kissing me, it was nothing to do with . . ."

"You think I believe that?" Holly hisses softly so the children don't hear, trying to sound angry, upset. Trying not to smile, for she believes Saffron, and she can see how this works to her advantage. "You think I didn't see your arms around her? How many other times have you done this? How many other women have there been?"

"None," Marcus almost shouts. "I swear."

"Right. And I'm supposed to believe you. And another thing, Marcus, don't you dare tell the children this is my fault. Not now. I've never said a word against you, even after last night, and I expect you to do the same. I'm going now. I don't want to talk to you anymore," and she ends the call just as she turns into the driveway of the house.

The house seems empty when they get back. The only person around appears to be Will, and Holly doesn't want to be around him right now. She feels guilt and shame, and mostly she feels stupid for thinking that Will was going to be the one to rescue her, that Will was her soul mate when he so obviously isn't.

She doesn't know what to say to him anymore. After all these months of telling him everything, sharing all the tiny details of her life, she doesn't know how to act or how to pretend that everything is normal, when nothing is normal.

Nothing about her life is normal. Nothing is as it was. It is, she realizes, like having an accident. One minute you are fine, the next you have sliced your hand open on the food processor blade, and it is ridiculous to suddenly have blood pouring down your wrist when a second ago there was nothing.

It is true, she realizes, how everything in your life can change in an instant. Tom was Tom—a husband, a father, a friend—and in an instant, Tom was gone. Sarah thought she knew where the rest of her life would lead her, and now she is going down a completely different path.

And Holly, Holly who has defined herself all these years first as a wife, then a mother, is realizing that if she is no longer a wife, she has to replace that with something else, and being a girlfriend, being Will's girlfriend, is not the right choice.

She knows that on some level she has to trust that it will all work out the way it is supposed to. Just this morning she was realizing that despite everything, she wouldn't change a thing about her life. She has her two beautiful children after all, and these fourteen years of marriage have brought her to where she is today, forced her to a place where she can acknowledge that she has wants and needs and that she is no longer willing to stay in a situation where those needs are not met.

People can change. This she knows. But even if Marcus changed it wouldn't matter. Even if he was granted the gift of humility, even if he started being an attentive, loving, adoring husband, it wouldn't matter, because Holly doesn't love him. Holly has never loved him.

"Where is everyone?" Holly asks, finding Will on his own in the kitchen.

Will puts the hammer down and comes over to help Holly unbutton the kids' coats.

"It's Olivia," he says gently. "She was bleeding. They've taken her to the hospital."

Holly takes a sharp intake of breath. "Oh God, the baby. Is she losing it?"

"I don't know. She was having some cramping as well, and they just bundled her into the car and took her to the Gloucestershire Royal Hospital. Paul said they'd phone when they knew something."

"When did they leave?"

"About an hour ago."

Olivia is scared. She doesn't like hospitals, has never liked hospitals, and wishes that she could turn the clock back to yesterday when everything was fine. Except it wasn't fine. Yesterday she was pregnant, and until this morning when she went to the bathroom and discovered blood in her underpants, she wanted to turn the clock back to when she wasn't pregnant, to when it wasn't something she ever, *ever* thought about.

Anna sits on a chair in the corner of the room. Paul and Saffron are outside in the waiting room as the radiologist places icy cold gel all over Olivia's bare stomach.

"I'm sorry," she says. "I know it's cold but it won't last long."

Olivia is transfixed by the television screen. Her head is turned uncomfortably, eyes glued to the screen, wanting to see. Not wanting to see. This is a blessing, she keeps trying to tell herself. This is a blessing in disguise. I don't want this baby.

She steals a glance at Anna, who looks far more terrified than she does. *This is the way it's meant to be,* Olivia thinks. *Now I won't need to make a decision. This is God's way of taking the decision away from me.*

There is silence in the room as the screen lights up with a grayish triangle. In the middle of the screen, there is something pulsing, and Olivia squints at it, trying to make it out.

"What do you see?" she says after several minutes of

silence as the radiologist scans and clicks and types numbers into the screen. "Is it dead?" she whispers.

"Very much alive I'd say," the radiologist says. "Look, can you see?" And she moves the scanner on her stomach, and Olivia and Anna both gasp, for there, quite clearly, legs furled up, arms reaching out, is a baby.

"You have a thumb sucker there," the radiologist says as the baby lifts a hand toward its mouth.

"It's a baby," Olivia whispers. And she bursts into tears.

"So the bleeding? The cramping? What was all that about?" Paul looks at Olivia, who has walked into the waiting room with such a huge smile on her face he assumes she has lost the baby and is thrilled.

"I've got a tiny subchorionic hematoma. It's basically a collection of blood between the placenta and the uterine wall. They said that, given the size, it's probably going to be fine, but I'll need to be carefully monitored."

"You're keeping the baby?" Saffron is the only one who dares to ask.

"I have to." Tears well up in Olivia's eyes. "I mean, I don't know about adoption, or Paul and Anna . . ." She turns to look at them as the tears spill out. "I'm so sorry, I know you want me to make a decision but I just can't do that, not yet. The only thing I do know is that I can't have an abortion. Not now."

Paul looks at Anna, then back at Olivia. "We understand," he says, walking over to Anna and putting his arm around her. "It's your baby and your choice. Just know that we're here if that's what you decide."

"What the hell is going on?" They are about to turn into the driveway when they see cars lined up and down, parked on the grass, men running around, stepladders everywhere.

"Oh fuck," Saffron whispers, just as someone turns and shouts, pointing at the car. "They've found me."

"Saffron! Saffron!" Dozens of paparazzi swarm the car, lightbulbs flashing in the windows as Saffron buries her head.

"What the hell do I do?" Paul, in his panic, has frozen, not knowing whether to try to reverse out of there, or whether to keep going. Either way, he's convinced he'll run at least six people over.

"Let's just get inside," Saffron says. "They're not going anywhere. I guess it was too good to last."

"Olivia! Are you okay?" They get inside, slamming the door in the face of what feels like a pack of wolves, and Holly gives Olivia a huge hug as Will explains he's covered the windows with sheets, that they just about managed to get reception on the cell phone, and the police are on their way.

Paul's face is grim as he directs everybody into the kitchen, then goes to the front door, opens it wide and waits for the photographers to stop yelling for Saffron, to quiet down enough to hear him speak.

"You are standing on private property," he says

calmly and clearly. "The police are on their way, and I would suggest you all get off my property immediately, or you will be arrested for trespassing."

"Where is she?" someone shouts. "We just want one shot," another says. "A quick comment," says someone else.

"You have two minutes to get off my property," Paul says, and grumbling and swearing, the paparazzi start moving their equipment to the top of the driveway.

"Will it make a difference?" Olivia asks.

"Not much," Saffron says. "They've all got these superpowerful zoom lenses. The best thing to do is exactly what Will did—cover up the windows."

"It's just like a movie," Olivia says. "Now we're all prisoners in the house."

"Saff," Holly says quietly, pulling her aside and taking her hand. "There's someone upstairs to see you."

"*What*? Who?" Saffron is immediately suspicious.

"You need to go," Holly says. "Your room."

Saffron walks upstairs, shooting quizzical looks at the others who shrug, and when she has disappeared Olivia looks at Holly and raises an eyebrow.

"Who?"

Holly starts to smile. She had been sitting at the kitchen table with Will, both of them sharing their concern for Olivia, when they heard the noise of the first cars arriving. She was stunned when she looked out of the window and saw all the commotion. Stunned but unsurprised. A part of her had been waiting for this. And then she heard a frenzy outside and, as she watched a black Jaguar with tinted windows pulled up and Pearce Webster climbed out, striding quickly and purposefully toward the front door, ignoring the shrieks and shouts and the frenzy that his arrival inspired.

"Shit," she whispers as Will turned toward her questioningly.

"Mummy!" Oliver piped up. "You just said a bad word."

"Look!" She pulled Will over to see. He immediately ran to the front door and opened it, pulling Pearce in and slamming the door in the face of the snappers.

"I'm Will." He extended a hand as Holly quivered in the corner. She'd never been in the presence of someone so famous before, and even though she tried to think of him as merely Saffron's boyfriend, or lover, the fact was she had seen every film he'd ever been in and read almost every piece of gossip ever written about him, and here he was! Two feet in front of her!

"And I'm Pearce. Good to meet you," he said, shaking Will's hand, then he turned toward Holly.

"Hello." She blushed like an idiot. "I'm Holly. These are my children, Daisy and Oliver."

Pearce was so . . . ordinary. If you didn't know, you wouldn't know. He came into the kitchen and sat down as Holly made tea. He asked questions about the house, about them, and then, finally, about Saffron.

"She's not good," Holly said. "I mean, she's great, obviously. She's Saffron. But she's drinking."

"Out-of-control drinking?"

"Shit-faced," Holly nodded.

Pearce shook his head, lost in thought. "Do you know if she's called her sponsor?"

"I don't know," Holly said. "I just know that we all feel lost. None of us know what to do."

"It's okay," Pearce said. "You aren't supposed to know. That's why I'm here."

Saffron doesn't say a word. As she walks in Pearce rises from the bed he was sitting on in the darkened room and flies into his arms.

They stand there, hugging each other tightly for a long time, as the photographers' shouts recede. Nothing else matters except these two people, locked together in this darkened room.

"You've got *some* friends," Pearce whispers, kissing her hair, her cheeks, her nose, her mouth. "They're worried about you. They called."

"You're here!" Saffron wipes the tears off her cheeks as she pulls back to look at him. "I can't believe you're here. Oh God. The press. Everyone will know."

Pearce shrugs. "They know. They got me on the highway and now they have pictures of me walking into the house. Fuck it."

"What about Marjie?"

"I just had to be here," Pearce says. "I couldn't bear hearing that you were struggling. We'll figure it out."

"A day at a time, right?" She smiles up at him.

"Exactly." He pulls her into him, marveling at how perfectly her head fits under his chin. "A day at a time.

I have the Big Book downstairs. Would you be willing to have a meeting? Right now? With me?"

Saffron looks up at him, feeling for the first time in days that she can breathe, that everything will be all right. "Yes." She exhales loudly. "It's exactly what I need."

CHAPTER THIRTY

The first flakes come quickly, swirling slowly over the Connecticut countryside, twirling around trees, floating softly down to the grass. Softer, fatter, wetter, the snowflakes fall faster and faster, no longer swirling, now simply settling on the ground, turning the trees and barns white, landing on the tongues of overjoyed children bundled up in snowsuits and sent outside to play in the first snow of the season.

They are warning drivers to stay inside. Warning that this snowstorm will be a big one, that unless it is absolutely necessary, people should stay inside.

However, there is a small contingent of cars that will not be turning back. They are crawling along the highways, slowly and carefully, on their way to the Mayflower Inn for a birthday party. Some are making their way along the Sawmill Parkway from New York. Others are on their way from JFK, having flown in from Los Angeles, London, Gloucestershire.

They are gathering in Washington, Connecticut, for Saffron's birthday party. Her fortieth. People she hasn't seen for years. People she hasn't seen for months. Some since a gathering in a yet-to-be-renovated barn in deepest, darkest Gloucestershire.

"Holly!" Saffron squeals as she walks out of the Tap Room, turning into the lobby and seeing her friends. She rushes across, feet flying noiselessly over the carpet, flinging her arms around Holly, then holding her at arm's length to look at her.

"It's so good to see you." She squeezes her again. "I'm so happy you're all here." She turns and hugs the others, stepping back to wipe the tears from her eyes.

"I cannot believe we are here," Anna says, looking at the grand staircase behind them, the faded Persian rugs on the floor, the whole air of faded elegance. "I mean, I cannot believe you sent us tickets for your birthday." She turns back to Saffron. "Organized a plane . . . This place is gorgeous, and I just . . ."

"She feels guilty." Paul grins. "She doesn't think you ought to be paying for everything. I think she wants to pay for the room."

"Darling girl." Saffron links her arm through Anna's as she walks her through the lobby to a small, cozy living room to one side, with a blazing fire and shelves lined with books. "Between Pearce and me, we get paid a fortune, and, frankly, I can't think of anything I'd rather do than gather my friends together for my thirty-seventh birthday."

"Don't you mean fortieth?" Anna is confused. "I thought you were all in the same year at school."

"Sssh." Saffron holds a finger to her lips. "As far as everyone here is concerned, I'm thirty-seven. Hollywood birthdays always have a few years shaved off."

"Everyone?" Holly raises an eyebrow. "It's not just us, then?"

"God, no!" Saffron says. "It's all the people we love. Close friends and family. We've flown people in from England, LA, there are even a couple from Australia."

"I take it things are great with you and Pearce?" Anna grins. "I just keep thinking of that whole fiasco when it first came out and you came to stay in the country. You did not expect, well, *this,* did you?"

Saffron laughs. "I didn't expect anything. I was too bloody drunk. But no, I didn't think he'd leave Marjie and, even if he did, I didn't expect us to be together."

"You look so happy." Holly looks at her and sighs as Saffron tears up again.

"Okay," she leans forward and whispers. "We're not supposed to be saying anything until tonight, but you're not here for my birthday . . ."

Anna squeals and gasps, knowing what she's going to say.

". . . we're getting married!"

Shouts of delight and hugs all around, interrupted only by the sound of footsteps approaching and a baby crying.

"That is Tommy!" Anna leaps up and goes out into the lobby to get him as Olivia appears in the doorway.

"I'm sorry," she says. "He desperately needs a nap but he won't go down."

"Do you want me to take him for a walk?" Anna says, rocking the baby up and down on her hip as he starts to gurgle.

"Would you?" An exhausted and grateful Olivia sinks into the sofa and reaches for a cup of tea from the tray that has just appeared with a silent, smiling waitress. "This place feels like Buckingham Palace." Her eyes are wide as the waitress disappears.

"I know!" Saffron smiles. "And the whole place is ours for the weekend. Now that you're here, I've got some news," and soon the only sound in the room is the excited chatter of a group of old friends who want to know all the details, with nothing left out.

It is a road Saffron never expected to walk. How long ago was it, those days when she fell apart, hit rock bottom when she had vowed never to hit rock bottom again. Nights of drinking and blacking out, days of vomiting and nausea, Pearce staying with her, holding her hand, promising he'd never leave her.

Then rehab. Three months. AA meetings all day, therapy, group therapy. Her family and friends coming in and telling her what she was like when she was drunk, the shame of being in that dark, lonely hole again. So lonely that nothing and no one could fill her up.

She finished rehab and walked out with head held high. A new sponsor, a new resolve. For the past year she has been to a meeting every day, and Pearce has been right by her side.

He finally stood up to his manager, his agents, and

said screw his career. He wasn't going to pretend any-more. He wasn't going to continue to stay in a marriage that was dead. It was against everything he believed in.

He moved into his beach house in Malibu, and Saffron joined him a month later. The press drove them crazy. There were times Saffron didn't think she could do it, didn't think she could cope with the loss of nor-mality, because there was nothing about her life that was the same.

She couldn't run to the corner store for a pint of milk, couldn't dash out in the evenings to grab a movie and a burger with Pearce. They tried, but even if they man-aged to escape the press, they'd be sitting in a restaurant trying to pretend that the buzz wasn't singing in their ears, that they didn't know that all eyes were upon them, that people's heads kept swiveling toward them. People constantly coming over with words of praise or words of criticism. It didn't much matter, there was no such thing as privacy anymore.

The job offers started pouring in. Saffron has worked constantly this past year, and between recovery, Pearce, and work, she hadn't had time for much else. She hasn't seen her friends since that time in the country, but knew she couldn't get married and not have them here.

Married! Saffron, married! Who would have thought? Pearce proposed on the beach one night. It should have been romantic but the dogs had been swimming in the water and had soaked them both, and it was freezing. When Pearce put his arms around her and said he loved her and wanted to marry her, she said, teeth chattering, "Fine, can we just go inside?"

He asked her again inside, and this time she burst into tears, crying so hard she forgot to say yes. The third time he asked, she said yes.

Pearce is planning to relay the story tonight during his speech.

It has taken months of planning to keep this secret, to keep the press away. They have taken over the inn for the weekend, have had everyone involved sign confidentiality agreements, have managed, thus far, to keep it private, largely by not telling even their friends and family, by gathering them here under false pretenses.

Pearce comes into the living room to greet everyone, and Holly watches Pearce and Saffron together with a smile on her face, for their joy is infectious, their love for one another is genuine and real. And as she watches, her mind wanders over the ocean to her little Georgian house in Maida Vale.

She isn't divorced, and it has not been easy, largely because Marcus has made it as difficult as he possibly can. He is, just as she suspected, unwilling to pay alimony, unwilling to pay a decent amount of child support, unwilling to do anything because, as he puts it, "*You* wanted this divorce, why should I have to pay?"

The only times when she has felt really low and wondered if she has the ability to do this on her own have been when she is ill, but thankfully those early days of staying in bed all weekend when the children were at their dad's, those days when her headaches were so blinding she thought her head was going to split open, have passed.

Marcus has kept the house. She thought she would mind, but, in fact, she found she just wanted to close the chapter and move on. They went through the inventory of furniture in the house, all of which had been chosen by Holly, and Holly found there was little she wanted.

Marcus demanded he keep the master bed, and Holly had laughed at the irony. Who would want the marital bed from an unhappy marriage? But then she remembered the bed was a Hastens, a bed made of natural materials from Sweden, a bed that cost more than some people's annual salaries. *Of course he'd want the bloody bed,* she thought, *if nothing else just to bring up the subject at dinner parties—"Oh, you only have a Dux? I have a Hastens, it's* glorious."

The best thing she ever did, her greatest moment, was spending the afternoon at Dream Beds Superstore and choosing her own mattress, her own bed.

Of course the worst thing she did, she now realizes, was buy a king-size. When she was married, she couldn't think of having anything smaller than a king, just in case she should wake up in the middle of the night and become aware of Marcus. Now, though, she wishes the bed was smaller, wishes she could cuddle up to Jonathan, finds herself frequently waking up squeezed against him in the middle of the bed, his arm across her chest, her legs across his.

Jonathan. Ah Jonathan. Just thinking about him, she smiles. I love him, she whispers to herself over and over as she goes about her day, delighting in the joy of loving, of having found someone who not only adores her, but who she, in turn, adores too.

He is her neighbor, three doors up. Such a cliché, she smiles to herself, too good to be true. He came and introduced himself on the day she moved in, returning twenty minutes later with his toolbox to put up shelves, pictures, flat-pack furniture for the kids' rooms that was delivered from Ikea.

She thought he was lovely, but nothing else . . . perhaps just a smattering of intrigue. He has two children, the same ages as Daisy and Oliver, who are with him every other weekend and one night during the week. They started doing things together on the weekends, just because both were lonely, and the kids liked one another.

She didn't think about him other than to think how much she liked seeing him when she did, and soon she would look for his car as she returned home. When she heard his voice on her answerphone, she would smile—there was something about him that made her feel good. Happy.

It has been five months since they kissed. They had both been in to kiss Daisy and Abigail good night—Abigail was having her first sleepover—and as they stood outside the door in the darkened corridor, smiling at each other as they listened to their girls' happily chatting away, Jonathan kissed her.

Five months on, it has been five months of the happiest, healthiest relationship Holly has ever had—a relationship that surpasses anything she might have dreamed of. She is constantly astounded by their kindness to each other, the sense that each of them values the other, and the appreciation they have for one another.

This, she finally realizes, after all these years, is love.

She remembers with shame her marriage to Marcus. Because however awful he might have been, she played a large part as well. She was guilty too. Holly was never kind to him. Never treated him gently or carefully. Choosing instead to engage in a battle of words and wits until she didn't have the strength to continue, and withdrew.

These days she has never felt so peaceful. So safe. And watching Saffron with Pearce, Holly can see echoes of her own relationship with Jonathan. She can see that despite what the newspapers may report about Saffron and Pearce, despite what the outside world sees, and the difficult start to this relationship, they have what she has with Jonathan, and it is only because of her own marriage to Marcus that she knows how rare and precious this is.

"I am so happy for you," she reaches over and whispers into Saffron's ear. "You deserve this, my darling." And Saffron squeezes her hand and nods. For the first time in her life, she does think she deserves this. She thinks she is good enough. She deserves to be in this wonderful relationship with this wonderful man.

"So how do you find single motherhood?" Holly

turns to Olivia, who rolls her eyes at the question, then laughs it off.

"It's amazing," she says. "Exhausting. But amazing. I never thought I could love anyone as much as I love Tommy. I never thought I could do the mothering thing, never thought I wanted to, but it works. It's working. He's the light of my life and I'm managing."

"And how is Fred doing?"

"He's actually been fantastic. After I told him, he wanted to get involved. I never asked anything of him, but he's been right next to me the whole time."

"Is he still coming over every few weeks?" Paul asks.

"He's over every month, and talking about coming over more."

"And things are okay? I mean, are you two . . ." Holly doesn't want to pry too much.

"No, we're not. And it's fine. I know to other people it looks weird, but we've made a decision to co-parent and to raise Tommy together even though we're not together. I have to say, I wouldn't recommend falling pregnant with someone you barely know, but in this case Fred's really come through."

"I guess Tom didn't do so badly with his choice after all." Saffron smiles.

"He obviously saw things I couldn't," Olivia says as Anna walks back in, shushing everyone as she parks a buggy containing a sleeping baby, by the door.

It is strange for Anna to think that there was a time when she wouldn't have been able to take a friend's baby for a walk without feeling inadequate or being eaten up with jealousy. Without thinking of everything in life she was missing, instead of everything in life she is lucky to have.

There is indeed something large missing from her life since we last saw her. Fashionista was sold several months ago to a huge public company, Anna retaining a role as consultant and getting paid far more money than she could ever have dreamed of.

She didn't do it for the money. She did it because she realized that Fashionista had been her baby for too long and that the stress of running it was probably contributing to her problems in getting pregnant. She wanted to stop, to jump off the conveyor belt and see what it was like to be a real person again.

Of course somewhere in the back of her mind was that secret, nudging hope that as soon as she left she would fall pregnant—it happens all the time to other people, so why not her—but seven months later she is not pregnant nor has she contemplated another course of IVF, even though these days they can certainly afford it.

What she has done, these last seven months, is to find herself again. She has taken up Pilates and yoga. Has learned to cook wonderful meals for herself and Paul and has taken seriously her role as Tommy's godmother.

For the first time in years, Anna is accepting her life as it is. She read somewhere recently that the key to happiness is not getting what you want but wanting what you get, and she smiled when she read it. She was able to think of all the things she has—all the good in

her life and all the people around her whom she loves—
and, all of a sudden, she knew that she was whole and
complete, and that it is enough.

The whole room is crying. Tears of joy, the joy that
comes when you know, you absolutely know, that two
people who are supposed to have found each other have
found each other and are not about to let the other go.

Pearce stands and clears his throat, so handsome in
his dinner jacket, better looking than even he has a right
to be, and he speaks of the reasons he loves Saffron. He
speaks of being the best man he can possibly be when
he is with her, of the gifts she has given him, and of the
ease and serenity he feels every day when he wakes up
and knows she is by his side.

"Most of you know," he says, safe in this room of
family and close friends, "that my situation before was
quite different. I didn't know it could be like this. I
didn't know it was possible to be this contented and this
calm. I feel as though my Higher Power has graced me
with a second chance, and given me this incredible
opportunity to have a new beginning.

"I thought it was too late. I thought I didn't have the
right to be happy. I had everything you're supposed to
want in life—movies, money, marriage—and I didn't
think I had the right to think that there could be more.
I was so ashamed at wanting more, at feeling that those
things were not enough.

"But what I never knew until I met Saffron was that
none of it is ever enough when you are with the wrong

person. I feel so blessed to have found Saffron, to have found the woman who graces me every day with her strength and her beauty and her joy. She is the greatest gift I have ever known, and I want each of you to witness our bond and know that I will love her and look after her forever."

Paul turns to see Holly wiping a tear from her eye, and he nudges her and rolls his eyes. "Oh for God's sake," he says. "Couldn't he have been a bit less Hollywood?"

"Nah," Holly laughs, "his whole life probably feels like a movie. Oh shut up. Do we have to start being bitchy now?"

"It's just that it's a bit sickly sweet, no?"

"No. I think it's just sweet."

"Do you really? Where's my cynical old Holly gone?"

"Gone for good. This new improved Holly's madly in lurrve and thrilled by oversensitive film stars waxing lyrical about how wonderful women are."

"I can't believe we haven't met Jonathan yet," Paul whispers as the applause dies down. "Why don't you bring him down to the barn? We could have a reunion."

Holly raises an eyebrow. "I take it you've got a bathroom that needs tiling? Or a roof that needs replacing, then?"

"Thankfully not. Anna's windfall took care of everything. We've even got radiant heating under the floors now. Go on. Come down. Let's get everyone down and start fresh. A new beginning, and this time the beginning of the best times. Isn't it all supposed to start after forty anyway?"

"Only for women, I've heard." Olivia leans forward with a grin and raises her glass. "But cheers. Here's to new beginnings and second chances!"

One by one, they all raise their glasses to toast, as the band begins to play.

Read on for chapter one of
Jane Green's exciting new novel,
THE BEACH HOUSE

CHAPTER ONE

The bike crunches along the gravel path, weaving around the potholes that could present danger to someone who didn't know the road like the back of their hand.

The woman on the bike raises her head and looks at the sky, sniffs, smiles to herself. A foggy day in Nantucket, but she has lived here long enough to know this is merely a morning fog, and the bright early-June sunshine will burn it off by midday, leaving a beautiful afternoon.

Good. She is planning lunch on the deck today, is on her way into town via her neighbor's house, where she has spent the morning cutting the large blue mophead hydrangeas and stuffing them into the basket on the front of the bike. She doesn't really know these neighbors—so strange to live in the same house you have lived in for forty-five years, a house in a town where once you knew everyone, until one day you wake up and realize you don't know people anymore—but she has guessed from the drawn blinds and absence of cars they are not yet here, and they will not miss a couple dozen hydrangea heads.

The gate to their rear garden was open, and she had heard around town they had brought in some super-swanky garden designer. She had to look, and the pool had been open, and the water was so blue, so inviting, it was practically begging her to strip off her clothes and jump in, which of course she did, her body still slim and strong, her legs tan and muscled from the daily hours on the bike.

She dried off naturally, walking naked around the garden, popping strawberries and peas into her mouth in the kitchen garden, admiring the roses that were just starting, and climbing back into her clothes with a contented sigh when she was quite dry.

These are the reasons Nan has come to have a reputation for being slightly eccentric. A reputation she is well aware of, and a reputation she welcomes for it affords her freedom, allows her to do the things she really wants to do, the things other people don't dare, and because she is thought of as eccentric, exceptions are always made.

It is, she thinks wryly, one of the beautiful things about growing old, so necessary when there is so much else that is painful. At sixty-five she still feels thirty, and on occasion, twenty, but she has long ago left behind the insecurities she had at twenty and thirty, those niggling fears that her beauty wasn't enough, not enough for the Powell family; that she had somehow managed to trick Everett Powell into marrying her, and that once her looks started to fade, they would all realize she wasn't anyone, wasn't anything, and would then treat her as she had always expected when she first married into this illustrious family . . . as nothing.

Her looks had served her well. Continue to serve her well. She's tall, skinny and strong, and her white hair is glossy and sleek, pulled back in a chignon, her cheekbones still high, her green eyes still twinkling with amusement under perfectly arched brows.

Nan's is a beauty that's rarely seen these days, a natural elegance and style that prevailed throughout the fifties but has mostly disappeared today, although Nan doesn't see it, not anymore.

Now when she looks in the mirror she sees the lines, her cheeks concave under her cheekbones, the skin so thin it sometimes feels that she can see her bones. She covers as many of the imperfections as she can with makeup, still feels that she cannot leave her house without full makeup, her trademark scarlet lipstick the first thing she puts on every morning, before her underwear even, before her bath.

But these days her makeup is sometimes patchy, her lipstick smudging over the lines in her lips, lines that they warned her about in the eighties, when her son tried to get her to stop smoking, holding up photographs in magazines of women with dead, leathery skin.

"I can't give up smoking," she would frown. "I enjoy it too much, but I promise you, as soon as I stop enjoying it, I'll give it up."

The day is yet to come.

Thirty years younger and she would never have dared trespass, swim naked in an empty swimming pool without permission. Thirty years younger and she would have cared too much what people thought, wouldn't have cut flowers or carefully dug up a few strawberry plants that would certainly not be missed, to replant them in her own garden.

But thirty years younger and perhaps, if she had dared and had been caught, she would have gotten away with it. She would have apologized, would have invited the couple back for a drink, and the husband would have flirted with her, would have taken the pitcher of rum punch out of her hand and insisted on pouring it for her as she bent her head down to light her cigarette, looking up at him through those astonishing green eyes, flicking her blond hair ever so slightly and making him feel like the most important man in the room, hell, the only man in the room, the wife be damned.

Thirty years younger and the women might have ignored her, but not as they do now, because they think she's the crazy woman in the big old house on the bluff, but because they were threatened, because they were terrified she might actually have the power to take their men, ruin their lives. And they were right.

Not that she ever did.

Not back then.

Of course there have been a few affairs, but Nan was never out to steal a man from someone else. She just wanted some fun, and after Everett died, after years of being on her own, she came to realize that sometimes sex was, after all, just sex, and sometimes you just had to take it where you could find it.

The village of Siasconset, known to all simply as Sconset, is burning with a bright morning light by the time Nan arrives on her bike. She cycles past the Sconset café, round the corner past Book Store that isn't a bookstore but sells liquor instead, and hops off to go to the general store to get some food.

All the way at the back there is still a refrigerator stuffed full of yogurt, milk, eggs—the bare essentials of life—but the rest of the store is taken up with gourmet foods: sesame crackers, delicious sweetmeats, designer candles and the necessary wall of T-shirts, baseball caps and tote bags advertising that the tourists had been to Sconset for a vacation, were wealthy enough to afford to come to a place where billionaires play.

As always, she heads to the back, nodding at the tourists, waving hello to the woman behind the cash register.

She is a familiar sight in Sconset, her long linen skirts floating behind her as she cycles on a rusty old Schwinn, one that she and Everett bought when they spent their first summer here, back in 1962, when she was twenty, and he'd brought her home to Windermere to meet his parents.

It is not a bike you see often these days. A huge oversized basket on the front, Nan cycles slowly, one hand lightly balanced on the handlebar, the other wielding a cigarette. She waves at everyone she passes, greets them with a smile, stopping to chat if the whim takes her, or if she sees a neighbor busy in a garden.

Most wave back, but more and more often she is noticing the change in the people around here, the people who don't wave back, who pretend they don't see the crazy blond lady on the old bicycle, the people who are so bright and shiny, so clean and perfect as they walk down Main Street tapping on their iPhones, it almost hurts to look at them.

This wouldn't have happened had she been thirty years younger, she thinks from time to time, when yet another young, glamorous New York couple hesitates as it approaches her, she weaving wildly on her bike as she attempts to light her cigarette without stopping. Thirty years ago he would have pulled a lighter out of his pocket and lit it for her, instead of turning as his wife prods him with a sneer of distaste when her cigarette lights and the smoke wafts, as if planned, right under her nose. The woman coughs dramatically, and Nan happily gives her the finger as she cycles off, as the woman gasps in horror and attempts to shield the eyes of the toddler who is with them.

What has happened to *people*? Nan thinks as she traverses the cobblestones. When did we become so *precious*? A family of six passes her, father, mother, then four little ones, like four little ducklings with sparkly aerodynamic helmets on. When did our children have to wear helmets? she thinks, turning her head to watch them wobble into the distance. When did we all become so scared?

She thinks of Michael, at seven, falling off the monkey bars and splitting his head open on the concrete floor. She didn't panic; it was just one of the things that happened to everyone. She bundled him in the front of the car and drove him to Dr. Grover's house, where he was stitched up in the Grovers' kitchen as Mrs Grover served them lemonade and gingersnaps.

She never knew where the children were when they were growing up. Someone had a boat on the marshes, and the children once got stranded for the day. Nan only knew when they ran in the kitchen door, shrieking with excitement at what swiftly became their near-death adventure. Whatever adults were around would smile affectionately, one ear on the conversation, the other somewhere else, because life, in those days, revolved around the adults. Not around the children.

The first time Everett brought her to their summer-house, Nan hadn't known what to expect. She had barely heard of Nantucket. Had vacationed only on the Jersey shore, knowing little of what she later came to think of as "old America," true Yankee families, old money that had sailed over on the *Mayflower* and could trace their families back hundreds of years.

Her own parents had been English, had sailed to New York hoping for a better life than the one they left behind in Birmingham, and had moved to Ossining because of a distant cousin who lived there.

She had been this naïve little girl, still known to all as Suzanne, who hadn't known what to expect when Everett brought her home. There was no Googling to find out about the Powells, no one who could have told her the family was famous in Massachusetts for funding the majority of the renovation that has made Cape Cod what it is today, no one who could have explained the money she was marrying into, the privilege and history that came with the Powells.

She married Everett because she thought she loved him, and as a wedding present his parents bought them an apartment in New York City. Nothing fancy, she would say years later, but it was utterly fancy, and for the first two years of their marriage Nan would wake every morning and think she had died and awakened in a Grace Kelly movie.

And nowhere did she feel this more than at Windermere. Built in the 1920s, just off Baxter Road in the village of Sconset, it stood high on a bluff, over-looking the Atlantic Ocean, its shingles gray and weary from being buffeted by the wind, but its lines graceful and elegant, the porches always abuzz with people.

Not a big house, Windermere now sat on nine per-fect acres. Originally a modest saltbox, over the years various additions had turned it into a sprawling estate. The developers had started to circle, like vultures look-ing for their kill. The house would be torn down, Nan knew, if she ever let them get their hands on it, and it was a place that held too many important memories for her to let it go that easily.

It was the Powells' summerhouse—their idyllic retreat from Memorial Day to Labor Day each year, a home filled with naked children, clambakes on the beach and so much joy.

It was one of those naked children who caused her name change, that very first trip. "It's Suzanne," Everett kept saying to the little three-year-old—someone's daughter, or cousin or something—who kept trying to drag her off to build another sand castle. "I want Nan to come," the little girl kept saying, and Everett had laughed, so handsome then, his blue eyes crinkling in his tan face. "Nan," he turned to Suzanne. "Nan in Nantucket. I like it." And since that time she had only ever been called Nan, had mostly forgotten her given name, often found herself crossing out Nan when filling out forms that requested her full name, only realizing at the end that she hadn't written Suzanne.

When Nan thinks back to those early days at Windermere, she can almost hear the tinkling of drinks being poured, of lanterns strung up around the house, of votives hanging from the trees as musicians played and people laughed, and drank and danced all night.

There were dinner parties that went on all night, Everett's parents—Lydia and Lionel—the first to lead their guests through the dunes for their notorious midnight swims, the shrieks from the guests as they hit the cold water audible almost in the center of town.

Friends were always coming to stay, often not leaving for entire summers at a time, but Windermere was big enough, and the overspill could always stay in one of the four cottages on the far edges of the compound.

Two of the cottages were sold off after Lionel died, and Lydia developed Alzheimer's, eventually going into a nursing home in Boston where Nan tried to visit as often as she could, sometimes bringing her son until it became too painful, toward the end, when Lydia wasn't even a shadow of her former self, but a tiny, shrunken, white-haired old lady whom Nan had walked straight past when she first walked in.

Everett had died by that time, or, as Nan put it for so many years, had gone. She had woken up one morning and the bed had been empty, which was not particularly unusual—he would often wake up and go for an early-morning swim—but it wasn't until he failed to return that her heart quickened with a trace of anxiety.

She went down to the beach, and still she remembers that she knew, knew from the moment she turned over and saw his side of the bed empty that there was something not quite right.

His T-shirt was roughly folded, weighted down by his father's watch. No note. Nothing. And the sea was particularly rough that day. Nan had stood and looked out over the waves, listening to the ocean crash around her as a tear rolled down her cheek. She wasn't looking for him, she knew he had gone.

She just didn't know why.

It turned out to be no coincidence that Everett's grandfather had won Windermere in a poker match. Gambling, it transpired, skipped a generation and landed quite solidly on the shoulders of Everett.

Nan knew he loved his poker games, but had no idea they were anything other than fun, anything other than a reason to spend a night out with the boys, drink a few single malts and smoke a few cigars, or whatever it was they did.

But after he died, all those years ago, she received phone calls from the banks, then from various people to whom he clearly owed money, and finally, from his accountant.

"It does not look good," he had said.

Luckily, there were assets. The two remaining cottages on the edges of Windermere were sold, and, then, a few years later, the New York City apartment. A big decision, but she had always loved Windermere, had loved the thought of making it a permanent home, and Michael was small enough that she thought he would benefit from a quieter life, a life that was simple, in a place they had always loved. It was in the late seventies, just before the boom, and she got so much money for the apartment she thought she would be fine forever.

"I leave it in your hands," she had said to her stockbroker with a laugh, knowing that a pot that sizable would be fine.

She doesn't have a stockbroker anymore. Stockbrokers used to be revered, but she doesn't know anyone who calls himself a stockbroker these days. These days she hears the summer people use phrases like M&A, bond derivatives and, perhaps more than anything, hedge funds. She still doesn't understand what a hedge fund is, knows only that the people who are building the biggest houses on the island, the husbands who fly in for the weekend on private jets and helicopters, joining wives, nannies and housekeepers, all seem to work in hedge funds.

She herself has her money in a hedge fund. Every month she receives a statement, but mostly she forgets to open it. Her mail has a tendency to pile up on a kitchen counter before being swept away into a cupboard some-where, for Nan has no patience for the prosaic—bills bore her, and the only envelopes that are opened and responded to immediately, are handwritten and personal.

Today her financial adviser is coming for lunch, although Nan thinks of him less as a financial adviser and more as a friend. Not that he is much of either—she has not seen him in person for four years, and he doesn't advise her particularly, other than to have told her, all those years ago, that the hedge fund she was investing in was a good one, started by one of the brightest traders at Goldman Sachs, and it would be a wonderful place for her to put some money.

The phone is ringing when she walks in. She dumps the hydrangeas in the sink and grabs the phone, running the water as she picks up.

"Hi, Mom." It's Michael, ringing, as he so often does, on his way to work.

"Hi, my love. How are you?"

"Tired. It's hot and muggy and revolting in the city. I'm deeply jealous of you on the island—is it beautiful?"

"Not yet." Nan smiles. "But it will be. Why don't you come out? I miss you. It's too quiet here with just me rattling around."

"What about Sarah? Do you still have Sarah?"

"She still comes once or twice a week to help me out," Nan says, "and I love having her around, but I miss my family, miss this house ringing with the sounds of people having fun. Remember when you used to come up here with all your friends for the summer? Remember how much fun it was? Why don't you come up with some people? Wouldn't they all kill for a vacation on Nantucket?"

Michael smiles. His mother never changes. "They would undoubtedly kill for a vacation on Nantucket, if only they could take the time off work. And most of them are married now, with kids. It's different, they can't just sweep their families up and bring them out."

"But why ever not?" Nan is genuinely perplexed. "I adore children, this is the perfect place for children."

"I know that, but it's just . . . hard. People are busy, everyone's running all the time. But I would love to come. I'd love to see you. I can't make it up at the moment, the bosses are away for another week or so, I need to be here, but maybe I can come at the end of the summer."

Nan turns off the faucet and reaches for a cigarette.

"Oh, Mom. You're not still smoking?"

Nan ignores him. "How are things going with the girl . . . what's her name? Aisling?"

Michael smiles. "Interesting. I like her. Still very early days, but so far so good. She's fiery. Independent. You'd like her."

"I'd love to meet her." Nan is careful not to ask too much. "Bring her."

"Maybe I will. What are you up to today?"

"Making lunch. Andrew Moseley is coming."

"Your financial adviser?"

"Exactly!"

"Is everything okay?"

"Why wouldn't it be?"

"It seems unusual for him to travel up to see you."

Nan shrugs. "I think, after four years, it's probably just due. Anyway, lovely to have some company. I'm making delicious salads straight from the garden, and Sarah has promised to drop off a lobster salad she made yesterday."

"Sounds yummy." Michael smiles, instantly picturing the table set on the deck, his mother's ballet slippers kicked off as she curls her legs under her after lunch, cradling a large tumbler of white wine in one hand, a ubiquitous cigarette in the other. "Don't drink too much."

Michael says good-bye with a sad smile, clicking his phone shut as he reaches his bike, chained to a lamppost on Ninety-fourth and Columbus, outside his apartment, unaware of the admiring glance he got from a tall brunette walking her dog.

Michael has always been unaware of his appeal, taken for granted his large green eyes, inherited from his mother, his easy smile, his all-American clean-cut looks.

At forty-two he looks much like the college football player he used to be, tanned and rangy, and utterly comfortable in his skin.

He undoes the lock and secures his helmet, slipping the phone into his backpack and weaving off down Columbus, making a mental note to phone Sarah, just to make sure that Mom is okay, to make sure that someone is looking out for her, that she isn't quite as alone as she sounds.

Coming June 2008

978-0-670-006424-3

www.janegreen.com

Available wherever books are sold.

Viking Canada
Published by the Penguin Group
www.penguin.ca